BY ALI BENJAMIN

The Thing About Jellyfish
The Smash-Up

THE SMASH-UP

a novel

THE SMASH-UP

ALI BENJAMIN

RANDOM HOUSE
NEW YORK

Copyright © 2021 by Ali Benjamin

Published in the United States by Random House, an imprint and division of Penguin Random House LLC, New York.

RANDOM HOUSE and the HOUSE colophon are registered trademarks of Penguin Random House LLC.

Library of Congress Cataloging-in-Publication Data
Names: Benjamin, Ali, author.
Title: The smash-up: a novel / Ali Benjamin.
Description: First edition. | New York: Random House, [2021]
Identifiers: LCCN 2020023010 (print) | LCCN 2020023011 (ebook) | ISBN 9780593229651 (hardcover) | ISBN 9780593229668 (ebook) | ISBN 9780593243244 (international edition)
Classification: LCC PS3602.E66346 S6213 2021 (print) | LCC PS3602.E66346 (ebook) | DDC 813/.6—dc23
LC record available at https://lccn.loc.gov/2020023010
LC ebook record available at https://lccn.loc.gov/2020023011

Printed in the United States of America on acid-free paper

randomhousebooks.com

9 8 7 6 5 4 3 2 1

First Edition

Book design by Diane Hobbing

FOR A WOMAN NAMED SILENCE

"Eros has degenerated; he began by introducing order and harmony, and now he brings back chaos."

—George Eliot

"I had the sense that the deeper meaning of the story was in the gaps."

—Edith Wharton

THE SMASH-UP

INTRODUCTION

WHAT HAPPENED?

Everyone asked the question, had been asking since the election. They asked while watching the news, that storm of headlines, jump-cut footage of marches and speeches and hand-sharpied cardboard, an endless, swirling blizzard—a siege, really—of protests and counterprotests, action and reaction, people screaming at one another in the street, neighbor versus neighbor, friend versus friend. (Or too often: friends no more. We were in new territory. People had their limits.)

What happened? Reporters asked in small-town diners over $7.50 lunch specials, BLTs cut into neat wedges and Heinz bottles perched like microphones atop scratched Formica tables.

What happened? People asked one another in church basements, community centers, gyms, coffee shops, living rooms where they came together to weep, process, scrawl on placards, plan the revolution.

What happened? Parents snapped off NPR mid-story, not wanting to answer questions from the backseat. College students organized walkouts, staged sit-ins, blocked freeways. A giant inflatable chicken appeared behind the White House lawn, some sort of protest that no one entirely understood. Everything was some sort of protest now.

What happened what happened what happened what

Everyone had their answers, and as is generally the case in these situations, everyone's version of the story was a little different. It was impossible, it was inevitable, it was surreal, it was unreal, it was scandal, sea change, enthralling, a coup. It was some bad sort of smash-up: just the right-or-wrong elements at just the right-or-wrong time: anger and alienation, misinformation and disinformation, resentment and rage, hucksters and hackers, bots and Nazis (literal Nazis! As if they hadn't been the unequivocal villains in every film for the last half century! For heaven's sake, hadn't these people ever even seen Indiana Jones?). It was all of these things, it was none of these things, it made no goddamned sense, that's the point, and the only thing any of us knew for sure was this: on the eighth day of the eleventh month of the year of our lord two thousand and sixteen, our nation—and with it the world we'd known—had turned upside down.

Once, a lifetime ago it seems now, I interviewed a geologist. This was in the Before—before the world smashed to pieces, back when we could count on tomorrow unfolding more or less like it had today, which of course was more or less like yesterday and all the days before that. *Find something interesting,* my editor had told me. He'd said it vaguely, with a wave of his hand. *Make geology relevant.*

The geologist I'd interviewed was athletic and lean, pale as parchment. For two hours, she and I sat together in a windowless basement office in the science building of a mid-sized college campus. She explained that the Earth's crust is always in motion, tectonic plates shifting endlessly, like jigsaw puzzle pieces shuffled around a table. The plates move so slowly that changes are largely imperceptible.

But sometimes the jagged edges snag. The plates can't get free, so they push against each other, like lovers who can neither separate nor get close enough. Pressure mounts, moment upon moment, decade upon decade. Eventually the planet cracks open, and nothing is ever the same again. *We think of an earthquake as a single moment in time,* the geologist told me that day, *when in fact it's a centuries-long event. It happens bit by bit by bit, then all at once.*

She shared other things in that conversation—that the Americas and Asia will someday be a single landmass, one enormous supercontinent. That our oceans sometimes belch enormous boulders into open sky; recently, a stone two and a half times the weight of the Statue of Liberty was hurled from the sea off the coast of Ireland. It sailed hundreds of feet through the air, then landed, to the bewilderment of locals, smack-dab in the middle of an open field.

But it was the earthquake part that I found myself thinking about in those days of *what happened.*

Bit by bit by bit, then all at once. That was how it felt: like pressure we hadn't even noticed building had cracked wide open the ground we'd been standing on. Only after fissures had become chasms did we realize they'd been there all along. Sometimes the people who had been next to us just moments ago were now on the other side of a sharp divide, a canyon no one could cross.

It ripped people apart, this thing that happened. That's what I'm saying. It tore entire lives asunder.

IF YOU'VE EVER been to Starkfield, you know the post office. And if you know the post office, you know it's the last place you can reliably get any sort of cell service until you reach Corbury.

It was a mile south of the post office, well into the dead zone, that I came upon Ethan.

It was March, then: twenty-eight months since the election. I'd spent the last two months traveling the country, interviewing artists and academics, scientists and entrepreneurs. I was gathering notes for an anthology of big ideas. *This Is Genius.* Its pages were to feature change-makers, innovators, thought leaders. These were the folks who delivered TED talks, won PEN Awards, who might, any day now, be invited to fly to Sweden to accept their Nobel. (None of them, it should be noted, knew what happened, either, nor had they seen it coming.)

That week, I'd been at a small Berkshires college trying to understand the work of a neurobiologist, a MacArthur winner who studied birdsong—one of those quiet academics whose research seems charmingly irrelevant until the moment people realize it upends tenets of Darwinism.

I was nearing the end of my research phase for the book, staying in an Airbnb apartment above the garage of an aging widow, Mrs. Nathan Hale, near the center of downtown Starkfield. For the most part, my book research had taken me to big cities and hip college towns—young places where I'd stood in long lines at pour-over coffee shops, listening to the whir of espresso machines as tattooed baristas rattled off the precise textural differences between flat whites and café au laits.

Starkfield, by contrast, is a quiet place. Humble. Though it's surrounded by communities with world-class museums and expensive ski lodges, celebrity-studded theater festivals and performances by the Boston Symphony Orchestra, Starkfield somehow manages to have none of these things. Downtown boasts only a nondescript village green, around which are scattered a handful of small businesses, no more than one of each variety: one coffee shop, one hardware store, one bank, one barbershop, one pharmacy. There's a recently shuttered UPS Store, a chain pizza shop, a dive bar called the Flats, and a nail salon with a tanning bed in back. A person can pass through the business district in forty seconds without breaking the speed limit.

Starkfield, in other words, is a closed-off sort of place—the kind of town where a person might be able to hide from all those screaming headlines, all that action and reaction. Maybe find a little quiet amid the noise.

So there I was: on Route 7, returning to my rented one-bedroom after my final interview with the biologist. And there *he* was: Ethan.

He stood on the shoulder, in front of a battered Subaru wagon, just past the painted WELCOME TO STARKFIELD, A HISTORIC VILLAGE sign, the threshold between Starkfield and everywhere. He was long and lanky, wearing Carhartts and Warby Parkers, a knit cap pulled over his ears. He held his cell phone toward the sky, and something about his posture—the lift of his chin as he squinted at his screen, the rigid way he held his shoulders—reminded me of a statue, some long-forgotten figure, frozen forever in bronze.

The man's tire was flat. Any fool could see that.

I didn't want to stop. I had work to do, deadlines to meet, a book to finish, plenty of other concerns too. I considered waving, rolling past as if I didn't understand he was in trouble. But as I got closer, Ethan glanced up from his phone. His eyes drifted through my windshield, met mine.

He nodded in greeting, a single dip of the head.

Poor man's not been the same since the smash-up. The Widow Hale had said that to me just this morning, confessing that she'd left a casserole on his porch. She'd said it almost apologetically, as if there were some shame in helping out a neighbor. I took pains to reassure her: it's always a lovely thing, looking after those who live among us. Isn't that what the world most needs these days?

Now I lifted one hand from the steering wheel, waved. Then I sighed, slowed, cranked the steering wheel to the right. I rolled down my window. "Need some help?"

He had a car jack back at the house. Shouldn't take long.

I nodded. Waited until he was buckled in before I put the car into gear. We rode in silence, Ethan staring out the window until we reached the edge of downtown. It was not quite the end of a long, bleak winter. The village green—presented as bright and alive in all the official town promotional materials—was now nothing but dead grass and gray patches of ice. Ethan turned away from the window as we passed. He leaned down to lift a book that lay at his feet: *String Theory for Dummies.* I'd been using this book while writing a particularly obscure chapter of *This Is Genius.* Ethan opened to a random page, began to read. "Ten to the five-hundredth power separate universes, each with its own laws of physics."

I kept my eyes on the road. I couldn't shake the feeling the wrong response might have the effect of a gunshot near a skittish horse; poor guy might throw open the door of the car, pitch himself right the hell out of the moving vehicle.

"Well, that's what some say, anyway," I finally answered. I flicked my left blinker, started up Schoolhouse Hill. "But it's not like any of us will get to know for sure."

He set the book down, looked out the window again. "There are so many things in this world I don't know about."

Was that wonder in his voice, or regret?

Just past the old cemetery, we turned into a rutted driveway. A hand-painted sign, faded almost to bare wood, hung from an oak: THE FROMES. The driveway, like the lawn, was all dug up, mud frozen into hard lumps like boils on skin. Flapping tarps covered bare clapboards—a renovation project, begun during more optimistic times, now permanently stalled. Ethan opened the car door, swung his feet onto the driveway. "Might as well come inside." He didn't look at me as he spoke. "Could take a minute."

I hesitated. Wouldn't it be easier, faster, less . . . *involved* . . . if I just waited out here? But then a blast of cold wind blew through the front seat. Too cold. I opened my own door and followed him up the sagging porch.

Inside, it took a few seconds for my eyes to adjust. The place was dark. Cramped. Construction tarps hung from the ceiling, blocking off an entire side of the house. On this side of the plastic, a stack of furniture stood like some sort of conceptual sculpture: a coffee table on top of an armchair atop a sofa. There were two dining-room tables, top to top, legs reaching both toward the floor and toward the ceiling, like a variation of Dolittle's pushmi-pullyu. Two rolled carpets, one still in its original plastic, leaned against the wall, while half-filled boxes covered the floor. Ethan glanced around, as if he were seeing the place for the first time. "Been trying to organize," he said. An apology, I think. "Car jack's around here somewhere."

Across the room, an old dog lifted her head. Her tail thumped two times. Three.

Ethan opened a box marked GARAGE—KEEP. He peered inside, frowned, then began to open another. The old dog, tired, lay back down, began to snore.

As Ethan stooped over those boxes, attempting to decipher the chaos of his own life, I turned around, shifted my attention to a built-in bookshelf. It wasn't a book that captured my attention. It was a photograph: taken outside on some bright, sunny day. Green grass, summer leaves, dappled light. Three faces, all of them laughing. In the center sat Ethan, eyes dancing. In this photo, he looked about twenty years younger than the man who had gotten into my car.

What happened?

You can imagine a thousand lives for a person, tell any number of stories based on a single image. You can try to put words to it: who he'd been and what he'd lost, and how, exactly, those canyons of worry had been carved into his temples.

It had affected him, too, this thing that happened.

There are no closed-off places, it turns out. The rupturing, the quake, could be felt in every floorboard, in every home. There wasn't a window anywhere that hadn't been rattled. Even here, even in this quiet nowhere, *what happened* had fractured even the quietest of lives.

TUESDAY, LATE SEPTEMBER 2018

1

HOW TO WAIT

*Maybe you're standing in the shadows. Near that old spruce tree, probably.
Maybe needles poke the back of your neck, and there's a leash in your hand,
and at the other end of the leash is an arthritic dog. She's patient, the old
mutt—a little confused, perhaps, about why you've taken to standing in this
particular spot at this particular time of night, but not so confused as to make
a fuss. She wags her tail a few times, then lowers herself, resigned, into a sit
position.*

Good girl.

*Maybe it's a Tuesday night, late September, and you're standing on the
Ledge.*

*The Ledge isn't a real ledge, not any sort of cliff. It is, instead, a tiny dip
near the bottom of Schoolhouse Hill Road. Here, after a steady half-mile
downward slope, the pavement rises ever so slightly before dropping, sharp
and steep, into its final, vertiginous descent. When drivers hit the Ledge too
fast, it can feel like the car is flying off the road altogether. Kids love the sensation: the unexpected weightlessness, the stomach drop, free fall, whoosh,
like a roller coaster, almost.*

But you've never much liked roller coasters, have you?

*Besides, you're on foot tonight. And as it happens, if you pause here, the
Ledge offers the clearest view of downtown Starkfield, Massachusetts, a person will find anywhere. That's where you look now: at three figures standing on the village green.*

No, actually; that's not quite right. There might be three figures down there, but your eyes are fixed on just one: the girl.

Blue hair. Yellow streetlight.

The girl brings something to her lips. Inhales. She holds her breath, count of five. When she exhales, wisps of smoke rise toward the sky. Diaphanous, that breath, like a prayer, or a spirit escaping the body. It's unclear where her breath ends and the dark night begins.

The girl hands whatever she's smoking (oh, who are you kidding? You know exactly what she's smoking and you wouldn't mind a little yourself, thankyouverymuch) to one of the two guys. Tall drink of water, this kid: clean-shaven, in too-short khakis and an old-man cardigan. Looks pimply, too, with hi-tops that seem too big for his stick legs. Skinny Pimple takes the joint, and just for a moment, you allow yourself to imagine that you're him, that you're curling your lips over the place where Maddy's had just been. You picture lipstick marks on white paper: purple, maybe, or cherry red, the color of a beating heart.

Thumping music from the Flats bar, AC/DC. What is it, 10:30? 10:45? Must be damn near last call by now.

Somewhere else—in Brooklyn, say, which you called home a lifetime ago—the night is just getting started. In those places, people are leaving apartments. They're stepping into the street, ready to eat, drink, dance, fuck.

Here in Starkfield, most of the windows have already gone black.

Skinny takes a toke, passes the joint to the other guy. This kid, the one you recognize, is more compact, almost stocky, with a beard that's trimmer and darker than yours. Not a speck of gray in his.

Perhaps you reach up to feel your salt-and-pepper tangle—more salt than pepper, actually—its length nearly to your sternum.

You don't head down the hill, don't even consider approaching those kids. Come on, you're no dummy. You know exactly what people—neighbors, say, or even your wife—would assume if you were to get any closer. They'd think you desperate. Some middle-aged fool. A modern-day Prufrock, pathetic in his longing.

But for the record, they'd be wrong: That's not who you are. It's not who you've ever been. This thing that's happening now—the thing that's brought you here tonight, and all the other nights—is something else alto-

gether, something you haven't yet put into words. Whatever it is, it feels important, urgent. The one thing you know for sure is this: it's only on these nights, these walks, that you can finally breathe.

My God. It feels good to breathe, doesn't it?

A screech owl. A guitar wail. This clear, cool night.

The hour is coming—if we're counting hours, we're down to the double digits now, and the clock is ticking fast—when this view won't be so peaceful. Mere days from now, an observer standing exactly where you are will be witness to a different scene entirely. But that all lies in the future. The unknown future, the impossible future.

In. Out.

Maybe that's when the phone call comes.

THE PHONE. *SHIT.*

Ethan jams his hand into the pocket of his fleece, flicks his phone to silent. The sudden motion startles Hypatia. The dog rises, collar jingling. Her wagging tail makes a soft swish against the branches. Ethan brings his finger to his lips, as if the animal could possibly understand. *Shh,* he wills.

He lifts his hand, the signal to sit, and she does. Good dog.

Did they hear anything, those three down there? Inside the circle of light, the blue-haired girl throws her head back, laughing. Some joke Ethan didn't get to hear. No one looks up.

Inside the bar, AC/DC gives way to Guns N' Roses.

Not long ago, trees would have blocked this view. When Ethan and Zo moved to town nearly sixteen years ago, a row of massive elms flanked the bottom of Schoolhouse Hill. The trees were nearly two centuries old, miracle beasts that somehow survived the Dutch elm epidemic, only to be drowned, seven years ago, in the floods of Hurricane Irene. The town replaced the elms with blue spruces, but death came for these new trees, too, just as it did for the ornamental pears that followed, and the emerald ash after that. Last year, town officials announced they'd given up on trees altogether—*Sorry, folks, the climate's changing too fast, no hope for it, we're in the apocalypse now, might as well enjoy the view.*

Ethan sees the bearded kid take his toke. Lean in. All greedy-like.

He knows this kid's name: Arlo O'Shea. Son of that dot-com millionaire from Corbury, the next town over. Back in the mid-'90s, Arlo's dad launched and sold some mediocre-but-brilliantly-timed medical website. That was back in the days when venture capitalists hurled suitcases full of cash at any idiot with a URL. Rumor has it that Arlo's dad, then still in his twenties, took in a cool $112 million when the company was acquired by AOL. Built himself an eight-bedroom home with killer views over on Mount Corbury and never looked back.

Now, apparently, the lucky millionaire's son has decided to slum it in Starkfield. And for the record, he's standing way too fucking close to Maddy.

Also, the sugar maples. They're dying too.

Ethan's phone vibrates in his pocket. Two calls in a row. Must be Zo, clearing her own mind of some to-do item by passing it on to him. *Did you write that tuition check yet?* Or: *Faucet leaking again, ugh.* Or: *Need paper towels!*

Except: no. That can't be right. Zo's women's group was still at the house when Ethan left, and they didn't look anywhere near ready to leave. When the women are meeting (and let's be honest: even when they're not), Zo's not thinking about Ethan at all.

When his phone comes to life a third time, Ethan takes a look: Not Zo. It's Randy. His old Bränd partner. Finally returning his calls.

Damn, he really has to take this one.

Ethan takes a few steps up the hill, to the far the side of the spruce. Hypatia follows dutifully. When she sits again, her back rounds, head droops, like she's an infrequently watered houseplant just barely hanging on.

"Randy," Ethan whispers into his phone. He'll make this quick, keep it friendly, find out why the last couple of checks from Bränd haven't arrived. It's been two whole quarters, half a fricking year, who does Randy think Ethan is, anyway? Randy will be filled with excuses—*Sorry, had to fire the finance guy,* or

Screw-up in the accounting software, you know how it is. Or even— maybe more likely—something that sounds like a scene from a bad movie. *Sorry, was on Richard Branson's private island, some things you don't say no to.* Randy's been filled with excuses ever since they met at Kenyon, which was—Ethan does a quick calculation— nearly three decades ago.

Jesus. Longer than Maddy's been alive.

"E!" Randy's voice in Ethan's ear is loud, insistent. "They're coming for me!"

Ethan sighs. There are a few things he's come to expect from Randy's calls. First and foremost is theatrics, some kind of urgent, pulsing drama.

They're coming for me. Drama: check.

The next thing that's going to happen, Ethan knows, will be some sort of name-dropping. Randy loves mentioning all the fa- mous people who run in his circle: *On my way home from a premiere, Cate Blanchett's in the limo with me, hey Cate, say hi to my buddy E.*

Or: *I'm at an after-party. Britney Spears is here, chatting with Salman Rushdie, is that some kind of whacked-out convergence or what?*

What's Randy going to say this time? *Hanging with Leo D. and Bradley Cooper. Bastards keep trying to get me to do more shots.* In spite of himself, Ethan smiles. Randy's exhausting, but his theatrics have their own sort of charm. Besides, everything Ethan has—including the freedom to stand here watching some twentysomethings smoke weed while Axl Rose sings about wanting to go where the grass is green and the girls are pretty—is due in part to the swirling maelstrom that is Randy Riverstone.

So, okay. Whatever it takes. He just needs his money.

"Who's coming for you this time, Randy?"

Through the branches, Ethan can still see Maddy. He can tell by the way her hands are in her pockets, the little jumps she's starting to make, that she's getting cold. The temperature must be, what, in the high forties? Not yet October, but winter's coming. It's not so far away now.

"The women. They're coming for me." There's something about Randy's voice. A strain, just a little too high in pitch. Ah, so this is the *other* version of his friend: the ranting, hysterical Randy. "They're after me, E. Oh God, I'm freaking out here."

"Randy," Ethan says. "Slow down, man."

"It's my turn," Randy says. "My fucking turn, and I'm gonna need your help."

"Your turn for what, Rand?" Just like that, Ethan's back in his old role. The soother. The fixer. The rational one. The straight-man foil to Randy, ever the entertainer.

"For the firing squad, E. Word on the street is that Bränd is next. *I'm* next, my balls on the chopping block. Gavin says they're out for blood."

Gavin. Ethan has to think. Gavin is Randy's agent. Or maybe his publicist? Manager? What's the difference between an agent, a publicist, and a manager, anyway? All these roles—like the fitness trainer, the nutritionist, the personal attorney, the one Randy calls his "money guy"—are all "AE"—After Ethan. They showed up after Randy and Ethan decided to part ways—or more precisely, after Zo refused to follow Ethan to Los Angeles, which meant Ethan sold off most of his personal stake in the company he'd co-founded just before it began making money hand-over-fist.

"Back up, Randy," Ethan says. His voice is even. It's his job to reassure, to get Randy un-spooked. "How exactly are your balls on the chopping block?"

"Jesus, are you not watching the news?" Randy says. "Do you *get* the news out in Amish country? Do you even have an Internet connection out there? Or electricity? There's a whole *thing* that's been happening to guys like us."

Like us? Ethan and Randy have almost nothing in common, not anymore. "I'm in the Berkshires, Randy. Western Mass. You know that."

"Berkshires, Amish country, same difference, you all make your own soap. Point is, we're in hot water here." Randy's words spill out, disconnected phrases in that familiar machine-gun staccato, *pow-pow-pow,* so quickly that even if you're paying attention, which Ethan isn't, not quite, you can still only catch about a third of what he says.

"Everything we built . . ."

"Never been an angel, but you know I'm . . ."

Ethan holds the phone away from his ear, watches Arlo lean in toward Maddy. Yeah, there's definitely something about that kid that Ethan doesn't care for.

". . . decide they're going to cash in . . ."

". . . tried to fix this . . . let's just say that backfired . . ."

Greedy: that's how Arlo looks right now. He looks way too fucking greedy. Meanwhile, Skinny Pimple is just standing there watching them, a dopey grin on his face. Ethan's struck with the urge to smack Skinny right in his stupid little smirk.

". . . I'm telling you . . . could really fuck up everything."

Jesus, he can't think clearly with Randy in his ear like this.

"Randy," Ethan interrupts. "Come on, man. Deep breath." It's like he's playing a character in a sitcom that's had too long of a run. The part went stale long ago, but somehow here he still is, reciting the same tired catchphrases.

God, he wishes he had some of what those kids are smoking.

"Randy, listen," Ethan tries again. "I haven't gotten my last two checks—" He wants to sound like he doesn't actually need the money, hasn't spent it already.

"You don't *get* it, do you?" Randy screeches. "Everything's on *hold,* that's what I'm saying. Money's frozen. Fucking board's quaking in their wingtips. Bränd's about to be the latest collateral damage in whatever the hell new war the women have declared."

Ethan's silence must betray his confusion.

"Seriously?" Randy asks. "Hashtag Me Too? You've heard of it, haven't you?"

Oh. So that's what this is.

Just for a moment, Ethan feels himself hurtling through space, feels the Earth spinning beneath his feet—roughly eight hundred miles per hour at this latitude if he remembers correctly. He reminds himself that gravity—that mysterious, invisible force—will keep him from flying off into the black night, alone.

"Truth is, I didn't think anything of it at first," Randy's saying, "but—"

Down the hill, Pimple grinds out the joint on the pavement.

"Now I've got *New York Times* journalists calling me. Swear to God, any second now, I'm gonna pick up the phone and it'll be Ronan Fucking Farrow on the line."

No, Ethan decides. He's going to stay out of this one. He doesn't even work at Bränd anymore; the checks he receives are payment for the work he already put in, for helping *found* the darn company, for keeping the whole enterprise together back when he and Randy were equal partners—as equal as can be, anyway, when only one of you is able to front the cash. This whole Ethan-cleans-up-Randy's-mess thing ended two decades ago.

Besides: Randy will land on his feet. Randy always lands on his feet.

"Randy, listen: I want to be clear. Whatever is or isn't happening with the company has nothing to do with me. What *I* need is for you to release my money."

"*Christ,* E, that's what I'm trying to *explain*! None of us are gonna get money until this thing blows over. So as a matter of fact, this *does* have something to do with you. And if it's ever going to be fixed, I need you to—"

And now Maddy's walking up the hill. Away from the others. Toward Ethan.

"Randy, I'm gonna have to call you back," Ethan interrupts.

Maddy's twenty-five paces away. Her head is down, her face lit by the glow from her phone.

"You hear me, right?" Randy presses. "Because I don't know if you're really listening here. Doesn't really seem like you *get* it."

Twenty paces away.

"This is trouble, my friend," Randy continues. "With a capital *T* and that rhymes with *P,* and that stands for poorhouse. You feel me?"

Fifteen paces.

"This is the motherfucking apocalypse, E. This is—"

But by now, Maddy's almost reached the Ledge. She's close enough that Hypatia—who's half-blind, half-deaf these days—is already rising, tail wagging. Ethan doesn't have a choice: he cuts off his oldest friend, his former business partner, his college room-mate, with a single motion of the finger.

End call.

Hypatia strains at her leash. She barks, a single yap of greeting.

Maddy startles, stops in her tracks. Then, almost as quickly, she laughs. And this time Maddy's laughter is for Ethan alone. "Ethan!" Hand on her heart. Her lip curl is just barely visible in the dark. "Scare the fuck out of a person, why don't you?"

2

HOW TO BE WHOLE

It's true that it's not what people would think, whatever this thing is, but let's be honest: it's also not not-what-people-would-think. It's some in-between thing, some third option. It defies, somehow, the usual categories.

That is what you would say, if anyone were to ask, which no one does. Right now, you and Maddy are the only ones here.

Soon—mere minutes from now, a half mile from here—you will be back in your usual roles. You will be Dad, you will be Husband. You will be the Guy Who Does Dishes and Laundry. Dude Who Recycles Even Though He's Not Certain the Recyclables Don't All Just Wind up in a Landfill Anyway. Responsible Father Who Picks up the Kid's Adderall and Drives Her to and from School (never more than five miles over the speed limit, not unless you're running really late). Man Who Pays the Bills, or Who Tries to Anyway.

And apparently now too: Chump Who Somehow, All These Years Later, Still Has to Worry About Randy Riverstone's Fucking Problems.

But these categories are two-dimensional; they're flat. Constricting, like a suit that's grown too tight. You can't fit a whole person inside of them.

These nights, these occasional walks home through deserted Starkfield, are for the rest of you: the parts that have mostly atrophied, but not quite. You can still feel them sometimes, like phantom limbs. On these walks, just for a while, you are pure possibility, untethered to the weight of expectation.

So fuck the usual categories. Whatever this is, you will allow yourself to have it. You will give yourself this.

So then. Let us go.

MADDY CROUCHES IN the dark to greet Hypatia. She rubs the animal's scruff, allows the dog to lick her cheeks, her eyes, her chin, the delicate stretch of her neck.

Ethan's hand, in his pocket, is still curled around his phone. *None of us are gonna get money until this thing blows over,* Randy had said. *Trouble,* he'd said.

Annoying, the way Randy's words still rattle around inside Ethan's skull, the way they resist his attempts to give them the old heave-ho. It's only when Maddy stands and punches Ethan lightly on the arm—"Well, *hey*," she says—that Randy and all his panic flit away like bats into black sky. *Sayonara, suckers.*

A pause. Maybe awkward, maybe not.

Wordlessly, Ethan and Maddy fall into step next to each other, start heading uphill. Five steps. Seven.

"Fun night?" Ethan asks. A dumb question, he knows, the dumbest, the kind that only gets asked as a way to fill up space, to stave off discomfiting silence. It's the kind of question that makes a guy wonder if maybe those judgmental neighbors wouldn't be so wrong after all. Maybe he is just another Prufrock: Old. Pathetic. A joke.

"Well, I mean . . ." Maddy begins. "It is *Starkfield,* after all." It's the tone of her voice. Playful. Ethan knows without looking that she's smiling, not *at* him but with him (relief then, instant relief).

Through his own grin (involuntary, this), he replies, "Right? There's nothing *but* fun in Starkfield." Her laughter, in response, feels like a gift.

Yes, here it is. The banter. The easy back-and-forth, maybe the only easy thing in his life these days.

"And you and Zo actually, like, *chose* to move here, huh?" Maddy asks. Hands deep in the pockets of her hoodie. Slow steps. She's in no hurry, and neither is he.

"We sure did."

"From . . . like . . . *New York*."

"Brooklyn. Yeah."

"And you did this because . . . ?"

Fifteen years after he and Zo made the move, even he can't fully recall the reasons why. It had something to do with the way New York felt in those years after 9/11—precarious, on a knife's edge. All those police officers searching backpacks at the entrance of the subway stations, the briefcase-sniffing K-9s, the way every helicopter in the sky felt like an ominous warning. Besides, Bränd had moved west by then, and Ethan had placed a tiny diamond on Zo's finger (handmade platinum band, purchased with cash at the Clay Pot on Seventh Avenue in Park Slope, back when the store sold at least a handful of clay pots). Moving to the Berkshires felt like clarity, sanity. Zo could make her films in peace, Ethan could write novels, maybe a screenplay or two. It was a chance to live a little more simply, *I went to the woods to live deliberately* and all that.

Now he tries to explain it to Maddy the only way he knows how: "Seemed like a good idea at the time."

"Well," Maddy answers. And this time there's no laughter in her voice. "I definitely know *that* feeling."

Ethan's phone buzzes. Stops, then begins again, almost immediately.

Poorhouse.

Motherfucking apocalypse.

Ethan pulls the phone out of his pocket just long enough to glimpse the image of Randy that's stored in his contacts: the silver-blond mane, just rumpled enough to look like he's not trying too hard, the fake horn-rims, those perfect teeth. The smile of a man who has never doubted the world is his.

"Oooh, what's that, an actual, like, phone call?" Maddy asks him. "Old-school." Maddy hates the phone—or rather, hates talking on the phone. In truth, she uses her phone constantly, flipping at dizzying speed between her camera and texts and Instagram and Snapchat and Candy Crush and FaceTime and God-knows-what-else. But the one way she won't use her phone is as an actual phone. It's one of Zo's biggest frustrations with her. *The main reason Maddy's here is to help out with Alex,* Zo has complained on more than one occasion. *But how are we supposed to leave our kid with someone who won't pick up when I call?*

"It's an old buddy of mine," Ethan tells Maddy. Then he adds, "Hollywood guy." He feels the urge to say more. Not about the conversation he'd just had—not about *balls-on-the-chopping-block* and *out-for-blood*—but the better, more impressive stuff. He could explain that Randy's kind of a big deal, actually, that his name appears regularly in *Variety* and *The Hollywood Reporter,* and even, from time to time, *Vanity Fair.* He could tell her that he and Randy launched Bränd together, just the two of them, after college, and that it was exhilarating. That sometimes, even now, Ethan still lies awake at night, remembering how it all felt back in those heady New York days, when their whole lives still lay ahead, all doors open, nothing yet impossible.

But even if helping launch one of Hollywood's most successful influence companies *did* happen to be the kind of thing that Maddy cared about, all she'd have to do is take a look around at Ethan's life today. What about any of this—the dying town, the sour wife, the ADHD kid, the picking up dog shit on nighttime walks—is likely to impress her?

Maddy takes a deep breath, looks up at the trees. "Holy wow, that was some righteous flower. Arlo's gonna make *bank.*"

Ethan has to piece together the meaning: *righteous, flower, bank.* "Wait. Arlo's a . . . dealer?"

"Entrepreneur," Maddy corrects. "You know Green Arts Wellness? That's his." Green Arts is a dispensary, or it's trying to be anyway. Set halfway between Starkfield and Bettsbridge, it's one of a gazillion Massachusetts businesses waiting for their recreational marijuana license. Any day now, the state will go the way of Colorado: all pot shops and open toking, hundreds of millions of dollars in revenue to be made, maybe more. That's what they say, anyway, although years after legalizing weed, the state has yet to approve a single facility.

"Ohh, I see." Ethan laughs. "*That's* what you were doing with those guys down there. *Market research*."

He's teasing her, but damn: what he wouldn't do for some of that righteous flower right about now.

"Dude, have you *seen* Green Arts? It's like an Apple Store in there. That guy we were with tonight? He's, like, a top cannabis consultant, and he says Arlo's going to be rich as . . . wait, who's that king?"

"Croesus?" Ethan frowns. He doesn't care for this line of conversation. "Well, we'll see. For the moment, Green Arts seems more like Schrödinger's Dispensary." Meaning, it'll open or it won't. Arlo will be rich as Croesus or he won't.

Though, come to think of it, wasn't the kid born rich as Croesus? *Entrepreneur, my ass.* Arlo's just a greedy, spoiled-ass son of a guy who lucked out in the dot-com bubble and now has money to burn on the Next Big Thing.

Cripes, he wants to think about Arlo O'Shea as much as he wants to think about Randy. "Listen, how come you don't have any girlfriends, anyway?" he asks Maddy.

"Why do you care?"

"I think you need some girlfriends, that's all."

"Okay, first of all," Maddy says. "Why does it matter if my friends are girls, or guys, or both or neither? And second, do *you* happen to know a whole lot of girls my age who live in Starkfield, Massachusetts?"

To her first point, it does matter. It matters to him, anyway. And to her second, well, she's probably right: it sometimes feels like he and Zo are the youngest people in this town, and they're well into their mid-forties. "I'm going to find you some girlfriends," he says.

The sound of gravel beneath their feet. And then Maddy's voice, more hesitant now. "So . . . is Zo still pissed at me?"

There had been another misunderstanding. Zo had been certain that Maddy was supposed to pick up Alex at the end of the day. Maddy, though, swore they'd never had a conversation about it. Seething, Zo had thrust her phone toward Maddy, showing her the calendar entry: M. TO PICK UP A. "I wouldn't have *added* it to my calendar unless we had *talked* about it," Zo had said. It had been too much, that phone-thrusting, and Ethan had found himself— not for the first time—siding with the person who wasn't his wife. The truth is, Zo *is* almost certainly still pissed at Maddy, but Ethan does his best to reassure. "Oh, I'm sure she's forgotten about it," Ethan says. "Besides, she's got her group over tonight."

"All them witches. Right, I forgot."

That's what Zo's women's group calls themselves: All Them Witches. Twice a month for the past two years, sometimes more often, the witches have shown up at Ethan and Zo's home (half of them wearing pink hats, all wearing their wrath like suits of armor) to make posters and write postcards and process the dumpster fire that is the news these days.

"Well, I know for a fact that Zo didn't tell me to pick up Alex," Maddy continues, and is it possible she's leaning into Ethan now? Just a little bit? "If she *had,* I would have told her I couldn't. I had . . . a call scheduled for that time. An important one."

A call? Probably a job interview, which Ethan knows should be a good thing—there's not much in Starkfield for someone Maddy's age. But he doesn't want to think about Maddy moving on, and even if he did, he almost certainly couldn't find the words right now, because, yes: Maddy most definitely *is* leaning into him, and frankly, he's starting to feel a little dizzy.

This. The feel of her arm against his. This is something new.

And then it is just their footsteps, and the rustle of leaves overhead, and a single, late-season cricket. If it weren't for the streetlights, or the occasional television flicker from otherwise-darkened homes, Ethan could almost convince himself they're walking not just through space, but also backward, through time. Might as well be a hundred years ago.

"So, Mad . . ." he begins. He hasn't any idea what's about to come out of his mouth. He feels reckless, almost dangerous.

"Mmm?"

Finally, he says, "You shouldn't take Zo personally. She's just . . . stressed, that's all."

"Oh, I don't take it personally," Maddy says, voice bright. "When people get pissed at me, I try to be . . . just . . . like, *whatever*. You know?"

He smiles. Maybe that's the advice he should give to Randy. *Take it from a Millennial, Rand. Be, just, like, whatever.*

MADDY CAME TO Starkfield in June. It had been Zo's idea. In college at Sarah Lawrence, Zo had worked at a coffee shop called Mornin' Jo's, run by a single mom, JoAnne Silver. The woman's daughter, Madison, often hung out at the café after school; Zo sometimes helped her with homework. After graduation, Zo lost touch with the Silvers. But a few years ago, Madison—now in her twenties—found Zo on Facebook. In the intervening years, she'd shortened her name to Maddy, graduated high school, attended two years at the University of Denver, dropped out, lost her mom to ovarian cancer, then followed a dubious boyfriend to Leadville. There, she worked a series of part-time jobs, waitressing and bartending, as her relationship with Dubious Boyfriend became increasingly volatile. Early this spring, Maddy had posted to Facebook that the relationship was finally done for good. She was desperate for a new start—somewhere else, *anywhere* else—but had only a few hundred dollars to her name. Did anyone know of any opportunities, *anywhere*?

Zo had seen the post and gotten an idea: Maddy could stay in their spare bedroom for a few months, in exchange for help with Alex and the occasional errand-running and transcribing of Zo's interviews.

"You want her to live *here*?" Ethan had bristled. The renovations had just started; already, they were crammed into a fraction of their usual living space. Besides, the last thing he wanted to do was make small talk with some stranger, some *Millennial,* before he'd even had his first cup of coffee.

Zo had pressed. It would be temporary, a few months tops, just long enough for the girl to figure out her next move. The poor kid *needed* this, she'd been in such a bad relationship—Zo had said those two words, "bad relationship," pointedly, some sort of code that Ethan didn't fully understand.

Besides, Zo argued, couldn't they both use the help? Zo's new film project was big: a commission from ESPN of all places, the first paid gig she'd had in a long, long time. "Plus you'll be busy with your Dr. Ash thing," Zo said. *His* latest paid gig was overhauling a website for an ethically dubious "wellness guru," an Instagram influencer at least fifteen years his junior, known to her growing fandom as "Dr. Ash"—never mind that Ashleigh Skelfoil's sole credential is a PhD in holistic healing, issued by an online university, accredited only in Liberia, with no apparent physical address.

Finally, Zo had lowered the boom, said the inarguable thing, the thing for which Ethan had no sound comeback: "Besides, don't *you* think we need a little help with Alex?" And what could he say to that? Of course they needed the help. At eleven, Alex was somehow still as exhausting, as challenging, as, *spirited,* as she'd been in the days of velcro light-up sneakers.

So on an unseasonably cold and drizzly day in late May, Maddy had pulled into their driveway in Yoda, her twenty-two-year-old Toyota with a mismatched driver's side door. They'd all gone outside to greet her—this girl with long, mermaid-blue hair and thrift-shop overalls, this person they recognized only from social media. Maddy had climbed out of her car and taken a long, slow look around. Then she'd tossed her hands in the air and laughed. "Where the fuck *am* I?"

Even though Alex was standing right there, even though his daughter hadn't yet finished fifth grade and shouldn't be hearing language like that, Ethan couldn't help but laugh too. It wasn't just the juxtaposition of Maddy's buoyant laughter with that hard expletive. It's that in those five words, Maddy had formulated the words to a question that Ethan hadn't even realized had been building up inside him for years.

Where the fuck *was* he, anyway?

Spring came and went, and then summer too. Maddy did some babysitting here and there. She searched for jobs online and researched various degree programs, though her next move still hadn't quite materialized. Now here it is, almost October, and Maddy's still staying with them. Not that Ethan minds. To the contrary, and to his great surprise, it turns out he doesn't mind at all.

THIS EASE NOW. Just the two of them. The faint scent of manure from some distant farm. A faraway dog bark. Almost home.

And is it so wrong, this? As long as it's *just* this—just a walk home, a little conversation, that's all—need it be necessarily *wrong*?

They reach the edge of the old Starkfield cemetery, the last milestone before home. It's dark in there. Ethan can just make out the faded gravestones, jutting from the ground at haphazard angles like crooked teeth.

Skeletons beneath soil. Once, those bones were covered in flesh, in muscle and sinew. They were human beings, as real as he, who walked on these same streets, looked upon these very same houses. If they woke now, these old ghosts, what would they think? Of him? Of Maddy's blue hair? Of the fact that vibrating in his pocket at this very second—Randy again, he's sure of it, guy's a pain in the ass—is a tiny computer, ready to give him the answer to every question he could ever ask? What would these dead souls think about this tap-of-finger *connection* to everything, everyone, the whole world, the universe beyond?

And for all of that, would the skeletons see much difference between him and them?

Then it's almost as if they have traveled back in time, like they're in some sort of Jane Austen novel, or maybe a postmodern mash-up, with everything old and new all at the same time, because Maddy slips her arm through his. They walk like this, elbows linked, and oh, man: what would the neighbors think if they saw him now? Would they declare it scandalous that he's arm-in-arm with someone nearly twenty years his junior? On the other hand, there's something so *goofy* about the gesture. It's the sort of thing Alex would do: *Come on, Dad, you be the scarecrow and I'll be Dorothy.*

Yes, this is fine. He's almost certain. He and Maddy are off to see the wizard, that's all.

Ethan lifts his eyes toward the dome of stars overhead. A miracle, the universe suddenly seems. It's all a fucking miracle, and never mind the dead: Ethan is alive, and now he knows this for sure.

He longs to tell Maddy everything. He wants to tell her how it felt to grow up outside an old Pennsylvania steel town, how he could stare out the window behind his house and see nothing but farmland, then walk to the front door and see a whole neighborhood, with mothers unpacking groceries and kids in Toughskins playing a game of tag so big, so sprawling, it seemed to comprise the whole world. He wants to tell her about the first time he went to a museum—he was fifteen, it was a school trip—and he'd stared gaping and incredulous at the Gauguins, all those bold blocks of color, those flattened, feminine forms. His heart had pounded, he wanted to reach out and touch those figures, he half believed that if he had, they might come to life, they'd turn around and smile at him from inside their canvases. He wants to tell Maddy that there's still so much he hopes for, things he can't even name, things that feel like a word you can't quite remember, it's on the tip of your tongue, and as soon as you hear it, you'll be all, "Yes, that's it. Yes, that's exactly right."

That's how it is with the things that he hopes for: they're inside him, still, and he'll remember them any second now. The veil that's keeping him from them is gossamer thin.

But he says nothing, because he doesn't want to spoil any of this: Maddy's arm in his. The lone, determined cricket, not yet silenced by cold, trilling in the leaves. This night. The unlikeliness of any of it.

Just past the graveyard, the empty street gives way to parked cars, nearly all plastered in bumper stickers:

RESIST.

PERSIST.

IF YOU'RE NOT OUTRAGED, YOU'RE NOT PAYING ATTENTION.

INJUSTICE ANYWHERE IS A THREAT TO JUSTICE EVERYWHERE.
LOVE EVERYBODY NO EXCEPTIONS.
MY OTHER CAR IS A BROOM.

His driveway. Ethan stops walking, his arm still linked with Maddy's, and takes in his home: the scraped paint, the halted construction (he needs that Bränd money, he really does). Shafts of light hurl themselves from the windows, dissolve into nothing in the darkness.

"Need to steel yourself?" Maddy asks.

"Something like that."

From inside, music starts up, a sign that Zo's meeting is almost over. Each week, one member gets to choose a song that's inspired them. Last week, they played Patti Smith's "People Have the Power." The week before that, it was the Beatles' "Revolution." Before that, Martha Wainwright's "Bloody Motherfucking Asshole." Since the witches started meeting, he's heard Marvin Gaye's "What's Going On," Helen Reddy's "Ain't I a Woman?," that old "Ain't No Stopping Us Now" song, who the hell knows who wrote it. "Do You Hear the People Sing," from *Les Miz,* has come up more than a few times. But whatever song they're playing tonight, he doesn't recognize it.

On the front porch, weedy vines hang like abandoned streamers from a long-ago party. Ethan feels his breath enter his lungs, then exit.

Out there is a planet made of diamonds.

Out there is a planet that rains rocks and reaches 4,000 degrees.

Out there is a rogue planet, tied to nothing, wandering the universe alone and never seeing a single dawn.

Yes: he wants this moment to keep going. He wants to walk and walk—past his house, into the fields beyond. He wants to stand in the open meadow, look up at all those glimmering lights, to feel, fully, that fist-sized muscle, his heart, beating behind his ribs.

What if he could just let it roll off of him—the bills that haven't been paid, the checks that haven't arrived, the bygone days with Randy, the witches in his living room, all the news that everyone's so pissed off about all the time, the broken house, the kid's prescriptions and homework, Randy's hysteria, this deathly quiet town filled with ghosts and bones?

What if he could let it all go? What if he could be just like, *whatever*?

June 1995

Bränd's First Leap of Faith is a painting. Street art–style, but these brushstrokes cover not some brick facade of New York's Lower East Side but rather one of the most prime advertising sites in the city: the Forty-second Street/Eighth Avenue billboard—a spot that has always, until now, been reserved for the Stetson-clad Marlboro man.

According to the eyewitnesses who will go on record with the *New York Times,* the canvas had not been unfurled at 2:30 A.M. But now, as the first beams of sun break over the East River, it's there. It won't last long—a couple of hours if they're lucky. Newspapers will document not only the painting itself, but also its speedy removal. Pundits will wonder aloud: What exactly *was* that? Some sort of protest against Big Tobacco? An advertisement? And if so, for *what*?

The subject of this painting is a man—one that anyone who ever took freshman lit, or ever read T. S. Eliot, will recognize: the poor bastard whose hair is growing thin, who shall grow old, who has seen the moment of his greatness flicker. The man, seen from behind, stands stiffly in a dark suit and bowler hat. Something about his posture suggests hesitation. Toward the edge of the frame, the viewer glimpses, through a crack in the door, technicolor nebulas, pinwheel galaxies, the entire magnificent universe.

The image bears just four words. The first three form a simple question: *Do I dare?*

It's 1995. The world is post–Cold War, post-Perestroika, post-reunification. The Internet, that information superhighway, is still novel; the world it will create, like the new millennium itself, lies just over the horizon. Right now, as Ethan and Randy, barely a year out of college, stand here looking up, a billion-dollar telescope perched hundreds of miles in outer space beams down images of the heavens. Scientists huddle over DNA in labs, mapping the entirety of the human genome.

Everything feels new, limitless, there for the taking. Do we dare?

Over the next few days, similar paintings will appear around the city: this same, sad man hesitating before reaching for a peach. Standing at the shore, ear tilted as if trying, and failing, to hear some siren call. Trapped against a corkboard by an oversized pushpin. Two dozen images in total, appearing collectively on walls and sidewalks in SoHo, Alphabet City, Chelsea, the Meatpacking District, Brooklyn Heights.

But this one, astride the massive DKNY mural in the heart of Times Square, is the first, and the biggest, and the boldest, and the most surprising. This is the one that seems to best capture how it feels to be alive right now.

Within months, the artist who painted this canvas, a woman, will have a solo show at the Gagosian. Within a few years, the Whitney. But the artist's name, today, appears nowhere. There was a cost to this anonymity, but everybody has their price— and Randy, who commissioned the work, has an instinct for such things. Where the artist's signature would ordinarily appear, in the lower right-hand corner, is a single word: *Bränd*.

Randy, on the ground, stares up at the billboard.

"Fucking Prufrock, man," Randy says. His mouth curls into a smile.

Watching him, Ethan realizes: No. The painting is *most* of us. But not all of us. It's not Randy, not even a little.

Unlike Eliot's Prufrock, Randy fucking dared.

3

HOW TO COME HOME

You think you know what to expect. You assume, when you open the door to your home, you'll see the usual group of women, planning their next protest, or finishing up a card-writing campaign, or staring at a gerrymandered map of some district you've never heard of.

It'll be grim faces. Dark eyes. Protest. Resist.

But you're not the only one who's chosen to escape the usual categories tonight. You're not the only one who longs to feel the thrum of life moving through you.

Here is what greets you: a swirl of pink, a crush of bodies in motion. Limbs and feet and hips and breasts. Lurching, swaying, bobbing, writhing. Dancing. The music blares. Your living room—the part that isn't covered up by contractor plastic, that is—has become a dance floor, some strange, surrealistic night club, all bumping pelvises, rolling shoulders, bodies that gyrate and bounce and flail in only-sort-of-sync with the pulsing beat.

And here is the oddest part, the truly unnerving thing: amid all this movement there are no faces whatsoever. You see no noses, no freckles, no chins or cheeks, eyebrows or eyeglasses or earrings or, for that matter, ears. No distinguishing haircuts, no hair at all. In place of all of these things, there is only pink yarn.

What the . . . ?

And where, in this crowd, is your wife?

◆

Sᴋɪ ᴍᴀsᴋs. Tʜᴇ women in Ethan's house are wearing some sort of ski masks.

Except that's not quite right: their head coverings aren't for winter sports. They're . . . what do you call them? *Balaclavas,* that's right: headwear for both criminals and dissidents. The women are wearing cheap acrylic pink balaclavas, every last one of them, as if the group that calls themselves All Them Witches have, in an instant, transformed from aging small-town activists into some sort of girl gang, a posse, goddamned lady-burglars.

Actually, Ethan realizes, that's not a bad idea for a story. *The Burglarettes.* Could be a film, maybe, or a TV series. He'll pitch the idea to Randy one of these days, if—*when*—things get back on track.

Ethan doesn't recognize the song that's blasting through his home, but every bar seems to end with the same line: *Don't play stupid, don't play dumb, Vagina's where you're really from!*

He searches for his wife among the dancers. None of them is Zo. All of them are Zo. Ethan is struck by the odd sensation that he doesn't actually know what his wife looks like now. It doesn't help that the room is so crowded! It's not just the number of dancers—there are probably a dozen or so, jammed so close they might as well be a single organism—or that half the square footage of the first floor lies on the far side of contractor tarps. It's also that what little space they have is crammed with furniture, far more than one family needs.

Zo's fault, that furniture. For some reason she won't stop *buying.* Their contractor has explained that if their renovation is ever to move beyond the demolition phase, he'll need the next payment installment. And for *that* to happen, they need either Ethan's late Bränd checks, or a new check from Dr. Ash, or for Zo to finish that ESPN documentary. Instead of working on the project, though, Zo seems to spend hours shopping for furniture online, as if they already have their skylights, their recessed lighting, their open floorplan. Just this afternoon, a new sofa arrived, even though their current sofa is less than two years old. Ethan had been in the process of turning away the delivery, explaining that there must be some mistake, until Zo appeared behind him. "Yes, that's ours," she confirmed, leaving him standing there like an idiot, like a dope. Now as the women dance in balaclavas, two sofas (one new, one definitely-not-old, both the same dingy shade of gray) sit back-to-back. Everyone's sardined into a space that also includes three rolled carpets (two still covered in plastic), two coffee tables (one made of chrome and glass, an obvious disaster-in-the-making for a family with a kid who's been diagnosed hyperactive), four armchairs, and some sort of tufted ottoman.

With nowhere to move, each dancer is simply repeating the same motions over and over. It looks like a cross between the Irish Republican Army and the Charlie Brown dance scene. Ethan scans the moving figures, tries to ascertain who's who. Nearest to him is a set of gyrating hips, slow and heavy in baggy, elastic-waist pants. No question who this is: the oldest of the group, in her late seventies, maybe. Short hair, dyed jet-black. Name's Eleanor. He's pretty sure it's Eleanor, anyway. Could be Ellen? Elna? Something like that, definitely begins with an E-L.

Elastic, Ethan thinks. *Elastic Waistband. Ye shall know me by my pants.*

Next to her is a stick figure in athletic gear, all elbows and fibrous muscle. This can only be Running Mom, the one he sees sprinting through town, a permanent scowl on her face.

Running Mom hip-bumps a figure in paint-splattered jeans: the artist, no doubt. Last spring, Ethan and Zo went to one of her openings at a gallery over in Bettsbridge; there, Ethan drank boxed wine from a plastic cup and tried to make sense of the woman's paintings, which were of . . . meat cleavers. (Canvas after canvas, nothing but meat cleavers! There were bloody meat cleavers, gleaming meat cleavers, meat cleavers on beds, and on sterile trays! Pairs of meat cleavers facing off, blade to shining blade!)

Those are the women he can pick out. The others, including his wife, are indistinguishable.

Don't play stupid, don't play dumb, Vagina's where you're really from.

He longs to leave this scene, maybe disappear into his bedroom—
it's right there, on the first floor, next to the dancing women ("A
first-floor master so you can age in place," said the real estate listing when he and Zo bought the place, back when aging anywhere
was an abstraction, wholly hypothetical). But Maddy's already
plopping down on the brand-new sofa, sprawling across it with
her shoes still on. (She's so comfortable! Everywhere she goes!)
Maddy pulls her sapphire hair into a loose bun on top of her head,
begins tapping on her phone.

There. The one down by Maddy's feet: Torn jeans, oversized
L.L.Bean sweater, holes at the elbows. That's his wife. That's Zo.

Above this entire scene, CNN plays in silence. The screen shows
a protest in the Capitol Rotunda: all women, all in black, many
with duct tape covering their mouths. The chyron at the bottom
of the screen reads: SUPREME COURT BATTLE HEATS UP. Ah, yes, the
newest outrage: a SCOTUS nominee who has been accused by a
high school classmate of a long-ago assault.

Ethan's phone buzzes. He pulls it out, expecting Randy. In fact,
it's Maddy, texting from three feet away. *OMG,* she writes.

He texts back a wide-eyed emoji.

Maddy: *White ladies, am I right?*

His finger hovers over his phone. He could tease, "Aren't you a
white lady?" But he looks up at Elastic Waistband, at the short,
jerky thrusts of her pelvis—that's entirely too much thrusting,
frankly—then remembers how Maddy looked beneath the streetlight: her smooth curves, the gentle lift of her head as she drew
that smoke into her lungs.

No, Maddy seems like a different sort of being altogether.

He sends Maddy a laughing-face emoji, then a shrug emoji.
And that's when Ethan notices that one of the balaclava-clad dancing women isn't a woman at all. It is, in fact, an eleven-year-old
child. *His* child. Alex.

Ethan weaves his way into the throng of women, taps his daughter on the shoulder, motions for her to remove her balaclava. She
does, but she continues bobbing up and down in rhythm to the
beat. "Kiddo, it's time for bed," he says.

Alex continues dancing, mouthing the words of whatever song this is: *My pussy, my pussy, is sweet just like a cookie.*

Jesus Christ. He puts his hand on her shoulder. *"Alex. Bed. Now."*

Alex has a way of going dark. It happens instantly, like someone's yanked a shade down over a window. Her eyes go black, her jaw hardens. Ethan, undeterred, stares her down, reminds himself that he's doing the right thing. It's late, she's a kid, it's a school night, this is perfectly fair. He's doing what fathers are supposed to do, he's *parenting* for Chrissakes, no matter what the heck her mom is doing.

"Fine," Alex snaps. She stomps toward the stairs.

"I'll be up in five minutes to make sure you're asleep," he calls behind her. In response, Alex whirls around. Lifts her hands like they're claws, and hisses at him. Bares her teeth.

Sixth grade, this kid, and she's still hissing like a feral cat.

"I'm serious, Alex." Alex narrows her eyes, gives him a final snarl, and disappears into the upstairs, leaving him alone with the dancing Burglarettes.

WHEN THE MUSIC ends, the women peel off their masks. And just like that, guerrilla soldiers become again moms and grandmas, small-town neighbors with ordinary lives. They're women who hold down jobs, care for kids, volunteer, who-the-heck-knows-what-they-do.

They're laughing now. Even Zo's laughing, which means, just for a moment, she resembles the person he thought he'd married—the woman he *had* married, the one who was clever and grounded, who could find the funny in anything, until anger settled inside her like an unwelcome squatter. Zo wipes a trickle of sweat from her forehead with the back of her hand. "Wow," she says. "That felt great."

"What's that?" Elastic Waist asks. Can't hear worth a damn, this woman.

"I SAID THAT FELT GREAT," Zo repeats.

"Boy did I ever need that," says Running Mom with a laugh. "Especially this week."

"Right?" says the artist. "I think we all needed that this week." Then, to Elastic Waist: "WE ALL NEEDED THAT."

By now, though, Elastic Waist's eyes are on the television.

There, on the screen, is Bill Cosby. It's not the Bill Cosby that exists in Ethan's mind, not the man who once sold him Pudding Pops and danced around in colorful sweaters with the rest of the Huxtables. This is an older version: slower, more grizzled, nothing funny here. Sad Bill Cosby is in handcuffs, and he's shuffling out of a courtroom guided by a uniformed officer. The chyron: BILL COSBY SENTENCED TO PRISON. The ultimate walk of shame, this: a once-beloved comedian being sent off to prison for things that Ethan still somehow can't quite connect to the man. (Bill Cosby? Host of *Kids Say the Darnedest Things*? Seriously?)

And then Cosby's gone, and CNN's on to the next segment, which means the women are looking at a smiling headshot: the new Supreme Court pick, the one who denies everything. (There will be a hearing. The man plans to fight this, he'll stick it out, emerge a martyr or a champion but he won't fucking cower, won't be shamed, won't crawl away with his tail between his legs. That's not how this is going to go down.)

The women boo, and someone shouts "motherfucker," and someone else lifts a middle finger, and then they're all doing it, the whole lot of them, standing there with their fingers up, like some rebel army flashing their salute to one another.

Whatever the hell new war the women have declared, Randy had said. It hits Ethan: Bränd could be in trouble. Real trouble.

But come on: Randy's no Bill Cosby, is he? Sure, the guy's a pain in the ass, can be a bit of a dick, to be honest, always with the showman thing. But Ethan's known him nearly three decades, since their first day of college. Whatever accusations face Bränd, they won't stand up in the face of real scrutiny. Ethan's sure of that. Almost sure.

So why does he feel so uneasy?

Feeling eyes on him, he looks up. Elastic Waist, the only one not flashing her middle finger to the screen, is watching him. Assessing him somehow. Or maybe judging him. He can't discern what the woman's look means, exactly, but he doesn't like it, doesn't like *her,* if he's being honest, and isn't it time all these women go home?

Zo clicks the remote control, and the screen goes dark.

Hugs all around. Murmurs of encouragement. *We'll get through this* and *Take care of yourself, try to get some sleep,* and *We'll stop him, we will,* and *Will we?*

Whatever it takes, they say.

Hell or high water, they say.

Good night, they say, picking up purses and backpacks and notebooks and reading glasses and balaclavas. *GOOD NIGHT,* they say, a little louder, to Elastic Waist. Hypatia lumbers around the abandoned dance floor lapping up cookie crumbs and popcorn bits. Maddy, still sprawled across the new sofa, smiles at something on her phone. Ethan empties a wineglass into the sink, sets it in the dishwasher. *Drive safe, stay strong, is this your bag,* they say, and then, at last, Zo closes the door.

And then it is his house, theirs, again.

A beat.

"So that was—" Ethan begins to say. The next word is going to be *interesting.* Meaning, the dancing, the masks, because it was. It *was* interesting. He's not going to say *ridiculous,* he's not going to say *absurd,* he's definitely not going to say *fucking insane,* he's not an idiot for heaven's sake, but it doesn't matter. Zo holds up her hand, stops him midsentence.

"Don't," she warns. "I swear to God, Ethan, just don't, because it'll just lead to a fight, and I cannot take one more thing this week."

He's acutely aware of Maddy, the way her finger pauses over her phone screen just for a beat before she continues tapping.

He drops a plate into the sink with a clatter. Let Zo clean up. He didn't make this mess, or ask for it. He heads upstairs to check on Alex.

4

A SWISH OF covers. A body diving. A flash of light disappears beneath a pillow, and then there is Alex: instantly still, eyes squeezed shut, blanket to her ears, her snore too conspicuous to be real.

"Hand it over," Ethan commands.

Alex sits up. "Ugh. *Fine*." She pulls a cracked iPad from beneath her pillow and hands it to Ethan. The device is the vestige of a brief, failed experiment at her private school. Last year, all families with students in fourth grade or higher were required to purchase iPads—the cost, mind you, was on *top* of the five-figure tuition they were already paying. In exchange, administrators promised project-based learning, coding classes, access to libraries and resources around the world. Whether any of those promises were kept is unclear. What's certain, though, is that school servers accessed Pornhub and similar sites so often that administrators shut down the iPad program midyear. The school's latest round of marketing materials declares them proudly screen-free, as if that had been their intended policy all along.

Ethan steals a quick glance at the iPad, just to check on what Alex was doing. Not porn, thank goodness. Instead, it's open to a fan site for *Wicked*, the Broadway musical. Her latest obsession.

Alex sits up. "So, Daddy. Do you think the song that Mommy's group was listening to is transphobic?"

"Transphobic?" Ethan frowns. "It's definitely *inappropriate*. Definitely not for *kids*. But how exactly would it be—"

"It was about vaginas. Not all women *have* vaginas, Daddy. Some women have *penises*. Duh."

Sometimes Ethan gets this feeling: like he's lost his grip on some critical thing, accidentally untethered himself from the world's orbit. Now he finds himself in some new galaxy, everything he once took for granted faded to a distant fleck.

"Right," he says. "That's a good point. Alex, how do you know about transphobia?"

"*Everyone* knows about transphobia, Daddy. Plus, they teach us about it at school."

The Rainbow Seed School had gone decades without any sort of sex-ed programming. That is, until Zo got some sort of bee in her bonnet about the whole thing. She raised money to bring what she called a "whole-health curriculum" to the school, an effort that wasn't entirely without controversy. There had been a series of meetings, Zo versus what she called the *ostrich moms,* the ones who, as she described it, believed that "jamming their heads into the ground is a viable alternative to informed reality." Zo had emerged victorious, as Ethan had known all along she would, and for six weeks last year, a sexuality educator had stood in front of the kids speaking frankly not just about anatomy and the mechanics of reproduction, but also—he learned only later—about the realities of pornography, about blow jobs and masturbation, with such apparent frankness that Alex had no reservations raising these topics as dinner-table conversation.

"But actually," Alex says now. "Don't you think 'vagina' is a great word? Just listen to it." She draws the word out slowly. "Vaginaaaaa. Vagiiiiina. If I ever have a daughter, I want to name her Vagina."

Ethan coughs. "Well, I suspect you'll change your mind by the time you're old enough to—"

But apparently Alex isn't interested in his prediction, because she talks right over him. "Mommy says that one of these days she's going to let me pick the song at the end of the meeting. I know exactly what I'll pick, too. Can you guess? I'll bet you can guess."

She lifts her chin and begins belting out into the darkness, *"I think I'll tryyyy . . . Defyyyyying gravity. . . ."*

Alex's life has been a string of fixations, a fact that has long driven Ethan and Zo bonkers. There are, after all, only so many times one can watch the same *Phineas and Ferb* episodes, or listen to Taylor Swift's country phase, or hear *Nancy* cartoons read aloud frame-by-frame. Everything—literally everything, save perhaps the *Hamilton* soundtrack—wears thin after six months of nonstop play.

Except not, apparently, for Alex.

"Tell them, IIIIII'm defyyyyying gravity!" She holds her hands out, wide, as if she's about to take flight.

From downstairs comes Zo's voice: "Alex. BED."

Okay, first of all, Alex is *in* bed, no thanks to Zo or her ski-mask dancing friends. Ethan's the one who's here right now, getting their kid settled. Besides, Zo of all people should know that there's no stopping Alex when she gets this way, all stream-of-consciousness and random blurting.

"Daddy, did you know that the guy who plays Fiero in *Wicked*—Fiero's the Scarecrow, he falls in love with Elphaba—is named Norbert Butz? That's funny. *Butz. Norbert Butz.* Also, what was Mommy's group meeting about tonight? Because they said the F-word a *lot.*"

Two years ago, as the presidential campaign took some uncomfortable turns, Alex's school sent home a notice called "Talking to Children About Difficult Subjects in Current Events." Their instructions: answer your child's questions honestly, but avoid giving more detail than necessary. Ethan tries that now. "Well . . . the president appointed a judge to serve on the Supreme Court. Which the president is supposed to do, that's part of checks and balances, remember we talked about those? But someone the judge knew a long time ago says he once . . . um . . . did something bad."

Good. That was good. That's the story, more or less, the broad outline anyway, told delicately, in a kid-friendly way.

"Oh." Alex's voice is matter-of-fact. "You mean that lady he raped."

"Uh . . . not exactly, he . . . tried. Maybe. I don't know." Ethan feels like he should explain about innocent-until-proven-guilty, about due process, but then he thinks about all of the women in the Capitol Rotunda, those BELIEVE WOMEN signs he's been seeing everywhere, all the stories that have come out, one after another, over the last few years. He thinks about Zo, and the witches, and he doesn't know *what* to tell Alex. What is the right thing to say about a very real crime that almost always comes down to one person's word against another's?

"Probably," he finally says. "These . . . are difficult cases."

But Alex is already moving on. "Also, Daddy, guess what? Idina Menzel—she plays Elphaba, the Wicked Witch of the West— missed her final Broadway performance because she fell through a trapdoor onstage. But get this: the lady who played the Wicked Witch of the West in the *movie* version of the Wizard of Oz *also* got hurt during filming, so some people say there's a *curse* on that character. Still, I'd take the part if I could. I'd be, like, super freaked-out, but I'd totally do it, oh, and you know what else? This is so cool: sometimes NASA wakes up astronauts by playing 'Defying Gravity.' They play that song *all the way in outer space!*"

"Okay, well, we can talk about that tomorrow. Right now, though, it's time to sleep."

He pats the pillow, and Alex falls backward onto it, hard. He smooths down her hair, kisses her on the temple. "Good night, Norbert Butz," he whispers.

A mistake. Alex pops right back up again. "No, I'm *Elphaba,*" Alex says. "She's wicked, *and* she's the only one who gets to fly, oh, and *ohmygod Daddy!* I forgot to tell you the most important thing! They're making a *movie* of *Wicked*! It's not going to come out for three years, but Daddy, we *have* to see it on the night it's released, okay? Promise me, Daddy, okay? You have to *promise*. Do you think Idina Menzel will play Elphaba, because I can't imagine another Elphaba, and . . ."

And on and on she goes, not even taking a breath.

Forget the Burglarettes. What he should write is a how-to book: *How to Not Lose Your Mind. How to Live with a Hyperactive Child Who Drives You Frigging Bananas. How to Put Your Kid to Bed or Die Trying, Because Seriously: Some Nights It Feels like It Might Actually Kill You.*

ALEX WAS A challenge from the moment she arrived shrieking in the world. A colicky infant, she slept badly, couldn't suckle, ate tepidly, grew too slowly. That last bit earned her a failure-to-thrive diagnosis, complete with a bunch of VNA home visits. The nurses reassured them: *Things will get easier as soon as your daughter starts putting on weight.*

The nurses were wrong.

As she grew, Alex proved sensitive to the mildest changes in temperature, to low-level noise, to the feel of particular blankets against her skin. She hated baths, diaper changes, being set down even for a few moments . . . and she was *always* awake.

Ethan and Zo tried everything to help her sleep. They tried Ferberizing and co-sleeping. They watched those Happiest Baby on the Block videos, wrapped Alex like a human burrito. They took turns staying up with her into the night, shushing her and swaying as she screamed. They tried feeding schedules, nurse-on-demand, skin-to-skin marathons, white-noise machines, some Putumayo lullaby CD that one of the parents in their birthing class swore had some kind of magical soporific powers and was *truly the only thing a baby really needs to fall asleep.*

Alex got older: three months, then six months, then a year, and as she grew, the list of things that made it impossible for her to exist peacefully in this world expanded exponentially. By the time Alex was a toddler, she couldn't bear clothing tags, the feel of denim, synthetic fabrics, hats, barrettes, elastic socks. She raged at camera flashes, other children's cries, scented shampoos, cheap baby wipes. Night lights. Total darkness. Bright sun.

Ethan and Zo did what they could: ordered organic cotton clothing from Hanna Andersson, tinted their car windows, drove two hours each way to Springfield to work with a $200/hour sensory integration coach. They installed dimmers in their light switches, spoke in whispers, tiptoed around their own home like cartoon burglars mid-heist. They hissed at Hypatia when she barked, and at each other every time a wayward utensil clattered to the floor. And all the while, they endured an endless stream of advice from fellow parents who happened to have hit the Easy Kid Jackpot and took their winnings as proof that they knew everything.

A year went by, then four more, and with each new milestone, Alex found a new way to challenge their best intentions. Then came kindergarten.

From the start, Alex despised school: the transitions between classes, the noise of the lunchroom, the fluorescent lights, all that tedious sitting still! One afternoon, she came home with an abrasion on her forehead, angry and raw; Alex had apparently found circle time so excruciatingly dull that she'd rubbed her face back and forth on the carpet until she'd worn away her derma entirely.

The irony of the whole thing? For all Alex's inability to process the world around her, she was perennially unable to keep her own volume, her own energy level, her own awareness-of-self, in check. As she grew, Alex became a loud talker, an interrupter, an impulsive blurter of anything and everything that popped into her head.

While some of her sensory issues had diminished in recent years, her volume issues hadn't. Then two years ago, she discovered musical theater, and that's when things really got loud. Now here she is, babbling away about some elixir that Elphaba's mother drank while pregnant, wondering if the potion that turned her green was the same thing that allowed her to fly, and *how exactly did Elphaba fly, anyway?*

"Well, for starters," Ethan says, "she probably had a good night's sleep . . ."

"Daddy. I'm *serious*. How *would* someone fly? I mean in real life."

"Alex, people can't fly. You know that."

"Okay, but that's what they say about bumblebees, isn't it? And yet they *can* fly. So maybe the same thing is true for witches."

"You're in sixth grade, Alex." His frustration is mounting. "You *know* that witches aren't real. Now, once and for all, *good night*."

"Wait! Hold on! I just realized something, Daddy: if you say good morning, or good afternoon, or good evening, you're saying hello. But if you say good night, you're saying *goodbye*."

His voice is tight: "Good. Night."

"Good *evening*, Daddy." And then: "Good afternoon? Good morning?"

Ethan can feel it coming now: his patience bending, bending until it breaks. At which point, he will yell, and Zo will hear, and then Zo will come upstairs and add her own yelling to his. Alex will cry, and everyone will feel crummy, and tomorrow they'll start the whole thing over again.

Except tonight, Ethan is saved, mercifully, by a rap on the door. Maddy peeks into the room, grins at Alex. "Hey, girl." Maddy enters, sits on the foot of Alex's bed. "You having trouble falling asleep?"

"I *hate* sleeping," Alex declares, before telling Maddy the thing about the NASA astronauts, repeating more or less the exact same sentence structure as she just used with Ethan.

"Cool!" Maddy says. "You know, *I* heard an interesting fact, too. About witches, actually."

Alex raises her eyebrows.

"So you know how Massachusetts was once filled with witches?"

Alex nods.

"Well, guess how they figured out which girls were transforming into witches?" Maddy pauses, glances over one shoulder, then the other, like she's about to reveal top-secret information. She lowers her voice to a near-whisper and leans in. "Girls would start dreaming the same thing. All over the village. The *exact same dream*."

Is Maddy making this up? Ethan doesn't even care. Alex is spellbound, and no one is yelling, and see, this is what Zo doesn't understand about Maddy. In some ways, Maddy's not the best babysitter, certainly not the most responsible—she does sometimes forget to pick up Alex, she does ignore phone calls, and several times, he and Zo came home late to find their daughter plopped in front of reality TV, hand at the bottom of a bag of chips, the carefully prepared, nutritionally balanced dinner they'd left still untouched on the counter.

But Maddy's *good* with Alex. Kind of a natural, actually.

"So here's what I'm thinking." Maddy's voice is conspiratorial. "I think *you* should put your head on your pillow, and I should go into my room and put *my* head on my pillow, and then we should both just . . . let sleep come. Tomorrow when we wake up, we'll compare dreams."

"You think we'll dream the same thing?" Alex asks. Ethan can tell she wants to believe this, wants to believe that witches are real, and that she might yet become one, and that it could be this simple, as easy as closing your eyes.

God, he forgets sometimes: eleven years old is still so young.

"I don't know. But if we do . . ." Maddy pauses dramatically. "Then we'll *know*."

Maddy meets Ethan's eye, gives him a tiny shrug. Like, *Okay, maybe it won't work, but what's the worst that could happen?* And just like that, Ethan's ever-wired, never-tired daughter closes her eyes and starts taking long, slow breaths like she's willing herself to sleep.

Out in the hallway, Alex's door finally closed, Ethan whispers to Maddy, "Thank you."

"Kinda genius, right?"

"Amazing, actually." Ethan looks down, shakes his head. "I don't know why it's still so hard to get her to sleep. Maybe it's her medicine, maybe we need to have it adjusted. I just wish she could settle—"

"Hey, Ethan?" Maddy places a hand on his arm. "You worry too much. You know that, right?"

He doesn't know that, not at all. What is the exact right amount of worry? Light without being negligent, serious without being burdensome? He's never known, and having a kid like Alex doesn't make it any easier.

Maddy seems to read his thoughts. "Alex is fine." There's no joking now. This is as earnest as it gets. "Alex is *great*." She gives his arm a tiny squeeze, and just like that, it's all true: Alex *is* great. Everything is okay after all. It's good enough, *he's* good enough. Maddy's saying it has made it so.

Something passes between them, silent, unnamed.

"Well," Maddy finally says. She removes her hand. "So . . . good night, I guess." She slips into the guest room, the one right next to Alex's. There's nothing left for Ethan but to head downstairs to the master bedroom, to his wife.

Behind him, Maddy closes the door so gently it doesn't make a sound.

5

Zo stands motionless before the new sofa, her eyes fixed straight ahead, as if she's having a stare-down with a phantom. She's holding her phone, and through the speaker, an automated voice asks, *Do you want to talk about a recent order? Or something else?*

"Something else," Zo tells the voice.

Ethan knows without asking that Zo's called the customer-service line of a major brand, some corporation that's fucked up somehow. Maybe they did business with the NRA, or with some totally ordinary-sounding nonprofit that turned out to mask a virulently homophobic hate group. Or who knows: perhaps the company just advertised on the wrong television show, some cable news outlet whose host said something terrible, or at least clumsily, and someone tweeted it, and now the company's 1-800 number is fielding furious calls from all over the country.

Okay, says the automated voice. *I can help you with that.*

Ethan moves toward their bedroom, but Zo stops him. "Ethan, wait."

If you want to speak with a customer representative, say, "Speak with a representative." If you want something else, say, "Something else."

"Speak with a representative," Zo says to her phone, at the same moment Ethan asks, "What's up?"

I'm sorry, I didn't hear that, the automated voice says. *If you want to speak with a customer representative, say, "Speak with a representative." If you want something else, say, "Something else."*

Zo leans in to her phone. "SPEAK WITH A REPRESENTA-TIVE."

Okay, then, says the voice. *I'll connect you to a customer representative.* Some kind of godawful New Age music starts piping through the speaker.

"Ethan, what do you think of this sofa?" Zo asks.

"It's . . . nice," Ethan says. He pauses, then adds, "The old sofa was nice too."

"But what color would you say it is?" Zo asks.

"It's gray. Like the old sofa."

Zo frowns. Wrong answer. "You don't think it's *blue*?"

This new sofa, like the old sofa, is most definitely gray. The sofa is gray, the walls are gray, the carpet is gray, their lives are gray. They're trapped inside a black-and-white photograph, that's what they are.

"I guess it's sort of a . . . bluish gray?" he offers. But he can tell that this answer, too, is incorrect.

The automated voice returns. *We are experiencing an unusually high call volume. Please stay on the line enjoying our specially curated musical selection until the next available representative can take your call.*

"Well, if you'd have seen the fabric swatch, you'd have expected it to be blue too." Zo tells him.

"So let's return it."

"We can't. It was custom-made."

Behind his wife, on the wall, there's a framed print, something Zo had gotten for him on his fortieth birthday. A silk-screen, block-letters, all-caps: GUESS THIS IS YOUR LIFE NOW.

"You had a sofa custom-made?" he asks.

"Online. One of those sites that cuts out the middleman, so it's less expensive."

It's less expensive, he supposes, unless it happens to be your third sofa in two years, a gray sofa ordered to replace a different gray sofa, which had replaced the perfectly fine, nothing-wrong-with-it-other-than-some-wine-stains-and-a-whole-lot-of-dog-hair olive sofa.

Zo pulls a yellow throw pillow from a nearby chair, sets it on top. "Does that help?"

In the great gray room, there's a yellow square, and an angry wife, and a print on the wall, GUESS THIS IS YOUR LIFE NOW.

"Sure, yeah." He gestures vaguely toward the furniture pile, the carpets. "Zo, can we return *any* of this?"

"The carpet?" she says, a little vaguely.

"Which carpet?"

"Maybe that one?" she says, pointing to the largest, fattest one, still in plastic. "I hadn't really made up my mind, but I don't love it."

We are experiencing an unusually high call volume. Please stay on the line enjoying our specially curated musical selection until the next available representative can take your call.

Ethan resolves to return the carpet. Maybe Zo hasn't made up her mind, but he sure has.

FIVE MINUTES LATER, the same *specially curated musical selection* fills their master bath. Zo opens a jar of cream as Ethan unspools a line of dental floss. "So Randy finally called me back," he says.

"'Bout time." She scoops out some white glop, begins rubbing it onto her chin.

Ethan leans into the mirror. "So, it turns out, Bränd's in a bit of a . . . transition. Randy says it's been challenging."

"Not your problem, Ethan." Zo's fingers move in tiny circles up to her cheeks.

"Well . . ." He wonders how much of the conversation he should share. "It kind of is."

"Don't let Randy turn his problems into your problem. He'll try to, you know he will. That's his thing."

"That's not his 'thing,' Zo."

"It's totally his thing. It's always been his thing. Randy's whole life, other people have had to bend over backward to fix problems that *he* created, and for which he takes zero responsibility." Zo leans into the mirror, lifts up the skin on her forehead with her palm, making her fine lines disappear. She lets go, lifts again. In the mirror, Ethan takes in his own swelling gut, the gray of his beard, those white chest hairs.

Jesus, when did this happen to them?

And is it wrong? Is it so wrong if part of him is still outside, with the stars and the whispering leaves? If the walk home with Maddy still lingers in his senses, the way a whiff of perfume might persist, or a particularly good dream?

We are experiencing an unusually high call volume. Please stay on the line enjoying our specially curated musical selection until the next available representative can take your call.

Ethan changes the subject. "Zo, you probably shouldn't play songs like that in front of Alex."

"Songs like what?"

"Like . . . the one you listened to tonight. At the end of your meeting." *The one where you wore ski-masks and danced like insane terrorists while our child mouthed words about her you-know-what being sweet just like a cookie.*

"It's that band, Ethan. The feminist punk rockers who were thrown in prison in Russia a few years ago."

He doesn't know that band. "Well, regardless. It's not appropriate. Not for Alex."

"Hmm. And why's that?" She says this vaguely, but Ethan can't help feeling like Zo's just laid some sort of trap.

"Because she's *eleven*," he says. "What happens when she goes into school and says . . . that word?"

"What word?"

Yes. It's a trap. Obviously he means the P-word, the *sorta like another way to call a cat a kitten* word. Zo knows better than anyone that Alex lacks an internal filter, an Edit button. So Zo can treat him like he's ridiculous if she wants, but no: Alex isn't ready for any words she wouldn't be allowed to use in school.

Ethan tosses the floss in the wastebasket, which is filled to overflowing with crumpled pages, all covered in Zo's writing. Notes, it looks like. That's a good sign, actually. Maybe she's finally making some progress on that ESPN documentary.

He moves toward the toilet, lifts the lid. "Come on, Zo, Alex is

struggling enough in school, you know that. Can you even imagine how those administrators would respond if she interrupted
their *kumbaya* singalongs by blurting out the P-word?"

"Oh! Actually, that reminds me, Ethan. We've got that conference at school tomorrow—"

But then the music on her phone breaks, and finally there's an
actual human voice, not an automated one, on the other end.
Male, vaguely British-sounding, impeccably polite: "Good evening, this is Roger, how may I assist you tonight?"

Zo takes the phone off speaker, presumably because Roger in
customer service doesn't need to hear the sound of Ethan's piss hitting the bowl. "Hi, Roger," Zo says coolly. "My name is Zenobia
Frome. I've been a loyal customer for many years. . . ."

She walks into the living room, leaving Ethan in peace.

That poor bastard, Roger. Some late-shift customer support
worker having the worst night of his life, his politeness his only
defense against an army of pissed-off liberals yelling at him as if
there's anything he can personally do about whatever the mega-
corporation he works for happens to have done wrong.

Ethan flushes, washes, brushes, spits. Drops his jeans in the
laundry basket. Heading into the bedroom, he hears Zo say, "I
know they gave you that statement to read, Roger. You've done
your job well. Now, I'd like you to tell your superiors that their
statement has failed to convince me. This is a deal-breaker for me.
I'll never again . . ."

Ethan crawls into bed, listens to Hypatia snore. On his phone,
there are, like, a million messages from Randy:

Randy: *E, u there?*
Randy: *Don't worry. I've got a plan*
Randy: *It's a simple plan, the right word at the right time,
remember?*

That had been their original tagline at Bränd: *the right word at the
right time,* back before Randy declared that the world was post-
words, that people didn't want to read, *words are dead, long live words.*

Randy: *Maybe ur thinking you'll ignore your old pal Randy and eventually Randy will move onto something else and life will return to normal*

It was never good when Randy started talking in the third person.

Randy: *except ur wrong*
Randy: *there's no more normal, this is do or die, my friend*
Randy: *you do, or we all die*

WHEN ZO JOINS Ethan in bed, they lie back-to-back, each scrolling through their separate phones. "Hey, listen to this," Ethan says. "Great Britain has appointed a Minister of Loneliness."

"Huh," says Zo. Hard to tell if she's listening.

Ethan turns the phrase over in his head. *Minister of Loneliness.* It would make a great title for something. A novel, maybe. Sci-fi, maybe, about the last man alive at the end of the world. Maybe the protagonist has deluded himself into believing there's a whole society surrounding him, and that he's been appointed to find a cure for their despair, which turns out to be his own. Actually, maybe it would be better as a screenplay, a high-concept one.

"There should be other jobs like that," Ethan muses. "Minister of Despair. Minister of Disgust. Minister of Shame."

"Minister of Rage," Zo quips, not looking up.

He laughs. "You could do that job, actually."

She says nothing in response, and Ethan wonders if he's gone too far. "So it looks like you got some good work done today?" he asks.

Zo's new film is about Lionel Trilling. Not, as Ethan had assumed at first, the Columbia University writer and critic, the darling of the New York Intellectuals. It was only weeks into the project—weeks of Ethan wondering why his wife, who had never before shown the foggiest interest in sports, kept watching old NCAA basketball clips on YouTube—that he discovered *this* Lionel Trilling was a nineteen-year-old basketball star. Some up-and-coming kid, the #3 draft pick last year, which is something Ethan would know if he still paid attention to basketball. But that part of him—the one that hung out with Randy in sports bars, drinking beers and shouting at the television only to return to the office for a few more hours when the game ended—was, after a decade and a half of living in Starkfield, buried, gone.

A few long moments pass before Zo says, simply, "I guess."

The Trilling project has been a bit of a disaster, frankly. Soon after Zo signed the contract, Trilling hit some sort of career slump. The kid started missing free throws, committing egregious fouls. Around that time, he fired his agent; his new agent came in, guns blazing, and began hollering at Zo. *The documentary needs a whole new approach! We need less childhood, more locker-room gossip!* Zo reached out repeatedly to Trilling for his opinion on the matter, but her calls went unreturned. Sometimes his assistant got in touch, filled with excuses—*Lionel is under the weather, looks like the flu. He feels really terrible.* Then the next day, Zo would see his image on some gossip-tainment site, strolling into a wine bar with a model on his arm.

Point is, the air date's been pushed back four times now, and with it the next installment of Zo's payment. Which would be okay, if Ethan's Bränd checks weren't so late, but . . .

Ethan rolls over. "I was kidding, Zo," he offers to the back of her head. "About the Minister of Rage thing."

"Okay." She says this absently, as if he's said, *I bought some new kitchen garbage bags, Zo. I reorganized my sock drawer, Zo.*

Ethan leans down and kisses his wife's shoulder, smells the lotion on her skin. Other than a single muscle twitch in her arm—she's scrolling again—Zo doesn't respond at all. He inches a little closer, presses his torso, his hip, to hers. Still nothing. When she finally turns to face him, it's just to say, "But you do plan to be there tomorrow, right? For the nine o'clock conference?"

"What conference?"

"With Mr. McCuttle and horrible Shreya Greer-Williams? Did I not tell you about this?"

"What conference? Who's Shreya? I have a phone call with Dr. Ash in the morning."

"You know, *Shreya*," Zo says. She props herself up on her elbow. "She drives the Range Rover with the BE KIND, GO VEGAN bumper sticker on the back? We went to her potluck a few years ago? Her entire house is filled with Ojibwe dreamcatchers. Remember?"

Ethan shakes his head. He doesn't remember the potluck. He doesn't know the car, or the dreamcatchers, or anyone named Shreya.

"*Tristan's* mom," Zo says.

"Oh, okay." Then: "Wait. Tristan's mom is named Shreya?" Tristan's mom, like Tristan, is blond and fair-skinned, real Connecticut country-club look to her.

"Well, that's what she *calls herself,*" Zo says. "But I guarantee that she was born Sandy or Shelly or something. Stacy maybe."

"And what are we meeting about?"

"Well, you know how every single year Shreya has it out for a different kid in the class?"

"She does?"

"In third grade it was Digby. In fourth grade it was Zeppelin. In fifth grade it was Heidegger. Every year, there's a new one. Shreya decides that this one kid is to blame for everything that goes wrong that year, then she turns all the other parents against that kid."

"How do you turn parents against a child?"

"You talk trash about the kid, point out their flaws, tell all the other moms what the kid does wrong. Shreya always does it with an air of concern, like she's *really* looking out for the poor child. But really, it's just her way of whipping everyone into a frenzy."

"Okay, and so?"

"So this year, she's got Alex in her crosshairs."

"Wait. Are Digby and Zeppelin and Heidegger even *at* the school anymore?" Every year, it's a thing at the Rainbow Seed School: Which kids are returning for the next year? Which kids are transferring to the public school? Which families are leaving the area altogether so they can go full-on Waldorf, or whatever?

"No, Ethan, they're *not.* That's the point. Because Shreya pushed them out. And she's had it in for Alex ever since that sticker debacle, first week of school."

"Sticker debacle?"

Zo reminds him: the kids had been doing some sort of project involving stickers. One of the stickers featured a carton lemur holding out a heart that read KISS ME. Alex had stuck it on Tristan's shirt, teasing him that he wanted to give it to a girl in the class, someone he was rumored to have a crush on. "It wasn't a *great* thing for Alex to do," Zo admits. "But it was pretty typical sixth-grade stuff. Except Tristan ran crying into the coat closet and refused to come out."

"He cried over a sticker?"

"Honestly, Ethan, did I not tell you this? Then the teachers told Alex *not* to apologize, because Tristan wasn't 'ready' for the apology yet, and apparently being apologized to at some point other than the exact-right moment would have contributed to his trauma? Except of course nobody ever told Alex when the right time actually *was,* so she didn't apologize, and then Shreya was mad about *that*?" Zo stares at him. "Does *none* of this sound familiar?"

"Why are they doing sticker projects in sixth grade?" Ethan's seriously starting to wonder what kind of education Alex is getting at the Rainbow Seed School.

"That's not the *point,* Ethan. The point is, ever since that day, Shreya Greer-Williams has been after Alex like a new-age Ahab stalking her white whale. And by the way, those dreamcatchers in her house? That's cultural appropriation. Where was Shreya Greer-Williams when Standing Rock protesters were getting blasted with firehoses in subzero temperatures? That's what I'd like to know."

Ethan figures it's a rhetorical question. It's not as if Zo was out there with the Standing Rock protesters either.

"She was busy trying to get other people's children kicked out of school," Zo answers herself. "That's where she was."

"So . . . you're saying I should cancel my call with Dr. Ash?"

"*Yes,* Ethan. Obviously, you should."

Truth is, he's relieved. He can't stand this project. The work is tedious, first of all, requiring that he sort through years' worth of chat room discussions, blog posts, and e-commerce data. But he also doesn't care for Fake Doctor Ash. When Ethan was first bidding on the job, she'd declared proudly that every product she sold, every recommendation she made, was backed up by scientific studies. She cited them, right there on the site. But as Ethan delved into the content, he began to understand: Ashleigh Skelfoil is mighty selective about which studies she posts. She seems interested only in those studies that support her business model, even if they have tiny sample sizes, even if they haven't been peer-reviewed, even when their data are undermined by voluminous meta-analyses.

Not that her fans seem to care—they adore Dr. Ash with an almost religious fervor. Her fan base grows by the day, and the Dr. Ash brand seems poised to explode. She told Ethan recently that he needs to work faster; apparently she's in talks to go on the Dr. Oz show.

Zo returns to her side, her back again to Ethan. She's silent for a few moments, no doubt scrolling again through the latest outrage. It's all outrage these days, an infinite loop of outrages, like some sort of existential hell.

Ethan tries again: kisses her shoulder, lets his lips rest there, on her freckled skin. He places his hand on her hip, moves it down the outside of her thigh, then up again. He waits a beat before curving his hand beneath her T-shirt.

"*Jesus,*" Zo hisses at her screen, as if Ethan's palm isn't cupping the soft curve of her belly. "These assholes."

Ethan nuzzles his nose into her neck. "Well, you can't do anything about that tonight." Her hair tickles his skin. "Tomorrow is another day, Zo."

He inches toward her a little more, and she scoots away from him—as far away as she can get without falling off the bed. "Tomorrow will be worse."

He sighs, rolls over onto his back. Lies there on the pillow scratching his beard.

◆

IT WAS SEX, his longing for it, that made him grow the beard in the first place. He'd always been clean-shaven, even on weekends—Zo hated stubble scratch, and he himself never much cared for the itchy feel. Then last winter a bad stomach bug left him weakened and dizzy, barely able to stand, let alone shave. After three days—newly bewhiskered and filled with the ardor of the healthy—he'd stood in the bathroom, razor in hand, examining the rugged shadow on his face. Maybe, he decided, he wouldn't shave just yet. He could make a joke of it, kissing Zo in bed that night. She'd laugh, say "ew," and make a no-kissing rule for that night's action. Or who knows, maybe she'd get a kick out of experimenting with the feel of stubble on her nether region. It'd be a joke they could share. Then the following morning, he'd shave the whole thing off.

Things didn't work out as he'd planned; that night, Zo stayed up late working on the newsletter for All Them Witches, and the day after that, she worked until almost dawn, sorting game clips for the Trilling documentary. The day after *that* came another school shooting, this one at a Florida high school, which left both of them numb for weeks.

And on it went. Even on the rare occasions when the conditions were right—when they happened to get into bed at the same time, Alex quiet, the news not quite as horrific as it had been the day before, or would be again the next day—Zo didn't respond to his advances. By now, his beard falls nearly to his clavicle, representing—what—seven months of unintended celibacy?

He's like the loneliest damn lumberjack on the planet.

ETHAN SIGHS NOW, heads to the bathroom. Pees one last time. When he's done, he picks up one of the crumpled papers in the trash.

It doesn't seem to have anything to do with basketball.

◆

THE ONES WHO whooped at you from construction sites. The ones who yelled from car windows, even though you were still a kid, and walking alone. The ones who made slurpy kissing noises as you passed, which you understood reflected something about you even though you couldn't say what, or why. The ones who sat next to you in public, and made perfectly ordinary, friendly conversation, until the conversation shifted, became something else entirely.

The ones who left you wondering what you should have done differently.

The ones who told you to smile, put on some lipstick, show a little leg, why don't you. The ones who said don't worry, it's better to have an interesting face than a beautiful one. The ones who said they liked you because they were tired of pretty girls, pretty girls are more trouble than they're worth. The ones who said flaws are what make a girl truly beautiful.

The ones who made lists: best body, best ass, best rack, most likely to squeal. The ones who made rape lists. The ones who passed the lists around, and the ones who laughed. The ones who taught you that laughter can be dangerous, something to be avoided, a lesson you will never, in your life on this Earth, unlearn.

The ones who offered to drive you home from a party, then pulled the car over to the side of the road. The ones who listened when you said this wasn't what you wanted. The ones who didn't. The ones who pretended not to hear.

The ones you hated.

The ones you still fucking hate.

WEDNESDAY

6

Early morning. Dim and formless. Ethan drifts through a strange, in-between place—between night and dawn, sleep and wakefulness, swirling dreams and rational thought. Indistinct fragments appear and disappear in his consciousness, like waves lapping on a shore. They're detached from context, no sense or structure.

> the comedian in handcuffs (Suspenders. He was
> wearing suspenders)
> America's dad, hawker of pudding, on a hard prison
> bed, right now, surreal
> lipstick marks on white paper, smoke rising to yellow streetlight
> need to steel yourself?
> just like, whatever
> that motherfucker

The clock radio kicks on, NPR. This is the same way Ethan's woken for decades; he and Zo had this very clock radio in their Brooklyn days. It, too, is an in-between thing: digital numbers keep the time, while an analog radio dial never quite finds a static-free station. Through the fuzz comes the president's voice, something about North Korea. If Zo were here, she'd groan, yell at Ethan to shut it off, *I abhor that man's voice, can't stand it even for a second.*

Not that he wants to hear the man either.

He should roll over, hit Snooze. But that would require action, change, an object at rest becoming an object in motion. Not possible, not yet.

Besides, Zo is already gone, off to the gym. Not to her usual one, either. For a decade, Zo went to the fitness center on Corbury Road—the one that's small and clean with the treadmills and ellipticals. A few months ago, though, she switched to a different gym altogether, one that's halfway to Bettsbridge. At this new gym, his wife wears boxing gloves. She punches things: a bag, mostly, but sometimes she gets into a ring and spars with actual human beings. Unnerving, really.

The president's voice gives way to newscasters. The reports are dire: warming oceans, rising interest rates, bump stocks, crippling smog, the whole world splintering, descending into some kind of sinister entropy.

You do, or we all die, Randy's text had said. Ethan lets that wave, too, roll up onto the shore of his mind, then watches it ease back into the deep. Now there's the president's voice again. He's talking about the Supreme Court situation, some of the accusations against the new nominee: ". . . *she said she was totally inebriated,* . . . *she was all messed up. And she doesn't know—*"

Cripes, who can bear this guy? Ethan rolls over, slams the clock radio with his palm. He picks up his phone, sees a notification that Randy has texted him twenty-seven times. He sets the phone back again, facedown. He places his feet on the floor, runs his fingers through his hair.

A new day begins.

THE SMELL OF butter in a cast-iron pan. The clank of the radiator, the first groaning efforts of the season. Ethan cracks an egg, measures out a scoop of dog food. Outside, an old Pontiac in need of a muffler slows, tosses a newspaper in a blue plastic bag, motors on. The refrigerator kicks on, hums, then stops.

Each day the same as the one before.

Ethan eats his egg alone, in silence. In fifteen minutes he's going to wake Alex, start the infernal, exhausting process of getting his child ready for another day of sixth grade. Alex will fight him, as she always does, and he will plead, as *he* always does, saying that if she can just get started—if she can just *begin,* get out of bed and start the morning routine without a fight, move through her tasks one at a time—then maybe *just this once* they won't have to rush, he won't yell, the whole thing can be just a tiny bit easier. If only Alex could just *try.* And all the while he's pleading and cajoling, Zo, theoretically his partner on this parenting journey, probably won't even show up.

These days, his wife rarely returns until after Alex is already at school.

Ethan checks the clock: he's still got a few minutes before any of that has to happen. He grabs his keys and a travel mug, then steps outside into the crisp late-September morning.

ETHAN DRIVES THE half mile down Schoolhouse Hill, hits the Ledge cautiously, then continues down to the heart of Starkfield, such as it is.

It's a hollowed-out sort of town, this place where he and Zo have landed. No matter where a person goes in Starkfield—the one-block business district that circles the village green, or either of the two-lane highways that take a person out of here, one sees ghosts of hopes come and gone. The Kmart gone. The tack shop gone. The single-screen movie theater gone. The hospital gone. The first attempt at an urgent-care clinic gone. The second attempt at an urgent-care clinic gone. The Grand Union, the Price Chopper, the Kwik-Stop convenience store: *gone, gone, gone.*

Three hours south of Starkfield, a city—once his—rises toward the sky. Ethan imagines those New York sidewalks now: crowds already flooding into the streets from the subway depths, jackhammers, honking taxis, drivers flipping one another off through car windows, food vendors in silver carts handing over foil-wrapped egg sandwiches and coffee cups emblazoned with Greek columns. He pictures men in dark suits barking into phones, women tucking loose strands of hair behind their ears, adjusting their handbags, then striding forward, chins high. All those *people,* old and young, rich and poor, from every corner of the globe, every language on Earth streaming from their collective tongues: they're all weaving around one another, a river of energy, movement, urgency. The click of heels, the slap of wingtips, the whooshes and whoas and watch-its of bike messengers dodging traffic, everything thrumming, humming, *alive,* even at this hour. They're *hustling,* those people, ready to conquer the street, the day, the world.

When Ethan steps out of his car, the sole movement on Main Street is his own.

He throws open the door to the Coffee Depot, feels instant relief as sound washes away silence: the swirl of frothing milk, the murmur of voices, a single clap of laughter, the ting of a metal spoon against ceramic. Above the din, Frank Sinatra's "Fly Me to the Moon" pipes through overhead speakers. No, this isn't New York, not by a long shot, but it's some sort of life, and he welcomes it all, welcomes the noise, and the mustard walls filled with amateur landscape paintings, and the handful of others, familiar, every one of them, who have risen early to be here, together.

He knows without having to look who is in this café, and where they're seated. He knows the trivia crew will be nosed up against the window in the near corner, the *New York Times* Arts section open to the *Jeopardy!* Clue of the Day. He knows, too, that the ancient plumber in coveralls will be watching the news on his phone without headphones—the sound annoying everyone, but not enough for anyone to confront him. Ethan knows that the craggy poet who teaches at the community college three towns away will be in the back corner scribbling on her yellow pad, that the maternity nurse, the one who delivered Alex more than a decade ago, will be studying Spanish at the center table.

Behind the counter, a server (Nancy: retired third-grade teacher, two grandchildren, had hip surgery last spring) sets a cup on the counter, shouts, "Jane!" And from her usual table in the far back corner, Jane (former New York City punk rocker, partied with Warhol and Basquiat back in the day, moved to Starkfield after 9/11 just like Ethan and Zo did) stands to retrieve her latte. Ethan listens to the two of them make small talk about the weather (*spectacular*), Nancy's grandson (*a handful, but getting bigger every day*), Jane's back pain (*better, thanks, the cortisone shot really helped*).

It could be yesterday, this whole scene. It could be the day before that. It could be fifteen years ago.

A voice from the corner: "Yo, Encyclopedia Brown!" It's one of the trivia crew: a retired logger in a VFW cap, looks like Willie Nelson with a bit more meat on his bones. Other members of the trivia crew include a wispy, thirtysomething yoga instructor, and a practical social worker in horn-rims, whom Ethan would place around sixty: three individuals who seem to have little in common beyond the fact that they happen to show up here, every morning, to debate the Clue of the Day.

"Get over here, Encyclopedia Brown," Willie Nelson calls. "We need you!"

"What's the question?" Ethan asks. He doesn't really care, but isn't this what you do in a small town? You go through the motions, give everyone the gift of small talk, of sameness, of predictability—a courtesy that they, in turn, extend to you.

"The category is Authors," says the social worker.

Ethan reads: *After this woman's death, her daughter wrote, "As far as we in the family are concerned, the alphabet now ends at Y."* Ethan turns the question over in his mind. "The alphabet ends at Y. Huh."

"First or last name has to be *Y*, am I right?" asks Willie Nelson.

"Yumi," suggests the social worker. "Yvonne."

"Yasmeen," says Yoga. "Yoshiro. Yakira." Apparently the strategy here is to grab names at random and hope one of them happens to be right.

The answer hits Ethan at once. "Sue Grafton!" The mystery writer, woman protagonist, every book begins with a different letter of the alphabet. *A is for Alibi, C is for Corpse, M is for Murder.* Zo read a few of them back in New York. Grafton must not have made it all the way to *Z* before her death.

"That's it!" Yoga's delighted.

"Who the hell is Sue Grafton?" asks Willie Nelson, which prompts a debate—this, too, is part of the routine—about whether there's actually a mystery writer named Sue Grafton, and if so, why Willie, who has read every John Grisham and Lee Child novel ever written, has never heard of her.

Ethan feels himself falling backward into all of this, lulled by the sleepy sameness of it all. Sure, he gets pissed off at Starkfield sometimes, as if the town should somehow fight harder against its own inertia, should rage, rage, against the dying of its light. But there's something so easy about this predictability, so comforting and soft. Sure the world out there might be cracking to pieces, but here, at least, is something a person can count on.

IT WAS GOOD until it wasn't. All of it: The town. His marriage. Their finances. The world.

Ethan can draw a line through his life: the break between before and after, then and now. It would look, he supposes, like the thick brown band embedded in the fossil record, the one that demarcates the age of dinosaurs from all that followed. The K-T boundary of his own life was Election Night 2016, nearly two years ago. A party, held at the home of some parents from the Rainbow Seed School. It was to be a huge celebration. The mothers showed up in pantsuits, the dads got slapped with I'M WITH HER stickers. Kids ran through the finished basement like a pack of puppies, emerging only to ask for more Pirate's Booty or Newman-O's. Television reporters filled the airwaves by showing Susan B. Anthony's grave covered with I VOTED stickers. Nearby, bottles of Veuve Clicquot chilled on ice.

It was to be an early night, that's what everyone said. A historic night. There was a rumor even Georgia might go blue.

Then stunned faces, serious voices. Projected winner checkmarks, and the godawful *New York Times* forecast needle moving steadily, bewilderingly left—deeper and deeper into the red. The party got quiet, then quieter still. Just as it started to look bad, impossibly bad, Zo had stood. She smoothed her pants, adjusted her blazer, and walked to the kitchen, chin high. Ethan watched as his wife bent at the waist, tucked her head beneath the faucet, and vomited right into the couple's hand-hammered copper sink.

Ethan did his best to comfort Zo—that night, and through the days that followed. He was upset, too, of course he was. But it would be *okay,* he was certain. This was America! There were checks and balances. Regulatory limitations. So much bureaucratic red tape! He reminded Zo that the founding fathers—they were geniuses, those guys!—had crafted the Constitution so that sudden changes, about-faces, were nearly impossible. Why, in the last decade alone, federal agencies had created something like 85,000 government rules! You can't just undo all that!

But Zo stubbornly refused to be comforted—seemed, in fact, to barely hear him. About a week after the election, as Ethan yet again tried to reassure her, Zo had leveled her eyes at him. "What I want to know, Ethan" (and this was the beginning, he realizes now: this was the start of the rift between them), "is why you would assume that I need *you* to tell *me* whether and how much I should worry." Ethan had been stunned by the hardness of her voice, by the fact that his wife would direct her fury at him.

Him, of all people! And he was only trying to help!

Now Ethan sits in the familiar coffee shop, listening to the trivia crowd argue good-naturedly about whether the fact that Willie Nelson has never heard of Sue Grafton says more about the author or about him. When a delivery truck attempts to back into a narrow alley on the far side of the green, the three of them pause from their debate to rate the truck driver's skills (*B minus,* says Willie, *A minus,* says Yoga, *that's harder than it looks*), then they squabble about which grade is the correct one.

Ethan imagines that Zo is by his side, that he can hold up the scene like an exhibit in a court case. *See?* he says to Imaginary Zo, the Zo who isn't here, the version of Zo who isn't at this very second wearing a mouth guard, a face mask, and boxing gloves, punching something, or someone, again and again. *Things go on,* he tells her. *Look: there is Nancy pouring the same variety of beans into*

*the same coffee grinder. There is the framed art on the walls, the peaceful
Starkfield green on the other side of the glass.*

*Yes, the world out there is a mess. Yes, we have to stay vigilant, vote, do
what we can. And we will. Of course we will. But look around at how easy
things can still be if we let them. If we trust in time, in the world, in each
other, in the arc of history bending toward justice and all of that, everything
will be okay.*

You were right, he insists, but I was too.

That's the thing he longs to say above all: *I was right. Because here
we are. See all the normal that still exists? See the way other people are able
to go on with their lives? The world is, at its heart, still ordinary.*

What is there to fear in such an ordinary world?

WHICH VERSION OF Alex will Ethan find this morning? It's a daily
question, the answer never sure. It could be Foggy Alex: disorga-
nized and dreamy, poky about getting ready but generally pleasant. It could be Big Energy Alex, the child who bounces all over
the house like an overcaffeinated Tigger. Or, in a worst-case sce-
nario, it could be Angry Alex: the kid who loses her temper, slams
doors, refuses to put on her shoes.

He's surprised to find Alex already at the table shaking out a box
of Cap'n Crunch—healthy breakfasts have become another post-
election casualty. "Maddy woke me up," Alex announces brightly.
She pours a carton of oat milk on top of the cereal, from a height
that guarantees a mess. "She said I was going to be late for school."

So perhaps this is the rarest version of all: Easy Alex, the pleasant, right-side-of-the-bed variety. Ethan kisses Alex on the head,
notes that her hair smells vaguely ripe—the kid's old enough to
have BO, but not yet old enough to care.

Alex gulps down a spoonful of cereal, then allows a series of
tiny burps to escape her lips. "Well, *that's* odd," she says, as if pondering Aristotlean metaphysics. "I thought I was going to make a
big burp, but it turned out to be just a bunch of little burps."

A pause. Alex holds up an index finger, then releases a loud, juicy belch, so deep it sounds like it's coming from her toes. "Ahhhh. *There* it is." She pats her belly, satisfied, then jams her spoon back in the bowl and begins slurping.

Ethan smiles. Yes, it's definitely one of the good days.

He pulls a prescription bottle from the cabinet, twists the cap off, shakes out a single tablet, red and oblong. Adderall: Alex's daily dose of executive-functioning skills, prefrontal cortex in pill form. He sets down the medicine and a glass of water on the table. She groans. "Do I have to?"

"You do," he insists. "And you'll have a better day because of it." The truth is, *everyone's* day will be just easier because of this pill. Not just Alex's, but also his own. Zo's. The teachers. Her classmates.

Ethan peers into the prescription bottle: only one dose remains. He pulls out a piece of notebook paper, scribbles *Get More Adderall,* sets it on the counter as a reminder.

And because this is a good day, maybe Alex won't resist a little academic help. "What do you say we practice some math?" The kid's mastery of multiplication is horrid, just embarrassing. "Six times nine." In response, Alex takes another spoonful of cereal, smacks her lips together loudly—possibly deliberately, to bother him, but it's equally possible that her table manners are on par with her math skills and he's simply failed to notice.

"Come on," Ethan urges. "Six times nine."

Alex grabs a number from thin air. "Twenty-one."

He takes a slow breath. How can she still not have her multiplication tables down? What are he and Zo even *paying* for at the Rainbow Seed School? "You know this, Alex. *Think.* Six times nine."

Alex furrows her brow, thinking hard. Then her face brightens. "Daddy, is it true that when you eat carrots, your skin turns orange?"

"I don't know. What's six times nine?"

Maddy strolls into the room, her blue hair pulled back into a loose bun. She's wearing a threadbare camisole and what may or

may not be Ethan's basketball shorts. He does his best to stay focused, but when Maddy flashes a smile at him, the corners of his
own mouth turn up involuntarily.

"Because I'm thinking . . ." Alex continues, oblivious to her
dad's idiot grin, "that if *carrots* turn your skin *orange,* then maybe if
I eat a lot of *spinach,* my skin could turn *green.*"

Yes. Those are definitely his shorts. Ethan coughs, takes a sip of
coffee from his travel mug, lets it linger on his tongue before swal-
lowing. He has to fight to keep his attention on Alex, who's sitting
right there yammering away about . . . what, exactly? Spinach?
Skin? Not math, that's for sure.

"Six times nine, Alex. Show Maddy you know the answer."

But apparently Maddy doesn't care about the answer either. She
turns to Alex. "Why do you want your skin to turn green?"

"Witch stuff," Alex says. "I'm doing a science project on
witches."

"Cool." Maddy picks up Ethan's coffee from the counter, takes
a swig.

"Six times nine," Ethan repeats. And then: "Wait. You're doing
a *science* project on witches?"

Alex nods, slurps. The table is covered with oat milk.

"You mean you're doing an *English* project on witches," Ethan
says. "A creative-writing assignment, maybe."

Alex makes a face that—if he had to put it into words—could
only be described as *Dad the dumbfuck.*

"Or maybe you're doing a history project. Something about the
old New England witch trials," he suggests.

"*No,*" Alex says, like *he's* the one who doesn't know what he's
talking about. "I'm doing a *science* project on witches. Duh."

Ethan glances at Maddy, looking for backup. What the heck
kind of science project could she be doing on *witches*? Maddy simply shrugs. "Sounds like she's doing a science project on witches."

"Alex. Honey." Ethan tries to appeal to whatever common
sense his kid might have. "You *can't* do a science project on
witches."

"Mr. Boorstin says I can, and *he's* the science teacher. So there."

Ethan rubs his temples. Nearly thirty thousand dollars a year they're paying for this education. "Alex, there's nothing remotely scientific about witches. They're fictional."

"Wrong," Alex answers. She says it like the president does sometimes, like it's a cartoon sound effect. *Boing. Splat. Pow. Wrong.* "There are more than two hundred thousand registered witches in America. I read that on Wikipedia. And there are plenty more like Mommy, who are *unregistered*."

"First of all, Mommy's not an actual witch, that's just the name of her group." The name All Them Witches came from an article in the *Bettsbridge Eagle*. When the group was first forming, the women had chartered a bus and traveled together, still relative strangers, to the Women's March in Washington, D.C. The *Eagle* had done a story about the trip; the reporter interviewed not only the women who'd attended the march but also some of the men back in Starkfield, the ones who watched the scene on the overhead televisions at the Flats bar. The article quoted a retired dairy farmer named Harmon Gow, who had shaken his head, eyes on the screen, and muttered, "All them witches screeching like hoot owls for no goddamned good reason." The women had howled with laughter when they read this line. The name stuck: *All Them Witches: we screech like hoot owls.*

"It's a *joke*," Ethan assures Alex now. "Mommy would tell you that if she were here. Also, there might be two hundred thousand people who have *registered* as witches, but that doesn't mean they *are* witches."

And that's when Easy Alex gives way to Angry Alex. She shoves her cereal bowl away, glowers at him. Black eyes, hard jaw. Her nostrils flare.

"Sweetie, I'm just saying . . ." Ethan tries to make his voice sound friendly, show Alex he's on her side. "Maybe we can come up with an idea for a story about witches. Like that musical you love. Or you can write your own musical! I'll help!"

"Ugh, *whatever*," Alex snaps, disgusted, apparently, with his *dumbfuckery,* except that he's right and he knows it. Alex marches upstairs and slams her bedroom door so hard the house shakes.

And now he's alone in the kitchen with Maddy, who's still holding his travel mug full of coffee. He turns to her. "I mean . . . am I *wrong*?"

Maddy leans against the counter. She clicks her tongue in a *tsk-tsk-tsk*. "Daddy, you are *so* mean."

"Whoa. Nope. Please don't call me *that*."

"Call you what, Daddy?" Maddy's teasing him, trying to make him uncomfortable, and boy is it working.

"Seriously, Mad." He scratches his beard. There is literally no appropriate way for him to respond to a twenty-six-year-old who wears his shorts and calls him Daddy. "I just—yikes. Also, can you *please* give me back my coffee?"

Maddy holds out the mug for him. But when he takes it from her, she doesn't let go. Ethan tugs at the cup, pulling it—and, by extension, Maddy—closer. They stand like this, both hands on the cup, her eyes squarely on his. One beat. Two.

She lets go only when he looks away.

"A science project on witches," he says. "You think the kids are learning anything at that school?"

"They're learning those peace songs, I guess."

He laughs, because it's true. Every Friday, the whole school gets together for a weekly assembly, to which families are invited. They invariably sing old peacenik songs while the music teacher strums a guitar: "Last Night I Had the Strangest Dream," "This Little Light of Mine," "If I Had a Hammer." Last week, the teacher tried to mix it up with a homemade rap. Ethan had stood in the back of the room, cringing as his sixth grader and sixty other kids beat-boxed and recited lines like *"Kind is fun! Kind is cool! We all love to be kind at school!"*

"Fifty-four," Maddy says.

"Hmm?" He looks up, not sure what she means. She's still so close to him he can feel her heat.

"The answer to your question, Ethan. Six times nine. It's fifty-four, in case you still need an answer."

"Well, I'm glad someone in this house knows her times table. Cheers to that." He holds out his mug to her. Maddy brings the coffee to her lips. She takes a long slow sip, keeping her eyes on him the whole while.

This time, he doesn't look away.

ETHAN HAS ALWAYS been faithful. He was faithful to every girlfriend he ever had, even the ones who weren't faithful to him. And since he met Zo, he hasn't had any moments of real temptation. Okay, maybe one. But it was a long time ago, and it was before they were married. And he didn't act on it.

A few years ago, he'd read an article—this was *The New York Times,* he thinks, or maybe it was *Slate*—about fidelity. The article claimed that every married person, faithful or otherwise, faced some occasional temptation. The difference between cheaters and non-cheaters was simply this: when temptation arose, the faithful removed themselves from the situation. They didn't flirt. They avoided extraneous conversations. They stayed away from circumstances where love or lust might have the chance to flourish. It's as if the non-cheaters closed a metaphorical window, just shut those possibilities right down. Ethan was about a decade into marriage when he read the article, and at the time, he was relieved: *He* was no Bill Clinton, no Eliot Spitzer, no Gary Hart, all those guys who blew up their lives by having affairs, pathetic, really.

He, Ethan, was a window-closer. One of the good guys. Such good fortune, that. A blessing, really.

These days, though, it feels as if he's lingering, just a little, near a window that someone accidentally left open. Giving himself permission to sneak the occasional breath of fresh air. And he's started to wonder: what if he'd confused *lack of opportunity* with some sort of innate *tendency*? After all, he's spent most of his marriage *here,* in Starkfield, where even now, in middle age, he's still younger than the median age by nearly two decades. He doesn't work in an office, doesn't go out to bars, rarely spends time with women when Zo's not around.

What if he's not a window-closer, after all? What then?

◆

THE REST OF the morning goes badly. Alex dawdles while taking her shower. She has to be reminded (one time, two times, five times, more) to brush her teeth, comb her hair, find clean socks. When all that's done, she dashes around the house, snatching up scattered pieces of her homework.

"Come on, Alex!" Every day—every damn day—Ethan swears he won't raise his voice. Yet here he is again, just like all the other mornings: frustrated and screaming. Alex jams a worksheet into her backpack as he hollers, "I keep telling you that *your homework isn't done until it's put back in your bag where it belongs!*"

But Alex isn't listening, because now she's rummaging through a pile of shoes and boots. "Where's my *other* sneaker?" She tosses a flip-flop in the air as Ethan grabs his keys, his wallet, his phone. Ethan searches in a mad rush for the errant sneaker, finds it in the back of Hypatia's dog crate. It's damp, with teeth marks on the sole, one lace frayed and noticeably shorter than the other. But the shoe's still wearable, so he tosses it to Alex. "Put it on in the car. *Come on, come on, come on,* let's *go!*"

And through all of this, Ethan can't help but wonder, where is *Zo?* Absent. That's where.

Zo's absent, entirely, until after he and Alex are out the door. They're rushing toward his old Subaru wagon when Zo's car— newer than his, but otherwise identical—screeches to a halt in the driveway. She rolls down the window, cuts her eyes at Ethan. "What, were you planning to go to the conference without me?"

7

THE CONFERENCE, THAT'S right. With Shreya Greer-Williams. He'd forgotten.

"What conference?" Alex asks as she climbs into the backseat of Zo's wagon.

"PTA thing," Ethan answers, strapping himself in, just as Zo says, "playground fundraiser."

Zo flies down Schoolhouse Hill Road, hits the Ledge way too fast (stomach drop, *whoosh*). At the bottom of the hill, where Ethan turned left this morning to go to the coffee shop, Zo flicks her right blinker, away from downtown. The Rainbow Seed School lies twenty-three minutes south of here, in what feels like a different world altogether.

Corbury's posher than Starkfield—a whole lot more expensive too. It's one of those iconic Berkshire towns beloved by weekend leaf-peepers and second homeowners; it's also a refuge for independently wealthy New Yorkers who want to raise their kids "in the country," even as they hold on to a two-bedroom pied-à-terre in Chelsea. When Ethan and Zo first moved to the area, they'd toured a few Corbury homes. But even then, Corbury struck them as unreasonably expensive—a bubble unto itself. Meanwhile, at every Corbury open house they met only other couples like themselves: New Yorkers hoping to escape the Big Apple. Finally, after making three offers and being outbid on all, Zo had put her foot down. "I don't want to be the people who leave New

York only to be surrounded by a bunch of people who *also* left New York," she said.

At the time, Ethan was relieved by the sentiment. It wasn't that they couldn't *afford* Corbury, he reassured himself. This was a *choice*. In a way, it was even a *noble* choice! All those other families would be *playing* at rural life. He and Zo, by contrast, would have the authentic country experience. They would live among locals, people who passed their winters hauling firewood, or keeping the cows warm, or whatever it was that rural New Englanders did. (Ethan would soon discover that people here do pretty much the same things as anyone else: consume too much sugar and booze while watching viral video clips on Facebook. In Starkfield, they just happen to do these things without seeing their property values rise.)

Point is, now Ethan and Zo live in Starkfield, but they make the twenty-three-minute-each-way, twice-daily drive to Corbury just so they can send their kid to school with *other* children of former New Yorkers.

It's twenty-three minutes, that is, if everything goes smoothly. Which today it doesn't. Just a hundred yards outside of town, a neon-vested police officer steps into the road and holds up one palm. Zo grimaces, presses the brake.

Corbury Road is under construction. Corbury Road has been under construction since they transferred Alex to the Rainbow Seed School three years ago. Corbury Road will never *not* be under construction, at least that's how it seems. In the passenger seat, Ethan shifts impatiently, watches a yellow loader inch toward a pile of dirt.

He turns on the radio, begins flipping through stations. Everything is news or a commercial.

. . . Supreme Court testimony scheduled for tomorrow.
. . . can finally shed that weight that's been holding you back . . .
. . . more Americans are opposed to the nominee than in favor . . .

. . . talk of a coming "sex war . . ."
. . . new Toyota with no money down . . .

On the other side of the windshield, the loader crawls toward the dirt at the wrong angle, backs up, tries again. Zo grips the steering wheel and takes a long, deliberate breath, like she's willing herself calm.

. . . Common effects include headache, nausea, vomiting, diarrhea, palpitations, seizures or even . . .
. . . ask your doctor about what Cialis can do for you. . . .
. . . Fed announced it's raising interest rates . . .
. . . this week a third accuser claimed . . .
. . . still denies all allegations . . .

Zo reaches down, snaps the radio off. By now, several construction-crew members are directing the loader, each worker waving his arms in a different direction.

Ethan sighs. "I shall grow old, I shall grow old." A line from "The Love Song of J. Alfred Prufrock," T. S. Eliot's ode to longing. Once, Zo wouldn't have missed a beat in repeating the next line. *I shall wear the bottom of my trousers rolled.* For years, they've gone back and forth like that.

Today, though, only Alex responds. "Huh?"

"It's a poem," Ethan explains. "Your dad once built a whole marketing campaign around it, actually."

Alex brightens. "I wrote a poem this week! Well, technically it's a rap. It's about Pompeii, listen: *Vesuvius is smoking! And everyone is choking! On the py-ro-clastic FLOW! Pyroclastic flow is superheated ash and gas! With lava chunks that flow downstream and come at you real fast! Four hundred miles an hour, there's no chance to get away . . . I guess that sucks, I thought I'd live, To see another DAY!*"

"Hey, that's actually pretty good," Ethan says. He nudges Zo. "Isn't that good, hon?" Zo keeps her eyes fixed on the loader, whose driver is apparently giving up; he hops out of the vehicle, allowing one of the hand-waving crew members to climb into the driver's seat instead.

"I wrote the rap for Latin class," Alex says.

Ethan considers this. "Did you translate it into Latin?"

"No. Why?"

A rap for Latin class that's written in English. A science report on witches, with no discernible science in it. Maybe next, Alex will submit an interpretive dance as a math project. Yes, he definitely wants to talk to Mr. McCuttle, the head of school, about their curriculum. He can do it this morning, after the conference with Shreya.

But of course he'll only get to do that—or anything else, for that matter—if his family can ever move beyond this particular construction zone. But they won't, it seems, not ever, because even when the loader finally moves out of the way, a dump truck rolls forward to take its place. It begins unloading a second pile of dirt so slowly that Ethan wonders if they're being punk'd. Swear to God, sometimes his life feels like slow death, like reading Proust, like a John Cage song, like the self-checkout machines at the grocery store, the ones where the scales are calibrated wrong so the machine keeps jamming, a friendly robot voice saying, *Wait, help is on the way,* except the lady with the key, the only one who can restart it all, never arrives. It's like he's trapped in some never-ending Beckett scene, tedious and nonsensical and freaking eternal.

Next to him, Zo's fingers are wrapped so tightly around the steering wheel that Ethan can see her tendons bulge.

Guess this is your life, he thinks grimly. *I guess this is your goddamned life.*

WHEN THEY FINALLY get to Corbury, scrappy yards give way to sweeping lawns, most of them bordered by stone walls so exquisitely built they appear to have sprung from the earth just-so. Ethan had priced out one such wall as a part of their renovation; the price was laughable, solidly in the six figures, nearly as much as he and Zo paid for their whole house.

The Rainbow Seed School occupies forty-six rolling acres, a former dairy farm that had been in the same family for five generations, until the entire New England dairy industry went bust a couple of decades back. Today, the barn that once housed 120 Holsteins and Jersey cows features a fake cupola, a $20,000 copper weather vane in the shape of a rooster, and more godawful kid murals in neon paint than anyone should have to look at.

Zo, who hasn't spoken since Starkfield, follows the school's curved driveway up the hill, into the drop-off zone. A hanging banner reminds everyone that tonight is Parents' Night, although it's spelled *Parent's Night* on the banner, which means either the world is post-apostrophe, or the whole evening exists for exactly one parent only.

Not it, Ethan thinks.

"Parents' Night, yay!" Alex shouts. She's putting her sneakers on, as if she hasn't had nearly half an hour to do exactly this. "That means I have Kids' Night at Persimmon's house! She's having all the girls over. We're gonna watch movies, and make pizzas, and eat ice cream and—" She's still talking as Ethan shoos her out of the car. He watches as his daughter spring-trips toward the front door, laces untied.

Once she's gone, Zo doesn't roll forward, doesn't clear the way for the next car to drop off their own Rainbow Seedling. She simply stares outward.

"Zo?"

"I mean," Zo says vaguely, as if picking up on a conversation neither of them actually started, "*you* wouldn't do what he did, right?"

Ethan glances behind them; a line of luxury SUVs waits. Any second, the passive-aggressive parking monitor will appear, knock on their window with a smile that's far too huge for the circumstance, and remind them that *other Rainbow Seedlings are waiting, my friends!* "What wouldn't I do?" he asks.

"Hold a girl down. Cover her mouth. Laugh while she tries to scream."

It takes a second before he understands: the Supreme Court

thing. She's talking about the nominee, the things the man's been accused of doing. *"No,"* Ethan says. "Obviously I wouldn't. *Jesus, Zo.* You know I wouldn't."

Behind their car, a horn blares. When Ethan turns around, a mom in aviator glasses, behind the wheel of a Range Rover, lifts her hands, palms up, as if asking whether they're ever going to get out of the way. Zo, though, seems oblivious to their ongoing drop-off-zone infraction. "See?" Zo says, as much to herself as to Ethan. "They can find someone else. It doesn't have to be this guy."

Aviator Mom lays on her horn a second time—this time for five whole seconds. Zo snaps out of it, glances in the rearview mirror. "Yeah, namaste to you, too," she snaps. She rolls forward, swings the car around to the visitor parking lot, where, presumably, they'll wait for a few minutes, until it's time for the conference.

It's almost a relief when Ethan's phone comes to life. *NEED TO TALK TO YOU. NOW!!!!!!!!!!*

It's, what, five-something in the morning in L.A.? What the hell is Randy even doing awake?

RANDY HAD BEEN the first person Ethan met at Kenyon. He'd breezed into their freshman dorm room in seersucker shorts and a paint-splattered tee, his skin golden from a summer by the sea. Randy tossed a monogrammed bag on a bed, and gave Ethan a firm, fist-pumping handshake. "Let the mayhem begin!" he'd announced, a mischievous grin on his face.

Randy was a prep-school kid—he'd attended three of them, actually—from one of those old New England families that tossed off mysterious phrases like *in the Blue Book* and *third form,* and *on Chappy.* Ethan, by contrast, was a steel-country kid, the first in his family to attend college, able to do so thanks only to a near-full merit scholarship for which he'd worked himself to exhaustion in high school. Somehow, though, from that first instant, Randy never doubted that he and Ethan were two of a kind, that they'd be buddies for life.

His confidence about that had been enough to make it true.

Their life at Kenyon had been a string of adventures and misadventures: disco balls and beer Olympics, thrift-store costumes and late-night victory laps up and down Middle Path, Randy bellowing, "Behold the new kings!" as they ran. Everyone on campus knew and loved Randy, and Ethan's proximity to him became a kind of currency in itself. Their whole shared experience was so wonderfully bewildering; Ethan had been a loner in his high school, the studious, skipped-a-grade oddball always with his nose in a book. Thanks to a single twist of fate from the Kenyon housing-lottery gods, he'd become, almost overnight, the center of the action on a rarefied campus filled with spires and glass.

After Kenyon, Ethan had planned to go to journalism school, but Randy had a different idea. "Move to New York with me," Randy suggested, late in their senior spring. "Let's start a company together." The company, as Randy explained it, was to be a marketing firm—but different from any that the world had yet seen.

It would be smarter. Stealthier. Way more fun.

"Guerrilla marketing," Randy said. This was the first time Ethan had heard the phrase. "I'm talking about marketing that's so sly people don't even *recognize* it as marketing. Marketing that's so clever people actually *welcome* it into their lives. Marketing that tells people not what they want to have, but *who they want to be.*"

Ethan shook his head. No. He'd been accepted to the Medill School, at Northwestern. He'd worked his ass off for that spot, and he'd already applied for his student loans. Maybe they could work together in a few years, once he finished grad school.

"We don't *have* a few years, E," Randy insisted. "The time to do this is *right now.*" As Randy saw it, the entire relationship between brands and consumers was about three nanoseconds from revolution. That change would happen so fast that nobody—especially not the big boys, the Young & Rubicams, the J. Walter Thompsons—would understand what hit them. "You and I have the miraculous fortune of entering the world at a once-in-human-history moment. This Internet thing is the next big bang, it's gonna remake everything. Mark my words, E: if we play our cards right, we'll land million-dollar accounts within a couple of years. Three, tops."

Three years? To go from being college kids tossing a frisbee to overseeing million-dollar campaigns? Even for Randy, the time-line seemed audacious, absurd.

"Three years," Randy insisted. "But only if we go balls-out—do something that really makes people take notice—and only if we act *now*."

Randy's plan was simple: they'd take whatever clients they could get, using whatever contacts they had. Of course they'd do *that*. They'd help these companies figure out how to navigate this new cyberspace thing—get them online, drive traffic to their sites. But since *those* clients were likely to be smaller, with tepid budgets, Randy and Ethan would simultaneously invest in a handful of major campaigns for which they had no clients at all—Three Great Leaps of Faith, as Randy called them.

Each Leap of Faith would create a branding campaign for some-thing so unlikely, so totally *out-there,* the company would generate instant industry-wide buzz.

"We'll use that buzz to catapult ourselves into the major leagues," Randy finished. "I'm talking the best brands out there, E: Absolut. Philip Morris, Rolex. I'm talking *Hollywood*."

Already, Randy had arranged everything: the rent-free two-bedroom at the northeast corner of Washington Square Park—owned by a family friend with apartments all over the world, who claimed to be glad to see the place get some use for a change. The U-Haul that would take them from Gambier to Manhattan the day after graduation. Randy had even picked out a company name: Bränd, with that gratuitous, nonlinguistic umlaut.

Most important, Randy said: he had access to start-up funds. A *lot* of start-up funds.

Apparently, Randy had approached an uncle, some hedge-fund manager with more money than sense. He'd convinced the man that what the world most needed as the millennium hurtled toward its completion was a couple of Gen-Xers with fresh ideas and no experience whatsoever.

Randy leaned in to Ethan then, eyes glinting. "Come on, E. Let's go get rich."

It was a tale as old as America: use someone else's wealth to make your own. Generations of Fromes had watched from the sidelines as other, more fortunate, types did exactly this. Now, here it was, in front of Ethan: the good life for the taking.

And so Bränd was born.

"CHRIST ON A cracker," Randy barks into the phone now. "It's about time you picked up my calls."

Ethan's standing at the edge of the Rainbow Seed parking lot, far enough away from the Subaru that Zo won't hear, even with the window down. "Listen, Randy, I've got a meeting in a few minutes, so make it quick. What's going on, and when can I get my money?"

"Relax, you'll get your money. But first I need your help."

Randy explains: There have been some accusations—harassment charges. Against Randy. A slew of them, actually. "At first there was just one," Randy says. "Some no-name actress, hoping to cash out after she failed to become famous. Suing me is her Plan B, apparently. My lawyers weren't worried. It was a nuisance suit, that's all; they figure we'll settle, cases like that come cheap. But *her* lawyer smells money, won't let this thing drop."

She's been calling around, this attorney. Talking to former employees, some models and actresses Randy's worked with through the years. Trying to establish some sort of pattern on Randy's part. And somehow, she's managed to get a bunch of others to sign on to the lawsuit. "Mind you, this attorney's a nobody, she's a Michigan State grad in a polyester suit, has no clue how things work out here. Do you know how many *careers* Bränd helped make? Think about all those girls who walked through our door as nobodies, and who walked out as legit actresses, or sought-after models, or publicists and agents themselves. *We* did that, E. You and me. We gave them work, or we connected them with other people who did, or at least we fucking tried."

Ethan glances toward Zo's car. He lowers his voice. "Seriously, Randy. Not much time here. Get to the point."

"So far, the suit includes Jennifer Philpott and Amy Judson and Hazel Patterson and—"

Ethan tries to attach faces to these names. In his mind, the women who came through the Bränd offices blend together. They're a long parade of flat bellies and $300 jeans, hair in conspicuously messy buns, and ruby lipstick—beautiful, bright-eyed women who always made Ethan feel both bumbling and forgiven, as if his awkwardness in their presence had been its own kind of charm.

"But here's the kicker, E. Here's the goddamn punch line. You ready for this? This lawyer reeled in a fish, all right. She got a big name to sign on. One helluva big name." Ethan says nothing. He's probably supposed to ask Randy who the big name is, but he also knows that if he waits, Randy will just blurt it out.

"E, it's bad." Randy's voice is uncharacteristically serious. "They've got Evie Emerling."

October 1995

Light flickers on stone. Some sort of silent film, sepia-toned, forty feet in height, dances on the Beaux-Arts marble exterior of the New York Public Library's main branch. A woman moves across the frame, draped in fabric so sheer she might as well be naked. She's gorgeous, this woman. Darn near ethereal.

A pause. The woman glances toward the camera, surprised, as if caught off guard by the Fifth Avenue pedestrians, some of whom have literally stopped in their tracks at the sight of her. Then she smiles.

Playful. Coy. Bewitching.

"Lust *sells,* E," Randy had insisted as they brainstormed this, Bränd's Second Leap of Faith. "To be worth anything in marketing, we've got to show we can tap into people's *desire.* We need to deal head-on with hard-ons."

A campaign about desire? Sure, okay. But how might such a campaign stand out? It's the 1990s, for heaven's sake: a person can't throw a stone without hitting one of those Calvin Klein ads—all those monochromatic, barely clad postcoital waifs. Abercrombie, also, has gotten into the softcore game, with endless images of prepsters in playful near-orgies. Meanwhile, news kiosks and flea markets are filled with stacks of back-issue magazines for every predilection: *Big Butt*. *Asian Dolls*. *Black Tail*. *Barely Legal*. And now there's this whole *cyber* thing! Must be a million pornographic images online by now, more uploaded by the minute. There's something for everyone in this new space, all of it just a couple of finger clicks away. Where, Ethan wonders, can Bränd possibly go from here?

Backward. That's where. Ethan and Randy will make the old new again, reinterpret some bygone longing to suit these modern times.

As they brainstormed, Ethan proposed—and Randy in turn rejected—numerous possibilities: La Madeleine cave paintings, with their fifteen-thousand-year-old images of reclining nudes ("Cave paintings? Who cares about *cave paintings*?"). The Kama Sutra ("Ugh, come on, E, that book's been done to death."). The Marquis de Sade ("Too French. Americans hate the French."). But when Ethan stumbled upon a short article in a back issue of *Smithsonian*—about Audrey Munson, America's first supermodel—he knew he'd struck gold.

Born at the end of the nineteenth century, Munson had lived a life of scandals. She was the first actress to appear nude on film! A prominent doctor had murdered his own wife just for the chance to be with Munson! There had been a nationwide game show–like contest to find Munson a husband! But Munson was no mere scandal-maker. She *also* happened to be the muse and model for such major artists as Daniel Chester French and Alexander Stirling Calder. All these years later, New York City was *filled* with glorious works of art for which Munson had been the model.

The grand, gilded figure atop the USS *Maine* monument at the Columbus Circle entrance to Central Park? Munson modeled for that. The twenty-five-foot copper sculpture towering above Manhattan's Municipal Courthouse? Munson posed for that too. Munson was immortalized in the bronze fountain at Grand Army Plaza; the seated sculpture at the entrance to the Manhattan Bridge; the granite porte cochère relief at the entrance of the Frick, multiple pieces at the Metropolitan Museum. She's even right here, at the New York Public Library, just south of the main entrance, in the form of a statue: Beauty, personified.

Audrey Munson, in other words, is at once tawdry and highbrow—an object not only of ordinary lust but also of the grandest human aspirations. And until now, the woman's been hidden in plain sight.

Not anymore. Over the next few weeks, Bränd arranges a series of these film projections, each telling a piece of the Audrey Munson story. These films will mysteriously appear and disappear from buildings all over the city. Each will feature the same stunning silent film star and end with the same yesteryear-sounding tagline: *Heaven Is a Gal Named Audrey.*

It won't take long before Bränd starts fielding calls from journalists, including reporters from both business and cultural desks. The company will get calls from talent scouts, too—from Hollywood agents and modeling firms. All will ask a few perfunctory questions about Bränd, about their intention for this campaign. But invariably, each comes around to the same question: who *is* the actress playing Munson in these silent films?

She's *got* something, this woman. Some kind of star power.

They're not wrong. Within a few short years, the actress playing Munson will appear on the screens of multiplexes around the world. Before long, hers will be a household name. For the moment, though, as the Second Leap of Faith becomes a reality in front of their eyes, Ethan and Randy are the only ones who know it: *Evie Emerling*.

———————————————

8

EVIE EMERLING. GOD.

Ethan stares up at the Rainbow Seed murals, pressing the phone to his ear. He turns the name over in his head. Just hearing those five syllables out loud is enough to make Ethan's stomach lurch.

When Evie had responded to Bränd's casting call for the "Heaven Is a Gal Named Audrey" campaign, she was one of a thousand aspiring actresses and models who pinned their hopes on a mysterious project being put together by a marketing firm no one had ever heard of. Randy had sorted through stacks of head shots and résumés, narrowing the talent pool down to a dozen or so finalists. Each had followed Randy, one at a time, into the closet that he'd converted into Bränd's "audition room."

The audition room was Randy's domain. Ethan was the serious, silent partner, busy with contracts and schedules and spreadsheets, with building anodyne websites for their handful of paying clients. He was too busy, or perhaps too shy, to pay attention to these women, as gorgeous as they were.

But when Evie walked in, it was different. Ethan *felt* Evie's presence before he even laid eyes on her. Some shift in the air, an electric crackle, something he still can't quite explain all these years later. Maybe it was chemical—some blast of pheromones. But when he looked up, he was thunderstruck.

Evie had flashed only the briefest smile before disappearing into the audition room with Randy. It had taken everything Ethan had to stay focused on his work.

Ethan tried to remain nonchalant, later, as Randy raved about Evie. *This girl's got everything, Ethan. I'm telling you: Evie Emerling is going to be a superstar. And we'll be the lucky bastards who discovered her.*

Now, as Ethan stands in the parking lot of the Rainbow Seed School, watching his wife step out of the car and try to catch his eye—time for the conference, apparently—he hears Randy say, "You know how much Evie Emerling earned in her latest movie? Twelve million dollars." If Ethan's not mistaken, Evie's latest movie was *Pandora,* a Guillermo del Toro fantasy about the woman formed from clay as a punishment from Zeus. *Opulent,* the reviews had called it. *Lavish.* The film had been greeted by nationwide protests from conservative Christians, who saw too many parallels between Pandora and Eve. Ethan had wondered, at the time, if those protests had been artificial—a sly way of generating buzz. For all he knows, Randy himself had staged the protests; this was precisely the sort of thing Bränd did for clients these days.

Guerrilla marketing at its best.

Ethan hadn't seen *Pandora*. He didn't like seeing Evie's movies; he could never quite reconcile the onscreen star with the human being he'd known, the person with whom he once stood in late-night Manhattan, traffic swirling around them as late night gave way to early morning. Her movies made him feel uneasy, like he couldn't trust his own memory.

Across the Rainbow Seed parking lot, Zo waves her arms at Ethan, taps an invisible wristwatch. *Time to go.*

"You know what the kicker is, E?" Randy asks. "Evie Emerling knows what Bränd did for her. She knows we're the difference between Zac Posen designing a custom gown for her Oscar ceremony and the clearance rack at Marshall's. So you tell me. You tell me about all the ways I've damaged her life, okay? I *made* Evie Emerling's life, that's what I did."

It occurs to Ethan, though he doesn't say it out loud: Hadn't Evie, in a way, made *them*?

"Randy, I don't see how any of this involves me."

"I need you to talk to Evie."

By now, Zo's motioning with a wild swing of her arm: *Come on.*

"*You* talk to her, Randy."

"Right, sure, that'll work. You think Evie's going to talk to the very person she's trying to sue? Evie *liked* you, E. The girls *always* liked you. You had that whole choir-boy thing, you were the good cop to my whatever."

Ethan's suddenly not sure what, exactly, Randy's "whatever" was.

"So . . . you think I can just call Evie Emerling," Ethan says. "The *movie star*. Like, I'll call her home number and say, 'Oh, hey, Evie, I just happened to be thinking of you, and by the way, will you drop the lawsuit against my old friend Randy?'"

"No, you're going to run into her. Be all, *Oh, hey, Evie, what a nice surprise,* or whatever. Do that whole sheepish good-guy routine of yours."

Across the parking lot, Zo's given up trying to signal to him, given up on him entirely, and is marching toward the Rainbow Seed front door alone.

"Sure, Randy, okay," Ethan says. "If I run into *Evie Emerling* out here in the middle of—"

"Well, it just so happens that Evie's in your neck of the woods this week. She's doing a reading of a new David Mamet play up at that theater near you. What's it called, the Hampton. The Hemingway. The Hurley. Something like that."

The Humphrey. A mostly summer theater festival in a small college town about forty minutes north of Starkfield. A celebrity favorite, the Humphrey: one of those theaters that gets *Times* reviews, because the shows are considered a prequel to a Broadway run. If Evie Emerling was going to be anywhere around here, of course it would be at the Humphrey.

"Okay, she's at the Humphrey. So?"

"So the reading's Friday afternoon. Go see her there. Remind her where she came from." Randy pauses, lets this sink in before continuing. "Bränd can settle with the rest. None of the other women will generate news and they know it. Without star power, all of this goes away. But if Evie's with them, we're talking *head-lines*. Front-page. And that, my friend, means massive payouts from Bränd—to lawyers and to these women. We're talking bags of money."

Bags of money. *Ethan's* money. Those checks he needs.

Texts from Zo now:

ETHAN. COME ON.
STACY/SHREYA IS ALREADY WAITING
FOR GOD'S SAKE DO NOT MAKE ME DEAL WITH THIS
WOMAN ALONE.

Ethan sighs. He's already exhausted, and it's not even nine in the morning.

"I'm telling you, everyone out here is spooked," Randy says. "That scene of Harvey walking through New York City in hand-cuffs? It's got folks shitting in their skivvies."

Ethan remembers that morning, the one when Harvey Weinstein, one of the biggest movie moguls on the planet, turned himself in to police headquarters in Manhattan. Zo had turned on the news so she could watch the scene over breakfast. Alex had peppered them both with questions. *So the bad guy is wearing the blue sweater? What are those books he's carrying? What exactly did he do? Why did the women go to his hotel room? How come nobody told the police? Aren't you supposed to go to the police when something bad happens? Mom, what do you mean "systemic power imbalances"? Wait, what's patriarchy again? Daddy, Mommy's not answering so will you please?*

And now here's Randy, explaining that "Harvey" might actually have something to do with him. It's the strangest sensation, as if a fictional character has reached right through the TV screen and grabbed Ethan by the throat. Ethan waits a long time before asking, "Did you do something, Randy? To Evie? To any of them?"

"Did I *do something* to them?" Randy roars. "I made them famous, that's what I did. Or even if I didn't, at least I fucking tried. And I tell you what: everything I said or did was to help *them*.

Because I'm the guy who knows what sells. Like it or not, beautiful women sell. No, you know what? Women who *feel* beautiful sell, which means yeah: sometimes I reminded them that they're beautiful. So sue me. Oh, wait, they already *are* suing me. E, I'm warning you: this is not a moment to go all knight-in-shining-armor. In this day and age? A lawsuit like this could end us. Kaput. Lights out for Bränd."

Ethan holds the phone away from his ear as he moves toward the school's entrance.

"Listen," Randy's saying. "The world sucks, women have it tough. Really tough. I *get* that. But I'm the guy who was trying to *help* them. I didn't *make* the rules of this game. I just *explained* the rules, so these girls had a fair shot at stepping into a better life. And by the way, E, you're welcome."

Ethan, almost to the front door, takes in the kid-painted murals on the side of the building. REPECT OUR EARTH, says one, with exactly that spelling. KINDNESS MATTERS, says another. NAMASTE TO EVERYONE, a third.

"What exactly am I thanking you for?" Ethan asks.

"For being the guy who was willing to go out front, to take some risks. You got to play it safe, futz around with spreadsheets, declare yourself holier-than-thou. Meanwhile, I was out there placing my balls in a fucking vise grip. So you're welcome, and fuck you very much."

Ethan's about to hang up on Randy for the second time in as many days, when Randy lowers his voice. "I've got tapes, E."

"Tapes?"

"Yeah. Tapes. Stuff Evie wouldn't want the world to see, you follow?"

"Like, you mean . . ."—Ethan glances around nervously—"*sex* tapes?"

"No," Randy says. "God no, Jesus, I *wish*. What I've got is way worse than sex tapes."

Ethan closes his eyes, tries to imagine what Randy might have, worse than a sex tape, that could convince Evie to drop a lawsuit.

"Look, I can't explain it now," Randy says. "The walls have ears these days. Check your messages. I'm sending you a file that I swear will make this whole thing disappear once and for all."

There's a click, then Randy's gone, and Ethan's opening, at last, the door to the Rainbow Seed School. He does his best to put on his best Good Dad face. But apparently something new's been added to his to-do list: Save Bränd.

9

THEY HADN'T WANTED to send Alex to private school—Ethan and Zo believed in public schools, that was the thing. But Alex's energy, her outbursts, her difficulties with transitions, her inability to stay focused on whatever early elementary task was at hand proved more than the Starkfield Elementary School seemed equipped to handle.

The school's go-to disciplinary action? Missing recess. Alex missed recess for making armpit farts during an all-school assembly. She missed recess for tipping in her chair. She missed recess for letting the sand out of the sand table, and for writing *I hate you* on the board, for eating a classmate's Oreos, for swiping a Beauty and the Beast cake topper from some kid's birthday cake, then flushing it down the toilet to hide the evidence.

When Zo and Ethan learned that she'd missed, collectively, an entire *month's* recess, Zo had fumed, "Alex needs recess more than *any* of those kids." They began looking around for other options. When they visited the Rainbow Seed School and saw the colorful RECESS IS A RIGHT mural outside the head of school's office, Zo's eyes filled with tears.

Then they saw the acres and acres of property. The frog pond. The petting zoo (Goats! Sheep! A flock of chickens whose eggs students collected for use in the school lunches!). At Rainbow Seed, Alex could learn about fractions not from worksheets but instead by baking apple pies using fruit handpicked from the campus orchard!

They decided on the spot: this was what they wanted for their child. And they'd give it to her. Whatever it took.

ONE OF THE things that had most charmed them at that first visit was that Rainbow Seed School had a real, live mascot, a rabbit called Mr. Pancake FuzzyPaws, who lived in a rabbit hutch next to the lower school playground. Last spring, though, coyotes discovered the poor animal. Children found tufts of fur and smears of crimson in the grass; a first grader found a bloody ear in the sandbox. Now there's a new Mr. Pancake FuzzyPaws who lives in the foyer, which means the school smells like a rabbit hutch.

Amid the stink, Zo and Shreya Greer-Williams wait together outside the principal's office. Neither looks up to greet Ethan when he enters. Shreya, all decked out in Lululemon, is twirling her blond ponytail with frantic energy. Zo, in turn, keeps her eyes fixed on a bulletin board decorated with children's handiwork: diamonds of colorful yarn wrapped inexpertly around popsicle stick crosses. *God's eyes,* Ethan once called these crafts. Except, of course, they're almost certainly not called that anymore. Perhaps these days they're just called yarn diamonds, though he's pretty sure diamonds, too, are problematic, even if he can't quite remember why. Whatever these crafts are called, he's troubled to see Alex's name next to one. Is this what they're doing in sixth-grade art?

Add art curriculum to the things he needs to ask about.

Except, wait. Hold on. If Randy is right, if Bränd really is in trouble, he and Zo might need to ask for financial aid next year. He's not sure why that changes the dynamics of whatever meeting they're about to have, but it does. For him, it very much does.

THE HEAD OF school, Mr. McCuttle, greets them slowly, as if he's Fred Rogers speaking to a television audience of toddlers. The man's outfit seems perfectly curated: colorful bow tie, fleece vest, khakis, Converse sneakers. Ethan looks the man up and down, remembering something Randy used to say: *Everything about us is a symbol, every choice a way of telling the world who we aspire to be.* In this case, McCuttle's outfit seems to be screaming, *I can be serious, and I can be fun! Both, at the same time!*

"So, I tend to approach conversations with *parents* as I do with *students*," Mr. McCuttle says, in his PBS singsong. Next to Ethan, Zo's arms are folded tight against her chest. Shreya sits on the other side of Mr. McCuttle, rod-straight.

Ethan smiles at the man, a little ridiculously. *Be a good guy,* he wills himself. *Show Mr. McCuttle what a great family we are, in case we need some financial aid. Temporary.*

And it *would* be temporary, right? Surely this Randy thing will settle itself, or blow over eventually. It's a minor setback, that's all.

"We'll follow a *three-part* approach." Mr. McCuttle smiles, seemingly oblivious to the energy in the room. "First, I'm going to ask you to place a pin on our *mood board*."

He points to a cork board, divided into four quadrants, each painted a different color. He explains that each color represents a set of emotions. "See, up *here* we have yellow. That represents *high-intensity positive,* like joy, or eager anticipation. Green is *low-intensity positive.* Think of green as a nice, calm focus. Blue is *low-intensity negative,* like sadness or boredom. Red, as you can probably guess, represents *high-intensity negative.* For example, irritation, impatience, frustration. *Anger.*" McCuttle's voice goes quiet on the word "anger," the way Ethan's mother used to drop her voice to a whisper whenever she said the word "cancer."

Mr. McCuttle hands Ethan a pushpin in the shape of a cartoon dog. Or maybe it's a wolf. A jackal. Ethan glances at Zo, who's staring at a pink flamingo. Shreya's lips are pressed together: she's holding a squirrel.

No one approaches the mood board.

"Go ahead," Mr. McCuttle encourages, like they're five-year-olds hesitating before show-and-tell. "Place yourself somewhere on the board. Wherever happens to feel *right*. As your mood changes, you can move your pin. I'll tell *you* the same thing I tell the children: whatever quadrant you're in is okay with me. *All* feelings are important, *all* have their uses. What's important is that we *know* where we are on the board."

Ethan looks down at the jackal. It's not the worst idea, this mood board. Might be useful with Alex, at home. But for a parent conference? Really?

Zo jabs her flamingo into the intersection of the four quadrants. "I'm neutral," she says, in a voice that suggests otherwise. Ethan places his jackal not far from Zo's pin, but firmly in the green zone. *Low-intensity positive.* Mellow. Good-natured. No need to start in a negative place.

Shreya slams her squirrel smack-dab in the middle of the blue quadrant, the morose zone. She looks right at Zo. "I'm *sad,*" she says, though to Ethan's ears, her voice sounds more like red-zone-fury. "I'm *sad,* because your *daughter* bullied my *son.*"

"Good, that's *very* good," Mr. McCuttle says. "What a great beginning. Thank you, Mrs. Greer-Williams, for stating your feelings so *clearly.* Feelings are *always with us,* see how that works? Now, for the *second* aspect of our three-part approach . . ."

On the whiteboard behind his desk, he writes, "PARKING LOT." "This here is our *parking lot,*" McCuttle explains. "Sometimes in conversation, *issues* arise, concerns that perhaps are a little *off-topic.* Not *unimportant,* mind you, just *off-topic.* When *that* happens, we park these topics *here,* in the *parking lot.* We can return to them later, after we've resolved the *issue at hand.* Does that make sense?"

Zo and Shreya stare at Mr. McCuttle. Ethan finds himself nodding. He can't help it. He feels sorry for the guy.

McCuttle smiles at him gratefully. "And then finally, we follow *these* rules." He points to a poster:

1. TELL THE TRUTH.
2. LISTEN AS MUCH AS YOU TALK.
3. CHOOSE KINDNESS.

4. ASSUME GOOD INTENTIONS.
5. KNOW THAT PEOPLE HAVE DIFFERENT EXPERIENCES.
6. REMEMBER, AT THE RAINBOW SEED SCHOOL, WE ARE ALL FRIENDS!

"So." Mr. McCuttle settles into his chair. "Let's turn our attention to the . . . *interaction* . . . that the children had last week."

" 'Interaction,' " says Shreya. "Is *that* what we call it when one child tries to *sprain another child's arm*?"

Zo closes her eyes, too long to be a blink. "Alex did *not* try to sprain Trenton's arm. This was an accident."

"*Tristan*," snaps Shreya. "Our children have been in the same class for three years. I would hope that you know by now that his name is *Tristan*."

Zo takes a long, slow breath. "Alex acknowledges she twisted his arm, but context is important: they were having a *thumb war* at the time. She was trying to get leverage in a *thumb war*. It was exuberance, that's all. She got a little carried away, as children sometimes do."

"Yes," says Shreya pointedly. Eyes fixed on Zo. "It *does* seem to be what *some* children do."

Mr. McCuttle shifts in his seat, suggests that this is a good moment to look at rule number four: *Assume good intentions*. "I checked in with Ms. Miller, the art teacher, about the matter," he says. "She tells me that the children had been laughing before, during, and *after* the incident, and that there was, indeed, some sort of thumb . . . *competition* . . . going on. So I think in this case, we can assume good *intentions* on Alex's part. . . ."

"Thank you," says Zo.

"*But* at the same *time,*" Mr. McCuttle continues, "we *also* must keep in mind rule number five: *Tristan* seems to have *experienced* the incident in a *different* way than Alex did. It's important to honor *his* experience *too*."

"Well," Shreya says, "even if Ms. Miller were correct that this was all in fun—an assumption I'm not yet ready to grant, by the way—I suspect it's difficult for Tristan to give Alex the benefit of the doubt about anything. After that whole Valentine sticker thing at the start of the year."

"And . . . there it is," Zo mutters.

McCuttle turns to Zo. "Is there something you wish to say, Mrs. Frome?"

"Mr. McCuttle, I have to be honest," Zo says. "I'm a little confused about why we're still talking about the sticker incident. It happened weeks ago, and really, it was a *sticker*. A sticker of a cartoon lemur. Alex placed it on another kid's shirt, that's all."

Shreya bristles. "Excuse me, but the sticker said *kiss me,* and when Alex stuck it on Tristan, she said, 'You want to give this to Imogen.' And he said *no, he didn't. He didn't want to give it to Imogen.* But Alex kept teasing him, *which he did not consent to,* and before long he was—"

"Yes," Zo interrupts. "He was huddled in the closet crying from the 'sheer humiliation.' I have heard this story a couple of times by now. I think we all have."

"It took your daughter *weeks* to apologize," Shreya snaps.

"And as I've explained, Alex would have apologized *that day,*" Zo presses, "except that Trevor said he wasn't 'ready' for the apology. And for some reason, everyone decided to indulge his feelings instead of helping the kids to move on."

McCuttle leans forward. "Perhaps, Mrs. Frome, you'd like to move your pin into one of the quadrants on the mood meter?"

Zo stares at Mr. McCuttle. One beat. Two.

Three.

"Mr. McCuttle, can I ask you something?" Zo finally asks. "Why did the school even *have* a Valentine's Day sticker?"

"Well . . ." he begins, confused. "I suspect it was left over from last February . . ."

"No, I mean, why would you perpetuate a holiday like Valentine's Day?"

Mr. McCuttle's eyes flick to Ethan's, then back to Zo. "I'm afraid I don't understand the question."

"At its best," Zo says, "the holiday is saccharine and benevolently sexist. But it's also got an atrocious history. A fact of which I'm sure you're aware. Being an educator and all."

A little snort escapes Shreya's nostrils as Zo explains that Valentine's Day has its roots in violent pagan ritual. "Men slaughtered animals, then beat women and girls with the hides. And when *that* was done, the men pulled the names of women—and, yes, girls— from a jar, and then dragged them off to . . . um . . . force themselves upon them."

Mr. McCuttle stares at his sneakers as if canvas and rubber are suddenly the most interesting things in the world. Shreya tosses her hands up. "*Why* are we talking about pagan rituals right now?"

"Oh, gee, I don't know," Zo snaps. "I'm just wondering if there's a connection between that sort of history and the fact that here we are, yet again, elevating a boy's feelings over the good of everyone else."

Mr. McCuttle coughs. "What an *interesting* point, Mrs. Frome. See, this is the sort of thing that we can put in the *parking lot*: a valuable discussion to which we can return *later*. After we've re- solved the *issue at hand*."

McCuttle stands up, writes HISTORY OF VALENTINE'S DAY on the Parking Lot board. Smiles broadly, like he's pleased with himself. Like he expects *them* to be pleased.

"I happen to *like* Valentine's Day," says Shreya. Eyes on Zo. "If you ask me, the world needs *more* love, not less."

Zo ignores her. "Another question, Mr. McCuttle: what ex- actly does the Rainbow Seed School do to teach boys about mas- culinity and vulnerability?" When the man can only blink in response, Zo presses. "I'm asking whether and how you actively teach boys to accept and be accountable for their own feelings *without* the expectation of comfort from girls?"

Ethan leans forward, touches Zo on the arm. Isn't that what the mood board is for? "Hon," he begins. "That's—"

But Zo shakes Ethan off. "Our long cultural inheritance as- sumes that if a male of any age feels vulnerable, or sad, or afraid, or lonely, that these feelings need to be *fixed*. And of course it's always women and girls who are expected to do the fixing. I don't know a woman on the planet who hasn't felt that pressure, so, Mr. McCuttle, what I'm wondering is this: does the Rainbow Seed School actively teach healthy forms of masculinity, or do you just allow your students to passively absorb toxic messages from our surrounding culture?"

"Why, that's another *very good question!*" says Mr. McCuttle. He adds MASCULINITY—TOXIC OR HEALTHY to the Parking Lot.

"You know what?" Shreya speaks directly to Mr. McCuttle. "I really don't appreciate the way Alex's mother twists everything around . . ."

"I'm right here, Stacy," says Zo. "I'm a human being who's sitting two feet from you."

"My name is *Shreya,* and my son's name is *Tristan,* and for the record, I'm trying very, *very* hard to be civil."

"Great. And *I'm* trying to raise a girl who doesn't believe it's her responsibility to assuage every bad feeling a boy ever has."

"Well." The corners of Shreya's mouth turn up like she's smiling, but her lips are thin and it's clear from her eyes that this is no smile. "You've certainly succeeded in doing *that,* haven't you?"

Ethan wants to press Pause, Rewind, move through this conversation a little more slowly. Give him time to catch up to whatever is happening in this room. The women are no longer talking only about the children, he's sure of that. He's not entirely sure *what* they're talking about, but it feels like Zo had been talking about *him* just now. Like maybe she's implying that somehow this is something *he* asks of *Zo:* to coddle him. And even if that's not what she meant, doesn't his wife understand that it might look this way to the people in this room?

"I have *tried* to show compassion," Shreya says. "Again and again, I have explained to Tristan that Alex has *impulse-control issues,* that none of this is *personal,* that Alex's behavior is hard on *everyone.* Tristan—like me, like the teachers, like *everyone* who knows your daughter—is doing his utmost to be patient."

And that's when Zo tosses her hands in the air, exasperated. "I'm sorry. But my God: why are we even talking about this? Does anyone even care that we are about to confirm a would-be rapist to the Supreme Court? Or that Nazis are marching in the streets?"

Ethan tries to meet Zo's eye, send her a *Let's stay on topic* signal. That was one of the things he always loved so much about being with Zo—the way they could meet each other's eye and have an entire conversation without saying a single word. They might be standing at opposite ends of a crowded room, but with one glance they could communicate everything they felt. *God, this party's a drag.* Or, *Sorry you got stuck talking to the guy who only wants to talk about how much money he's made flipping houses, we'll have a good laugh about it later.* Or, simply, *Let's get the fuck out of here, now.*

But the conversation-without-words thing only works if Zo looks at Ethan. Which she's not doing. Not at all.

Does she ever do it anymore?

As McCuttle scribbles on the Parking Lot board, Shreya stares at Zo, incredulous. "I beg your pardon?" she asks. "Nazis?"

"I mean, maybe you haven't been following the news," Zo says. "But yes, they're in the streets: literal Nazis. And by the way, our government has been separating families and locking children in cages and hurtling us into a dystopian future by doing nothing about the climate crisis, which means our kids may actually get to witness the end of life on this planet. But sure. Let's keep talking about a sticker."

Shreya's eyes harden. She grits her teeth. "So you think that because there are problems *out there,* we should just—what—ignore the *problems* that are right here at home?"

"You're calling my daughter a problem," Zo says. "The way, say, Nazis and human-rights abuses and melting ice caps are a problem."

Shreya sits up straighter, lifts her chin and looks out to some vague place in the middle distance. "I call 'em like I see 'em."

Zo's eyes are hard. "Lady, you talk a good game about peace and love, but it's clear the only thing you actually care about is your Aryan boy-child."

"*First* of all, Tristan is not Aryan."

"Sure, Stacy."

"Excuse me, but I was an anthropology major at Wellesley," Shreya insists. "So I happen to know that *Aryan* refers to people who settled in the region that is today modern-day Iran, and *second* of all—"

"You know exactly what I mean when I use the word 'Aryan.'"

"And second of all, I feel sorry for you. I feel sorry for *you*, and for your *husband*, but most of all for your *daughter*, who is clearly suffering from the lack of a positive female role model in her life."

Zo reaches into her bag, pulls out her phone, starts tapping furiously on the screen. "Mr. McCuttle, please tell me: what precisely, is the statute of limitations for the high crime of placing a cartoon sticker on another child? I want to be sure the date is in my calendar."

McCuttle makes a sound that resembles a laugh, but is in no way laughter. Shreya's face is frozen in a smile that is not a smile.

Zo glances back and forth between them, her finger poised above her phone. "Six weeks? You think we might be done by Thanksgiving? No? Okay, maybe by New Year's then. Just let me know, please, because when that day finally comes, I'm opening a bottle of Champagne."

Shreya stands, wraps her sweater a little tighter over her yoga leggings. "Well. I can see that Alex isn't going to get the help she so desperately needs. Excuse me for trying to show you the impact she has on the others around her." She moves toward the door, then turns around. Her voice filled with false cheer, she says, "Oh, and I imagine you've forgotten by now, Zo, but tonight is Parents' Night, and you volunteered to help serve lasagna. Will you be there? Or do you intend to shirk this responsibility too?"

"Oh, I'll be there," says Zo through gritted teeth. "Wouldn't miss it for the world."

Mr. McCuttle points lamely to rule number six: REMEMBER, AT THE RAINBOW SEED SCHOOL, WE ARE ALL FRIENDS! He opens his mouth, begins to read aloud, but Shreya snaps at him. "Save it. You know where I stand." Then she's gone.

In the long silence that follows, Ethan stares at the Parking Lot board:

HISTORY OF VALENTINE'S DAY

MASCULINITY——TOXIC OR HEALTHY

NAZIS

THE SUPREME COURT

KIDS IN CAGES

CLIMATE CHANGE/END OF LIFE ON EARTH

WHAT IS ARYAN, REALLY?

LASAGNA!

FOR HIS THIRD date with Zo, Ethan had taken the train out to Brooklyn to meet her at a tiny organic restaurant near the entrance to Prospect Park. He hadn't kissed her yet, hadn't even reached for her hand. But he wanted to, badly, which is probably why he found himself nervous-babbling through the entire meal. At some point, he found himself inexplicably blabbering about foreign words for which there were no exact English translations. He loved these words, he told Zo, loved that these words proved that experiences can be deeper, more complicated, than the words we have to describe them. He began listing some of these words: *trepverder* (Yiddish: the witty comeback you think of too late), *duende* (Spanish: the feeling a person gets when a work of art grabs them by the throat), *weltschmerz* (German: the melancholy one feels when comparing the way the world is and the way it ought to be).

Later, Zo would confess to Ethan that this conversation was the moment she *knew*. She knew not only that she'd be inviting Ethan back to her apartment after dinner but also that by the time they woke up together the next morning, their lives would be forever entwined. It was that last word, "weltschmerz," that had done it; Ethan had, unknowingly, given her the word to describe how she felt nearly all the time.

Now, in McCuttle's office, after Shreya sweeps out of the room, sucking all the energy with her, Ethan wonders if perhaps there's a word, in some language, for the feeling you get when you realize that a person you once loved—maybe the most grounded, thoughtful, real person you'd ever known—has changed beyond recognition, maybe even gone off the deep end.

In which case, it's up to Ethan to get this conference back on track. *Time to show McCuttle that this isn't how we are, we're quite a likable family, really.*

Curriculum. Financial aid.

McCuttle returns to his seat, takes a deep breath, and restarts his singsong. "So, I've been *eager* to meet with you both for *some time,*" he says.

There's something off about this guy, Ethan realizes. Phony, maybe. It's like McCuttle's whole *schtick*—the outfit, the singsong, those earnest eyes—is a performance of some sort, like he's practiced in front of the mirror at home a few too many times.

"The thing is," McCuttle continues, "it strikes me that Alex sometimes needs more . . . uh . . . *support* . . . than perhaps *we* at the Rainbow Seed School are able to *offer.*"

Ethan glances at Zo just in time to see the way she lifts her eyes. Quick. Something in there that he can't read.

"Don't get me wrong," McCuttle says. "Alex is a wonderful, *spirited* child. I imagine that as she matures, she'll get better at harnessing all that . . . uh . . . *vitality* . . . for good. But I must be honest: we are a small school, and our resources are limited. I sometimes wonder if . . . well. . . . if the Rainbow Seed School is the right place for her."

"Hold on." Zo leans forward in her seat. "*What* are you telling us?"

McCuttle coughs. "I'm *suggesting* that Alex might be better off in a school with more *specialists*. The kind of setting where they're accustomed to meeting a wider variety of *needs.*"

There is a long, still moment as his words sink in.

"Mr. McCuttle," Zo says, "you told us this was a great school for kids who were square pegs. You said we'd be amazed at Alex's transformation here."

"I *did* tell you that, it's true," says McCuttle. "And I did so based on years of seeing children who hadn't quite fit into their previous school environments. Most of these children find their places at

Rainbow Seed *very* quickly. But it's possible Alex needs a little more, uh, one-on-one *attention* than we're able to give her."

Zo stares at him. "You think, what, the public schools have the resources to give her one-on-one attention? We've been there. Done that. It didn't work. *That's why we're here.*"

And when Mr. McCuttle responds only by looking yet again at his stupid sneakers, Zo adds, "She's gotten better. You *know* she's gotten better." She glances at Ethan for support, but he feels topsy-turvy. He'd planned to use this conference to question McCuttle about the school's dubious curriculum, about whether it's good enough for their kid. Now here's McCuttle questioning them about whether their kid is good enough for the school's dubious curriculum.

McCuttle speaks quietly. "We never guaranteed that we'd be able to meet her needs. Only that we'd try. Please try to see the situation from our perspective. We don't have classroom aides, we don't get state funding, and Alex . . . does seem to command higher than her share of attention."

By now, Ethan can read exactly what's in his wife's eyes: some sort of panic. Zo came prepared for Shreya. But she wasn't prepared for this.

"Hold on," Ethan says, then realizes he doesn't know what to say next. Even if they can convince McCuttle to tough it out with Alex, what chances do they stand at receiving financial aid if the school doesn't even want their kid?

Ethan flashes to his first day at Kenyon—the way he'd stood there looking at all those rich kids getting out of their parents' shiny, foreign cars. He'd looked down at his Sears-purchased chinos, then out toward his parents' battered twelve-year-old Oldsmobile. He'd understood right away: he didn't fit, didn't belong, had no place there.

He was an outsider. Until Randy decided he wasn't.

And now here's McCuttle trying to turn their whole family into outsiders again—*unwanted,* not enough—and what can he possibly do about that?

"If I may," says McCuttle. He clears his throat again. "Perhaps *these* would be clarifying." He lifts from his desk a manila file folder, filled with paperwork, holds them out.

Ethan flips through them. There's a stack of incident reports:

Alex wrote "English sux" all over her textbook.
Removed from class for repeated talking, even after six warnings.
Refused to stop saying "Uranus" during science class.

There are also a bunch of homework assignments, marked with red:

Next time read the instructions.
You only filled out half of this worksheet.
Even your name is spelled wrong!

The math assignments, in particular, demonstrate rising frustration on the teacher's part:

If you don't show the work I cannot help you.
Is this graph meant to be a joke?
Nonsense!
ENTIRELY WRONG.
You are so far from getting the right answer, I wonder if you have paid any attention.

Ethan sets down the papers, rubs his temples. To be honest, these comments seem to him at least as much an indictment of the math teacher as they are of Alex. Can McCuttle really not see how unhelpful these comments would be to a child? Maybe McCuttle *is* a giant phony. Maybe he doesn't actually know a damn thing about education or kids. He's like a variation of that old TV commercial: *I'm not a real school administrator, I just play one on TV.*

And McCuttle is rejecting *them*?

Ethan takes a deep breath. "Okay, let me get this straight. Alex left behind her old elementary school, all her friends. At *your* recommendation. And now you don't even want—?"

Zo interrupts. "*She'sonthewaitlistatBostonChildren's.*" And then slower: "We've been trying for a while to get an evaluation from the pediatric neurology department at Boston Children's Hospital. It's the best in the country, the wait list is years long. What if I can get that appointment?"

Mr. McCuttle looks down at the floor.

"I'll convince them to let us come in," Zo presses. "They'll do a whole workup, evaluate Alex on everything—medication, doses, behavior-management plans . . ."

Ethan had forgotten about that appointment. They've waited at least a year and a half by now.

Zo continues: "Until now, Alex's medications have been managed only by her local pediatrician, not by a specialist. Her doctor's wonderful, but she's a *generalist*. For all we know she's gotten the dosage wrong—maybe Alex isn't even on the correct medicine. The experts at Boston Children's will *know,* they'll be able to tell us. If we can just get that appointment, maybe we can—"

She breaks off, takes a deep breath, and stares at Mr. McCuttle.

"Please," she finally says. "At least let us try. At least let us hear from the experts before you make any final decisions."

1 0

NEITHER ZO NOR Ethan speaks as they walk to the car. They're silent as they buckle in, as Zo drives down the Rainbow Seed drive. Ethan watches the painted murals get smaller and smaller in the side-view mirror.

It's only when the Rainbow Seed School disappears entirely from view that Zo says flatly, "That was an ambush. A total fucking ambush."

"It was definitely not what I expected."

"Didn't I tell you Shreya had it in for Alex? Didn't I *tell* you that, Ethan?"

"You did."

"I just didn't think it would happen this quickly, that's all. I didn't think the school would be so quick to jump on board. Like it's already a fait accompli." Zo presses on the accelerator, takes a curve a little too fast.

Ethan starts to say maybe it's for the best, that it's not clear that Alex is learning anything, and they *are* spending an awful lot on tuition these days. But he's struck by a memory, something from back in kindergarten, during Alex's *Star Wars* phase: He'd picked her up from school, and the teacher had pulled him aside. "Mr. Frome, you really shouldn't let your daughter watch *Star Wars* anymore," she said. She looked around, then added in a stern whisper, "Alex is playing *shooting* games."

Ethan had felt like the world's worst parent for about two

weeks, until he'd observed something curious: every little *boy* on the school playground played shooting games, and nobody seemed to say a thing.

Now, to his wife, he says, "Sometimes I wonder if people would respond differently to Alex's behavior if she were a boy."

"Oh, you think?" A bit too much sarcasm in Zo's tone, in his opinion. Zo rounds another curve without slowing, then says, "Yes, of *course* they'd respond differently. Obviously. They'd say, 'boys will be boys,' they'd declare that our kid has a future in comedy, they'd ask everyone to be patient, *boys don't mature as quickly as girls*. That's how they'd respond."

"But . . . they can't *do* that," Ethan presses. "That's sexist."

"Misogynist," Zo corrects. "And welcome to my world, Ethan."

Ethan hates how helpless he feels, hates that McCuttle, that singsonging nitwit, that *poseur,* doesn't see his own double standard. And the man can get away with it, too, simply because he's the one with the power.

By now, Zo is careening along Corbury Road at what seems to Ethan a harrowing speed. She begins to imitate Shreya: "*I assume you don't remember this, but tonight is Parents' Night.* Did you hear her, Ethan? I mean, did you even *hear* her?"

"I did," Ethan answers, as if his wife is actually asking him whether he heard, as if maybe he hadn't been sitting right there in the room, right next to her. "Maybe slow down a little?" he suggests. But the closer they get to home, the more furious Zo grows . . . and the more frantically she drives. By the time they cross the border into Starkfield, Zo's going all Indy 500 along the narrow two-lane road.

"*It took your daughter* weeks *to apologize.*" Zo takes a left curve so fast, Ethan's right shoulder slams against the passenger door.

"Seriously, Zo. Slow down."

"*I think the world needs more love, not less.*" Zo yanks the wheel to one side, then another. Ethan's body follows, like one of those crash-test dummies in a driver-safety video.

"I was an *anthropology* major at *Wellesley.*" Slam, his shoulder's pressed against the door.

"Zo. This is way too fast."

"I'm trying very hard to be civil here."

Ethan places his hands against the dash, presses his foot into an imaginary brake. By now, they're nearing the Corbury Road construction zone. An orange sign—SLOW: CONSTRUCTION 1500 FEET—comes into view. Zo whooshes right past it. Then another sign: CAUTION: ROADWORK AHEAD.

Zo doesn't so much as tap the brakes.

Must be lunchtime, because none of the neon-clad construction workers are out there, thank God. No forklift drivers, no loaders or diggers or dump trucks, no police officers in their neon vests, earning their time and a half as days turn into years. There's just a long stretch of orange cones lined up like toy soldiers.

WORK ZONE: SPEED FINES DOUBLED. Zo grits her teeth, sneers, *"I call 'em like I see 'em."*

It's only when she's bearing down on the cones that she finally hits the brakes. Tires screech on asphalt. Ethan feels his seatbelt cinch as the Subaru comes to a sudden stop. *Thud.*

Ethan watches a single orange cone sail into the air. It rises, arcs, descends, a perfect parabola. The air smells like brake fluid, like burning rubber.

The cone bounces on the ground a few times then comes to rest on its side. He and Zo turn to stare at each other, stunned.

One side of Zo's mouth curls slowly into a smile. She throws the car into reverse.

The car hurtles backward, ten yards, twenty. Zo presses her lips together, then shifts into drive and guns the accelerator. The car blasts forward like they're in the chase scene of a movie, except that doesn't make sense because this is Zo, and she doesn't even *like* movies with car chase scenes.

Bam. Bam. Bam. Zo hits one orange cone, then another, then the next. She slams every cone in their path, a dozen of them maybe, all the way down the line. She's like Thelma without a Louise, or maybe one of those new girl Ghostbusters, cackling with laughter while blowing the ordinary world to smithereens.

Ethan meets his own eye in the passenger-side mirror, as if his image were a friend with whom he could commiserate with a single glance, the way he once did with Zo. *What the hell is happening here?* he asks his reflection.

The reflection responds with wide eyes. *No idea.*

He asks: *What am I supposed to do?*

Tell her to pull over. Tell her you'll drive. Tell her this isn't okay.

And then it says, *Whoops, too late.* Because apparently, the cops in orange vests have been there the whole time, sitting in their car on their lunch break, just slightly out of view.

Even before Zo's reached the final cone, the sirens have already started to wail.

THERE ARE TWO officers. From the passenger's seat, Ethan watches them emerge, notices the cautious way they step out of the cruiser, all stormtrooper boots and mirrored sunglasses. They approach the Subaru with hands on their holsters. When they see Zo behind the wheel, their shoulders visibly relax.

The bigger one does the talking. He's all paunch and beef, this guy. His badge catches the sun as he flashes it. "License and registration?"

This cop is older than Ethan, or at least less in shape, maybe had a few too many beers with the guys over a few too many years. Behind him stands a younger kid, baby-faced. A constellation of pimples still dots his chin.

"Are you aware that you hit a few cones, ma'am?" asks Beefy.

Hit a few cones. All of the cones are strewn across the road haphazardly. The place looks like it was hit by a hurricane, a tornado. Maybe a war.

"I am aware. Yes." Zo opens the glove compartment, then her wallet, handing the man the paperwork.

Beefy glances down at her registration. "And do you know that in Massachusetts, fines in work zones are doubled?"

"I believe I read that on a sign."

Ethan stares out at the cones. Yes, he thinks: more like a war. All those orange corpses. Lying where they fell.

The cop looks over her license. "Zenobia Frome." He sounds it out. "Ze-NO-bee-ah. Interesting name. Well, Mizz Zenobia Frome, are you also aware that your license has expired?"

Ethan's heart sinks. What's *this* going to cost?

Beefy passes the paperwork to the younger kid, who walks it back to the cruiser without a word. Beefy removes his glasses, peers a little closer at Zo. "Ma'am, have you had any alcohol in the last few hours?"

"Not a drop."

"Any marijuana in your system?" He pronounces it with five syllables: *Mary-Joo-Wah-Nah.*

"No."

"Any other substances?"

"Just cortisol and bile," Zo answers. "My drugs of choice these days."

The cop's eyes are sharp and quick.

"No," she says, quieter this time.

From the cruiser, Ethan can hear muffled voices over the radio. Static, then more voices, too garbled to make sense of. Beefy stands there like he's making a decision. In the distance, a cloud of swallows lifts off from a tree, twists and swirls in formation before swooping down again.

"Mrs. Frome," Beefy says. "Please step out of the car."

Ethan watches through the windshield as the cop commands Zo to recite the alphabet. "Start at V and go backward." She does it surprisingly well, eyes straight ahead. Then the cop holds a single index finger in the air, tells her to follow its movement. She does: left, then right, up, then down. When that's done, Zo walks a straight line, heel-to-toe-to-heel. Zo's still in her gym clothes, fleecy running tights, a thick ribbed cardigan, hits at mid-thigh, covering her faded Sarah Lawrence tee.

Finally, the cop pulls out a tube: a breathalyzer. It's like the guy can't quite believe that anyone would drive like Zo while stone-cold sober. After she passes, he frowns. He commands Zo to place her hands where he can see them, and wait where she is. He returns to the car, peers in at Ethan. "Your wife always drive like that, Mister?"

For some reason—maybe it's the look on Zo's face, that cool stare, or her absolute stillness—Ethan feels a little desperate, like there's something he needs to ward off, some kind of foreboding he can't quite name. Ethan leans toward the steering wheel, smiles at the cop apologetically. He wants to connect, show this guy that the two of them are on the same team, just as he was attempting to do with McCuttle a short while ago. "This might be my fault, sir," Ethan says.

"Your fault." A statement. Skeptical.

There's no ring on the guy's finger, but years ago, at a bar in New York, Ethan had struck up a conversation with an off-duty officer. The man said that guys on the force rarely wear wedding rings—ostensibly to protect their families from the criminal element, though (he'd elbowed Ethan at this point) appearing unmarried had other advantages too. Ethan sizes up Beefy now; he's definitely old enough to have *had* a wife, at least one, even if he doesn't anymore.

"I was kind of . . . you know . . . giving the wife a hard time. Making fun of her driving." Ethan makes a point of wincing, like he's cringing at his own boorishness. "Teasing her about women drivers and such. Made her angry, I guess. Lesson learned. I'll pick up the cones if you'd like."

Zo's face is impassive. He can just make out the slow rise and fall of her breath. Ethan can't tell if she's heard his falsehood or not.

Babyface returns to the car, hands his partner the registration and license. "She's clean," the kid says. "Other than that expired license."

Beefy taps the license against the registration a few times. Then he turns to Zo. "Okay, Zenobia Frome. I'll let you off with a warning this time."

Ethan exhales inside the car. "Thank you," he whispers—as much to the universe as to the cop himself.

"Your husband's going to need to take the wheel," Beefy tells

Zo. "I advise you to renew that license *today*. And in the future, remember, will you? When you see orange cones, you're supposed to *avoid* them, not *aim* for them. This isn't target practice." He chuckles at his own joke.

Maybe Ethan and Zo, too, will have a good laugh about the whole thing on the way home. *Every single cone!* Ethan will say. *Ten points! Twenty! Nailed every one!* This can become one of those stories they tell and retell, to themselves and to others, their voices rising and falling together in a practiced duet, until the whole thing becomes cemented into legend.

Before any of that can happen, though, Zo needs to get in the car. Which, for some reason she's not doing.

Ethan's vague foreboding gives way to something stronger. Some sort of dread. *Get in the car, Zo.*

Please just get in the car, Zo.

On the other side of the windshield, Zo says something to the cop, Ethan can't hear what. Ethan doesn't like the way the man's head tilts, slightly and suddenly like he's newly alert to some lurking danger.

Get in the fucking car, Zo.

Beefy asks, "Excuse me?"

Zo speaks again, louder this time: "I'm supposed to be grateful now?" A pause. "I should thank you for merely having condescended to me, instead of, say, harassing me, or arresting me, or worse?"

The cop is motionless. His eyes flick to his partner's, then back to Zo. "Ma'am. I'm not sure what you're suggesting."

"I'm just wondering," Zo's voice is level, "whether you're this quick to let *everyone* off with a warning, or if my good fortune today is a result of being, I dunno, who I am, *rather than* whatever I did or didn't do."

Christ on a cracker, as Randy would say

"Lady." The cop's voice is guarded. He's warning her. "In case you don't realize it, I'm letting you off easy here. This could be a lot more painful."

"Oh, I absolutely realize that," Zo says. "You're giving me the criminal justice equivalent of a nice little pat on the head. I'm just wondering why, that's all. Could it be because you and my husband shared a nice little bonding moment? Or because my lady parts have aged out of any possible interest . . ."

Beefy's already taking a step backward, hands up, like he's the one at risk of arrest. "Hey, hey, no one said anything about your lady parts."

"Or perhaps there's something . . . else . . . that makes me seem harmless, docile, less of a threat than another person might in the exact same circumstances."

The guy blinks, trying to catch up. "You're saying I should consider you a . . . threat?"

"No. I'm saying that in America, white drivers like me are significantly more likely to get off with just a warning than, say, Black or Latino drivers."

Ethan does his best to communicate to his wife telepathically. *Shut. The fuck. Up.* But even as he thinks this, he has a sinking feeling. Why would she listen to his telepathy, when she no longer listens to the things he says out loud?

Zo continues, as if delivering the world's most ill-timed book report: "We're also half as likely to have our cars searched during traffic stops." A pause. "For whatever that's worth."

"Do you want . . ."—the cop scratches the back of his neck, squints at her—"to be searched?"

"What I want," Zo replies, "is equal justice, equitably applied in America."

Ethan closes his eyes, imagines All Them Witches chanting to their usual crowd of no one on the Starkfield village green: *What do we want? Equal justice equitably applied! When do we want it? Well, it would have been nice to have it several centuries ago, if we're being completely honest!*

Something in the cop snaps. He leans down and talks to Ethan through the car window. "Okay, Mr. Frome. We'll be taking your charming wife down to the station now. You can pick her up there after she's been booked."

And then Beefy's reading Zo her Miranda rights, *she has the right to remain silent, she has the right to an attorney,* as Babyface slaps cuffs on her wrists. As the kid steers Zo toward the cruiser, Ethan realizes he has no clue what he's supposed to do. He opens his car door, pokes his head over the top, and yells, "Should I follow you?"

It's Zo who answers. "No," she shouts over her shoulder. "I need you to call for that appointment."

"Appointment?" This is all happening so fast, Ethan's lost track of everything.

"For *Alex,*" Zo says. "The one at Boston Children's!"

"But what about . . . *you?*"

"Call Jackie. She's an attorney, she'll know what to do. You just get that appointment for Alex, okay?" Zo's got one leg in the back of the cruiser, but the cops aren't pushing her in. They're letting her have this conversation, this husband-and-wife back-and-forth, logistics and to-do lists and division of labor, unremarkable under any other circumstance.

"Who's Jackie?" Ethan shouts.

Zo looks exasperated—with him! *She* looks exasperated with *him!* "Thin, blond, runs a lot. Jesus, Ethan, it's been almost two years, how do you not know any of their names yet?"

Oh. Okay. She means Runner Mom. Jackie is Runner Mom.

Zo turns to the cops. "Seriously? You're allowing me to have a conversation with my husband? This is a privilege you extend to everyone that you arrest, I assume?"

The cops look at each other in disbelief.

"Wait!" Ethan shouts. "What's Jackie's last name?"

"Watters! She's in my contacts!" Then to the cops: "So you're really just letting me do this, huh?"

And no, they're not. Not anymore. Babyface cups Zo's head so she won't whack herself as she slides into the back of the cop car. It's just like in the movies, except that Ethan's inside this scene, and the criminal in handcuffs is his wife.

The cops climb into the front seat, turn on their lights with a single whoop. The lights flash silently as the cruiser pulls out onto the familiar road, the one he and Zo have driven down thousands of times without any incident whatsoever. Ethan watches the car carry his wife into the distance, then disappear around a bend.

He thinks about an article he read recently in *The New Yorker*: WHAT IF THIS IS A GLITCH IN THE MATRIX? Apparently it is. Apparently all of this is exactly that.

Ethan gets out of the passenger's seat, walks around the front of Zo's wagon, slides into the driver's seat. He feels around on the floor for Zo's phone, then begins scrolling through her contacts.

Wacha, Ariana, a filmmaker friend from New York.

Wadsworth, Jeffrey, a Rainbow Seed parent, dad of Sargent Pepper, and yes, that's the kid's real goddamn name.

Wang, Sara, an old Sarah Lawrence buddy.

Watters, Jackie. Bingo.

Ethan dials the number, gives Jackie the basic facts, not quite believing the words even as he says them: Zo's been arrested, she's at Starkfield Police Department, is asking for Jackie's help.

"You're serious?" Jackie asks.

He is. Yes.

"They targeted Zo?"

Targeted? "No, that's not—" Ethan begins.

"Ethan," Jackie interrupts. "Tell me everything that happened."

"Zo . . . well, I guess she hit a cone."

"She *hit a cone*?"

"More than one, actually. In a construction zone."

"Well, *that's* a bullshit charge if I've ever heard one. Oh my God, I can't fucking believe they're doing this."

"Doing what?"

"Hitting Zo with a bogus offense. Of course. This is how they do it. Political retribution is the oldest play in the book."

"No, Jackie. That's really not what—"

"*Think* about it, Ethan. Zo's an activist. Cops target activists all the time. But they're not going to get away with it this time, I promise you. *They are not fucking going to get away with this.*" And before Ethan has a chance to say anything else, there's a click, then silence. And then he is alone in his wife's car, staring at her phone.

Sitting there, Ethan wonders if there's a word, in some language, for the surreal sensation that your own life is a stage play that, after running smoothly for years, has veered wildly off-script. The other actors look the same, they're moving around the same stage, but for some reason, nobody is speaking the right lines.

And then there's nothing else to do but start the engine, flick his turn signal, and put the car in drive. He's just pulling out onto the road when the first of the construction workers return from their lunch break. In his rearview mirror, he sees them survey, confused, the wreckage.

11

MADDY'S CAR IS in the driveway, but the house is silent. Other than the jingle of Hypatia's collar as she lifts her head from the new-not-blue sofa, the house is still. "Maddy?" Ethan calls out. "Mad, you here? You won't believe what happened!"

As if in response, his phone rings: it's Fake Dr. Ash. Ugh, Ethan realizes he never rescheduled their call, he just blew the whole thing off. He should answer, apologize, try to explain. Instead, he flicks his phone to silent. He'll call Dr. Ash later. First, he needs to get his head on straight, to make those phone calls to Children's Hospital, to know that Zo's okay. He needs, also, to figure out what to do about this whole Randy thing.

Ethan sits down at his laptop, opens his email. At the top of his inbox is a message from Randy. From his personal account. The subject: EE TAPE FOR E—CONFIDENTIAL. Ethan hesitates, then clicks.

The message is only a single line, followed by a link:

E. Remember Riverstone Specials? Well, there's more where this came from.

RIVERSTONE SPECIALS? OF course Ethan remembers those. As he recalls, they were a colossal waste of time.

Most marketing firms found actors and models from headshots

and résumés—if they liked what they saw on paper, they'd bring someone in to read from a script, get a sense of how they look on-camera, how well they might represent the client's brand. Randy did the same thing, more or less, with one exception: he wrote the scripts himself.

Or . . . he paraphrased them, anyway.

Randy took existing texts, from the most random of places— theatrical monologues, political speeches, presidential addresses, key moments from the Larry Flynt trial, Marlon Brando's "horror" speech from *Apocalypse Now*, even the occasional clip from *The Partridge Family* or *The Brady Bunch*—then rewrote them. He'd remove each from context, then cast the whole thing in an entirely different voice, as if for a different *genre*. In Randy's hands, Carl Sagan's "pale blue dot" speech was given mob-boss intonations, making the whole "everyone you love, everyone you know . . . nothing but a mote of dust" thing sound more terrifying than awe-inspiring. Nixon's famous "Silent Majority" speech was given a James Joycean stream-of-consciousness twist, making it sound unnervingly like the ramblings of a madman.

And what, Ethan had wondered, was the purpose? Did rewriting Hamlet's soliloquy in the voice of a Valley Girl ("Should I, like, even, you know, *be*, or what?") reveal anything about aspiring talent that Shakespeare's original text couldn't? Ethan suspected not, but Randy insisted he was missing the point. *Don't you get it? Riverstone Specials are proprietary. This way, we get to tell clients we're doing something different, using methods that nobody else can. People love having access to something others don't. Barely matters what it* is, *just so long as their competitors don't have it!*

Ethan had known better than to argue—hiring talent was Randy's job, not his. And the truth was, Randy *did* find talent. He had a gift for recognizing people with that ineffable *something,* the star power that made audiences sit up and pay attention.

People like Evie.

But what could Riverstone Specials have to do with a harassment lawsuit? How would it convince Evie to drop the suit?

Ethan clicks on the attachment to find out.

◆

EVIE'S ON A couch. She's young, far younger than Ethan remembers her ever being—God, she looks like she's barely more than a kid here, had any of them ever been this young? Ethan recognizes the sofa, and the abstract print behind it: this is Randy's so-called audition room.

The sound on this video is turned off. For the first several seconds, Ethan just watches.

Evie's talking. She leans back in her seat, runs her fingers through her blond hair, pulls those full lips back into a shy smile.

That smile: Ethan remembers it well, remembers it flashing at him beneath New York's artificial skyglow on a night that now feels indistinguishable from a dream.

On-screen, on this sofa, Evie looks at ease, as if she's speaking off the cuff. Ethan can almost believe she *is* speaking off the cuff, that she's just making conversation, except for this: her eyes keep flicking ever-so-slightly leftward. Reading something, probably. Evie's good, though; her reading is subtle, barely noticeable. She's just barely old enough to order a beer in this video, but already, you can tell: she's a pro.

Ethan hits the Volume button.

"I mean, I just think it's so totally, like, *ironic.* All those people, our, like, ancestors? They came here, searching. For *freedom.* For like, equal *opportunity, rights,* all that stuff. And when they landed on these shores, they founded, you know, the greatest country in all of human history."

Ethan scratches his head. Evie didn't talk like this. She didn't use extraneous *likes* or *you-knows.* Evie graduated from Andover, spent two years at Yale before leaving to launch her acting career. Whatever this is, these aren't her words.

"I mean, those people who sailed to, what's that place called? Yeah, Plymouth, right?" she continues. "They were, like, actual heroes. *Scions.* And now they're, what, second-class citizens? In, like, their own country?"

Ethan hits Pause. It's the word "scions." Ethan remembers that word, remembers Randy repeating it in their kitchen, some sort of impersonation that Ethan never found funny. A political speech, maybe?

Ethan closes his eyes, now, wracks his brain. *Scions.* When it hits him, he feels a wave of nausea.

Yes, he knows exactly what this is.

This is a paraphrase of David Duke, the bayou Klansman turned presidential candidate. Back in the '80s and '90s Duke managed—either despite or because of his pointy-hooded past—to generate round-the-clock national media attention for his campaign. The guy got interviews with Dan Rather, Phil Donahue, Ted Koppel . . . an entire *hour* with Larry King. Most of these reporters *tut-tutted* about Duke's racism while somehow failing to notice that all their public hand-wringing was giving Duke the kind of publicity and legitimacy that money couldn't buy.

With every public condemnation, the man only grew stronger.

Randy had been fascinated by Duke—by what Randy called his audacity, his media savvy, his sneaky, duplicitous use of language. Never mind that Duke lost his presidential campaign, and his run for governor after that; the guy could win by losing, just so long as he stayed in the spotlight.

To Randy, Duke was proof: the key to getting big attention was a little bit of shock value and a whole lot of shamelessness.

Apparently Randy wasn't wrong about that formula. What, after all, is the current president if not the inheritor of Duke's toxic legacy? Took a couple of decades, sure, but Duke's strategy—and his odious message—made it all the way to the White House eventually.

And now, on the screen in front of Ethan, that same message is on Evie Emerling's lips.

Ethan watches Evie run her fingers through her hair. She looks beyond the camera, toward someone just out of the frame. "I'm sorry, do I have to say this next part?"

This is now all Evie, she's not reading anything.

And then, still Evie: "Please. I'd prefer to skip ahead. Or perhaps there's something else I can read?" But the answer, from the man whose face Ethan cannot see, is no. The answer is that a professional works through her discomfort. The answer is he thought he'd seen something in her, but maybe he was wrong. The answer is that there are a hundred other girls Bränd can audition for this role, and does she want this job or not?

And Evie does want the job, apparently, because after a pause, she takes a deep breath. Forces a smile, then makes that smile look genuine. Then she opens her mouth to read more.

No, no, Evie. No, don't. Ethan wants to reach through the screen, clamp his hand over her mouth, get her to stop speaking, to avoid saying the next part, and the part after that, and the part after that, because if Ethan recalls the speech correctly, it only gets worse, much worse, from here.

Don't say it, he wills Evie, even though he is decades too late. He knows, simply because this video is in his inbox, how it ends. He knows that Evie, in that audition room, is filled with ambition— you don't go on to have the career like hers if you're not hungry, if you don't have the feeling that you can *be* somebody (and you're right about that, young Evie: you *will* be somebody, you'll be one of Hollywood's most bankable actresses, you'll pull in millions of dollars per film, you'll be on the covers of magazines, you'll walk red carpet after red carpet, you don't need to do *this*). But right now, on this sofa, at this 1995 audition, Evie is still nobody. And reading the next part, says the man standing offscreen—the man who holds the power, the man whose face doesn't appear, the man who will hang on to this audition tape for decades, who will digitize it, file it away, who won't hesitate, someday, to edit it down into bite-sized clips and send it out into the world without context or explanation—is the thing she has to do to become somebody.

Ugly words emerge from beautiful red lips, and Ethan sees—he sees clearly now—he shouldn't have allowed this, not in the company he co-founded, not when he's right on the other side of the door futzing around with spreadsheets and contracts and HTML code. And the problem is that Evie's a terrific actress, because she says it all like she believes it. If Ethan hadn't seen her hesitate just now, he'd think she *does* believe it.

Ethan presses Stop. Tries to make sense of what he's just seen.

One of the reasons Randy Riverstone has been such a success is this: Randy understood long before most not only that the media landscape was changing but also what those changes would *mean*. It wasn't just that the news cycle would be firmly and forever round-the-clock, or that there would soon be hundreds of channels broadcasting the day's events, countless talk shows on television and radio. It wasn't that each of these sources would in turn splinter, then splinter again, into gossip sites, then blogs, then into the veins and capillaries of social media . . . or that any story, reported from anywhere in the world, could be shared with a single click. It's that all of these changes pointed in exactly one direction: the media was becoming a reaction factory. In an endlessly networked twenty-four-hour news cycle, few would have the time or resources to plan, to *think,* to analyze, to provide meaningful context. They'd all be too busy *responding.*

And this meant the media could be manipulated.

Put some raw meat in front of a news source—outrage or the outrageous, doesn't really matter—and the world will gobble it right up.

Ethan doesn't have Randy's instincts, never did, but even Ethan knows: if this clip of Evie were to be leaked to the press, even just a few phrases here or there, it would lead to a torrent of headlines— EVIE EMERLING CAUGHT ON TAPE! HOLLYWOOD STAR REVEALED AS A BIGOT! There would be no questions about context, no chance for Evie to explain, to apologize, there's no time for that anymore. The headlines would cease only when the world moved hungrily on to the next outrage, and by then it would be too late for Evie.

There's enough in this one tape to ruin Evie Emerling for good, and Randy says he has more.

And Ethan's the one who's supposed to tell her?

◆

I<small>T TAKES</small> G<small>OOGLE</small> just .77 seconds to return 123 million results.

EVIE EMERLING: WIKIPEDIA PAGE

Evelyn Rose Edelmann, credited professionally as Evie Emerling, is an American actress. She has received international acclaim for her work, including two Screen Actors Guild Awards, two Golden Globes, and one British Academy Film and Television Award. She was one of the world's highest-paid actresses in 2004, though in more recent years, she has eschewed the spotlight. . . .

Ethan clicks some links, finds himself scrolling through interviews on YouTube: Evie with Charlie Rose, the women of *The View,* Regis and Kelly, Kelly and Ryan. Ethan follows all this with an image search: There's Evie at the Golden Globes in an emerald gown. At Sundance in furry boots and a white parka. Stepping out of a limousine in an outfit that looks a bit like an *I Dream of Jeannie* costume. Ethan looks at image after image of the woman he once knew, the one whose career he once helped launch, and now is being asked to help to end.

God. He needs to talk to someone, needs to get his head straight.

"Mad?" he calls out again. Where *is* she, anyway? He goes to the bottom of the stairs, listens for noise. When he hears none, he climbs the stairs, still calling her name.

Upstairs, Maddy's bedroom door is closed. He raps lightly. When she doesn't answer, he cracks the door just enough to see pink toenail polish pointing toward the ceiling.

"Hey, Mad?"

Silence.

He pushes open the door a little more, pokes his head into the room. Maddy's lying on the floor. Totally motionless. Sleeping, except . . . no, wait. Maddy's *not* sleeping. Not at all. Her eyes are open, aimed at the ceiling. Her lips are parted, and her shirt's unbuttoned revealing a pierced navel and an orange lace bra.

There's no movement of the eyes, no movement of the body. Nothing at all. *Dead, she's dead.*

Jesus Christ.

A heart attack, a stroke, one of those aneurism things that nobody ever sees coming. Or no. Maybe some sort of overdose. Ethan's at her side in a flash, shaking her shoulder. "Maddy! Maddy, oh God, Maddy, wake up!"

Maddy opens her eyes. Frowns. *"Goddammit."*

Alive. She's alive.

"Are you okay?" His eyes move wildly over her face. "You're really okay?" He tries to calm his heart, which is pounding so hard it feels like an animal inside his chest, trying to shake its way free of his ribs.

Maddy sits up, looks annoyed. "I'm fine, all right? *Jeez.*"

Maddy buttons her shirt, just a single button, above her navel. She looks past Ethan. "Sorry dude," she says (to whom? To no one. No one's there, it's just the two of them, plus that cage-rattling creature in his chest). Maddy gets up, goes over to her laptop, starts punching the Volume button. "I really am sorry. I'll refund you."

The computer responds by making a noise, some sort of grunt, human and deep. That's when Ethan realizes there's a face on her computer. Male.

"You can hit me up again if you thought it was worth it," Maddy tells the grunter. "No hard feelings if not. Again, I'm *super* sorry."

The face grunts again. Nods. Disappears. There's a beep, like a call ending.

"What are you doing?" Ethan asks. "I thought you were . . ." He doesn't say the word "dead" aloud, doesn't dare.

Maddy keeps her eyes on the screen as she taps away at her keyboard. "I was *working,* okay?"

"Working?"

Tap, tap, tap. "As in, 'a job'? As in, somebody gives you money in exchange for your services?"

"Job? What job? You don't have a job." Her job is babysitting for them, isn't it? Her job is *looking* for a job. Her job is figuring out what comes next, that's why she's here.

"Whatever, Ethan."

"Wait." He's not thinking straight yet. This whole damned day has been so off-kilter. "But *do* you have a job?"

Maddy stops typing, finally looks at him. The expression on her face says at once, *You're really stupid,* and also, *But that's okay, I like you anyway.* Her voice is softer as she says, "I do, Ethan. I have lots of jobs, actually."

Ethan tries to piece together the facts. He thought she was dead, but she's not dead. She didn't overdose/stroke out/collapse in his house, not on his watch. It was a job, that's all.

The hell kind of job, though?

When he asks her that, *the hell kind of job,* she replies, "The kind that's my own damn business."

He gives her the look she sometimes gives to him. Lips together. Arms folded, waiting. A taste of her own medicine. He'll wait like this until she answers. Finally she tosses her hands in the air, re-signed. "Fine. You ever hear of Ten-Spot?"

He hasn't.

"It's one of those odd-jobs websites," Maddy explains. "Online marketplace for freelance stuff. You pitch your services, people bid. Gigs you can do from your home, starting at ten bucks."

"What sorts of gigs? Like graphic design?"

She smiles at him, amused—too amused, actually. She looks like she's talking to an idiot and is trying not to laugh at how slow he is. "Sure, Ethan. Like graphic design."

"But . . . for ten dollars?" He's trying to do the math in his head. What sort of design jobs can a person do for ten bucks? And how can there possibly be enough of them for the business model to work?

"Well, you have to offer *something* for ten bucks. So if it takes, like, a minute of my time, I charge ten bucks," she says. "Price goes up from there."

"Maddy, do you even know graphic design?"

Maddy stares at him. (Yes, he's an idiot, he doesn't know the first thing about anything, he admits it. He's old, he's irrelevant, ridiculous, a fool.) "To be honest, Ethan, I don't get too many requests for graphic design."

She bangs on her laptop, then turns the screen toward him. "Here. This is my shop."

Now Ethan's looking at a photo of her. He's almost certain that it's Maddy, anyway. It's a selfie, taken from above her head. The picture includes just a portion of her face—her chin and a portion of her jaw. Mostly, he's looking down on her body, which is sitting cross-legged on a white carpet. She's wearing a loose black V-neck, and it's almost impossible not to notice her cleavage, the hint of neon lace peeking out.

The headline: I'LL DO ANYTHING, KINDA' PROBABLY.

He scrolls down, reads the description: *I'll rewrite ur online dating profile. I'll correct ur spelling, or compliment your new haircut. I'll call your house when ur girlfriend's there and refuse to leave my name. I'll Skype with u and not say a word, no matter what u say to me. Heck, I'll even do that last one while licking a lollipop. I'll do other things, too. Who knows—if I'm in the mood, I might even do that. Or that. Yeah, I'd might do that, too. Try me.*

He looks up. "Maddy, you can't say this."

"Why not?"

"Because . . ." He pauses. Will Alex someday be in her twenties and still not know you can't say *this*? "Well, because there are creeps out there, Mad."

She tilts her head, stares at him. "Oh, really, Ethan? *Are* there creeps out there? I never would have guessed." Yes, he's a silly old man, obtuse, he doesn't understand. That's what she's saying with that look on her face.

"Maddy, I'm *serious*."

"News flash, Ethan: creeps are out there no matter what I do or don't do. And creep money is as green as anyone else's."

"Wait. So you *take* those jobs?"

"I mean . . . Sometimes I do, sometimes I don't. Depends on

my mood. I can refuse any job I want, just so long as I don't break a contract after it's signed."

"But . . ." Ethan can't shake the feeling that she's missing something, some essential point. "What do you *do* for them?"

"Honestly, most of the time it's stupid," she says. "One kid had me stuff as many cheese puffs in my mouth as I could, then say 'penis' a bunch of times. Another asked me to dance around to Ariana Grande wearing underwear over my face. It's mostly pretty juvenile stuff. Lots of teenage boys with dumb ideas. I think they're paying the ten bucks just to see if I'm for real."

He thinks about this, imagines himself as an adolescent with the power to ask a woman to do anything, anything at all, for the price of a movie ticket.

"But it's not just guys," Maddy continues. "Like, this one woman asked me to call her husband and start talking dirty to him. I don't know if she was spying on him, testing how long he'd stay on the phone, or if it was some kind of foreplay for the two of them, or what. Didn't really matter to me either way. Only took a minute or so before he moaned and hung up."

"And this guy, today?"

"Wanted me to lie motionless on the floor, mouth and eyes open. That's it."

"Like you were . . . dead."

"I guess, yeah. He wanted to watch."

"But . . . why?"

"I mean, I'm guessing that's how he busts his nuts, but what do I know?"

"Jesus, Maddy," he says. He sits down on the bed, presses his forehead to his fists. "That's horrible." Why can't she see how horrible this is?

"Better than him using an *actual* dead girl, that's what I figure. Plus I turned the sound down, so I wouldn't have to hear him. I could've turned the job down, but he was offering, like, *really* good money. So I was like, okay, sure, I'll take fifty bucks for lying on the floor for ten minutes. Hell yeah, I'll do that."

"Mad. You have to be careful. Some of these people could be dangerous."

She shrugs. "It's not like I *meet* them. They never even know my real name, or my location, or anything like that. The whole thing is, like, totally anonymous. Anyway, that's the gig economy for you, am I right?"

ETHAN KEEPS HIS promise to Zo. Despite everything, he forces himself to call Boston Children's, just like he said he would.

He looks up individual doctors, specific department staff, as if his wife isn't in jail as he does this, as if Maddy Silver hadn't just indulged some psychopath's murdered-girl fetish, as if his oldest friend weren't asking him to blackmail a movie star. Ethan dutifully calls every extension at Boston Children's he can find, explaining the situation into one voicemail box after another. *Been on the waiting list for nineteen months . . . really struggling in the classroom . . . need more help than is available locally . . . might have to change schools . . . just want information . . . please, isn't there anything you can—*

Very occasionally he talks to a live human. Those individuals take his name and number, promise nothing. Between calls, he dials Jackie's number. He leaves multiple voicemails for her, too, each time saying pretty much the same thing—he's at home, he's waiting by the phone, he'll come to the police station whenever Zo needs, can he do anything? Anything at all?

And when he runs out of people to call, he sits down at his laptop. Tries to work.

But the truth is, he's got bigger problems—much bigger problems—than the rebranding of Fake Dr. Ash's website. Try as he might, Ethan can't keep his mind on Dr. Ash's pseudoscience, her made-for-Instagram platitudes—*Your body cries out for wellness, will you answer the call? Your soul is a seed that needs light and nourishment to grow!*—or any of her supposedly health-boosting products.

Ethan frowns. His eyes drift from his computer, to the reminder he scratched out this morning, still sitting on the counter: *Get More Adderall.*

Never mind Dr. Ash. He'll go get Alex's prescription now. While he's out, he'll return the carpet Zo ordered and now doesn't want. Might as well do something productive while he waits for the phone to ring.

How to Get an Adderall Prescription, Part A

Don't think. Not about money, or about financial aid, or your wife in handcuffs. Don't think about what your old business partner is asking of you, or about beautiful women who do unsavory things. Put all of that out of your head.

Your only task right now is to get a prescription. Your kid needs her Adderall, and soon. You've got just one pill left in that jar.

Adderall's a Schedule II drug, so highly controlled that the Starkfield pediatrician won't prescribe more than thirty days at a time. Her office also refuses to fax the prescription to the pharmacy, as they would for antibiotics or antihistamines. So getting this prescription filled on short notice is trickier than it seems.

Don't call the pediatrician's office; they'll just connect you to an automated prompt—"Dial 3 to fill an ADHD medication." This path, you've learned, takes forty-eight hours. You don't have forty-eight hours: you'll be out of pills by morning.

Drive to the office instead. Ask for Tracy, the medical assistant whose full-time job seems to be managing ADHD prescriptions for kids. When she comes out to meet you, put on your friendly voice, your affable voice, your whole "sheepish good-guy routine," as Randy called it. You're sorry, you tell Tracy, so sorry, but you need a prescription today. Count on the fact that Zo used to take a yoga class with Tracy, back before Zo changed gyms. Count on the fact that you once brought cookies to the staff after a particularly rough office visit when Alex was four; you'd had to hold her down, Exorcist–style, so the doctor could remove what turned out to be a pair of bright purple Barbie shoes from her left nostril. Count on the fact that you're a dad; Zo says that fathers who are involved with their kids' care are forgiven for cluelessness in ways that moms never are. Use this. I'm just a bum-

bling dad who doesn't know the rules: but hey, look how much I care!

Yes. You'll wait here while she gets the prescription ready. You appreciate it, you really do.

Sit in the waiting room, surrounded by primary colors and restless infants and a snotty-nosed toddler whose whine is an endless drone. When the prescription is ready, hand over your driver's license. As they copy your license number—some precaution they claim to have to take, even though they know you—fill out the paperwork: patient name/date of birth/relationship to patient/yes I certify that this medicine will be used only for said patient/ yes, I understand that this is a Schedule II controlled substance and I'm personally liable if it gets into the wrong hands.

Drive the prescription to the local Rite Aid. Wait in line. When it's your turn at the pharmacy counter, hand over the prescription. Show your driver's license again. Fill out a new form, which says more or less all the same things that the first one did. Sign again. You'll have to do the whole thing— the driver's license, the form, the signature—a third time, when the prescription is ready to be picked up. It'll be a half hour, they say. You can wait, or not.

Not.

You'll come back for the filled prescription later. After you know your wife's okay. After you've returned that carpet, and after you've gotten an appointment at Children's Hospital, and after you've picked up Alex.

And maybe, too, after you've figured out how to get a little money so you don't need to do what Randy's asking.

How to Get an Adderall Prescription, Part B

After Maddy had arrived to live with them, Ethan had told her about Alex's ADHD. "She takes medication," he'd explained, his voice low as if someone might hear, even though they were alone in the kitchen.

"Cool," said Maddy. Unfazed. "I took ADHD meds for a while."

"Really? Did they help?"

"I guess so, yeah."

He asked Maddy why she stopped taking them, and she shrugged. "My supplier moved away. I guess just never bothered to find anyone else."

"Wait. You never actually had them officially prescribed?"

Maddy shrugged. "I mean, it's just Adderall or whatever."

ALEX HAD STARTED taking that red horse pill long before she knew how to swallow pills, or to spell her last name.

They'd tried everything else. No screens, no sugar, no red dyes, no wheat, no dairy. They tried vitamins, magnesium, omega-3s. They'd done an elimination diet that left Alex eating little but rice and turkey for weeks. They tried memory training, meditation, neurofeedback, acupuncture, forced early morning walks, then forced early morning jogs (Ethan cheerleading—*You can do this! It's so good to get our energy out!*—and Alex crying the whole while). When fellow parents recommended craniosacral therapy, kinesthesiology, Reiki, aromatherapy, qi-gong, crystal therapy, they tried those things too. And maybe some of it helped, hard to say, but not enough, because after all of this trying, they still marched up to the pharmacy counter with a prescription in hand.

It helped, the Adderall. It helped more than they had expected, and faster than they expected too. It didn't fix everything, but it made their lives—their child's life!—just a little bit easier, a little bit more manageable.

Okay, Alex still gets sent to the principal's office more than the average kid. And sure, a dad at the Rainbow Seed School once remarked to Ethan, "So your kid's got a real raised-by-wolves vibe, doesn't she?" When the man saw the look on Ethan's face, he added, too quickly, "It's really very compelling." But the truth is, Ethan couldn't even get mad, because the guy wasn't entirely wrong. *You should have seen her before,* he thought.

It took the edge off, that's the thing that nobody who hasn't been through it could possibly understand. Thanks to those red pills, Alex was a little *less* raised-by-wolves. Everything became just a little easier. For her, and for them.

1 2

BOY, IS A nine-by-twelve wool carpet heavy. Ethan huffs and puffs as he drags the rolled rug from the back of his wagon toward the UPS Store. He throws open the door, managing to heave the rug only a couple of inches before the door closes, wedging it in place. Damn thing won't budge. Ethan tries again: *Open door, heave. Door shuts, carpet stuck.* Then he does it a third time, and a fourth.

Behind the counter, a clerk watches this whole clown show. "Need some help there?" The clerk's younger than Ethan, with a beard that's as long and scraggly as Ethan's.

"Nah," Ethan pants. A bead of sweat trickles down his forehead. "I've got it."

Open door, heave, shut, stuck, fuck.

The clerk shakes his head, emerges from behind the counter to help. He moves slowly, this kid; bit of a limp, as if he's managing some kind of chronic pain, lower back maybe. His name badge, pinned to his shirt, says JARRETT K.

Jarrett K tells Ethan to hold the door open, then grabs the carpet. He lifts the whole thing onto his shoulder, and carries it easily to the front of the store. The kid might walk funny, but he's a friggin' musk ox.

Jarrett sets the carpet down, wipes his brow. "It's a nice carpet, hey? This is what, New Zealand wool?"

"No clue."

Jarrett peels back a corner of the carpet, rubs the yarns between his fingers. He nods. "That's New Zealand, all right. Felted. Yeah, that's real nice. Hand-knotted and everything." Ethan's surprise must show, because Jarrett shrugs. "Used to work over at Home Goods, the one over near Albany. Was one of the only guys who worked there—some days it was just me and a bunch of women, so naturally I hauled all the heavy stuff. You learn pretty quickly to dread a well-made carpet."

Ethan sets down the return label. Jarrett asks, "Your wife order this?"

"She did."

"And lemme guess. The color was ever-so-slightly off."

Ethan laughs. "Probably." *I don't love it,* Zo had said, who knows why.

Scanning the barcode, Jarrett says, "So your wife does the ordering and the rejecting, and you do, what, the paying and the hauling?" Jarrett's voice is friendly, and the truth is, he's not wrong—Zo *did* order it. She *did* reject it. Ethan *is* the one who has to haul it. Still, Ethan feels a little guarded as he answers. "Well . . . she had some stuff going on."

You know, like getting arrested.

Jarrett nods, tapping on a keyboard, eyes on the computer screen. "Sure, of course."

Also, not that it matters, but Ethan did pay. He's not complaining, not really. What's his is hers. Theirs. It's theirs. Although he wouldn't mind if Zo started bringing in some money again.

"You married?" Ethan asks. Hard to tell how old this Jarrett kid is. His body seems middle-aged tired, but there's not a speck of gray in his beard. Shaved head, but the stubble on his scalp looks dark, too. Could be anywhere from nineteen to thirty-five.

"No sir, no marriage for me," Jarrett says. He prints out a form, marks the places for Ethan to sign, flashes a grin as he hands over the pen. "I get to do enough hauling as-is."

"Well . . ." Ethan hesitates. "Marriage has its benefits too." He feels like he should name a few. Comfort, maybe. Friendship. Partnership. Predictability. But he suspects these words will sound banal, not remotely convincing, and are they even true? There's not much comfort coming from Zo these days. Or friendship, for that matter, let alone partnership. And predictability? Just a few hours ago, Zo slammed headlong into traffic cones, cackling like a madwoman.

No, "predictable" isn't a word he'd use to describe his wife at the moment.

"Aw, don't mind me," Jarrett says. "I'm jealous, that's all. As it happens, not too many girls swipe right for guys like me."

Lonely. The kid is lonely. "Sounds like you just haven't met the right girl yet," Ethan reassures him.

"Could be," Jarrett says, but he shakes his head as he speaks, like even as his mouth is saying that love is still possible, his body can't help but disagree.

Ethan sizes him up: the kid's not so bad-looking. A little unkempt, sure. Probably not a ton of job options, not around these parts, anyway, but Jarrett's clearly a hard worker, and he's friendly too. Ethan's Pennsylvania hometown is filled with guys like Jarrett. Heck, Ethan himself might have *been* one of them, if not for that Kenyon scholarship. If Ethan knew any girls Jarrett's age—other than Maddy, that is—he might introduce them.

"How about you?" Jarrett asks. "How'd you meet your wife?"

At Bränd, of course. He and Randy had been on the lookout for a filmmaker who could help out with the "Heaven Is a Gal Named Audrey" campaign. Zo was two years out of college when she walked into the Bränd office—all blunt bangs and big plans, wearing her take-no-crap attitude like a cloak. Randy had launched into one of his signature monologues: *Bränd isn't looking for a filmmaker per se. We're looking for someone who can do with video what the ancient poets—the ones who once sang the epic poems that Homer would later codify into texts—did: unify audiences, bring them together around some core ideas, symbols. Make people feel something, you know? Everyone together, all at once, you don't get that so much anymore, do you?*

By this point, Ethan had heard a variation of this speech about a hundred times. As usual, he stayed quiet through Randy's rambling. Three times, though, he met Zo's eye across the table. Three times, they'd both been unable to stifle a smile. As Randy went on and on, oblivious to what was unfolding in front of him, Ethan could hear, as if through Zo's ears, how absurd this all sounded. *Something was lost when Homer wrote those tales down, something essential, the creative juice, that feeling that you get when artist and art and audience are one in the same, I'm talking the feeling you get when you look at Picasso's* Guernica, *that what-the-fuck feeling, that sense of being on the edge. That's what Bränd is going for. Our goal isn't just to sell product, it's to wake people up, make them feel alive, see what I'm saying?*

By the time Randy finished, Ethan couldn't even look at Zo for fear of cracking up. There was a long pause while Zo gathered herself. "Well," she finally said, standing. "I'm not an ancient poet. Nor am I Picasso. I make films. Good ones. So if you ever need a *filmmaker,* feel free to give me a call." She'd started toward the door, then paused. She pulled out a business card, set it down in front of Ethan. "And if you, Ethan, would ever like to have coffee, here's how to find me." Then she'd walked out the door without looking back, and Ethan felt like he'd won the motherfucking lottery.

It wasn't long before he and Zo were sleeping with their feet entwined, spending long, lazy Sundays at a café near her Brooklyn apartment at Fifth Avenue and Carroll Street, what was then the far outermost edge of Park Slope. They'd sit there for hours, he and Zo, sharing sections of *The New York Times,* pausing occasionally to read a paragraph aloud to each other.

From the beginning, Ethan loved how grounded Zo was, how real. Around Randy, Ethan often felt whipped around, like he could never quite get his bearings. With Zo, by contrast, he knew exactly where he was, and *who* he was. She had a sharp wit, but she wasn't afraid to be goofy. Occasionally, she laughed so hard at her own jokes that she snorted.

Now, standing in the UPS Store, he longs to understand: where is that version of Zo now? Where is that humor, that ease, that laughter? The mutability, the sense of partnership, friendship? Where did all of it *go*?

It was buried by laundry, maybe, or eroded to nothing from too many nights of trying to put a hyperactive child to bed. Consumed by fury, perhaps, at the whole damn world.

Wherever it went, he misses it.

Jarrett's still waiting for an answer: how did he meet his wife? "Work," Ethan says, like the answer is simple. "More than twenty years ago."

"And you're still married. Well, kudos to that, man. You must be doing something right."

Ethan lingers at the UPS counter longer than he should. Maybe he needs the distraction, the friendly break from a world gone mad. He and Jarrett talk about the Corbury Road construction, about Arlo's dispensary ("I hear it's going to be like an Apple Store," Ethan tells Jarrett, and even as he says it, he's both pleased to have an insider's scoop and irritated with himself for talking up Arlo's business venture). Whether it will be a bad winter, how it is always a bad winter in Starkfield.

It's not the worst thing, talking to a lonely kid in a UPS Store. *What is there to fear in such an ordinary world?*

And then Jarrett poses a question for which Ethan has no answer: "Listen, I'm just curious. When was the last time you were like, 'I love my life, I just freakin' love it'?"

Ethan stares at the kid. "You ask all your customers this?"

"Only the ones I like."

"Sure, yeah. I love life."

"See, that's interesting, that answer. Because I didn't ask you if you love life. I asked if you love *your* life."

Ethan hesitates—does he?

He's saved from having to answer, mercifully, by the phone: Jackie. At last.

IT'S ZO'S VOICE, not Jackie's, on the other end of the phone. "It's me, your criminal wife."

"Are you okay? How's prison?"

Zo whoops with laughter, then says—not to him—"He wants to know how prison was." He hears a room full of women cheering.

"Who's there?" he asks.

"Everyone," Zo says. "Jackie called an emergency meeting. We're at her house now, plotting and scheming. But to answer your question, being arrested wasn't especially interesting. Mostly it was a lot of sitting around. And paperwork. Listen, Ethan, I'm going to be at Jackie's pretty late."

"Zo, we have Parents' Night, remember?"

"Oh, right. Parents' Night. Okay, so if you drop Alex off at Persimmon's house by six, I'll meet you at school. Speaking of which, did you get that appointment at Children's?"

"I've left a million messages," he tells her. "I'm trying."

"Great, keep trying."

"Zo, what exactly are you all plotting and scheming?"

"The revolution. Seriously. Check out our Twitter feed."

ETHAN PIECES THE story together from fragments. The way one does these days.

A week ago, it seems, the Starkfield Police Department sent out a tweet (because of course they have a Twitter account, who doesn't? Ethan's apparently the last man standing). The tweet itself was benign, a warning about a rainstorm that might lead to flooding. The tweet had included a screenshot of the Doppler radar, taken from a department computer.

But whoever posted the warning had neglected to crop the image; clearly visible was every browser tab that had been open at the time. Of the six open tabs, four were pages for area activist groups. One of those groups was All Them Witches.

Later that day, someone calling themselves @LeftyMama-Bear458, had tweeted:

@starkfieldPD: Why are you monitoring peaceful citizens' groups??? #Overreach #abuseofpower

Within minutes, the cops had deleted their original tweet, then reposted a new one with the image cropped so a viewer could no longer see their open tabs.

@LeftyMamaBear458 followed up almost immediately with a screenshot of the original tweet:

the @starkfieldPD surveils activists, then hides their misdeeds by deleting the public record #screenshotsare4ever #policestate #thisiswhatfascismlookslike

At this point, the police chief decided to nip concerns in the bud. He released a statement—by tweet, of course—which included the sentence: *To ensure the public safety, the Starkfield Police Department routinely monitors all potentially volatile public gatherings.*

The chief's later assurances—he didn't mean the activists *themselves* were volatile, he meant that the political *environment* was inherently volatile, the department remains committed to free speech, they protect peaceful protesters of every political leaning, Starkfield has had forty political protests since Inauguration Day 2017, all of which have occurred without incident—came too late. Already, several left-leaning publications reported on the incident, one even branding the Starkfield PD as "jackbooted thugs." The attention didn't last long, though; the world quickly moved on to the next outrage, and the incident was forgotten.

It was forgotten, that is, until a member of one of those activist groups was arrested for hitting some cones in a construction zone.

By the time Ethan knows any of this, the whole story has spun out of control.

Tweet from @AllThemWitches:

@StarkfieldPD, why did you arrest an activist with a clean record? @ResistanceNational, @ResistanceMass @ResistanceWesternMA, #thismachinefightsfacists #trumpedup-charges

Tweet from @ResistanceMass:

A seriously disturbing story from one of our chapters in western MA: #SisterResister with no criminal record

ARRESTED without cause. We have followed up with the @ starkfieldPD for more information. #Staytuned #FightThe-Power #protestispatriotic

Tweet from @ResistanceMass:

Update: we have learned the arrest was for hitting a cone in a construction zone. This peaceful activist/mom was ARRESTED and HANDCUFFED and TAKEN TO JAIL. She. Hit. A. Cone. WTF. #dystopia #MightDoesNotMakeRight

Tweet from @ResistanceNational:

Massachusetts activist harassed and arrested by police in rural community after hitting a cone. @Bostonglobe, @NYTimes, @washingtonpost.

Tweet from @BettsbridgeResistance:

Western Massachusetts Resisters, we are following up to see how we can be of support. Stay tuned! #Resist

Tweet from @ResistanceWesternMA:

We're on it. #nosurveillancestate #persist

Tweet from @NorthamptonPeaceBrigade:

Wow. Spread the word. Then call the @starkfieldPD to tell them what you think. #ActivismIsNotaCrime

Tweet from @MassFreedomFighters:

An activist arrested for her activism, folks! You know what to do! #WonderResistersActivate #ThisIsWhatDemocracy-LooksLike #America2018

And even as other accounts, representing opposite-and-amplified points of view begin to push back—*Don't do the crime if you can't do the time. . . . Another bored mom without enuf to do . . . Lock her up!!!*—Zo's story continues to spread, bit by bit and click by click, 240 characters at a time, through the strange, boundless geography-free territory that is our new world.

RT@CollegeProgressives
RT@ResistandPersistMA
RT@FourFreedomsMA
RT@JusticeWarriorsMass
RT@WomynforPeaceMassachusetts
RT@WomensMarchBoston
RT@WomenforJustice
RT@SmashthePatriarchy5789

February 1996

Ethan and Randy bet Bränd's third and final Leap of Faith on a philosopher.

By now, Ethan and Randy—these new kids in town, these youngbloods, these *Gen-Xers*—have gotten attention. Through their "Prufrock" and "Heaven Is a Gal Named Audrey" campaigns, they have proven they can generate buzz, grab headlines, make people stop in their tracks. They know how to make people *feel* things: loneliness and lust; nostalgia and trepidation; timelessness and time slipping away.

They've got moxie, these upstarts. They have smarts. Instincts. Creativity. *Youth*.

Now, Randy says, Bränd has one last thing to prove: that they can create a cult brand. Soon, after all, savvy advertisers won't need to reach customers en masse. They'll be able to microtarget customers, follow individuals as they move through cyberspace, nudge customers click by click into ever-increasing loyalty. The future of marketing isn't about going wide, it's about going *deep*—turning customers into superfans.

But what—or whom—should they feature in this Third Leap of Faith?

"Something esoteric," Randy suggests. It's after hours, they're at the apartment, and they've been brainstorming for hours. Randy takes a swig of beer, sprawls backward on the floor, stares up at the ceiling. "A scientist, maybe, or some obscure deity. Some random old scholar."

Ethan goes to the closet, pulls his Intro to Philosophy textbook from a box. Hasn't looked at this since sophomore year. He hands it to Randy, who opens it randomly, and places his finger on the page: Jeremy Bentham? No, Ethan tells him; utilitarianism is a snooze. Randy tries again: Wittgenstein? Nah, nobody understands that guy. They reject Thomas Aquinas (too religious), Claude Levi-Strauss (already branded as everyone's favorite denim), and Ayn Rand (a non-starter: Zo practically broke up with Ethan when she saw *The Fountainhead* on his shelf).

"How about this guy?" Randy hands the book to Ethan. Jean Baudrillard. There's a black-and-white photo on the page: Older fellow, tweed jacket, balding. Thin shock of white hair above his ears. Playful look in his eyes. He looks erudite. Comfortable. Intellectual. Like a Platonic ideal, actually, of a postmodern French philosopher.

Ethan reads the text and summarizes for Randy. "Okay, so Baudrillard talked about the nature of reality in the modern world. He argued that the line between reality and fakeness was becoming increasingly blurred. Eventually, we'll be so awash in advertisements, in symbols stripped of their original meaning, that reality itself will vanish altogether. Then we'll be in something called the hyperreality, the ultimate death of meaning."

"The hyperreality," Randy repeats. Then he turns to Ethan, eyes bright. "Bingo."

"I dunno, Randy. That's awfully cerebral, don't you think? And such a dystopian worldview."

"Think about it, E: we'll turn the guy who spoke *about* symbols into a symbol. They'll call us *geniuses*. I think we might be geniuses, actually!"

Ethan's not convinced, but walking to work the next day, Randy presses the point. "Look around, E. We're practically living in hyperreality already. Everyone's just walking around flashing symbols at one another." Randy shakes the flaps of his jacket. "Like this so-called barn coat. This is Ralph Lauren, I paid four hundred dollars for this. You think anyone who *actually goes into a barn* would pay four hundred dollars to keep themselves warm? This coat's a *symbol*. I'm using it to *signal* something to the world."

"What, that you're rich and spoiled?"

"Sure! Probably! But what I'm *not* signaling is that I shovel manure." Ethan's not so sure about that, but Randy continues. "Now think about *cyberspace,* E. Pretty soon, we'll live our lives there, which is hilarious, because nothing actually *exists* online, there's no *there* there. On the Internet, *everything* is detached from its original meaning. Everything becomes a symbol ripe for the taking."

Ethan chews this over. "Ripe for *exploiting,* you mean."

"Call it whatever you, want, E. But buckle in, we're going full-on hyperreality pretty soon."

Ethan's not sure if his discomfort is with Randy's proposed campaign, or with the world that Baudrillard describes. Already, too much of Ethan's world feels . . . manipulated. *Performed.* Like the simplest decisions—where he went to school, what kind of shoes he buys, where and how he cuts his hair— feel more like a statement of identity than of utility. But Ethan doesn't *want* that to be true. He doesn't want to live in a world where everyone's busy flashing symbols for others to decode, like some strange new language that he'll have to learn and then relearn.

Didn't he *do* that already, when he moved from a blue-collar world into this new one? Wasn't that transition enough? Is he going to have to continue learning the meanings for things, shedding old selves for new, like some sort of molting snake, forever?

Does he ever get to simply *be*?

Randy tries a different angle. "E, maybe think of this campaign as a cautionary tale: our way of making people aware of Baudrillard's warnings. If we do our jobs right, maybe folks will pay a little more attention to what's happening all around them."

Randy always did know the right thing to say.

The Baudrillard campaign begins simply, with stickers. Each sticker features a minimalist pen-and-ink drawing of the philosopher's face. Beneath the image, four words: WELCOME TO THE HYPERREALITY. Bränd makes these available at indie-music venues, coffee shops, skateparks, select college campuses renowned for their cool. Bränd also pays graffiti artists to tag buildings and bridges with Baudrillard's image, then hires street teams to plaster posters all over hip neighborhoods in big cities: SoHo, Silver Lake, Wicker Park. These posters feature the original pen-and-ink drawings, along with the line, WILL THE REAL JEAN BAUDRILLARD PLEASE STAND UP?

Ethan's not exactly sure what's supposed to happen next, and for a while, nothing does. Ethan figures this is it—the campaign over, the ultimate bust. Now, the Three Leaps of Faith will fade in people's memories, and Bränd will continue to eke out work from small-scale web-design products. Kind of a ho-hum business model, but it's a living.

And then, like magic, the images take on a life of their own.

Some hipster entrepreneur—Randy and Ethan don't know who, don't care—starts selling T-shirts and hoodies with their drawing. Then others do too. An anonymous artist creates a 'zine entirely devoted to Baudrillard's work. On the MTA, there's an underground movement to cover subway ads with Baudrillard's face. Before long, there are Baudrillard-themed stickers that Bränd didn't print, Baudrillard street art that Bränd didn't commission. There are Baudrillard-themed hoodies and caps and bumper stickers. The campaign spreads well beyond its creators.

It spreads because it's clever, or because it's subversive, or because it's an in-joke. Because people get that joke, or because they don't. Ethan's not even sure people know who the philosopher is, let alone what he said, but that hardly matters. *Having* the image is the point—it's insider code, available only to the few, the rad, the nonconforming. It all feels so *unlike* marketing, it's *anti-marketing,* really: a declaration of independence from consumer forces, except, of course, it's not: the whole thing can be traced back to two guys with corporate dreams.

Will the real Jean Baudrillard please stand up?

The campaign is turned inside out when the real Jean Baudrillard *does* stand up, in France, to claim that the campaign has "out-Baudrillarded Baudrillard." Ethan's so stunned by the philosopher's unexpected appearance (he and Randy had assumed the man died years ago) that he barely notices or cares that Baudrillard's declaration wasn't exactly a compliment. *The New Yorker* features the twist in a "Talk of the Town" story; this is followed by pieces in *Newsweek,* the *Times Magazine, Rolling Stone, WYNC, 1010 WINS.* Ethan hears a rumor, never confirmed, that over a six-month period, sales for Baudrillard's books increased by 8,000 percent.

But most important, Bränd gets calls: a sneaker company, a sports agency, a hotel chain, a movie studio, a craft distillery . . . even, hilariously, some of the biggest advertising firms in the world. Everyone wants the same thing: marketing that doesn't feel like marketing, campaigns that help them reach Generation X, all those skeptical cynics, oh, and by the way, is it possible to get the name of the woman who starred in the "Heaven Is a Gal Named Audrey" campaign?

Bränd borrows more of that hedge-fund capital, hires some staff: a receptionist, an office manager, more. Randy begins planning a massive bash, a coming-out party—at the Ritz-Carlton of all places! Right there on Central Park South!

It will be years before Ethan fully understands: it's Baudrillard and everything he represented—the death of context, the collapse of meaning, the rise of the manipulated symbol—that's ultimately responsible for Bränd's good fortune.

13

ZO HAS BECOME a symbol. This is what Ethan understands by the time he finishes reading the tweets about his wife's arrest. She *represents* something now.

An activist arrested for her activism. Well . . . sort of. But that story resembles the truth about as much as Dr. Ash represents an actual physician, or a reality-TV presidency resembles functional government. Something important, some essential thing, is missing.

Ethan mulls the situation over as he drives to Corbury to pick up Alex from school.

What happened?

When Ethan was a kid, "the news" meant a hometown newspaper. Maybe a national source too. Television? Sure, but there were only a handful of channels, and the news was on for, what, an hour or so each evening? A daily check-in, that's all you needed. Newscasters told you what was happening out there, and they'd get it over with quickly. *Just the facts, ma'am.*

Now the news is nonstop, with so many different outlets that it barely even matters what the stories actually *say*; everyone just cherry-picks the parts they want anyway. And all that's *before* social media, all those hashtag battles and back-and-forth tweets, reactions not equal and opposite, but rather *opposite and amplified*.

And all those social media accounts doing that amplifying: Are they actual humans? Are they bots? Are they paid propagandists sitting in a concrete office building across the ocean? Does it even matter? It's like we're all propagandists now.

Point is, two hours after a story breaks, Google returns so many different entry points, each one branching out into so many permutations of hyperlinks that within a few clicks, three or four taps of a finger, a person's adrift in a sea of disconnected fragments. It's up to you to choose what to do with them. *You decide,* Google says over and over.

It's like the world's given up on objective truth. *The post-truth society,* Randy would have called it. It all feels like those choose-your-own-adventure books Ethan used to love. *Choose-your-own-reality.*

We're plotting and scheming, Zo told him on the phone, *check out our Twitter feed.* There was delight in her voice, which means she *likes* what she sees online, she's *happy* to take on this role of Symbol of the Resistance.

But Ethan was *there.* He saw Zo's arrest with his own eyes, knows exactly how it went down. It wasn't the way those tweets suggest.

The atomization of truth, that's what this is. Truth so pulverized it's barely more than whizzing specks, like those particles hurtling underground in that supercollider, the one in Geneva, seventeen miles around. Slam the individual bits together, and you're basically re-creating the Big Bang.

He remembers telling Maddy about that supercollider recently. He'd talked with excitement about all that the experiment would reveal: why anything exists, how particles gain mass, what physics might exist beyond the standard model.

Maddy had asked, "Isn't that the experiment that everyone says is gonna end the world?"

Ethan assured her no, that was never a concern, and even if it had been, scientists have been running experiments for years now, slamming together protons at nearly the speed of light, and look: everything is fine.

But Maddy had grinned. "Or maybe this is what the end of the world looks like."

He'd laughed at the time, but honestly: he's starting to wonder if she might be right.

To ETHAN'S RELIEF, when Alex climbs into his car, she doesn't ask about her mother. Instead, she launches into a mile-a-minute monologue about today's active-shooter drill, and how she got in trouble for talking when the shooter was there, which made the other kids say that it's her fault that they're all dead, so she decided not to talk to them for the rest of the day, but then she forgot, and then *they* didn't want to talk to *her,* and anyway, can they please listen to *Wicked* now? She sings at the top of her lungs about *unadulterated loathing popular defying gravity dancing through life,* turning the music down only long enough to announce that no witches have ever been burned to death in America. "All of the witches that were found guilty in the Salem Witch Trials were *hanged,* except for one guy who refused to plead either guilty or not guilty. They crushed him to death with heavy stones for not taking a side."

"Gee, I'm glad you're learning so much in science," Ethan says dryly, but if Alex catches the sarcasm, she doesn't show it.

Maybe it's not such a bad thing if Alex can't stay at Rainbow Seed. The public school must have academic standards, right? Don't they have to report that stuff to the Department of Education? Prove their value on standardized tests? Besides, Alex would get bus service again. Which means Ethan won't ever have to make this horrible drive, not ever again.

But if Alex is going to school anywhere but Rainbow Seed, she's going to need to get up to speed academically, and fast.

HOW TO HELP YOUR CHILD WITH MATH HOMEWORK

Sit with her. Walk her through the equations, step by step. Speak patiently, in a calm voice. Don't let it be like last time, don't lose your temper, don't get so irate when she refuses to pay attention, or complains, or forgets where she is in the assignment.

Remind yourself how funny she is, how spirited and clever. She just needs to harness her energy, channel it toward the equations on the page. She can do this. With your help, you're sure she can.

"OKAY, ALEX. LET'S *try this. Eyes on the page. The page is right here, honey. Look."*

"*Can I get a calculator?"*

"*No, you can do this yourself. How many times does seventeen go into thirty-seven? This is why it's so important to know your times table. No. No, don't erase it that hard. Alex, come on, you're going to tear the paper again, Jesus Christ, okay, go get a clean sheet."*

"THIS PROBLEM'S EASY, *how do you reduce that fraction? Wait, why are you writing like that? Is that your normal way of holding a pencil? You're holding your pencil with just two fingers. Why would you do that? You need three fingers to hold a pencil, no one will ever be able to read that. Alex, what are you even doing?"*

TAKE A DEEP *breath as your child sings in an operatic voice,* "I haaaaate this! I haaaaaate this! Daddy is the woooo-oooo-ooooorst!"

"ALEX, STOP. FIRST *you have to do the multiplication."*

"*I did! It's right there: Nine times one hundred and seven!"*

"*Wait. No. When you set up problems like this, put the smaller number on the bottom. This'll make it easier to keep track of your work."*

"*As long as I got the right answer, what does it matter?"*

"*You didn't get the right answer."*

"*What? Impossible! Impossible, I say!"* That last part with a British accent.

"Try it again."

But now she's standing, doing a Mr. Magoo walk across the room, pretending to hold a monocle. "I dare say, old chap! Shall we take the lift to the lorry, or do you fancy a visit to the loo?"

"ALEX, PLEASE." BY now, you're begging. "Please. We've been sitting here over an hour, and it's almost time to go to Parents' Ni—"

But she's singing, now, "The Star Spangled Banner," in a raspy, jagged Janis Joplin voice. On the page in front of you, there are exactly two completed math problems, and you basically did this work yourself.

Her medicine's wearing off, you realize this, which reminds you that you still haven't picked up her Adderall prescription. You glance at the clock. There's still time to pick up that prescription. You can do it before driving— for the third time today—to the Rainbow Seed School.

This time for Parents' Night.

14

THE PHARMACY IS closed. Never mind that the store website claims that pharmacy hours run until 7 P.M.: the gate at the pickup counter is down. A sign lists new pharmacy hours, which end at 5:30 P.M. Luckily there's still one pill left for the morning.

For much of the drive, he follows a pickup truck: GMC, brown and battered, with two massive flags affixed to the cab with wooden dowels. One of those flags is the stars and stripes. The other bears the president's name: five huge block letters on a blue background. Each flag is enormous, as big as the entire truck bed. They ripple violently as the vehicle barrels along the road. Beneath the flags are a series of bumper stickers: PROUD DEPLORABLE, and ARE YOU TRIGGERED YET?, and DON'T TREAD ON ME, and a decal of a cartoon Calvin pissing on a snowflake. And also, mysteriously, a single small red oval.

The driver, whoever he is, has apparently decided to turn himself into a rolling billboard for resentment, the spirit that elected this president.

In the passenger seat, Alex gapes at the truck. *"Whoa,"* she says. "It's a good thing Mommy's not here, because she would *hate* that truck."

Ethan nods. Zo *would* hate the truck, but even so, he's not quite as quick to classify Zo's absence as "a good thing." It seems like an even *worse* thing that Alex still hasn't wondered where her mother has been all afternoon. Like it's Alex's new normal to never see her mom.

What exactly should Ethan do, he wonders, about the Zo-sized hole in their lives?

PERSIMMON'S HOUSE, WHERE the sixth-grade girls are meeting, is titanic, new construction in midcentury-meets-renovated-barn style. Probably designed by some Manhattan architect who never spent more than forty-eight hours at a stretch in the Berkshires. Looks like every light in the house is on, too; yellow beams spill from floor-to-ceiling windows onto the rolling fields beyond. If Ethan squints, he can almost convince himself that the house is some sort of spaceship, like the one that lands in the woods at the start of *E.T.*

It occurs to him that Alex has probably never seen *E.T.* He should organize a family movie night. A double-feature, perhaps: *E.T.* and *Jaws,* or maybe *E.T.* and *Raiders of the Lost Ark.* Spielberg, though. Definitely. Everybody loves Spielberg.

Ethan escorts Alex to the front door, where she's greeted by a freckled, pony-tailed nanny—just out of college, maybe, though it's hard to tell. "Mr. and Mrs. Prendergrast left about five minutes ago," says the nanny. "Come on in, Alex, we're making pizzas."

Ethan peers into the house: there's a gaggle of eleven-year-old girls seated around a gargantuan live-edge table set with bowls of pizza toppings. One of the girls glances up, sees Alex, doesn't say hello. Ethan watches the kid take a slice of pepperoni from a bowl and lay it carefully on top of her personal pizza as if she's Botticelli adding the finishing brushstroke to *The Birth of Venus.*

Back in the car, Ethan turns to the place where his wife would be, should be, and isn't. "We should do a movie night," he says to Imaginary Zo. "Spielberg."

He imagines Zo's response: "Spielberg. Hmm."

"What's wrong with Spielberg?" he asks.

"Nothing's wrong with Spielberg," his wife-who-is-not-there answers. "If you like sanitized, sentimental tripe."

Ethan decides it's not worth it to argue with a wife who isn't even present. He gives himself the last word—*Spielberg is a genius, and everyone knows it.* Then he backs down the crushed-stone driveway and heads, yet again, toward the Rainbow Seed School.

Zo ARRIVES LATE to Parents' Night. She bursts into the classroom, flushed, several minutes after the homeroom teacher has already begun talking. Ethan can't help but notice the way Shreya glances up, then presses her lips together.

Oh, but she's got a good explanation for her lateness, Shreya. She's a criminal now! He actually snorts with laughter at the thought. A couple of parents shoot looks at him.

For an hour, parents traipse back and forth across the Rainbow Seed campus, schedules in hand. They follow the pattern of their kids' day, listen to one teacher after another say some variation of the same thing. *Hands-on projects . . . joyful discovery . . . nurture the whole child . . . kindness . . . respect.*

Sometimes parents raise their hands and ask questions. They've been instructed that because this isn't a parent-teacher conference, *questions shouldn't focus on any specific child, but rather on topics that apply generally, to all children.* So every parent question is framed to appear as if it's not about their individual child, even though it clearly is. "Let's say a child is a reluctant reader . . ." asks Jett's dad (last name Mars, of candy fame).

"And how might you support a child who's *anxious*?" asks Muse's mom (divorced from a leveraged-buyout financier, rumored to be worth ten figures). "I mean *theoretically,* of course."

In English class, Willoughby's mom (did Ethan once hear that this woman is the stepdaughter of the artist Julian Schnabel? Or maybe it's Jeff Koons? Someone like that, Ethan's pretty sure) raises her hand to ask whether the children are reading diverse perspectives in English class. The teacher nods, responds with a straight face, that yes, they value *all* perspectives in this class. Currently they're reading *Our Town.* Before anyone has a chance to respond, Mr. McCuttle's voice comes over the intercom. "Wonderful Rainbow Seed families," he says gently, like he's Stuart Smalley from the old *SNL* sketch, "it's time to proceed to your next class."

The families rise, ready to move dutifully to their next location.

Zo and Shreya reach the classroom door at the same moment. "After you," Zo says.

"Oh, no," says Shreya tightly. "Please. I insist."

A pause. "Fine," says Zo. She lifts her chin and exits. "Thank you."

In gym class, the parents have to participate in something called "The Harmony Dash," which works like a relay race, except there's no winner, and instead of passing a baton, players must give each other compliments. Somehow Zo and Shreya get placed next to one another in line.

When it's Zo's turn, she says, "Shreya's *extremely* devoted to her son."

Shreya flutters her eyes and offers a practiced smile. "And Zenobia has so many interests *other* than home and family!"

Toward the end of science class, Ethan asks Mr. Boorstin a question of his own. "What if a child wants to do a science project on a non-scientific topic? Will you steer them toward a subject that involves *actual* science?"

Mr. Boorstin, who has introduced himself as a "recovering alpaca farmer," explains that *any* subject can be used as the basis for scientific exploration. "Well," Ethan pushes back. "I'd venture that some topics, like, say, witches and ghosts, don't lend themselves easily to the scientific method."

"Can you not apply the scientific method even to investigations of the occult?" Mr. Boorstin asks, smiling.

"Actually, no," Ethan says. "Because you can't prove a negative."

But there's McCuttle's voice again: "I hope you've enjoyed this class period, Rainbow Seeders! It's time to move to your next location. And if you've volunteered to help serve our delicious lasagna dinner, *thank you*. It's time to report to the kitchen."

◆

Dinner is served in the Sharing Room, which is what Rainbow Seed calls the cafeteria, although judging by the notes that are sent home on a weekly basis (*reminder: due to peanut allergies/dairy allergies/nightshade allergies/wheat allergies/gluten intolerance/lactose intolerance/veganism/soy avoidance/over-processing of our food supply, there is to be no exchange of food items at lunch or snack!*) no sharing takes place in this space whatsoever.

Zo's at the serving table; someone's assigned her to the vegan and gluten-free option, which, it turns out, is more of a lasagna soup. By the time Ethan gets in line, Zo's given up on the spatula altogether and is doling out servings with a spoon.

Ahead of Zo, Shreya slides a perfect square of turkey lasagna onto a parent's plate. She smiles broadly. "Free-range!"

Standing there in the food line, it occurs to Ethan: he should network. These are successful parents, with good incomes. Maybe one of them knows of a job for him—something permanent and well paying. If Ethan can land a real job, something with a decent salary, maybe the Bränd situation won't seem quite so dire. If Randy were here, he wouldn't hesitate to glad-hand these people, to make connections. In fact, the guy would probably manage to land a CEO position before dessert was served.

Ethan sizes up the parents in line ahead of him. At the front of the queue, there's a dad in biking gear. Made a mint in biotech, this guy—some diabetes therapy, or maybe it was cancer. Anyway, he's retired now. Behind him stands a gorgeous, leggy mom in black, an early investor in Bluetooth technology, also now enjoying early retirement. Behind her, a lesbian couple (one in Carhartt's: an organic farmer. The other, in a caftan: last name Marcus, apparently of Neiman fame). There's a venture capitalist who claims to be "mostly a dabbler these days." A former punk-rocker with two Grammys to his name. A couple with the last name of Dillard (because there's money in middle-end department stores, too). A mom with the last name Halliburton (nobody talks about it).

What could Ethan possibly offer any of them, job-wise? Even if he managed to work into a conversation that he once started a successful media company, he already knows what their next question would be: *Oh, when was that?*

Decades ago, that's when. In a different century. Literally. These days, he's just some Subaru-driving schmo from the wrong side of the tracks.

He longs to text Maddy, just to give himself a boost, a break from this place, but he's struggling to balance his food plate and rolled-up silverware and cup of watery lemonade, and anyway, here's Shreya now, holding out a spatula with a square of lasagna and wearing the world's most magnanimous smile. "What the cluck!" Shreya says. When Ethan doesn't understand, she clarifies, her facial muscles frozen in place. "The turkey is from What the Cluck Organic Farm."

Ethan has to admit, it looks delicious.

Shreya slides it onto his plate, "Enjoy!" she chirps. Ethan feels vaguely guilty, like taking a piece of turkey lasagna is some sort of betrayal—of Zo, at least, if not some more core principle he should be holding.

In front of him, Zo offers to Punk Rock a spoonful of lasagna puree. "It's a little runny," she apologizes.

The guy leans in. "That's okay, I enjoy *any* food that's served to me by a beautiful woman."

Zo takes the kind of long, deep breath she sometimes uses with Alex. "You know, I'd actually appreciate it if I could serve lasagna without being reminded that a man is assessing my looks."

Next to her, Shreya makes quick eye contact with the Dillards. Her tidy brows lift, as if to say, *See? Whole family's a problem.*

"Uh . . ." Punk Dad stares at Zo. "In case you weren't aware, that was a *compliment.*"

Zo dumps a heap of lasagna slop onto the man's plate. "It really wasn't."

Punk reaches for a slice of garlic bread with a pair of plastic tongs. Under his breath, he mutters, "Fecking *cunt.*"

As he turns around to hand off the tongs, he notices Ethan. "Sorry, mate," he says quickly. Ethan is still piecing the facts together: *That guy just called my wife a cunt, I should do something, I think*

I'm supposed to . . . kick his ass? as Punk scurries off to a table and takes his seat.

ETHAN DOES HIS best to play the role of Good Dad. He tries to pay attention as the other Rainbow Seed parents discuss whether there are enough parking spots in the parents' lot, makes a valiant attempt to nod along thoughtfully as they talk about the new homework policy: *no more than ten minutes per grade beginning in second grade, which means that the average sixth grader should get forty minutes, but doesn't that seem* excessive, *they're still just* children *after all*. He even manages a vague smile as a couple tells him about their home renovations: *The wallpaper is to die for, but we're going to have to fly to France to get it*.

But Ethan can't keep focused on any of it, doesn't care. He's a misfit here, he sees this now. Even if he wanted to fit in, he doesn't have family wealth, or Wall-Street-speculation-boom wealth, or dot-com-bubble wealth. There's not a job in the Berkshires that would let him come close to earning what these people take for granted. He never did write that novel, or screenplay. Instead, he's wasted his best years relying on Bränd checks while piecing together part-time jobs like Dr. Ash's Cornucopia of Snake Oil that would never, on their own, pay the bills.

The truth hits hard: He *needs* Bränd, needs his old company to stay afloat, to keep growing, to keep paying him. Whatever it takes.

At the front of the Sharing Room, McCuttle taps the microphone. Ethan knows the man's about to make a speech. *At the Rainbow Seed School, every child is treated as a gift! We wish every child could have this extraordinary education, too bad it's available only to families who can afford tens of thousands of dollars in annual tuition,* but of course McCuttle will leave off that last bit. Then will come a second speech—from a trustee, probably, someone who will ask for six-figure donations with a straight face. Then they'll all watch a slide show, three minutes of images captured by the marketing team: children standing in the school garden digging potatoes, tapping maple trees, painting en plein air. All the colors will be a little oversaturated, the whole thing set to a sentimental soundtrack to which they don't have the rights—Natalie Merchant's "These Are Days," maybe, or "In My Life" by the Beatles. If they pick just the right song, the room will fill with sniffles, and when it's all over, everyone will cheer. Ethan feels like he could make a Bingo card for the night, fill each square with phrases like "joyful learning!" and "power of community!" except he's probably the only one in the room who'd find it funny.

Mr. McCuttle introduces the school's next chair of the Board of Trustees. "This individual, himself a proud graduate of the Rainbow Seed School, is a *budding entrepreneur*"—for some reason, that gets a big laugh from the crowd—"who also happens to be brilliant, thoughtful, and kind. We're delighted that he'll help lead Rainbow Seed for a new generation."

And then out walks Arlo Freaking O'Shea, Maddy's friend who's about to open the marijuana dispensary.

Ethan thinks about Maddy's comment last night. *Arlo's gonna make mad bank.* Seems the Rainbow Seed School is hoping to get a little of that ganja cash for themselves.

That's it. Ethan can't take one more second of this. He stands, carrying his plate, just as Arlo "Gonna-Make-Bank" O'Shea begins recalling fondly his own days in the Sharing Room. Ethan finds a quiet hallway just behind the kitchen. He plops down, listens to the clanging of pans, the spray of water. No doubt there's an army of parent volunteers scrubbing and rinsing, each doing their part to keep the Rainbow Seed School humming. They're almost certainly knocking back wine too. When Ethan volunteered for kitchen duty two years ago—the only dad who did, by the way—he learned that one of the unofficial perks of the job is sneaking sips of alcohol like a rebellious teenager. By the time the night ends, the kitchen will be spotless, the parents will be tipsy, and everyone will pat themselves on the back for their generosity, their sense of community, the *extraordinary education* their gifted kids are getting.

Ethan drips some lasagna soup onto his jeans. He wishes he'd skipped this whole night, that he'd stayed home. He could have had a quiet night alone, or maybe Maddy would be there, which would be even better, because here's the truth: The question Jarrett asked him earlier? When was the last time he was like, *I love my life, I just freakin' love it*?

Ethan knows the answer. It's *last night*. Walking home with Maddy.

When he was young, he'd thought that life would unfold the way the books he loved always did: from emotion to emotion, a vast stretch of grand feelings, like an endless strand of pearls laid out before him. He'd imagined moving from one bead to the next, pausing at each to feel its full contours, its weight and heft, before moving to the next pearl, and the one after that. These days, though, Ethan feels like he goes for weeks, months, even—feeling nothing whatsoever. Just an endless line of empty string in his hand, not a pearl in sight.

But lately he's remembered what it is to feel, to believe that life might yet offer surprise, that there could be more ahead than a tedious slog, that maybe he does have miles to go before he sleeps.

Ethan taps out a message to Maddy on his phone: *Hey. Your weed-king buddy is giving a speech.*

Maddy: *Yeah? What's he saying?*
Ethan: *Dunno. I'm in exile on a hallway floor.*
Maddy: *U GOT DETENTION! LOL*

Ethan sends a shrug emoji in return.

Maddy: *Bad boy!*
Maddy. *Sounds like U need 2B punished*
Ethan: *Oh, is that a service I can buy on Ten-Spot?*

He hesitates before sending that one. And when he does, he follows it up with a wink emoji, making this officially the most flirtatious text exchange of his life.

Maddy responds almost immediately. A GIF: a scantily clad

woman spanking her own rear end in slow-mo. This one's followed by a quick succession of similar GIFs: a woman in a low-cut dress spanking the air. A gorgeous TV character repeatedly spanking the rear of her male co-star. A cartoon Tom spanking cartoon Jerry.

Ethan searches for just the right GIF to respond, but his thumbs feel clumsy and slow, and Maddy's GIF game is too strong for him. She sends another, then another: a late-night talk show host saying, *So naughty*. Austin Powers mouthing the words *Oh, behave*. They keep coming, the GIFs, one after another.

Ethan gives himself permission to sit back and watch them roll in. As he does, he catches snippets of the kitchen conversation:

. . . any dry dishtowels?

. . . a little more detergent

. . . What have you heard

. . . Still no room for Andrea's kid

. . . Full class

. . . so frustrating

. . . great kid, very kind, could really change the dynamics of sixth grade

. . . I mean how long will they let one child ruin things for everyone else?

. . . What's it going to take?

Ethan's not paying attention until he hears the name *Alex*. Then he starts listening closer. Yes, he recognizes some of those voices: there are a couple of sixth-grade moms in there.

. . . Started to create a paper trail

. . . Never belonged here

. . . Impulsive

. . . Discourteous, actually

. . . Shreya told me she's

. . . McCuttle says give it time, there's a procedure

. . . Wish they'd started documenting all of this years ago.

And then the women start discussing how large the slices of cake they're serving for dessert should be, and whether they should even serve dessert in the future, or whether that's poor role modeling given the toxicity of white sugar, *there's a reason people call it poison white/did you know that sugar is the new smoking/I thought sitting was the new smoking,* and by then Ethan's staring down at his disgusting, half-congealed lasagna, a sick feeling in his stomach.

Zo was right. About Shreya, about the woman's machinations. The Boston Children's thing probably doesn't even matter at this point. The paper trail's started.

They're planning to push Alex out. So they can give her spot to Andrea's kid, whoever that is.

From the Sharing Room, music starts up, and then the O'Jays are calling on people all over the world to *join hands, join the love train,* which means the slide show has begun.

Ethan stands, moves toward the kitchen. He stands in the doorway watching the women work. When they notice him, they startle, but they recover quickly.

"Ethan!" one of the women exclaims. Enormous, plastic smile.

"How's it going out there?" A little nervous.

Yes, they're drinking. He can tell by their pink cheeks, their glossy eyes.

He scans the room. Sure enough, there are some empties on the floor, and a fresh bottle of red sticking out of a Burberry tote. He grabs it, looks at the label. Mayacamas, Cabernet Sauvignon, 2014. Sure, that'll do.

Ethan takes a swig straight from the bottle. He wipes his mouth with the back of the hand, then lifts the bottle as if toasting them.

"Ladies," he says.

Then he exits, taking their wine with him. He walks outside, into the cool night. The trees above him carve black silhouettes from the stars.

He feels dangerous. Wild. Like he could fly right over the Ledge, lift off, and keep going. Never come down.

◆

A HALF HOUR later, he and Zo are at Persimmon's house, picking up Alex from the pizza party.

"How was Kids' Night?" Ethan asks as she plops down in the backseat.

"Okay," Alex says. "Except a bunch of the girls dared me to put *all* the anchovies on my pizza, so I did, and it turns out I don't like anchovies very much, and also then everyone said I smelled like old fish."

"It's okay, I don't like anchovies either," says Zo, more to her phone than to their child.

"But we played hide-and-seek," Alex says. "And I *won*. Persimmon told me that the best place to hide was upstairs, in the stairwell to the attic. It was *super* creepy up there, and I couldn't find the light, but I guess she was right, because they never found me."

"Good for you," Ethan says. "How long did they look before giving up?"

"Mmmm . . . about an hour, maybe?"

Alex has always been terrible at judging time. "An hour? That doesn't sound right, kiddo. Sixty minutes is a pretty long time."

"Yeah, I know how long an hour is. But by the time I finally came downstairs, they were already more than forty-one minutes into *Legally Blonde,* and I figure they must have looked for a *little* while before putting on the movie, right?"

"Hold on," Ethan says. "They started a movie while you were still hiding?"

Next to Ethan, Zo lifts her head, listening more closely now.

"Yeah," Alex says. "I guess they *really* couldn't find me. But you know what I can't figure out? Why didn't Persimmon come get me? *She* knew where I was, since she was the one who told me to hide there."

Ethan's heart sinks. He imagines Persimmon steering Alex up the attic steps, into the dark, then running downstairs, going straight to the sofa to start the movie. He thinks about Alex waiting, alone, the minutes ticking by while everyone else giggled and ate popcorn, letting Alex stay there indefinitely.

And it's almost like his picturing this is enough to make Alex see it, too, the cruelty of it, because she says, "Oh. Wait."

And then, sadder: "Oh."

Zo turns around. "Oh, honey," she says. She reaches for Alex's hand, but Alex turns away from her, folds her arms, stares out the window. Even in the rearview mirror, Ethan can tell she's trying not to cry.

They drive home in silence, Ethan's heart pounding the whole way.

Little bitches. Mean, rotten, stinking, sniveling little bitches.

ONCE HOME, ETHAN digs those crumpled papers from the trash, the ones he found last night that have nothing to do with Lionel Trilling:

The ones who called you a bitch, a cunt. The ones who said these things to your face. The ones who said these things behind your back.

The ones who talked over you. The ones who talked at you. The ones who told you things you already knew.

The ones who assumed you didn't know about oil changes. The ones who assumed you didn't know about geography. The ones who assumed you didn't know about Foucault. The ones who assumed you didn't know about congressional politics, or about wine, or about corner kicks, or about the Protestant Reformation, or about pescatarianism, or about NASA's Voyager, or about Bartleby the Scrivener, or about barefoot running, or even, in one gobsmacking instance, about the clitoris. The ones who assumed you didn't know about string theory (which, okay, you don't, not really, but let's face it: neither do they), the ones who assumed again and again, that whatever you happen to know, they knew more. The ones who seemed so genuinely happy to teach you things, you didn't feel right explaining that you already knew.

The ones who, while they're talking, look not at your face but at your chest. The ones who let their hand graze your arm, your back, your rear, the side of your breast, maybe it was an accident, it was probably an accident, except maybe it wasn't. The ones who were your teachers, your coaches, your uncles, your friends.

The ones who hugged you, which you were okay with, until they held you too long, and then you weren't. The ones who turned a handshake into a kiss on the back of your hand, or worse: who tickled your palm with a single, flickering finger. The ones who stepped out from behind a tree and rubbed their dick while you jogged. The other ones who also stepped out from behind a tree and rubbed their dick while you jogged (what, did you think it would happen only once?). The ones who sat next to you on a plane leaned in close, and asked if you were a virgin.

The ones who breathed on your neck, whose breath you can still feel, even today. The ones who followed you down the street late at night, a little too close, maybe oblivious, maybe to see if you'd get nervous, maybe for more sinister reasons.

The ones who pressed you against the wall of a dark room, saying please please please, can't you just please.

The ones who blocked the door.

THURSDAY

15

MORNING, DIM AND formless. The clock radio. The static. Zo gone. Another day.

The smell of butter, clank of the radiator, crack of the egg. The old Pontiac, still needs a muffler, tosses a newspaper in a blue plastic bag.

One last red pill in the bottle. Ethan sets it out on the table for Alex, then pulls out a red Sharpie. He starts to write "ADDERALL" on his wrist, then thinks better of it. What would Shreya say, if she should see it at drop-off? He can just imagine her gossiping to the other parents: *And I have it on good authority that they drug their child,* she'd say, shaking her head at this, the latest evidence of their shameful parenting.

Ethan changes the A on his wrist to an R. Instead of writing the name of Alex's medicine, he writes, instead, two words: "RED PILL."

He resolves: Today will be more productive than yesterday. Ethan types out a quick message to Dr. Ash: *Dear Ashleigh, I apologize for missing yesterday's call.* He pauses before adding, *My wife had a car accident.*

That's sort of true, isn't it?

He's just about to hit Send when the doorbell rings. He glances at the clock. It's only 7:13 in the morning.

Elastic Waist stands on the porch, Pyrex dish in her hand. "Zo's not here," Ethan tells her. He blinks, feels like he should say more. "She's at the gym."

And when Elastic Waist blinks right back at him, unmoving, he says, louder, "ZO'S NOT HERE."

"I KNOW," says Elastic Waist, her volume matching his. "But this needs to go in a low oven for about forty-five minutes. I thought I could drop it off while I run to the store to get all the other stuff we need." She holds out the dish to him.

He was awake too late. He's not thinking clearly.

Of course he was awake too late: Alex wouldn't go to sleep last night, she was so wired from the evening. She'd flopped down on their bed, refused to get up, tossed her body around in their sheets like a fish, or maybe like that kid from *The Exorcist*. Ethan's pleas to Alex hadn't worked. Zo's increasingly strained explanations about the importance of sleep to a growing brain hadn't worked. Nothing worked, nothing, until Zo finally lost her cool and yelled. Ethan left the room, sat on the gray-not-blue sofa, feeling angry at Zo, and sorry for Alex, watching TV with the vague hope that Maddy might come downstairs to watch with him, distract him, which she didn't. When he finally went to bed, he tossed and turned, listening to Zo snore and doing his level best not to think of the blue-haired girl above him, sprawled out on a separate set of sheets. So, yes: he's tired and confused now as Elastic Waist hands him a foil-covered dish of food. Why is she here? And who exactly is the "we" in the phrase *all the other stuff we need*?

"IT'S FOR THE TESTIMONY," Elastic Waist says. And then: "THE HEARING IS TODAY, REMEMBER?" Right. The hearing about the Supreme Court nominee. That's today. "IT'S A BREAKFAST CASSEROLE. COMFORT FOOD. I THINK WE'RE ALL GOING TO NEED IT."

Ethan pieces together what she's telling him: people are coming here? To watch the hearing? Zo hadn't mentioned that. What about her work on the Lionel Trilling film? Or his work? Or their privacy? Or the fact that he needs to get Alex ready for school? Or his feelings about having a house full of people, yet again?

Elastic Waist gives the dish a little shake, her way of saying it's time for him to take it. He does. "PREHEAT TO 250," she tells him. "PUT A LITTLE FOIL ON TOP, AND LET IT WARM UP FOR FORTY-FIVE MINUTES. THE HEARING STARTS AT TEN, BUT PEOPLE MIGHT START ARRIVING SOONER. I'LL BE BACK IN A JIFF."

And then she's gone, and Ethan is standing alone in his kitchen, staring at a breakfast casserole for which he's somehow now responsible.

"ENCYCLOPEDIA BROWN!" FROM the trivia corner of the Coffee Depot, Willie Nelson waves him over. Ethan isn't exactly in the mood for the trivia triumvirate, but he heads over, reads the clue:

One theory says a phrase for euphoria comes from plate no. 9 in an 1896 meteorological "atlas" of these.

"Hm," Ethan says.

Yes, here they are again: the trivia crew, the electrician in coveralls, the poet with her yellow pad, Nancy behind the counter, Punk Jane, every day on repeat, one upon the next until lights-out, and what will he have to show for any of it? Thousands and thousands of cups of coffee that he's pissed away, literally.

I shall measure out my life in coffee pisses.

Ethan looks around, sees white hair, gray hair, silver hair, dark-brown hair but like Zo's, with a defiant white stripe at the roots. Everyone a little longer in the tooth than they were last year, and the year before that. This, he supposes, is how it is in a small community: You watch your neighbors grow old. Maybe in a city, surrounded by strangers, you can convince yourself that some people just *are* old, that it's not a process that's happening to everyone, all the time, yourself included. In a place like Starkfield, though, you can't help but see it unfolding in real time.

Next to him, Willie Nelson argues with the others about whether the correct answer is "over the moon" or "starry-eyed."

"But euphoria and 'starry-eyed' aren't synonymous," Yoga explains. "So that can't possibly be right."

"Read the clue," insists Willie. "It says 'an atlas of *these*.' Plural. We've only got one moon."

"The stars are *over* the moon," presses the social worker.

Willie tosses his hands up. "Well, of course stars are over the moon, but I don't see what that's got to do with today's question."

They're arguing, but something's missing from their debate. Or, no, Ethan realizes: there's something present here that's too often missing.

Ethan interrupts. "You all . . . like each other, don't you?" The trivia crew stare at him. Ethan clarifies. "I mean . . . you disagree about something pretty much every day, but that doesn't stop you from being . . ." He trails off, because he's not sure what the next word is. Friends? Neighbors? Fellow humans who agree to share the same time and space on Earth more or less amicably?

The social worker waves away his comment. "Oh, please," she says. "I'm a three-time cancer survivor."

He hadn't known that.

"Two times breast, one time uterine. Walked right up to the abyss the third time. And I remember when my treatments were finally done, looking around the world and wondering: *When did we all fall so in love with our own opinions?* It felt like everyone was *shouting* at one another, clinging to their own hot takes, and missing all the best parts of being alive."

Yoga places a hand on her arm, gives it a little squeeze. Willie Nelson looks down, gives a little cough, stares straight ahead.

"Tell you what," the social worker adds. "You won't catch me forgetting to love my neighbor . . ." She pats Willie on the back before finishing ". . . even if this old fart doesn't know a damn thing about trivia."

Ethan excuses himself and gets a cup of coffee. Two cups, actually.

◆

AND THEN THE getting-ready routine—the breakfast-and-red-pill routine, the hairbrush-and-missing-shoes routine, the yelling and rushing routine.

Ethan does as Elastic Waist instructed: he pops the breakfast casserole in the oven just as he and Alex scramble out the door. He sets a timer and leaves a note for Maddy. "MAD PLEASE TAKE OUT WHEN TIMER GOES OFF." He sets the second cup of coffee on the corner of the page. "COFFEE'S FOR YOU," he adds with a smile.

WHEN HE RETURNS from driving Alex to school, Zo's car is in the driveway, along with half a dozen others. Inside, his note to Maddy is still on the counter, the coffee untouched, but the casserole's out of the oven, the house smells like butter and baked eggs, and everything is humming with energy.

The witches are there, and they've taken over. They're bustling around the kitchen, opening and shutting the refrigerator door, folding napkins, setting out utensils, pouring coffee from a Dunkin' Donuts Box O' Joe, and talking, talking, talking. On the table, there's a complete spread: not just the casserole, but also a basket of muffins and two different coffee cakes and a plate filled with varieties of chocolate, ranging from milk to bitter. Someone's hand-scrawled notes which are folded like tent cards all over the table: *SELF-CARE MATTERS. YOU ARE LOVED. REMEMBER: CHOCOLATE IS CALMING.* Which Ethan is pretty sure isn't true, but whatever.

A hand on his shoulder: Runner Mom (no, he corrects himself: *Jackie,* her name is Jackie. Jackie Watters). "*Ethan,* can you believe it? They're trying to put a predator on the Supreme Court, but they behave like *Zo's* the criminal. Unbelievable."

He refrains from pointing out that Jackie's conflating her "theys"—the ones who want to confirm this justice aren't exactly the same people who arrested Zo, the two groups have nothing to do with each other. He glances across the room at his wife. She's still in her gym clothes, surrounded by other witches in the two-sofa TV area. Everyone's talking at once.

This woman's my hero
Can't believe they're making her testify
Casserole is delicious
National travesty
Off caffeine these days
Oh boy oh boy oh boy

Ethan tries to meet Zo's eye, he tries to ask without words, *What the hell, why didn't you tell me about this little brunch party,* but before Zo looks back at him, Meat Cleaver bursts through the kitchen door holding the *Bettsbridge Eagle* above her head.

"ZO MADE THE PAPER!"

Starkfield Arrest Raises Questions about Police Tactics

September 27, 2018. STARKFIELD, MA. Zenobia Frome was driving home from a conference at her child's school, the exclusive, progressive Rainbow Seed School in Corbury, when she hit a traffic cone in a construction zone. She was pulled over by the Starkfield Police. Within minutes, the 46-year-old Starkfield mom had been handcuffed, arrested, and taken to the single jail cell in the basement of the Starkfield police headquarters, a 10 x 10 concrete holding area more typically occupied by drunks who need to cool down after a late-night bar brawl.

Those are the facts upon which everyone agrees. They are also where the agreement ends.

Frome is a member of a women's activist group formed in the wake of the 2016 presidential election. Registered officially with the Resistance Network as the Starkfield Women's Resistance, the group has informally dubbed themselves All Them Witches. Locally, they are known for their frequent stand-outs and protests on Starkfield's otherwise quiet village green.

"This arrest is shocking," says Jackie Watters, 41, a fellow member of the group. "A law-abiding activist was arrested, booked, and placed in a jail cell for a minor traffic infraction. We hear often about police overreach in the news, usually in the context of faraway places. This situation happened *here,* at home."

Chief of Police Stan Grapowski disputes that Frome was arrested for her political work. "The Starkfield Police does not target law-abiding citizens, directly or indirectly, for their political affiliations," he said in a phone interview. "Mrs. Frome was pulled over because she'd been driving recklessly, posing a danger both to herself and to others on the road. My officers tried to issue her a warning, but she became belligerent."

"I'm not exaggerating," Grapowski added, "when I say she was basically asking to be arrested."

Watters suggests that this particular word choice is revealing. "That phrase—she was asking for it—tells you everything you need to know about this situation. It's appalling that anyone, especially a powerful public figure like a chief of police, would use those words about a woman in 2018. It goes to show how much more work our society has to do." She adds that the Starkfield Police Department does not have a single woman on the force, nor any people of color.

Representatives from the Rainbow Seed School refused to comment, citing confidentiality of their students and families. But late last night, reporters reached the school's PTA president, Shreya Greer-Williams, who spoke to *The Eagle* by phone.

"Obviously, it's highly disturbing to think that something like this could happen within the Rainbow Seed School community," Greer-Williams said. "The Rainbow Seed School has long been known for its nurturing, child-friendly environment, positive role models, and peaceful engagement with the world."

Does the arrest raise questions about police overreach for Greer-Williams?

"It raises questions about many things," she said. She declined to comment further.

The Starkfield Women's Resistance has a rally scheduled for Saturday morning related to the latest Supreme Court appointment. Watters says that this protest will go on as planned, but they will add Frome's arrest to the list of issues being protested.

What exactly does a traffic arrest have to do with the Supreme Court nomination?

"Both situations involve strong women using their voices against a powerful status quo," says Watters. "But the days of silencing women are over. We demand to be heard."

IT's JACKIE WHO reads the article aloud, stopping to repeat several paragraphs at loud volume for Elastic Waist. When she finishes, everyone whoops. Zo moves through the women for high fives.

Ethan leans in the doorway, listening. Watching.

"Post the story, everyone!" Jackie shouts. On command, the witches reach for their phones. "Use the hashtag FreeZenobia. Tag different groups, everyone you can think of, and encourage them to come to Saturday's rally in solidarity."

"Zo," Ethan says. Across the room, his wife lifts her gaze, gives her head an almost imperceptible shake. *Not now, Ethan.*

"*Zo.*" In that single syllable he tries to communicate everything he possibly can: that the story in the paper isn't exactly accurate, that it left out some pretty important facts, doesn't she think? That perhaps her arrest had nothing to do with her activism, maybe nobody cares about a group of poster-making white ladies who shake signs in the middle of nowhere, and besides, didn't that comment from Shreya seem *ominous*? Isn't Zo the one who's so desperate to keep Alex at the Rainbow Seed School, and doesn't that outcome seem *less* likely now?

"Can I talk to you, Zo?" he asks.

"In a minute," says hashtag-Zenobia, who for the record is already hashtag-free.

"Now."

The witches glance at each other. An uncomfortable hush falls over the room. *Fine,* Ethan thinks. *Look at each other like I'm the jerk husband, like I'm nothing but another asshole* man. *And maybe I am, but at least I'm not a liar, at least not about this.*

"Certainly," says Zo. Her smile resembles Shreya's from last night: frozen and fake. Ethan can't read how much sarcasm is contained in that *certainly.* He has no idea what the state of his marriage is.

Alone in the bedroom, he stares at her. "The hell?"

"What?" she says.

"What are you, the new poster child for police overreach? You *know* that's not exactly what happened."

"Well, it's not *not* what happened," she says. "I *am* an activist, and I *did* hit a cone."

"You hit *all* the cones, Zo. Every last one of them! And I was there: you *were* belligerent."

"Belligerent?" Zo tilts her head, all faux-curious, like she hasn't a clue what he's talking about. "I asked a question. Those cops arrested me because they didn't like the question."

"Come on, Zo, your ladies are all out there hashtagging it like this is a simple story. But there's a bigger context, and they don't know it, and for some reason you're not telling them."

"My *ladies*?"

"Your friends, the witches, your whatever-you-want-to-call-them. They don't know the full story, and by the way, *why are they even here, Zo?*"

"We're not allowed to support each other?"

"Of *course* you're allowed to support each other! But it's a Thursday morning. I lost a whole day yesterday calling for that

Boston Children's appointment." This, too, isn't the whole truth. He also spent a long time thinking about Evie Emerling and talking to a stranger at the UPS Store, and stumbling into the uncomfortable discovery that Maddy is willing to do just about anything to make a buck on Ten-Spot, but never mind that.

"So what are you saying?" Zo asks. "You can't call for an appointment? For your own child? Maybe you think that's a job for a mother, but not a father?"

"Stop twisting my words, Zo. And what about *your* work? What about Lionel Trilling?"

A pause. And then her voice, bitter. "Excuse me, Ethan, but I'm not a child who needs to be managed, so please stop treating me like I am. And for the record, this thing that's happening today? It's big. We're talking about a lifetime appointment to the Supreme Court. This is a big and frankly fucking tragic event in history. So 'my ladies' and I are entirely in the right to support one another through it. Or maybe you don't think it's such a big deal?"

He takes a deep breath. "I *know* it's a big deal. Of *course* it's a big—"

"Alex will be an *adult,* she'll be a mother herself, and *this guy will still be sitting on the court.* He'll be making decisions that affect *her* body. Like she won't already have a whole world telling her that her body isn't her own."

"I understand that, Zo."

A beat. And then Zo's voice, flat. "I don't think you do, Ethan. I frankly don't think you can."

Whoosh. She's out of the bedroom, back with the witches who have colonized his home, his life, his whole crazy upside-down world.

1 6

#America2018, Act 1

The woman on the television screen begins with her eyes closed. She stands, chin raised, solemnly swears to tell the truth. The woman wears a simple navy suit. Her straight blond hair is curled at the edges, suggesting she's had a stylist apply a heating iron this morning. She's put mascara on, too, but it's hard to see her lashes through her glasses, which keep catching the light. When she sits, her posture is straight. The woman's movements are subtle, precise. She'd like a little caffeine, if that's all right.

What's important about the woman is none of these things—the tilt of her head, the suit, the hair, the mascara, the polite way she makes her request—but still: these things will be discussed, dissected, disparaged, denigrated, and she knows it.

The woman on the screen says *please* and *thank you*. She doesn't remember every detail about the night she's here to talk about, the event that happened decades ago, the thing she says the Supreme Court nominee did to her. She's clear about this: she can't remember every detail, but she does remember the most important part. She remembers what, and she remembers who. This is what she tells the unsmiling men in suits, the ones who are fanned out in a semicircle before her. Many of these men are not on her side, and she knows it. But still: she wants to be helpful, doesn't want to be difficult.

No, she no longer recalls how she got to the party. Yes, she's sorry about that lapse in memory.

She knows how the hippocampus works, this woman. She knows not only what she remembers, but also how, specifically, it became encoded into memory. She knows why she went to therapy, why all these decades later she needs two doors in her home, a second escape route, just in case.

Hers is a quiet street, a quiet life.

At moments her voice quivers, but she does not cry. No, that's wrong: she does cry. She cries when the people asking questions are kind to her.

She takes tiny sips of her soda. She laughs at other people's jokes. She removes her glasses, slides them on top of her head. She sets them down on the table, lets them rest at her side, then puts them on again. She never wanted to be here. But she's accommodating. Now that she *is* here, she does her best.

IN ETHAN'S POCKET, his phone vibrates. He pulls out the device, as noiselessly as he can. It's a text from Randy: *Just checking in, E.*

Then: *Remember Evie's reading is 2morrow. I mapped it all out. The Humphrey's about 40 minutes from you.*

And then: *Play reading starts at 2. Over by 4, I'd guess? Not open to the public so wait outside. Run into her. Work the lawsuit into conversation. Tell her you don't recommend going forward with it. Talk to her as a friend.*

Get there early, just in case.

Then: *E?*

Ethan returns the phone to his pocket.

THROUGH THE WOMAN's testimony, the witches form a kind of still life in the cramped TV area. They are motionless, transfixed. Their eyes don't stray from the screen.

A couple of them cry, but they do so noiselessly. Ethan watches as Meat Cleaver's shoulders shake, tiny shudders that in a different circumstance might seem like laughter. He waits for a sob to escape her throat. It doesn't come. Jackie reaches over and places a hand on Meat Cleaver's arm. A single quick gesture, then all is still.

In front of him, Elastic Waist folds her hands together, then brings them to her lips, a kind of prayer. She closes her eyes. Breathes.

Is ETHAN ACTUALLY considering doing what Randy wants him to? Is he going to drive to the Humphrey, pretend to run into the movie star Evie Emerling, and then, in an otherwise benign conversation, let it slip that Randy has information that could ruin her, so she'd best watch out?

That's not the guy he is. Not who he wants to be. He's a quiet guy, a good guy, the more-or-less silent partner who stays on the sidelines. He's always been the matter to Randy's energy: constrained, grounded. Maybe even a little dull. He really, really doesn't want Evie to see him as a villain.

But he's also the guy who needs those Bränd checks.

He left Bränd too soon, he sees this now. He should have gone to Hollywood with Randy, should have stayed in the business, should have kept rising. He would have, too, would have done it in a heartbeat, if it hadn't been for Zo. She hadn't forced him to stay in New York, it was nothing like that. He could go or not go, up to him. She just wasn't going to go with him.

He'd made the choice on his own.

Ethan had thought, at the time, that he'd earned enough money. Had figured that the cash he'd gotten from selling his shares to Randy would be, more or less, all the money he'd need in this world, or at least it was enough to get *started*. Surely he could live on it for a long time—at least until he'd launched his writing career. But there was so much he hadn't understood at the time. He hadn't understood how quickly the years would pass, and how easy it would be to produce nothing at all. He hadn't understood how much money a person truly needs. He hadn't realized how *skewed* the world would become: the way millionaires would explode into billionaires, the way the gap between the Corburys and

Starkfields would grow ever wider, a divide that would become impossible to cross.

No, of course he doesn't want to do this thing that Randy's asking. Not at all.

But if he doesn't: what then?

IN THE MIDDLE of the woman's testimony, Maddy shuffles downstairs, wearing a plaid wool flannel shirt over torn leggings. Ethan recognizes the shirt as his own: an L.L.Bean classic that Zo had bought for him their first winter here, back when they imagined that life in the Berkshires would be like a magazine portrait of the homesteading life: chopping wood, building sheds, raising goats and chickens, all that rustic stuff that they don't do even a little bit, never did, even once.

Ethan glances at Zo, unsure if his wife would recognize the shirt. Her eyes don't stray from the television screen.

Maddy steps over the women, strolls barefoot into the kitchen.

Another text from Randy: *I'm counting on you, E.*

THE DOORBELL. A delivery truck. Four boxes—Crate & Barrel, West Elm, Pottery Barn, Overstock. Collectively, the boxes contain a new comforter, a duvet cover, seven throw pillows, twelve new curtain panels, a Belgian linen sheet set, four faux-fur blankets, plus some sort of enormous macramé wall hanging. Ethan digs through the boxes, finds their packing slips, tallies the cost of the items.

He carries the boxes straight to his car.

When he returns to the living room, the woman on-screen has been replaced by a man. The C-SPAN logo is in the corner. "Our lines are open," the man is saying. "Give us a call to tell us what your reaction is to the hearing so far."

Some sort of break then. A rest before the nominee himself appears.

Ethan wades through the sea of witches. He looks at no one,

just goes into the kitchen. Maddy is at the table, bowl of cereal next to her as she plays Candy Crush. He doesn't interact with her, tries not to even look at her. He just makes himself some toast and eats it alone, standing at the counter and staring out at the back-yard.

With his back to the TV, to the women watching the TV, Ethan listens to the man take his first call.

He waits for all of this to be over, so he can figure out his next move in peace.

THE ONES WHO don't know how to act, don't know what to say. The ones who prefer to stay out of certain conversations, let women talk to women. The ones who know that their opinions are suspect, that their words could come back to haunt them, that whatever is happening—whatever is tilting the world off its axis—their safest bet is to keep their heads down and wait it out.

At some point, they might have to make a choice, their choice might be do-or-die, but for the moment it's best not to draw too much attention. Best to stay out of all this mess. Stay quiet, respectable, respected. Wait this one out as long as possible.

Maybe everything, soon, will return to normal.

#AMERICA2018: An intermission

Maddy's phone dings and blips, drawing glares from the witches. On television, the man from C-SPAN takes more calls.

"When I was fourteen," says Barbara, a caller from Tacoma, "I was attacked."

She's just a voice coming through a phone line, and she's saying this live, to the man taking calls, and also to the whole world. Ethan turns around in time to see the man's face shift, his mouth close. He's wearing a dark suit, a crisp white shirt, a red tie. Could be a senator himself, this guy. He's got a trustworthy face, serious but not unkind.

"I was walking home from a violin lesson," continues Barbara from Tacoma. "There were two of them." She tells her story: it was the suburbs, almost dinnertime. There was a patch of woods. Decades later, she still has panic attacks.

And then the twist: The woman they've just watched, says Barbara, is clearly lying. Barbara doesn't believe one word of that testimony. The witches boo. Meat Cleaver's face screws up into something grotesque, and this time she does sob aloud.

There are other calls: Martha from Bar Harbor, Marie from Orlando, Brienna from Scranton, Amy from Taos, Olivia from Chicago, Betty Anne from Salt Lake City, Vicky from Morristown. Also Chuck from Shaker Heights, Isaac from Bakersfield, Bob from Cedar Falls.

Thought I was over this.
Who puts a wet bathing suit on under their clothes?
Happened all the time
Circus
Frame-up job
Happened twice
She has nothing to gain . . . everything to lose
You feel worthless, you feel like you'll never get over it
Had to bite and kick.
So why hasn't her attorney marched into a police station and filed charges
He had not broken any bones, so they said nothing could be done
He's the perfect sacrificial lamb
My boyfriend's daddy
A terrible thing, you never forget it
Remember every little detail
Still feel like I'm trapped there

Bloop. Whoosh. Ding. Maddy keeps her eyes on the candy colors of her screen. She isn't taking hints, doesn't notice the way Zo keeps turning her head, narrowing her eyes, annoyed. Or maybe Maddy is being belligerent, maybe she thinks Zo is overreacting.

Either way, by the time Audrey from Corpus Christi calls in, *I was twelve . . . brother's best friend . . . drugged . . .* Zo has had it. She whips around. "Maddy, can you stop?"

Maddy glances up. "Stop. . . . what?"

"Your phone. Whatever that noise is. Stop. Now."

You get asked all these questions, and you just want it to be over. The man on the screen stares stoically at the camera. He couldn't possibly have expected this break to go the way it has, he couldn't have been prepared for any of this.

Maddy glances at Ethan, then back at Zo.

"And when you've finished eating," Zo continues, "perhaps you can, for once, put your fucking bowl in the fucking dishwasher instead of leaving it for someone else to deal with?"

Maddy thinks for a minute. "Yeah," she says. She draws out the word for several seconds. *Yeeeeaaah.* She gestures toward the women sprawled out on the floor. "Thanks, I appreciate the advice. Since *your* life is so under control."

There is a long moment of stillness, and in that silence, anything can happen, Zo could go in any direction, and Ethan holds his breath, and Kevin from Newport News, Virginia, is saying *it must come down to the burden of proof,* but then before anyone can force the moment to its crisis, the cameras are clicking and the man taking calls is no longer on the screen, and something new is beginning.

#America2018, Act 2

The man on the screen scowls, sniffs, snarls, sneers. The man on the screen is flushed and sweaty. The man on the screen leans forward, eyes hard. He wrinkles his nose, purses his lips, raises his voice, avoids answering yes or no questions with either a yes or a no.

The man on the screen is outraged, thinks this whole thing is an outrage. The proof is in his yelling: reasonable people yell about outrageous things. He uses terms like *last-minute smears, character assassination, orchestrated political hit, national disgrace, what goes around comes around.* His brows sink into a deep, angry V.

The man on the screen talks about Eagle Scouts, Five-Star basketball camp, busting his butt, football practice, volunteering at the soup kitchen, lifting weights, going to see Roger Clemens pitch at Fenway. He says going to church is like brushing his teeth: automatic, barely worth noting. Sure, occasionally he's had a few too many, but he insists, spitting, that he remembers everything, every time. You can see broken capillaries through his skin.

Where the woman was careful with her words, keeping them close to her chest, the man on-screen spews his own words everywhere, like a firehose. He is like one of those snakes that spits venom, or maybe more like a lizard that shoots poison from its eyes. When asked about whether he would support an FBI investigation into the woman's claims, he responds, "I'm innocent. I'm innocent of these charges." When asked about his drinking, he hollers, indignant, "I got into Yale Law School. That's the number-one law school in the country."

He breathes fire, this man. He doesn't care where it catches. He's willing to burn it all down if that's what he has to do.

THE ONES WHO remind you of where they went to school. The ones who hold up their pedigree like a shield, all those stickers on the rear window, names of universities splashed across their broad chests, best time of my life. The ones who have never questioned whether everything they have is deserved, they worked hard, don't you get that? Harder than you: the proof of this is in their success, and if you point out the circularity of this logic, you will feel their wrath.

The ones who are beyond question, beyond reproach. And don't you dare suggest otherwise, don't you dare try to overturn this, the natural order of things.

Don't you fucking dare.

WHAT IS HAPPENING?
  Is this real life?
  Are you watching this?

The witches ask these questions of one another, as if they're not all sitting right here, side by side, watching the whole thing unfold in real time.

But it's not just them. Ethan knows this, because by now he's scrolling online, looking at photographs from everywhere in the nation: A photograph snapped on a commercial flight, New York to San Fran: every seat-back screen on the plane showing the testimony. A scene in a pub, day drinkers on barstools, but the scene looks constructed, artificial, more re-presentation than representation; instead of slouchy, red-nosed drunks yapping and spilling out of their seats, these patrons are upright, rigid, deadly serious. Every single one of them is a woman.

There are images from nursing homes and college classrooms, the New York Stock Exchange and the New York City subway. Conference rooms and waiting rooms, delis and diners, bars and buses, gyms and cubicles from sea to shining sea. The whole nation has stopped, it seems. Everyone holds their collective breath. Whatever is happening, whatever this thing is, it's big, and there can be no compromise.

It will tip one way. Or it will tip another. And whatever happens then, who the hell knows.

ETHAN'S PHONE RINGS while the fire-breathing man sputters. A 617 number. Looks familiar, though Ethan can't place it. "Hello?" A couple of witches turn to glare. Ethan moves through them, toward the bedroom, holding the phone to his ear.

"Hi, Mr. Frome," the voice says. "My name is Ananya, and I'm calling from Boston Children's Hospital, department of pediatric neurology."

It takes Ethan a moment to make the connection.

Ananya explains that they've had two cancellations, which means there are two available appointments in the next couple of days. "We got your many, many messages, and given your family's circumstances, we wanted to offer you these openings before turning to our wait list."

"Oh!" Ethan says. "Yeah. Okay, great. Hang on one sec, lemme grab my wife."

He pokes his head into the living room and tries to catch her eye. *Sixty-five women,* the man on the screen is saying, *who knew me more than thirty-five years ago, signed a letter to support me.*

"Zo."

Zo keeps her eyes on the television. *"Shh."*

"Zo, it's Boston Children's."

Zo gets up reluctantly, follows him into their bedroom. She keeps her eye on the TV as long as she can.

"Okay, thanks for holding," Ethan says into the phone. "What are the options?"

"Well, it's short notice," says Ananya, "but our first option is actually tomorrow morning." There's a strange echo on the phone, and Ethan assumes it's the connection, until he realizes that Ananya, too, has the TV on, that even as she's talking to him, she's also watching the man say, *I have sent more women law clerks to the Supreme Court than any other federal judge in the country.*

"They can see us tomorrow," Ethan tells Zo. She nods.

"Tomorrow works," he tells Ananya. "What time?"

"The appointment itself begins at nine A.M.," Ananya explains. "But there's significant paperwork that you're going to need to complete—behavioral questionnaires and other assessments. Most people fill out this paperwork well in advance, but you won't have that option. So we'll ask you to arrive thirty minutes early to complete those. We provide lunch and snacks, and depending on how the day goes, you'd likely finish between three and four P.M."

"Wait, it's *all day?*"

Remember Evie's reading is 2morrow

Boston's nearly three hours away without traffic. If he takes this appointment, he'll miss Evie entirely. He's still not *sure* if he's going to do what Randy's asking, but he's not ready to shut down the possibility. Not yet, not until he has a better idea. "Tomorrow morning is too soon," he tells Ananya. "What's the next option?"

"Saturday," Ananya says. "Ten-fifteen in the morning."

"Yeah," he tells Ananya. "Saturday works better." But Zo stares at him like he's out of his mind, like he just announced that Saturday's the day Hypatia's going to transform into a three-headed dragon with purple scales.

"No," Zo insists. "Not Saturday. Let's do it tomorrow."

"I can't," he tells Zo.

"Why?"

Why indeed? *Because I might have to blackmail the person who was once Hollywood's most bankable star, that's why.* "I have to work."

"Your Dr. Ash thing? Ethan, you don't even *care* about that project."

He asks Ananya to hold on, they're discussing it. Then he puts on his best Voice of Reason tone. "Zo, tomorrow's appointment is too early. We'd have to leave tonight, which would mean getting a hotel. And what about Hypatia?"

"So we'll get a hotel," Zo says. "And Maddy can take care of Hypatia."

"Zo, hotels are expensive. And think about it: Alex would have to miss a whole school day. Saturday's better."

"Saturday's the rally, Ethan."

The goddamned stupid rally. The shaking of the handmade signs, the shouting at the few passing cars, as if this is how people make up their minds about anything, ever. *Well, I didn't know what I thought about the issue before, but then some ladies in pink hats yelled at me as I drove around the village green in downtown Starkfield, and that cleared everything right up!*

"Skip the rally," he tells her.

Zo glowers at him.

"I'm serious," he says. "Skip it. Let others rally."

And then he says: "This is for Alex, Zo."

And then: "You won't do this for Alex? For our daughter?"

In his living room, the man says, *I have not questioned that she might have been sexually assaulted at some point in her life by someone, someplace. But as to me, I've never done this; never done this to her or to anyone else.*

"Sir?" Ananya's voice comes through his phone. Ethan apologizes, reassures her they're working it out.

"Some of the protesters will come to this rally because of me," says Zo. "To support *me.* Jackie thinks we're going to draw a big crowd, *because of what happened to me.*"

"It's a bullshit rally then," Ethan says. "And it's based on a bullshit lie."

It's as if he's lobbed a stone into still water. He watches the shock of the impact, then the ripples moving one at a time through his wife, one at a time: from understanding to decision to steely resolve. "Tomorrow," Zo says.

"I told you," he says. "I *can't.*"

They stand like that, face-to-face. When Zo speaks again, it doesn't even seem like her voice. It's not the voice of the woman he married, not the woman he once made love to inside a tent on the floor of L.L.Bean's twenty-four-hour store in Freeport, some last-minute escape from the city some summer weekend during their Brooklyn days. It's not the voice of the woman who'd once read *Moby-Dick* aloud in bed, a few chapters a night for months, except her voice always lulled him to sleep so fast he couldn't keep track of the characters or plot. It's not the voice of the woman who'd laughed her way through his proposal on the Brooklyn Bridge, then again through their tiny wedding ceremony in the nearby River Café. (This was back when the River Café felt like a secret of sorts, still in the middle of nowhere, back before anyone knew the acronym DUMBO, *Down Under the Manhattan Bridge Overpass,* the final word added, as Jerry Seinfeld observed, because nobody wanted a neighborhood called DUMB. It was before the Jehovah's Witnesses sold their Watchtower Building, before Etsy and West Elm moved to town, before Times Square had morphed into Disneyland, before the High Line and Citi Bike and the Second Avenue Subway, before he and Zo had moved up to Starkfield expecting only peaceful, bucolic days ahead, not understanding that the city they'd known and the life they'd once lived there would, like the towers that appear in every wedding photograph, the ones that stood proud across the river as they exchanged their vows, crumble to ash, and if they ever looked back, if they ever tried to see fully what they'd lost, they'd fall to the same fate as

Lot's wife: nothing would remain of them but pillars of salt). No, it isn't Zo's voice at all, not really, but the voice of whatever fury's taken up permanent residence inside of her.

"So don't come, Ethan," the fury's voice says.

And with that, Zo pulls his phone from his hand. "Yes, this is Alex's mother," she says, turning her back to him. "I'll take tomorrow's appointment. Can you please give me the details?"

In the living room, the man on the screen issues his final words of the testimony: *I swear to God*.

#America2018, Act 3

It's a morality play, this whole thing. But something is wrong, very wrong, with the script. There are only two acts, and these acts have nothing to do with each other. They are played on the same stage, in succession, but together they make no sense. They are puzzle pieces that don't fit, they are apples and an iguana eating granola while riding an orange Vespa.

There must be a third act. That's the only explanation. There will be some dramatic denouement, some closing monologue, some grand finale that bridges the two parts, weaves them together into a coherent narrative. "Oh," the audience members will say when the curtain rises again. "Oh, *now* I get it. Brilliant, the way it all comes together in the end."

The third act is coming any minute, it must be, because otherwise, what is the way out of this situation? You can't just present these two opposite stories with no resolution.

The audience waits. And waits. They begin to shift in their seats, look down at the programs in their hands. Someone coughs politely. The curtain does not rise again. After a while, the house lights come on. The audience members glance around at one another. *That's it? Really?*

They stand, begin to exit—a few at first, and then more, and then everyone. They shuffle outside, blink, look around at the street traffic, at the world both changed and unchanged.

They wander home, bewildered.

✦

EVEN WHEN THE testimony is over, even when the punditry about the testimony ends, even when the TV goes off, the women don't leave. They pour more coffee. They arrange themselves in a circle on the floor. They strategize. They pull out their poster board, their markers, their weapons of choice.

"So it's decided," Jackie says. "We'll keep getting the word out on social media about what happened to Zo. We'll say that the best way they can honor her is to join in Saturday's rally."

Elastic Waist fills in letters on her poster: BELIEVE WOMEN, BE-LIEVE ZO.

SILENT NO MORE says Meat Cleaver's.

"Be prepared: we're going to get pushback," Jackie warns. "But that's a *good* sign. Controversy means people are paying attention."

By now, Ethan's fed up. He's fed up with the women, for having been here all day, as if they weren't here two nights ago, as if they won't be back again next week, and the week after that, ad infini-tum, as if nobody needs to work for a living, as if *he* doesn't.

He's fed up with Zo, too, for insisting that her thing is more important than his thing, even if she doesn't know what his thing is, shouldn't she *trust* him when he says he's got a thing? He's fed up with the way his wife treats him: like he's a has-been, disposable, like it doesn't matter if he's at his daughter's appointment. His own daughter! As if he hasn't over the past year and a half become the main parent-on-duty, the one it's just assumed will take care of the breakfasts and the morning routine and the endless driv-ing and the homework help and the bedtime routine, only to start again the next day. He's fed up with Zo for her absences, for not finishing that Lionel Trilling documentary, for her ceaseless *buy-ing*. All those stupid purchases, some of which are now waiting in his car—yes, he's definitely going to return them, he's not going to keep throwing good money after bad, not when they need every penny right now, not when their house is an unfinished construc-tion zone with no end in sight.

He thinks of that punk rocker last night, calling Zo a *fecking cunt.* Sure, maybe he should have punched the guy right then and there, in the lasagna line, as No-Balls McCuttle walked around tut-tutting about *sharing* and *community.* But Punk Rock was trying to be *nice,* to make her feel better, could Zo not see that? Are we *all* the enemy now?

Ethan's tired of being treated like some sort of enemy. Especially right here, in his own home. And meanwhile, not one of these women has asked what seems like a pretty essential question: *What if the story about Zo isn't true?* How would anyone *know*? Before he can stop himself, he's asking that question out loud, right now, in front of all them witches: *What if it's not true?*

The women all turn to stare at him.

It's like he's cast some sort of spell, *petrificus totalis,* frozen all those women in place. *(Yeah, who's the witch now?)*

Ethan can see by the women's faces that they think he's talking about the hearing, that he's asking what if the accusations against the Supreme Court nominee aren't true. He doesn't want to clarify what he's really saying, doesn't want to do that to Zo, so he takes a deep breath. "I'm just playing . . ." He pauses. A few weeks ago, in an argument about who-knows-what, he'd used the phrase *devil's advocate,* and Zo flipped out. *Thedevilhasplentyofadvocatesalrea-dythankyouverymuch.*

He tries again, his voice measured. "I'm just asking. What if someone told a story that wasn't true, or was only half-true? How would anyone *know*?" He's talking about everything *but* the Supreme Court thing, actually: about Zo and Randy and Bränd and Evie, and maybe something else, too, some bigger principle: critical thinking, asking questions, nuance. All those things that he once thought mattered but which nobody seems to have patience for now that everything's so highly charged.

"He did it," says the painter. She's still talking about the nominee, and she's no longer crying. Instead she looks like she's ready to come after Ethan with an actual meat cleaver.

"I'm talking more generally," Ethan says. "I'm asking: Are we *always* supposed to take one side's word, and not the other? Does *that* seem like the best idea?"

Zo's voice. Hard and icy. "That's pretty much what we've been doing for most of human history, Ethan."

It's meant to shut him up, but now that he's started asking questions, he's got a few others. "And anyway, what are we supposed to *do* with people who made mistakes in the past? Do we just throw them to the wolves? No matter how long ago it happened, or what the context was, or who they are today?" By now, Ethan's not even sure who he's talking about—Randy? Evie? Himself?—but suddenly the question feels urgent. "Don't we *want* people to be able to change? To grow? To learn more and then do better?"

Zo tilts her head to the side slightly. Watching him. Guarded. Like she's waiting to see what he'll do next.

There is a long pause, then Elastic Waistband stands. "SO. I THINK I'M HEADING HOME." He can't tell if she's leaving because she hasn't heard the conversation, or because she has. But something shifts. The spell is broken, and the other witches begin to gather their belongings. A few of them look around awkwardly at the mess they're leaving behind, like they're not sure what, exactly, they should do. Should they leave Zo alone with both a giant mess and her shitty husband? Not to mention that rude twentysomething who's still seated at the table, her phone blipping and whirring away? Or should they just get the heck out so whatever is about to happen can happen?

They move together, as a group, toward the door. Zo says nothing at all. Just stares at Ethan.

As Ethan closes the door behind the last of the witches, his phone dings: a text from Maddy, *Oooh,* she writes from the table. *You've done it now.* When he glances over at her, she makes a subtle *tsk-tsk* motion with her fingers.

Zo's eyes still on him.

Ethan tries again. "Look, Zo. I'm really not trying to be an asshole here. But the world is complicated. It's filled with context. You *know* this, I know you do."

"Is there something you need to tell me, Ethan?" Her voice cold.

At first he thinks she's asking about Randy, that she knows somehow what's happening at Bränd, what Ethan's being asked to do. Like she's read his mind, or his texts (and if she reads his texts, then how often? And how recently? Could she have read that flirty exchange with Maddy, all those spanking GIFs?). Then he realizes: no. She's asking if he, Ethan, ever did what this Supreme Court nominee is accused of doing.

She's asking if he's ever assaulted someone.

"No! Christ, no! My God, Zo, are you serious?" And when she responds only by lifting her brows, he throws up his hands. "There has to be some way to discuss things with you, Zo. Don't you see? If one side can't even have a *conversation* about these issues without lobbing accusations, then of course the other side is going to dismiss the whole thing as a witch-hunt."

"Witch-hunt." A statement, not a question. "Ethan, witch-hunts involved powerful men accusing innocent women and girls of practicing dark magic, then summarily executing them. Perhaps you'd like to rethink your wording?"

It's the way she's talking to him, like he's an idiot, like whatever words come out of his mouth—no matter what he says or how he says it—he will always be wrong, like he can never be right, shouldn't even have a bloody opinion, because whatever it is, Zo's just going to find the worst possible interpretation, distort his meaning beyond recognition.

Would he like to rethink his wording? Sure, how about *fuck off,* how's that for better wording? *Fuck off, Zo,* for assuming the worst of him, instead of the best.

Fuck off, Zo, for refusing to see now what she once knew beyond doubt: that he's actually not one of the bad guys.

Fuck off, Zo, for doing to him in his own home what Shreya's trying to do to Alex at school: barring the gates of the "we."

So that's what he says. Out loud and to her face: "Fuck off, Zo." He says it under his breath, the same way the guy last night muttered *fecking cunt.* Even with his eyes on Zo, he can see Maddy, at the table, lift her head, surprised.

Zo is motionless as his words sink in. Then she brushes her hands together, as if she's casting away invisible dirt. "You know what? I can't do this now. I need to pack some bags and find a hotel for me and Alex."

"You seriously think *this* is what the world needs from you?" he shouts. "You think that placing *yourself* at the center of a conversation about police overreach helps? You think *that's* going to lead to equal justice equitably applied, or whatever it is you claim to want?"

Just for a second, Zo stops, startled. Ethan watches Zo consider what he's just said: that maybe a middle-class white lady in a majority-white town, released almost immediately after her arrest, might not actually move this particular conversation as much as she hopes. He can see by her eyes that his meaning has sunk in, and for an instant, she looks shaken.

Good, he thinks. *Maybe now we can finally talk, just Ethan and Zo, for real.*

"Hon," he says. He takes a step toward her. He's ready to take her into his arms, start over. He reaches out toward her.

A mistake. Zo holds up her hands as if fending him off, and her face goes hard again. "No," she says. "I can't do this now. I'll pick up Alex from school. She and I can head to Boston straight from Corbury. We'll stay in a hotel tonight."

As she disappears into the bedroom, he calls after her. "If you think I'm one of the bad guys, Zo, if you push me away like this, I promise you: *you will have no one left.*"

But before the words are out, she's already gone.

THE ONES WE'RE taught to admire: Telemachus, who becomes a man only by telling his mom to STFU. His hero-dad, Odysseus, who loots women like property and spends years bedding goddesses, and somehow still manages to be celebrated through all time as the ultimate faithful husband. Aristotle for that whole superior-inferior thing, and more recent heroes too: Updike, that "magnificent narcissist," and while we're at it, his literary alter egos too: Rabbit Angstrom, Ben Fucking Turnbull, even poor dumb

Sammy-of-the-A&P, all these boy-men who can't recognize an honest-to-God human being when they see one, and whose blindness gets cloaked in dazzling prose (it's stealthy, that prose, like a boa constrictor, it'll steal your breath while you sleep). Nabokov, too: master of dizzying linguistic dips and loops. A person could almost forgive ol' Vlad his Humbert Humbert if it hadn't been for that one professor, the guy everyone said was such a fucking genius, who once stood in front of the classroom and declared, loftily, that never again shall a writer put a tween girl character in sunglasses without the reader envisioning Lolita.

(Lo. Lee. Ta, that tongue trip, palate, palate, tooth. Her name, for the record, was Dolores.)

Mencken, and Strindberg and smug-ass Flaubert. Roth. Bukowski. That '80s bad boy who grew, so predictably, into yet another cranky old man. That '90s postmodern cult hero, who gave that one glorious speech about compassion, may he rest in a peace he denied to the women in his life. Every dude who's ever written the trope, "she's beautiful but doesn't know it."

All those brilliants, from every era, invariably white, invariably male, who for all their vast talent couldn't imagine what it was to be Not-Them. Aren't these the guys who are supposed to be imagining the world?

The ones who, having failed to imagine, denied others their voices: the one who shot Joan Vollmer in the face before the world could hear her words. The one who stabbed Adele Morales—the second of six wives, disposable, really—with a penknife, then went on to literary glory while she struggled and died in a tenement house.

The darlings of the art world: Renoir and Picasso and de Kooning and Pollock and Dalí and Duchamp (Duchamp! Whose world-inverting 1917 Fountain was almost certainly the brainchild of one Baroness Elsa von Freytag-Loringhoven, who was weird and clever and practically no one's ever heard of her). And while we're at it, let's talk musicians. Elvis and Chuck and Iggy and Sid, and dammit, some days even you, too, Bruce, for tarnishing an otherwise-perfect song with an eight-word reminder of the inescapability of the male gaze. (I ain't a beauty but hey, I'm all right? At ease, Boss man, you're not such a looker yourself.)

And let's not even get started on Hollywood. Or D.C. Or Madison Avenue. Or Wall Street. Or Nashville. Or that urbanized stretch of land near the southern San Francisco Bay once known as the Valley of Heart's Delight.

I mean, let's just not. Who among us has the time, or can fully bear it?

ZO LEAVES THE house without saying goodbye. Never mind that expired license, either: fair is foul, foul is fair, apparently. Ethan listens to the slam of her car door, the engine starting. The Subaru backs out of the driveway, turns east, heads down Schoolhouse Hill Road.

In the silence after she's gone, Ethan opens his laptop, tries to remember what he should be doing.

Evie Emerling. He needs to look up Evie Emerling.

He's typing the name into his search engine when it hits him: with Alex and Zo gone for the night, he's got a whole night alone with Maddy.

17

HARPER'S BAZAAR:
The Great Disappearing Act of Evie Emerling

Evie Emerling is an enigma. Unless you live under a rock—and maybe even then—chances are good that Evie's face is indelibly etched into your mind from her starring roles in films in such wide-ranging genres as high-concept sci-fi (*Deep Space, Wormhole*), Disney (*Little Red, Kiss of a Toad*), art-house indie cinema (*Dancing in Antwerp, The Ivory Hunter*), and summer blockbusters (*Crime of the Century, Bite the Bullet*).

The multitalented actress, whose blue eyes are so pale they can be downright unnerving, burst into the Hollywood spotlight in the mid-late 1990s. But like a meteor that flames out after hitting Earth's atmosphere, Evie's light is hard to see these days. Where exactly *is* Evie Emerling now?

Is she, as some have suggested, a modern-day Greta Garbo, the reclusive starlet from the 1920s–'30s who once famously quipped, "I want to be let alone"? Or was Evie's retreat forced upon her—either by a youth-obsessed Hollywood, or by some sort of breakdown?

Ethan scrolls through more search returns. Most of the stories he rejects based on the headline alone.

Evie Emerling Canoodles with Mystery Man in Anguilla. Pass.
Evie Emerling Denies Plastic Surgery Rumors. Pass.
Evie Emerling Trolled by Anti-Semites. Definite pass.
Evie Emerling: Just Another Hollywood Hypocrite Driving a Hybrid. Pass.
All Evie Emerling's Roles Ranked from Worst to Best.

Ethan clicks on this one, moving through a series of movie posters for films he never saw. Each image offers someone else's vision of Evie Emerling—Evie as a sorority girl, flapper, disgraced ballerina, tarted-up mistress of an infamous white-collar criminal. But it's the poster for a 2008 film, *Phenomenology*, that makes him stop and stare. Beneath the poster is a brief description: "a brilliant mind-fuck about a universe-tripping cosmologist who may or may not be real. *The Matrix* meets *Girl, Interrupted*."

Ethan doesn't care about the plot, though. It's her expression in this poster. Something about this particular smile.

It all comes flooding back: the night he spent, long ago, in the company of someone who was not Zo.

June 1996

After Bränd's three Leaps of Faith pay off—in the form of eager calls from big-name brands, in their own swelling balance sheets, in a future that seems to expand ever-outward with new possibility—Randy throws a bash. It's time the world celebrated this daring new firm, Bränd, these Gen-X boy-genius newcomers.

The party, thanks to Randy's networking wizardry, is filled with A-listers: corporate suits with executive suites. Rising dot-com entrepreneurs. Street artists in conspicuous paint splatters. Art dealers eager to meet those street artists. A couple of Hollywood types. Nearly all of these individuals are men; for the most part, the women at the party are their dates, or aspiring actresses and models.

Evie Emerling's in the crowd, dressed in the classic black of Audrey Hepburn. Randy stays by her side for much of the evening, steering her from one circle of men to the next. "This one's beautiful *and* smart," Randy tells his guests. He holds up his glass again and again for a toast. "And thanks to Bränd, she just signed with an agent. A big one. Remember who discovered her, friends. Never forget that Bränd saw her first!"

The glasses clink, and Evie laughs. She seems to be having a terrific time. But when Ethan runs into her near the bathrooms, she's wearing a different mask altogether. Her skin is pale. Her eyes look tired and frankly a little sad.

He asks if she's okay, and she says only, "I'm ready to go home."

"Home?" But it's still early. And this is Evie's party, too, in a way. Everybody loves her, it's clear. "You sure? Okay, why don't I let Randy know—"

"No, Ethan." She stops him. "I was hoping to slip away quietly. Listen, would you mind seeing me into a cab?"

Ethan glances back at the party; Randy's at the center of a scrum of suits. All eyes are on him as he tells some sort of story. He gesticulates, and the huddle breaks into laughter. Randy takes a sip from his tumbler glass, pleased with himself.

Ethan turns back to Evie. "Okay, yeah," he says. "Let's grab you a cab."

It's June. Warm and wet. The city streets are slick and glossy, more mist in the air than actual raindrops. Nonetheless, every passing cab is occupied, light off.

Ethan holds his arm up in a futile attempt to defy the inalterable laws of New York City taxi supply and demand. After a few long minutes, he turns around. "Where exactly are you headed?" Ethan asks.

"A hundred thirty-first and Amsterdam." West side, up near Columbia.

He thinks about this. "We might have better luck over at Columbus Circle."

They head west. Ethan walks on the outer side of the pavement, closer to the street, just as his mother once taught him. Wet tires whish past, creating low sprays. On the far side of Fifty-ninth Street, Central Park lies shadowy and mute, two and a half straight miles of leafy wild, right here in the middle of concrete and glass.

Ethan tries to make conversation. "So I hear you're moving west," he says. "To L.A."

Evie smiles. "I am, yeah. Signed my agency contract last week." She crosses her fingers, holds them up as she walks. "Hope springs eternal, I guess."

"You'll do great, Evie." He means it too.

"And you?" Evie asks. "You're also moving to L.A., I hear?"

"Well," Ethan says, "Bränd is, anyway. Eventually." Randy has his sights set on Hollywood, on putting his guerrilla marketing savvy to use on behalf of major studios. Randy's prognostication from senior year—that the firm might land million-dollar accounts within three years—is looking conservative.

Evie's surprised. "You're not going with?"

No. He almost certainly isn't. By now, he and Zo are pretty serious, and Zo's made it clear: she's determined to stay put. The documentary scene is better in New York, she's explained—edgier, with more opportunity for a fledgling filmmaker. In New York, Zo can show rough cuts at DocuClub, pitch films at the IFP. In L.A., she insists, she'd be adrift.

So Randy's offered to buy out Ethan's Bränd shares, for what seems to Ethan like a staggering amount of money, low-mid six-figures, enough to live on for several years. Ethan will close out the smaller, non-Hollywood accounts here in New York. He'll also keep a small stake in the company—a still-unhatched nest egg that, if things continue to go well, will pay regular dividends for the foreseeable future. And who knows: maybe someday, if the company ever sells to one of the big firms, Ethan and Zo will have access to a larger lump-sum payout. Maybe even the kind that will set them up for life.

It all strikes Ethan as massive stroke of luck. By his mid-twenties, he'll have more in his bank account than his parents were worth at the end of their lives.

Ethan doesn't want to say any of this to Evie, though. He knows better than to talk about money, and he definitely doesn't want to talk about Zo. It's something about the feel of this mo-ment, this sweet, unexpected pleasure of slipping out of a party with Evie. The way late-night Manhattan feels right now: the air gauzy and wet, the slick streets shimmering with the reflec-tions of Manhattan's lights, like brushstrokes on a still-fresh canvas.

It's some sort of enchantment, this. He knows better than to break the spell.

They walk together in silence. When they reach Columbus Circle, Evie lifts her eyes. "And there she is."

Yes, there she is: Audrey Munson, subject of the Heaven Is a Gal Named Audrey campaign, more than forty feet high. Ethan gazes up at the USS *Maine* monument, marking the entrance to

Central Park. Here, Audrey takes the form of Columbia Trium-
phant, winged victory, riding proudly in her seashell chariot.

"She's still around, you know," Evie says. "Audrey Munson.
I looked her up. She's alive, if not exactly well."

Ethan looks at Evie, stunned. "Wait. For real?" Bränd had out-
Baudrillarded Baudrillard. Is it possible they'd out-Munsoned
Munson too?

"For real. But it's a pretty sad story. She's been in a psychiatric
institution in upstate New York since the 1930s."

"How *old* is she now?"

"More than a hundred. And get this: she didn't have a single
visitor for five whole decades. Not one. I tried to go see her. I
just wanted to meet her, that's all, but at the last minute, a nurse
called me and said it was best if I didn't come. She's really not
doing so great these days."

Ethan looks again at the figure above him, fulsome and powerful, her olive branch raised toward the heavens. It seems impossible that this gilded form, eternal and strong, could have
anything to do with a century-old woman who's spent most of
her life within the confines of a psychiatric hospital.

Evie turns to Ethan. "I don't want to keep you, Ethan. I mean,
if you want to get back to the party. . . ." She hesitates, then
adds, "But if you're up for it, I wouldn't mind sitting for a bit."

Ethan thinks about the Bränd party—that crowd, all those
back claps, the murmur of small talk punctuated by bursts of
laughter, the promise of campaigns he won't work on.

No, that's not for him.

"Yeah, let's sit," he says. "We'll keep Audrey company. Seems like the least we can do."

They lower themselves onto the monument's stone steps. Evie says she's all talked out, so Ethan does most of the talking. He tells her about his family—about losing both parents to cancer within eight months of each other, just last year. About what it's like to return to his hometown these days, how grim and surreal it all feels now that the factories have gone—and with them, so much of what made the town feel like a community. About his college experiences with Randy, what a heady escape those days had been. He tells her about books he's read, how he hopes to write his own book someday, to write something, anyway. As he talks, cars snake around them, red taillights blinking on and off like Christmas bulbs.

Minutes pass, then an hour, then more. People come and go—they emerge from bars and office buildings, galas and concerts. They're wearing suits and jeans and heels and fur. They talk, or they kiss, or they scurry off to the subway. Occasionally, a small group stumbles, singing, into Central Park. But what they don't do—what not one of these New Yorkers does—is bother to look up, to take in the magnificent, near mythological figure cast from the guns of a doomed naval ship, that's looming overhead.

Traffic dwindles. The sky clears. Subway rumbles shake the ground, then quiet. The silences between Evie and Ethan grow longer and more frequent.

After a particularly lengthy pause, Ethan rubs his thighs.

"Well," Ethan says. Zo, he knows, is in Brooklyn, waiting for him. She hadn't wanted to come tonight, didn't want to be a part of what she's taken to calling the Randy Show. He'd told her he'd come to her apartment when the party ended. Which it must have, a while ago. "I guess we should probably get you that cab."

When Evie doesn't protest, he stands. He walks to the curb, lifts his arm, half hoping it will be like before: that no cab will come, that he'll have no choice but to linger, the universe having decided his fate.

In an instant—too fast—an empty taxi swerves to the curb.

He opens the door for Evie. She pauses before getting in. "I really wish you'd move to L.A., Ethan. I don't know anyone out there, and I could really use a friend."

Ethan looks at his feet. "Yeah, well. Hollywood is probably more Randy's vibe than mine. He's got that whole Leading Man thing going. Me, I'm more of a back-room guy."

"I dunno, Ethan." Evie bites her lip. "You might have more Leading Man than you know."

Ethan looks at her, the strangest sensation flooding him. He could kiss her. He's almost certain of this. If he were to lean forward, move toward this bewilderingly beautiful woman, this actress who'd made half of Manhattan gape with little more than a flickering smile, she would respond in kind.

He can picture it, almost, as if it's something that's already happened: their lips pressed together. Tentatively at first, then more urgently. He sees the way she'd place her hand on his arm, the way he'd reach up to touch the space between her shoulder blades. They'd kiss and kiss, stopping to laugh only when the cab driver eventually shouts, impatient, from the front seat, "Hey, lady, you getting in or not?"

Ethan is *this close* to blowing up his whole life.

The moment is there, and then it passes, and then Evie slips into the cab. She squeezes his hand before closing the door. "Stay in touch, okay, Ethan?"

Ethan watches as the taxi rolls uptown, blending into a stream of other vehicles, then disappears.

The next time Ethan sees Evie Emerling, it is on a movie screen.

1 8

IT TAKES THREE trips from the car to get all the boxes inside the UPS Store. All these packages, all these new items that Zo ordered, that they don't need and can't afford. Ethan piles the boxes on the counter as Jarrett K shakes his head.

"My friend," Jarrett says. "Your situation is worse than I thought."

"You have no idea," Ethan says.

Jarrett peers into one of the boxes. "So . . . wrong color again?"

"Nope. I just don't want any of this crap."

"Aha. And how exactly did that go over with the wife?"

"Wasn't exactly a joint decision."

"Taking control, man. Respect." Jarrett offers Ethan a fist-bump. As their knuckles touch, Jarrett brightens. "Red pill!"

Ethan's momentarily confused, until Jarrett points to Ethan's arm: the reminder, in marker, that he needs to pick up Alex's Adderall prescription. Which he hasn't done. And now it's too late: Zo's gone, off to Boston with Alex, without the medicine they'll need in the morning.

He needs to call Zo. Tell her to turn around.

Across the counter, Jarrett grins at him. "There is no spoon." It takes a moment for Ethan to understand: this is a line from the film *The Matrix*. So that's why Jarrett was excited to see the words "red pill" on Ethan's arm. Early on in the film, the hero, Neo, is offered a choice between two pills, red or blue. Only the red pill lifts the shield of illusion, allows Neo to see reality as it truly is, which is to say a dystopian nightmare.

Sounds about right, actually.

"*Great* film," Jarrett says. He scans a return label. "One of the best." Then his eye catches something outside the store window. "Oh, jeez, here comes this one."

Ethan turns around. In front of the store, Elastic Waist is stepping out of her old hatchback. Ethan watches her lumber toward the door, heavy and slow, like a bear just waking from hibernation. "Yikes," says Ethan. Elastic Waist is probably the very last person he wants to see right now.

"You know her?"

"Sort of. She's . . ." Ethan decides not to explain about the witches, or about the scene he and Zo just made in front of the group. "She's not a fan of mine. Listen, I've got to make a phone call."

He'll call Zo right now. Tell her to stop driving. He'll pick up the medicine from the pharmacy, meet her at a rest stop. But Zo's voicemail picks up after just one ring. Ethan hangs up without leaving a message.

Still, as Elastic Waist enters the store, Ethan presses his phone to his ear and says, loudly, "UH-HUH." The truth is, he'd rather have a fake conversation with dead air than to make small talk with one of them witches right now.

When Elastic Waist sees him, he flashes a perfunctory smile, points apologetically to his phone. It's like he's saying, *Gee, I sure wish I could talk, but I happen to be on the most important phone call of my life, what a shame we can't talk.* "YES, THAT'S WHAT I FIGURED," he says to no one.

Elastic Waist greets Jarrett, too loudly. "ARE THEY READY?"

"Yeah," Jarrett says.

"WHAT'S THAT?" Elastic Waist asks.

"YES," Jarrett says. "THEY ARE."

"NO," says Ethan to nobody at all. With no connection, the phone against his ear sounds dampened, inert, like he's talking inside a coffin. "NO, TUESDAY WON'T WORK FOR ME."

He imagines describing the scene. *There I was,* he'll laugh. *A grown man pretending to be on a call, just to avoid talking to someone who calls herself a witch. This town is just too damn small sometimes.*

But to whom might he describe this, exactly? Not Zo. Maybe Maddy.

"BIG RALLY SATURDAY," Elastic Waist tells Jarrett. "YOU SHOULD JOIN US."

Jarrett, under his breath, mutters, "In your dreams."

"WHAT'S THAT?"

"I SAID MAYBE," Jarrett says. He sets a stack of posters on the counter:

BELIEVE WOMEN.

BELIEVE ZO.

RALLY: STARKFIELD GREEN

SATURDAY 10 AM.

Believe Zo. Sure, okay, whatever. Never mind that Zo has twisted beyond recognition the relevant facts about what happened yesterday. Never mind that under an hour ago, she seemed ready to accuse Ethan of having been a literal sexual predator. Never mind that she once promised to love and to cherish him forever, and *for the record, he doesn't exactly feel cherished right now.*

Yet somehow, bewilderingly, Zo's furious at *him.*

She's furious enough, apparently, that she won't even answer his call. She's driving straight on to Boston without an inkling that Alex won't have the medicine she needs in the morning, and Ethan is powerless to help.

But why must Alex's medicine always be his responsibility, and his alone?

Ethan keeps his phone pressed to his ear as Elastic Waist pays for the posters, waves goodbye. He returns the device to his pocket only after she exits the store.

Jarrett shakes his head. "Moron," he says, watching her climb into her car. "They're all a bunch of fucking morons. You know what those protests do? They hurt small businesses. Like this one.

It's hard enough to draw people downtown these days. Now when people do show up, they get screamed at? No wonder this branch is closing. Another empty storefront, and I'm out of a job again."

Ethan attempts to steer the conversation in a more elevated direction. Or at least one where Jarrett isn't unknowingly calling Ethan's wife a fucking moron. "The thing that I don't understand," Ethan muses, "is what those protests are supposed to accomplish." He means *here,* in Starkfield, a world away from anywhere that matters.

"Right?" Jarrett asks. "Like this Supreme Court thing. Most experienced justice in history. So they're protesting what exactly? The system working the way it's supposed to? Send these women just about anywhere else in the world, and they'll be kissing American soil faster than you can say, *Make me a sandwich.*"

Ethan laughs, not because it's funny, but because—well, it *is* sort of funny, imagining this kid saying "Make me a sandwich" to Zo and the other witches.

"I'm kidding," Jarrett says. He looks down at his feet, shakes his head. "Kind of. But I saw online that they're trying to turn this rally into a whole big thing. Bringing in protesters who aren't even from around here. People coming in just to make trouble. I don't like it. Don't like it one bit."

Ethan sees something flash in Jarrett's eyes. So Jarrett goes dark, too, apparently—the way Alex does.

Jarrett seals up Ethan's boxes. "Hey, you ever know anybody who topped himself?"

"Anybody who . . . *what*?"

"Danced with the train. Rode the comet. Caught the bus. Tried a little shotgun mouthwash. You know, who . . ." Jarrett forms a finger gun, points it at his own head, pulls the trigger.

Oh. Suicide. He's talking about suicide.

"Well . . . sure. Of course." There was a high school buddy. Shot himself while drunk. A neighbor of Zo's in Brooklyn who swallowed pills, maybe by accident, maybe not. Probably more than that these days, especially back in his Pennsylvania hometown. Places like that—all those communities, all across America, abandoned by factories then stripped for parts—are ground zero for despair these days.

"Any of them women?" Jarrett asks.

Ethan thinks about that. "I knew one girl who tried. No, two."

"But those girls are still around, right?"

Ethan nods. He's pretty sure.

"I lost four friends in the last seven months alone," Jarrett says.

Whoa. "Friends from around here?"

"Yeah right. I don't have friends around here. Nah, these were online buddies. But I tell you what, they were more real to me than the people I interact with in the so-called real world."

"I'm really sorry, man," Ethan says. He means it too.

"Eighty percent of suicides are men. Think about that. Eighty percent."

Ethan nods. Maybe that's right, men tend to choose more violent methods than women. But he can't see how this fact, if it is a fact, will help Jarrett right now.

"It's always guys like me and my buddies too," Jarrett says. "Guys who won what I call the fuck-you lottery."

"No. You didn't." Ethan's starting to get kind of worried about this kid. Is this a cry for help?

"Sure we did. We're the punching bags of the world, the last ones left it's okay to make fun of. We're just supposed to take it too. We have to grin and bear it while everyone else shouts about how *they're* the ones who have it rough."

"Well . . ." Ethan knows there must be a good response to what Jarrett's just said, he's almost sure of it. Zo would know how to respond. WWZD? What would Zo do?

But even as he asks himself this, he already knows: Zo wouldn't be talking to this kid at all, wouldn't feel sorry for him. She would have dismissed Jarrett entirely after his first sexist wisecrack. Might even have called UPS headquarters, actually, filed a complaint— *You have a misogynist in your store and if you don't dismiss him, I'll tweet about it and stir up a world of trouble for you.*

So what would Zo do? Who cares what Zo would do? She's not exactly a paragon of virtue herself these days.

"Hey." Jarrett's peering at him. "Are you okay, man? You're looking a little peaked."

"I'm just—life's complicated, that's all."

"My advice? Stop drifting. Be your own savior while you can."

Ethan looks at him, confused.

"Actually, that's not my advice," Jarrett admits. "It's Marcus Aurelius: '*Stop drifting . . . sprint for the finish. . . . Be your own savior while you can.*'"

The Matrix and Marcus Aurelius: Jarrett K contains multitudes, apparently.

"I think what he's saying," Jarrett says, "is that guys like us need to take back some control, you know? Refuse to accept the decline of our own lives."

"Refuse to accept the decline of our own lives . . ." Ethan repeats.

Yeah. He likes that.

THERE WAS A time, he can't remember how long ago, when Zo's notes to Ethan—even about mundane tasks—took the form of haiku:

> Toilet paper low
> Quickly running out of squares
> Ethan, can you help?

> Milk and yogurt gone!
> So, too, Hypatia's dog food!
> Stop & Shop awaits.

Today, when he gets home, he finds a series of notes, all in Sharpie, all in uppercase, each on the back of a different piece of scrap paper:

STAYING AT THE KIMPTON
HYPATIA PEED DID NOT POOP
HOME AROUND 6 TOMORROW

If Ethan squints at them, the notes resemble miniature protest signs. Ethan scoops up all of Zo's messages and drops them in the recycling bin.

He walks to the bottom of the stairs.

PEOPLE CHEAT ALL the time, that's the thing. And to be honest, Ethan's not even sure Zo would mind anymore if he did.

When the witches were just forming Zo confided to Ethan that one of the witches (she refused to tell him which one) and her husband were in a relationship with another couple. "You mean they're *swingers*?" he'd asked, incredulous.

"Polyamorous," Zo had corrected him. When she saw the look on his face, she'd shrugged, as if asking *who was he,* or anyone, *to judge*? So who knows. Maybe Zo—this new Zo, anyway, the one he barely recognizes—*wants* him to cheat. Maybe she'd be nonchalant, or relieved, or heck, even *excited* about the possibility.

For all he knows, Zo's breathing the occasional whiff of fresh oxygen herself, and if that's true, can he blame her? What if caring about somebody means occasionally turning your head away from what your spouse is doing, saying, *I see you need something other than me, and that's okay*? Couldn't a person make an argument that this attitude is just an extension of the thing Ethan himself has been doing for months now: taking on more and more of the childcare duties, just so his wife can feel whatever she feels when she puts on those boxing gloves?

Okay, maybe it's different. It's probably different. Sure, it's almost certainly very different. But who knows anymore. Once, there were rules, taboos, and they were clear. Nowadays, it feels like someone tore the rules into pieces, then tossed the fragments in the air, confetti-style, as if morality were a game of fifty-two-card-pickup.

Maybe it's time for him to pick up a card or two.

OUTSIDE MADDY'S DOOR, he takes a deep breath. Knocks.

It's almost like she's been expecting him, has been expecting whatever this next part is, because when she opens the door, she wears a knowing grin.

"Hey, so I was just . . ." He swallows, then looks straight at her. "Maddy, I don't know if you were planning to go out tonight, but I don't think you should."

Do her brows lift, ever so slightly? Does the tilt of her head shift a tiny bit? "Why, you got something in mind?"

"Maybe," Ethan says. He pauses. "Zo left for Boston."

"I'm aware."

"So we could get some take-out. Or watch a movie. Or something."

"Or something," Maddy says. A statement. But not without its own sort of question.

"Yeah. Or something."

She mulls this over. "How about I cook dinner?"

And now he's the one lifting his brow. "You cook?"

"Yeah, and by cook, I mean, I'll order pizza, and you'll pay."

"Perfect." If Zo were here, she'd ask, which brand of pizza? One of the pizza chains is on her boycott list, he forgets which, or why. But let's get real: all the pizza companies probably use tomatoes grown with pesticides and picked with migrant labor, cheese from cows in factory-farm conditions, herbs shipped with fossil fuels, drivers who don't earn a living wage. Scratch below the surface of anything today, you'll find venality. Probably that's why everyone's always shouting at one another on social media, putting their righteousness on public display: deep down, they're terrified that there's no escaping the cesspool that is the twenty-first-century global economy.

The world is rotten to its core. We're all fucking compromised. Might as well be honest about that.

"Cool," says Maddy. "Then we're on."

"We're on," he echoes. He hovers in the doorway, unsure if he should turn around and go downstairs, or what.

Maddy glances at her phone. "Oh, shit. Ethan, I need you to clear out for a bit."

"What, you have another . . . job?"

"I do."

Just like that, he's less interested in leaving than he was even a few seconds ago.

"Ethan, you have to go. I have an appointment."

"Yeah? And what exactly is this . . . appointment?"

"One of the better-paying ones, is what it is."

"Uh-oh."

"What, are you going to go full Dad on me now? Warn me about stranger danger or whatever?"

"This dad's off duty tonight. I'm just curious. Will it be underwear on the head? Or your charming dead-girl sketch?"

Maddy eyes him, like she's considering whether or not to answer his question. Then she reaches into her pocket, taps out something on her phone. Hands it to him. He reads: *I have never seen a woman pleasare herself to compleetion if you know what I mean, I want vry much to see that will you be the 1?*

He looks up from the screen. "You're not serious." She can't be. She can't possibly be about to pleasure herself on-screen. For pay.

"It's good money. Great money, actually. I bargained him up by a *lot*. Plus, he threw in an extra fifty if I'd do it while playing some band called Axis of Perdition. Some sort of heavy metal, not my thing, but whatever . . ."

"Maddy. You can't."

She raises one eyebrow, like it's a dare.

"But how is that not . . ." he starts. "I mean, doesn't this make you—"

"A whore, Ethan? Are you suggesting that this makes me a whore?"

"No! No, Mad, of course not! I just . . ." And, he *doesn't* mean that, not really. Maddy and this guy won't even be in the same room, so obviously it's not *prostitution*. Not *literally*. Also, is he even supposed to say "prostitution" anymore? He read somewhere that you're supposed to use the term "sex worker" now, and that there's no longer any shame about the work, and aren't they trying to unionize like twenty-first-century Norma Raes? "But will you actually . . . you know . . . do it to . . ."

"Completion?" She says the next part really slowly: "Am I going to have an orgasm, Ethan? Is that what you're asking?"

Well, yes. That is sort of what he's asking. *"No."*

"Hmm . . . Well, the answer to the question you're definitely not asking is this: I'll see how I feel in the moment. Maybe I'll fake it, maybe I won't; either way, I'll give him a good show. But to answer your other question, this is about me doing what I want, with my body. This is, like, the stuff that Zo talks about, you know? Empowerment or whatever."

Empowerment or whatever. Ethan's pretty sure this isn't exactly what Zo is talking about. In fact, he's pretty sure Zo would freak the fuck out if she knew that Maddy was jacking off for money mere feet from Alex's bedroom, and frankly, he's mighty uncomfortable with the idea himself.

Maddy glances at her phone again. "Look, you gotta go," she says. "Client's waiting."

He wills himself to leave, if only because he doesn't want to look like such a hopelessly stodgy old man, *Dad the dumbfuck.*

Maddy closes the door most of the way, then, almost immediately, opens it again, pokes her head out. "Actually . . . I don't mind if you watch."

It takes him a few moments to register what she's just said.

"As I see it," Maddy says, "the whole thing is already bought and paid for, so as long as you stay out of view of the camera, what's one more set of eyes? And honestly, Ethan? You seem like you could use a little more fun in your life."

And then, after a beat—after an eternal beat where he says nothing at all, just stands there turning her words over in his head, wondering if he heard her right, if there might be another possible interpretation—she shrugs. "Up to you."

Maddy disappears into the room, leaving the door half-open. He hears the tapping of her fingers on her laptop. A ding, then her voice, not to him: "Hey. I'm ready if you are."

Ethan doesn't move. Doesn't leave, doesn't watch. Just stands there frozen.

The music kicks in. *Baum chack baum baum chack.* The guitars are hardcore. Angry. He imagines the wails filling not just Maddy's bedroom, but also all the other spaces of his torn-apart home: the stairway and the cramped living room, the kitchen, the bedroom he shares with Zo, everything he has.

He keeps his eye on the space between the open door and the jamb.

Maddy steps back from the computer, only partially into his view. From where he stands, he can make out just a few inches of her left side: her shoulder, the edge of her T-shirt, her elbow, the sweeping curve of her hip beneath her jeans. Then she shimmies, bends, stretches, and now, where jersey cotton and denim had been, there's only a single elastic band over bare skin.

Her arm bends. Between her elbow and waist is a diamond of empty space, framed by flesh. The diamond begins to stretch. It elongates, then returns. Maddy's arm is moving. Up and down.

Ethan watches the slow stretch-and-return of the diamond.

The guitar wails, drums thump, the Axis of Perdition singer, or maybe there's more than one, screams. Beneath Ethan's feet, the floorboards shake. He could take one step to the side, just one, see everything.

You can watch if you want.

There's nothing stopping him from walking in. Just walking right into the room, standing there, taking her in, all of her, Maddy Silver. As long as he doesn't step into the frame of the camera, he could.

Would she look at him as she moved, or would her eyes be fixed on the computer screen? Maybe she would stare past both viewers, toward something else altogether, toward nothing at all.

No.

If Ethan were to enter the room, he'd walk straight over to that laptop and close it. Poof, the other guy would be gone, and then it would be just the two of them. Ethan would step right up to Maddy. He'd reach his hand through that diamond, wrap his arm around her waist, rest his fingers on the small of her back. Pull her toward him, breathe her in, the whole of her, all at once.

It would take nothing at all.

But Ethan doesn't do any of those things. He stands motionless in the hallway, eyes fixed on that shifting diamond, watching without watching, his feet as unsteady as if he were standing on the hull of a ship. His chest rises and falls. He's unsure where the music ends and his own blood, pulsing urgently through his veins, begins.

THE FIRST TIME he walked Maddy home was nearly six weeks ago, mid-August. The night was balmy and overcast, officially the start of the Perseid meteor shower, though not a speck of light could be seen through the clouds. Ethan had taken Hypatia for a longer walk than usual, hoping that the sky might clear long enough that he could catch a glimpse of a meteor or two. He'd been so busy looking up that he hadn't even noticed Maddy walking up School-house Hill Road, didn't see her until she was standing right next to him.

They'd fallen into step together naturally, and as they made their way uphill, he told Maddy about the show he'd been hoping to see. He told her everything he knew: that the Perseids, like all meteors, are tiny, smaller than mustard seeds. That meteors are remnants of disintegrating comets, and that comets, back in the Middle Ages, had been considered the smoke of human sin: full of stench and horror, set ablaze by an angry god.

When they reached the driveway, Maddy had stopped, pointed up toward the blank sky. "Oh, hey, look," she'd said brightly. "There's one!"

He was sure she'd been mistaken. Nothing up there but cloudy haze.

Maddy hopped onto the hood of his Subaru, leaned back against his windshield. "Look, there's another one. You see it?"

Ethan gazed up at the emptiness. He felt the late-summer air on his skin, listened to the crickets whir. He was vaguely aware of his wife, moving inside the house.

"Yeah, actually," he said, catching on. "I think I did see that one."

He climbed up next to Maddy, and for the next hour, maybe more, Maddy pointed out imaginary celestial fireworks streaming overhead. "You see that one?" she asked, again and again, and pretty soon it was almost like he *could* see them: streaks of light burning across the sky, fireballs that exploded, bright and green, some sort of magic visible only to them.

Every time Maddy asked, *Do you see it?* he said the same thing: *Yes.*

AFTER ETHAN FINALLY turns around, heads downstairs, feet shaky, fingers gripping the banister the whole way—after the music snaps off, after the godawful screaming guitar gives way to the stifling Starkfield silence—he decides that this is what he will do tonight: He will say yes.

It's early still, barely five P.M. Zo and Alex won't be back for at least twenty-four hours. He will say yes to wherever this evening goes, whatever is offered.

Yes to pizza, even if it's from that place Zo is boycotting. Even if he has to drive the box downtown to throw it away so his wife never sees it.

Yes to the thrum in his head, the pounding in his chest. To knowing that his heart is in there, his telltale heart, and sure, it might feel like it's buried under layers of snow, frozen beneath soil, but it's still beating with the force of life, and he can finally feel it again.

Yes to choosing to see meteors instead of gray sky, to doing what Jarrett says: refusing to accept the decline of his own life. Because what is the point of trying your whole life to be good—a good guy, good husband, good father, good neighbor, good sport—if you end up lumped in with the creeps anyway? Because yesterday he watched his wife slip into the back of a police cruiser, she *wanted* to be in that police cruiser, she chose it over returning to the car with him, driving back home, to everything they'd built. Because it was Jackie, not Ethan, she wanted at the station with her, because apparently Zo has decided her own husband is unnecessary, inessential, like some vestigial organ: an appendix, a coccyx. A male freaking nipple.

Yes, because who can say what's right and wrong anymore? Once, he knew, or he thought he did. But the old order's all torn to shreds, scattered in the wind, knocked clear in the sky like a construction cone in a two-lane highway. It doesn't even feel like there *are* any rules anymore. The world's just a bunch of people staking out their own territory, society be damned, and if that's true, then why shouldn't he, too, stake out a little something for himself?

He will say yes, because everything will dissolve, will crumble into nothingness, his life will be rounded out by permanent sleep sooner than he ever understood. But not yet.

Not tonight anyway.

He will say yes, because Prufrock might have been a coward, but Ethan does dare. He dares eat a peach, dares disturb the universe, dares blast everything he's known to smithereens if that's what it takes to continue feeling something. He will say yes, because #YOLO or whatever, because if he's going to morph from Good Guy Dad into one of the villains, if no matter what he does, people are going to lump him in with this dumpster fire of a president or any of his disgusting kakistocracy, then maybe Ethan should at least enjoy the fucking ride.

He will say yes, just for this one night. He will say yes and see where it takes him.

1 9

Yᴇs ᴛᴏ ᴛʜᴇ question "Do you like my hair?," which is what Maddy asks when she finally comes downstairs. She's rubbing the top of her head, and the question is apparently ironic, because for some reason there *is* no hair, not anymore, that's the point. Her long blue waves are gone, entirely: shaved down to stubble.

Ethan gapes. "Was that . . . a Ten-Spot request?" he asks. The words "Ten-Spot" feel sour in his mouth, but what else could this be?

"Nope," says Maddy. "Just felt like I needed a change. You like?"

"Yes." And actually, he does like it, quite a bit. Maddy looks like Natalie Portman in that *V for Vendetta* movie, or like what's-her-name from *Mad Max: Fury Road*. Freaky, sure, but also kind of weirdly super hot.

"You look badass," he says.

In response, Maddy makes a movie-poster face, eyes narrowed and lips pressed into a pucker. She points finger guns at him.

"Bang."

Yᴇs ᴛᴏ ᴇɪɢʜᴛᴇᴇɴ-ʏᴇᴀʀ Lagavulin, single malt and aged in oak casks. Maddy pulls the bottle from a lower cabinet, gives it a shake, grinning. Probably has no clue that those 700 milliliters cost him upward of $400.

And, yeah, why *not* drink it? The bottle has been sitting on the shelf for years, a relic from a brief scotch phase he and Zo went through. They'd read about malting and mashing, peat and smoke, nose and finish, unironically used words like "earthiness" and "hint of pepper," and "subtle notes of coffee and seaweed." They'd planned, someday, to host some sort of tasting party: maybe they'd set up tables in the backyard, in roughly the shape of the Scottish Isles, with each bottle placed in the location of its distillery. The party never happened. Maybe their interest waned, or they realized that drinking made them feel crappy the next morning, they discovered *Breaking Bad* on AMC, who knows why. Point is: a fat lot of good the booze is doing on the shelf.

So yes. Might as well enjoy it.

Ethan digs out the proper glasses (shaped like a tulip, a little narrow at the rim), but Maddy brings the bottle straight to her lips. She takes a swig, then shakes her head as if she's Hypatia fresh from a bath.

"Whoa," Maddy says. She smacks her lips, then shakes again. "Holy shit, that's intense."

She holds out the bottle to him, and he takes it.

Yes.

YES TO PIZZA straight from the box, to hand-feeding crusts to Hypatia. Ethan lets Hypatia lick the oil from his fingers, then he wipes his hands on his jeans. He and Maddy are both seated on the ancient marble counters (yes to this, too), facing each other with their backs on opposite walls. Their knees are bent, their toes just inches apart on top of the stove.

"Know what I read recently?" Ethan asks (because yes, too, to repeating for Maddy the same thing he recently said to his wife). "Britain just appointed their first-ever Minister of Loneliness."

"That's the greatest job title ever!" Maddy says. She tosses a piece of crust to Hypatia, who fails to catch it. Going blind, the poor creature.

"Personally, I think there ought to be one for all the dark emotions," Ethan continues. "Minister of Despair. Minister of Envy." Maybe *that's* the screenplay to pitch to Randy when this lawsuit thing is over: *The Ministers*. An anti-superhero film.

"Minister of Douchebaggery," Maddy suggests.

"Hey, you talking about me?" he jokes.

"You, Ethan, would be the Minister of Affability." The way she says it isn't necessarily a compliment.

"And you'd be, what?" he asks. "The Minister of Don't-Give-a-Fuck?"

She flutters her eyes, all innocently. Her voice sweet, she says, "Or maybe the Minister of Go Fuck Yourself?" Then she nudges his foot with her own. Leaves it there.

Yes to that. Yes.

YES NOT ONLY to flirtation, but also to real talk. About Maddy, her future. About what she wants, and doesn't. About whether she'll ever marry, or have children, or settle down.

"I'm just saying," Ethan says. "Don't rule anything out. When I graduated college, I thought I was going to be an itinerant journalist. *Never* thought I'd get married. Never thought I'd be a dad. Definitely never expected to settle in a town like this."

Maddy peels a layer of cold cheese from the top of her slice. "And yet here you are." She pops the cheese in her mouth, drops the rest of the slice on the counter.

"I'm just saying, someday you'll be somewhere, too, Mad. Actually, you know what? I bet you become one of those PTA moms. You'll drive a Range Rover a little too fast, yell at the other moms for taking too much time in the school drop-off line. Maybe you'll stand at the side of the soccer field with a thermos of cocoa and a tin of hand-baked cookies for the team."

"Not gonna happen," Maddy says. Like it's simple, like a person can predict where they'll wind up, and how they'll feel about it. Like life is something you choose instead of the thing that sort of just happens, in increments so small you don't even notice, and by the time you really get it—*this is it, this is your one and only life*—it's too late. "For one thing, who wants to be with the same person for, like, a century?"

Ethan laughs. "It only *feels* like a century sometimes." (Look at him! Sharing his own real talk too!)

"No, Ethan. I mean an *actual* century. Like, *literally*. I read that people my age might live to be a hundred and fifty, assuming we don't OD on heroin or blow our brains out or get nuked by a rogue state or whatever. So let's say I'm the ripe old age of thirty-five when I get married. That's still a hundred and fifteen years of marriage for me." She downs a long swig of single malt—probably twenty-five bucks, gone, just like that. "No thanks."

A hundred and fifty years. Ethan was twenty-six when he and Zo married, a baby, really. He tries to imagine being married for a hundred and twenty-four years: literally, he'd have more than a hundred years left with Zo.

"Jesus," he says. Then he points to the bottle. "Gimme some of that." When Maddy hands it to him, he slams a shot, just like she's been doing.

Because, man: maybe he does need to blow his fucking brains out.

Yes even, apparently, to talking about Zo.

"I just wish I knew what it accomplished, you know?" Ethan says. It's the whiskey that's making him talk, it's the warmth of his belly, the way his head is spinning just a little. "All that protesting. An endless stream of protests in the middle of Starkfield, Massachusetts, population next-to-nothing, and for what, exactly? Is it performance, or does it actually make some sort of difference?"

"Protest is the new brunch." Maddy shrugs. "At least, that's what Zo told me."

"See, but that's what I mean. If it's your alternative to *brunch,* how impactful can it really be? I mean, if someone could tell me, 'Yes, your standing out there and shaking a sign that you made with pasteboard and Sharpies that you bought at the local Rite

Aid, in a downtown that barely anybody even drives through absolutely helps change the world,' I'd be all in."

"Right? I'd be like, great. Lemme join you."

"But what difference *could* it make in a town like this? Also, for the record, I did go a couple of times. At the beginning, I did."

"And?"

"And when it was over, the world was exactly the same as when we started."

He lifts the bottle again, swirls the brown liquid around, watches the eddy it forms. "Anyway," he says. He wants to stop talking about Zo, but something inside of him can't stop, not yet, almost like his wife is some sort of problem he needs to solve, a circle that he might get square, he can't move on until he does. "Sometimes I wonder if Zo's having a nervous breakdown."

Maddy considers this. "I guess that depends on if she's getting closer to who she really is, or further away from it."

This seems like a pretty good insight, actually—one he'd stop to think about a little more if only his head weren't so woozy. "Meanwhile, she's not even *trying* to finish her film," he continues (and is he slurring his words a little now?). "God, she was such a good filmmaker."

He's telling the truth: Zo's documentaries were gorgeous. In Zo's hands, a snoozer of a story of a mathematician who explained non-Euclidean geometry through crochet became candy-colored, exhilarating, filled with wonder. Another, about an eccentric philosopher turned bus driver, got a brief mention in *The New York Times,* which called it "transcendent . . . as offbeat as it is sublime." Zo's shorts had made it into some good festivals: New Hope, and Vero Beach, and that one that Michael Moore runs in Traverse City. But her last big work was back in the early 2000s. Some family-owned pharmaceutical company in Stamford, Connecticut, had paid her what seemed like a gobsmacking amount of money to make some corporate videos about a breakthrough product for pain management. The family behind the company—famous billionaire philanthropists—loved her work: they promised to introduce Zo to important people at the Tate, the Smithsonian.

"So what happened? Why'd she stop making films?" Maddy asks. Ethan shakes his head. What happened? They left New York, that's what happened. They had a great kid who required a lot of work to raise. Zo still came up with terrific ideas, for both documentaries and features—one that Ethan remembers in particular was called *The Muses,* about an alternative-reality world in which the women behind famous artists had never met the men they supported—but she could never find the funding she needed to bring them to screen. A few years ago, she tried to get back into commercial work, but by then, the wonder drug she'd worked on was at the heart of a growing opioid crisis, which meant she couldn't even show that film, among her best, in her reel.

She bid on dozens of jobs, coming close every time, but never actually getting them.

"It's hard, the film world," Ethan tells Maddy. "But she's got a real *chance* with this Trilling thing. This could be her ticket back into the business, and I think she knows that. Maybe that scares her, because instead of working, she . . . punches things. In fact, she changed gyms *specifically* so she could punch things."

"Well, she didn't exactly *change* gyms, Ethan."

"She did. Her gym used to be right here in town, the one over on Broad Street, out near your friend's dispensary."

"Right, I know. That *was* her gym. Until they kicked her out."

"Wait . . . what?"

"They canceled her membership, said she couldn't come back. You don't know this story?"

Ethan's incredulous. *"Why?"*

"She kept flipping off the TV. I guess there were all these television screens all over the gym, and apparently every time she saw the president's face on any of them, Zo gave the guy a double-barreled salute." Maddy hops off the counter, stands erect, raises her arms above her head, and lifts her two middle fingers.

Ethan thinks about the women in his living room two nights ago, all in that same stance. Is Zo seriously so wrapped up in her rage that she doesn't realize a person can't actually do that *at the gym*?

Maddy climbs back up on the counter, downs another $10 or so of Lagavulin, then smacks her lips. "The gym owner gave Zo a bunch of chances, he apparently talked to her several times, but she didn't stop. So they booted her."

"She never told me any of that."

Maddy eyes him. "It's possible, Ethan . . . that you and your wife don't exactly tell each other *everything*."

Well, yes. That seems true.

MAYBE YES TO weed, maybe, if Maddy has any? He hopes she has it, he'd like to feel that carefree rush, the it's-all-good mellow.

Maddy shakes her head. "Sorry. But if you want, I can text Arlo, tell him to bring some samples over."

"*No.*" Ethan says it too quickly, but there's no way Arlo O'Shea is coming over tonight. Ethan waves his hand, all casual, dismisses the whole idea. "Never mind, it was just a thought."

Maddy brightens. "Actually, hold on. I know what we should do."

She pulls herself up to a standing position, feet on the counter, and reaches for a ceramic crock sitting on top of the cabinet. The crock is left over from Zo's fermenting phase. She'd read a book about gut bacteria and the human immune system, then ordered some expensive, hand-crafted crocks from a ceramicist in Ashfield. Zo filled the crocks with homemade sauerkraut and kimchi, pickled cabbage and radishes. For months, the house reeked of decay. Fortunately, she'd abandoned this effort, and now the crocks sit, unused—not unlike the mason jars from Zo's hand-canning phase, or the bag full of yarn from her knitting phase, or the gardening equipment from her grow-your-own phase, which failed to last even a single season.

Maddy climbs down, lifts the lid. "*This* is what we should do."

Ethan peers inside. There are a bunch of plastic snack bags, something gray and shriveled inside each: animal droppings, it looks like, or maybe desiccated corpses from the animals themselves.

"What's this?"

"*Psilocybe cubensis*. Picked by yours truly."

"Sillo-what?"

"'Shrooms, Ethan. You know: magic mushrooms? Keeper of secrets? Revealer of wisdom?"

Oh, that. He tried mushrooms, once, back at Kenyon. He remembers an absurdly long walk down Middle Path, as if time and space had been stretched like taffy. But the effect didn't last long, and looking back, he wonders if the whole thing had been in his head, some kind of placebo effect.

Maddy opens the bag. "How much you want? Two? Three?"

Does she mean two or three baggies, or mushrooms, or what? He tries to remember how much he'd taken, once upon a time, but all he remembers is laughing with Randy as gravel crunched beneath their feet. Had he chewed those dried mushrooms? Steeped them like tea? God, it was so long ago.

Maddy's waiting for his answer. Does he want two? Three? More? Maybe he should say *two* and take his chances? Two sounds like a good number. Reasonable. Not the lowest of the low, but it doesn't sound too risky.

But Maddy apparently takes his idiot silence to mean something else. "What, you want a *heroic* dose?"

Heroic. He smiles. He likes the sound of that.

"Yes," he says. *Whatever the night brings.*

Maddy raises her eyebrows. "Mmm-kay. So I'd better do just one or two. Can't have both of us out of our skulls."

Maddy gets to work, the way a professional might: she gets out a coffee grinder, a Pyrex cup, a bunch of lemon juice. Some sort of technique, she explains, to make them kick in sooner. She works efficiently, and before long, she's stirring the whole concoction into a glass of water.

"Don't worry," Maddy assures Ethan as she hands him the cup. "I'm a great fucking babysitter."

He knows from experience that this isn't remotely true. He drinks anyway.

2 0

THEN YES TO the waiting, and the creep of anxiety, the jittery fidgeting, the *What have I done?* and *Is this it?* and *Do I feel it yet?* and *What if Zo calls?*

"Relax," Maddy tells him.

"I am. I'm relaxed." His foot is jiggling a million miles an hour.

Maddy assures him it's okay, that scientists are doing research with mushrooms at places like Harvard and Johns Hopkins now, that the chemical inside them, psilocybin, is a breakthrough treatment for PTSD and anxiety. They've done studies with cancer patients, with alcoholics, he's going to be fine.

"Yeah, okay," Ethan says. Nods too fast. Cracks his knuckles. He feels sick to his stomach, maybe nerves, but maybe she poisoned him.

Wait. What if she poisoned him?

"Dude, you need to focus on something else. Here." Maddy bends at the neck, so all he can see is the top of her head. "Feel my hair."

He hesitates. Looks at the dark stubble on white skin. There's something vaguely indecent about seeing her scalp, like he's glimpsing something his eyes weren't meant to see.

"Come on, Ethan, it's just hair."

He places both hands lightly on her head, begins to rub.

Maddy was right. This helps. The stubble is softer than it looks. Velvety. Ethan moves his fingers apart, then together. In his mind, he hears Alex's voice, a joke she used to tell. *Know what this is? A brain sucker. Know what it's doing? Starving.*

He closes his eyes, feels Maddy's warmth, all that silky fuzz.

"Mmm," Maddy says. "That feels great, actually. Keep doing that."

He moves his fingertips over the curves of her scalp, down toward her ears, her neck. He imagines he's running his fingers through long locks. Above him the light fixture hums.

Maddy lifts her head. He opens his eyes and is surprised by how close her face is to his own.

God, he had forgotten what it felt like to desire someone like this, had forgotten that it's possible to feel your whole self hurtling toward another soul. He thinks again of those underground particles, just two bits of matter, whizzing around at light speed, ready to collide, to smash together, creating an impossibly vast explosion of energy, *Maybe this is what the end of the world looks like.*

He could declare himself post-faithful.

"Let's do you," says Maddy. And when he doesn't understand, not completely—when he stands there frozen and dumb—Maddy adds, "Let's give you a shave, I mean."

He touches his beard.

"No," she says. "I like the beard. I mean your head. Come on, you've got a few minutes before the 'shrooms kick in for real. And when they do, you are going to *love* how a shaved head feels."

He tries to imagine what Zo would say if she came home from Boston and found them both with buzz cuts, like that cult from forever ago, the one in California, all those tech nerds in Nike sneakers who were so certain the aliens were planning to beam them up. What was their name? He considers asking Maddy, then realizes she probably wasn't even born yet when that happened.

"It feels good?" he asks. "A shaved head?"

Heaven's Gate. That was the name. Bunch of lonely-heart computer programmers in sweatpants.

Maddy grins. "Feels like freedom."

◆

AT FIRST IT'S lovely. He sits on a stool in the bathroom, eyes closed. Maddy presses her body into his back as she works. The electric razor tickles his scalp. He opens his eyes, head down, sees a clump of hair land on the floor. He smiles, closes them again. The razor moves from the back of his neck to his forehead, from his ear toward the center of his scalp. He imagines his hair like an overgrown summer lawn, the razor a mower that leaves neat, satisfying tracks.

His spine tingles. It's a pleasant buzzing, a warm whir. It hits his solar plexus and expands outward, into his chest. And then, in an instant, everything changes. The buzz is a dentist's drill, then a jackhammer, and then worse, torturous, like some sort of demon.

"Stop," he says, and then he says it again, panicking now. He waves Maddy away, puts his fingers in his ears. He begins to rock. *Stop. Stop. Stop.*

Maddy kills the razor. Ethan inhales the silence, feels it cooling him, calming him,

Cold then. Cold sweat. When he closes his eyes he's hurtling through space, stars flying toward him at dizzying speed.

"Ethan," Maddy says.

A wave of nausea, of motion sickness, it's the stars, they're too fast, he wants to stop this ride.

"Open your eyes, Ethan," Maddy tells him, and when he does, the room looks different. The colors have gone Day-Glo, electric. The blue of the towel, Alex's clothes on the floor *red sweatshirt, green T-shirt, blue jeans, rainbow socks.* All of these things are saturated to the point of surreal.

Ethan? And this time Maddy sounds different. She's an aria, a thousand voices at once, a choir in a cathedral. He turns to her. He feels an urge to giggle like a child. Giddy, this feeling, euphoric, something he hasn't felt for years, and there is the music again, that swell in his chest.

Ethan, the music says, *you're only halfway done.*

The words come to him through a tunnel, he doesn't know what they mean, and that, too, strikes him as hilarious.

Ethan, your hair. Maddy runs her hands over his buzz cut on one side, air cool, then through the chunks of hair on the other. He understands now, she's only shaved half his head, she wants to finish, but all he can think about is how good her touch feels, magnificent, he can feel every nerve ending, millions of neurons every square inch, he knows this as a fact but he's never *known* it before, not like he does right now, my God. He rolls his head around beneath her fingers.

I guess you're feeling it, her voice explodes into color, sound is sight and sight sound, and people should touch each other more, should touch and touch and touch and touch, and now the hexagonal tiles are moving, shifting back and forth like connected gears. Ethan laughs because it's spectacular.

His heart pumps blood through his body, he can feel the liquid rushing, can *hear* it. He laughs again, because all this time he's never noticed this, that he can hear his own blood, and now the wall is vibrating, rippling like waves, the floral pattern of the old wallpaper turning into waltzing couples.

He closes his eyes: Stars. Opens them: Waltzers.

Stars. Waltzers. Stars. Wal—

And then the walls melt away. White-hot energy, some sort of electric jolt, ripples up through his spine. It is a cosmic big bang, this, and it's an absolute fucking miracle.

LIGHT RAINS, DROPLETS from the fixture, photons made visible, at last.

Ethan holds out his hands, palms flat and facing the ceiling. Particles move through his body, glittering ghosts passing through and beyond his skin. *So beautiful,* he says, not so much to Maddy, or even himself, but to some Other, and did he say it out loud? If he did, the words aren't right, they're not enough, they're just sounds coming from a hole in his face, from skin and saliva and muscle, a strange, inadequate monkey-mouth. Words can't convey what he means, can't possibly.

In the living room, pictures disintegrate, reassemble.

In the kitchen, he sees Zo's crock, still on the counter. He picks it up, holds it in his hands, feels the cool ceramic. The crock is saying something, or maybe something is speaking through it to him, but then it's not in his hands anymore, it's shattered, it's all over the floor, and so are all the plastic bags filled with those gray organic lumps.

He stares at them. *I need to go lie down,* he says, or maybe he doesn't.

IN THE BEGINNING, there were single-celled creatures. They were alive, but they perceived nothing: not light from dark, one color from the next, even their own movement through the expanse. The difference between no-perception and perception isn't incremental, it's existential, it's everything, and it's happening again right now. Ethan's crossing some threshold, moving from one way of being into another, like stepping through a door into a place that was always there, always around him, but that he'd never noticed.

It's some kind of super-vision he's gaining: a super-understanding, some new language that's flooding from the deep, dark empty.

MADDY STANDS IN the half-light of his bedroom. *Doing okay?* Energy comes off her in rays, glistening and golden.

Ethan hadn't known he loved her, but he does. He loves her. He loves everyone, maybe. Maddy's smile is so beautiful it is a wound.

She is Maddy, but she is also more than Maddy. She is the force that flowed through Aphrodite, Venus, Freya, she's the pulsing of life itself. He knows if he could be with her, if he could touch her, move with her, that they would combine to become something holy. He imagines the sweat that would pour from them, the way their perspiration would slickly mingle, every drop a tiny sparkling jewel.

He longs to reach out to her, but he cannot move.

I guess you are, she says. She slips out of the room, and when she disappears, he is more alone than before. Also, it is so hot.

ON THE COFFEE table,

the one on the floor,

not the one that is part of the monstrous stack of furniture looming beastly in the corner, don't look at that, don't, but the other one, safe,

there is a *New Yorker* magazine, pulp with markings: color and form, lines and dots, stripped of all meaning.

He sits on sofa number two, turns the pages. He looks at the ads: eyelashes like insects. Faces contorted into distortions. *Grotesque,* he thinks. They are on this page, these faces, because they are supposed to be beautiful, but they are all wrong, disfigured somehow. Twisted, overdone.

Hideous. Does no one see how hideous humans are?

He doesn't know where Maddy is, if Maddy is. Maybe he is the only one.

SILVER HOLE IN the bathroom wall, beast in the mirror, gray skin like pockmarked plastic, beard a disgusting tangle, made up of a thousand twisting creatures. His head is uneven, one half a forest of stubble, the other half writhing like the beard. *This is what you are,* the image in the mirror tells him. *You are an ugly thing, and weak.*

Lower than low.

BATHMAT BENEATH HIM, curled and crying, who knows how long he's there, a small child weak and scared. *Maybe it's time to get up and walk around.* That voice again, hers, thank God.

♦

OUTSIDE IS AN alien planet, at once cartoonish and exquisite. Rounded edges, ballooning middles, shimmering light. He wishes the world always looked like this. He understands the world always looks like this, it's his fault for missing it.

He walks to the edge of the place reached by the light of the house. Then he steps beyond it. He has the sense of being absorbed into some Other. He doesn't so much dissolve as he does become part of everything else, things seen and unseen.

The trees are breathing. Everything out here: breathing, for him and with him, a single organism.

In. Out. Expand. Contract.

He runs his hands up and down the bark of the tree, *You are me and I am you and we are breathing as one.* His fingers come across something: initials, carved in bark, EF + ZF 2003, and it is so jarring. He'd put those letters there himself, years ago, when they'd moved here. He'd done it with his monkey body and his monkey understanding, done it with a pocket knife in the middle of winter as he and Zo held mugs of coffee even though all those things— knife, winter, mug—emerge from some half-remembered dream he's not even sure is his own.

He is ashamed of these initials, this casual violence. He puts his forehead against the bark, feels himself breathing with the tree. *I'm sorry,* he says, not with words, *I promise we won't be around much longer.* By *we* he means *people,* and as soon as the thought exists, he knows that it's true. There's some cataclysmic event, some apocalyptic transformation that has not yet happened and yet somehow also already has. The entire human enterprise, from knuckle-walks to the coding of machines that will outlive us all, is on a collision course with some final Unspeakable. Ethan feels himself hurtling toward it right now, even as he can already see glimpses of it, like lost memory.

He knows what he said was true: we won't be around much longer.

He feels ripples of sadness rising from the ground, like shockwaves, like the heat that rises from asphalt on a summer day. These sadwaves are coming from every living thing, they move through him, and he releases his own waves too. Their collective sorrow drifts into the sky, beyond it, disappears.

It's around then that the beast appears.

IT IS LURKING: a wolf, not a wolf. A coyote, not a coyote. Something else, something he sees when he closes his eyes, but which is there even when he cannot see it. A jackal, like a creature he remembers from some long-ago life, a lonely creature adrift in a sea of blue.

The jackal tells him to come forward. The animal doesn't say it with words, he knows only the false things have words, the true things are untranslatable.

You are a god, the jackal tells him with a voice that isn't a voice.

I am a scared animal clinging to a rock, he answers.

Also true, says the jackal.

What is this experience? he asks the jackal.

This is all there has ever been, the jackal answers.

I am alone, Ethan says.

The jackal does not say yes or no.

ETHAN MADE UP everyone else, invented them from whole cloth. It was always just him, him and the jackal. Anyone else, everyone else, was a wish, an illusion, a delusion. Everything he ever thought happened to someone else had been happening to him all along.

OUT THERE. HERE. There is no difference.

Them. I. Again: no difference.

Causeeffect backforth actionreaction All these distinctions dissolve, are undone.

Never were.

Later, much later, when all of this is over, and he's trying to explain, he'll try to describe this place. He'll use words like "expanse." "Void." "Abyss." "Nothingness."

None of them will begin to capture it.

It is eternal solitude, loneliness without bounds, the worst sort of hell, and it will never end.

THE JACKAL IS still there when the world starts to return, when Ethan reenters his monkey body, with his monkey arms and monkey face and monkey ears and monkey toes and monkey ball sac and monkey knees. It is there when he relearns walls and windows, shirt fabric on skin, the yellow spot on the ceiling where the upstairs radiator leaks.

It's still there as words return, as he relearns the demarcations between things—hazy, at first, like figures seen through mist, but gaining clarity:

In, out, there, here, cause, effect.

Now, then. Self. Other.

It is still there, the jackal, as he feels the pieces of himself slotting into place, like he's a LEGO figure that had been ripped apart, left adrift in an ocean of LEGO bits, then reassembled, slowly, brick by brick. He knows it's there, because every time he closes his eyes, he sees it. Watching, waiting.

It's only when the final LEGO bricks are finally snapped into place, as the final window separating him from everything else seals shut, that the jackal speaks again. It still speaks with the words that aren't words, in that voice that is everywhere and nowhere, and it comes only, at last, when Ethan remembers he is a man with a past. With a wife.

That's all over now, the Jackal says, and Ethan knows the beast means all of it: the time he and Zo walked through Park Slope in the rain at two A.M. and it felt like the world was theirs alone, the time they fucked in a prairie preserve, somewhere in Missouri, maybe, or Oklahoma, halfway through a road trip to Texas for an aunt's funeral, the way during their daughter's birth he laughed and sweated through his shirt and smiled at Zo's pained brow and assured her everything was going to be fine, just fine, the sense they belong to each other, that they could make promises and keep them. All of these moments, all of the others, the ones he remembers, the ones he doesn't, their whole messy, complicated everything, has been distilled into a singularity that pops like a soap bubble and vanishes forever.

That's all over, and it's never coming back.

FRIDAY

2 1

OR MAYBE HE'S not quite put back together. Not entirely. It's as if one or two of the LEGO bricks didn't get put back where they should, because when Ethan wakes (midmorning, he can tell by the angle of the light, the lazy chirr of a late-season cicada outside his window), he's at once inside his body and outside of it. It's as if some part of him is watching himself, even as he lifts his head from the pillow, turns to look at the clock radio (11:42 A.M.! He's slept in as if he's a college student! A kid!).

He sits up. Rubs his hair. Half of his head shaved to stubble, the other half full.

He sees himself doing all these things—lifting, looking, sitting, rubbing—as if with some sort of third eye, disconnected from himself.

The room is bright, the air is clear.

Something happened last night, and he's not entirely sure what he's supposed to do now. The jackal is gone, but the animal's final words—*That's all over now*—linger in his bedroom like a forlorn spirit.

And yet.

And yet: look how beautiful the room is: the honey glow of the walls, the tangle of bedsheets, the eager way Hypatia's tail thumps at his rising.

His throat burns. The whiskey, maybe.

Maddy's nowhere to be seen.

He goes to the bathroom, sees his reflection: asymmetrical, uneven, a man who's half one thing, half another. Razor on the counter, hair still in clumps on the floor. He takes a piss, finishes shaving his scalp himself. Long hair on his chin, short stumps on his head. When he's finished, he scoops up all the hair, lifeless, useless, like fingernails that grow on a dead body.

In the kitchen, Zo's crock, the one where Maddy was storing her mushrooms, is in pieces on the floor. The ziplock bags are gone, though: rescued, presumably, by Maddy while he was wherever he's been. He stares at the shattered ceramic. Picks up the pieces one by one, placing each carefully in the garbage. He nicks his finger on one of the shards, watches blood pool on his flesh.

There's a swell in his heart he can't entirely explain, both mourning and joy.

He puts Hypatia's leash on, takes her out in the backyard, hears the wind in the leaves above. It's a shuffling of papers, that rustle: a kind of caress. He smiles. Watches himself smile. Then he watches himself steer Hypatia out of the yard, to the street, and begin walking slowly down the hill.

THEY'LL DIVORCE AMICABLY. That's what he decides as he descends into Starkfield. He glances around, as if he's seeing the town for the first time: the peeling clapboards, the buckled sidewalks, all the lovely, sad potential of this place.

Light lines the edges of the trees, like someone's painted strips of white. *Hello, trees, you magnificent bark-cloaked beasts.*

If he and Zo are to divorce—which maybe they won't, except maybe they will, doesn't feel like it's his to control, frankly—he'll make sure of it: they'll be amicable. They'll make great co-parenting partners.

If.

Which, now that bright sun is streaming through the leaves (high noon now, and look at him, just getting started on his day!) he can no longer entirely picture.

Sure, maybe at first they'll have to force themselves to be

friendly, but they can do that, of course they can. For Alex's sake. For their girl, their wonderful child who is, he realizes, right at that moment submitting to tests in some hospital office in downtown Boston.

The distance between Alex's "now" and his own is surreal, absurd.

Other couples have good divorces, remain friends. Surely he and Zo can too. They'll find a new rhythm, remember how much they liked each other in the first place, remember *why*. Their newfound distance will make it easy to see all the good in each other.

They'll all have dinner together once a week: he, Alex, and Zo. Maybe twice a week. Perhaps he and Zo can call each other for advice—not just about Alex, but about life, love. He imagines Zo saying something like, *He used to be my husband; now he's my best friend*.

The air is crisp, the sky the blue of a child's drawing.

IN THE VILLAGE green, signs rise from the grass like toadstools:

NO SCOTUS ABUSERS

I DO NOT CONSENT

BELIEVE WOMEN, BELIEVE ZO

RALLY, SATURDAY 10AM

That rusted truck is there, too, the GMC that he and Alex followed on the way to Parents' Night: the one with the behemoth flags and all those screaming bumper stickers. The truck is parked outside of the Flats.

Ethan looks back and forth between the truck and the rally signs, trying to make sense of the argument they're having: opposite and amplified. Both make him feel as if he's standing in a museum, peering through glass at some inexplicable artifacts from a long-extinct society. He can't possibly understand these messages, or even imagine their purpose.

He ties Hypatia to a parking meter outside the Coffee Depot.

The usual morning crowd is long gone from the coffee shop, the place at midmorning strangely empty and still.

Yes, look: there is Nancy pouring the same beans into the same coffee grinder. There is the whirring of the machines, the amateur art on the walls.

He pulls a plastic bottle of water from the cooler. This, too, is an artifact: transparent plastic bubble surrounding clear liquid, a snow globe without snowflakes. No dancing hula girl, no *Greetings from Florida* irony here. He pays for the water without speaking, the cash from his wallet almost unrecognizable. He sits in Willie Nelson's window seat, watches Hypatia through the glass, notices the white fur on her nose, the careful, arthritic way she lies down when she finally gives up waiting for him. Hypatia, like he, like everyone, is growing old. He observes this thought neutrally, with no attachment. Certain death as mere fact, untethered from fear.

He stays there, in that seat, blinking. He does not count the minutes as they pass.

By the time Ethan returns to the house, it's late, almost two P.M. His phone is on the counter. He'd set it down sometime at the start of an evening he thought would go another way. It is a sleek rectangle, not much bigger than a pack of playing cards. He presses it, and it blinks to life.

There are fifty-two notifications. Five texts from Maddy from earlier in the day:

hope you had a good trip. Wink emoji.
Find any infinite truth?
You're sleeping it off, I'm hanging w Arlo
See ya later.

Seven from Zo, also from this morning:

Just got to Children's. Wow, this place is really something.
Alex is bouncing all over the place—talking a million miles a minute
We forgot her medicine argh, I'm already exhausted

A clown just came into the waiting room.
I despise clowns.
Okay, they just called us in. Wish us luck.
Talk later.

There are four calls from Dr. Ashleigh, as well as a voice message, time-stamped to her final call at 11:22 this morning.

You know what, Ethan? I think I have enough information at this point to know that for whatever reason, this just isn't working. I'm going to wish you well.

All the other messages—voicemails and texts—are from Randy. These, too, are like messages from some far-off world, extinct. These have nothing to do with him.

Ethan imagines the humans behind the texts: Zo sitting in a waiting room with a clown, trying to quiet a rapid-talking Alex. Then in some doctor's office, watching doctors evaluate their daughter. He thinks of Randy, and of the people who work for Randy. People who surely need jobs, health insurance. They will be better off because of what Ethan is going to do today. He sends a single text to Randy: *About to go to the Humphrey. All good.*

He feels a warm glow as he opens his laptop.

First, he types out a message to Dr. Ash. He moves his fingers on buttons that translate his thoughts into ones and zeros, which will reassemble into thoughts again on the other side. *Dear Ashleigh,* say the ones and zeros, *I got your message, and I agree, this isn't a fit, but I wish you happiness, peace.* He pauses, thinks about the transparent, desperate need that lies beneath her business model—to be seen, to be needed—then adds: *Everyone is doing the best that they can.*

He presses Send.

He takes out two pieces of paper, a green pen. Then he opens Google, pulls up one of the stories he saw yesterday: *Evie Emerling: Just Another Hollywood Hypocrite with a Hybrid.*

He's not interested in the post itself—in some lonely writer's desperate clinging to his own resentment, as if enmity were some sort of lifeboat that could possibly save a person. No, Ethan's interested in the photos slapped across the top of the page: a series of images snapped in Montauk: Evie stepping out of a pale-blue Prius, then turning away, shielding her face when she notices the camera.

Ethan zooms in on the car: New York plates.

He zooms in further: the plates are fuzzy, but not impossible to decipher. The first letter is a K? No . . . an X. He moves between photos, piecing the plate numbers together one at a time.

XTP-334. He writes the number down on the first piece of paper, green letters against white.

Then he stares at a new blank page, trying to figure out what to say. What are the exact words that will convey his good intentions, that he—the anonymous writer of this letter, faceless and nameless, omniscient, benevolent—is really just looking out for her?

We are all connected, he wants to say, *you and me and everything else.*

He was right last night: words are the problem, they aren't adequate. All he has are twenty-six symbols—a pocketful of lines and dots—to convey the fullness of his heart, the ripples of sadness he now sees everywhere, all the world's love and longing and fear, inextricable from his own.

The fact that he may have loved her once, even if it was just for one night.

He sits for a long time. He's not sure how long. Then he picks up the green pen again, begins writing.

He's just setting the pen down when the kitchen door opens. He stands, expecting to see Maddy, home from her morning with Arlo O'Shea. He wants to tell Maddy about all that he's seen. All that he's come to understand. But it's someone else entirely who comes bursting into the house.

"Daddy!!!!!"

IT'S AS IF his daughter exists in two places at once. One version of Alex is in Boston, sitting in a neurologist's chair, answering doctors' questions, or completing spatial-recognition tasks, or watching the line made by some doctor's moving finger, or whatever it is they do at Children's. And then there is *this* version, the miraculous, grinning version who's slamming into Ethan with all the bone-rattling impact of an NFL defensive back, *force equals mass times acceleration*.

He stumbles backward. "Whoa, whoa, easy there." These are the first words he's spoken aloud since the mushrooms kicked in; they come to him from some murky, dark place, as if language itself is a long-ago dream, only vaguely remembered.

He touches Alex's hair, her shoulders. She *feels* real. "But how are you here?" he asks.

"Daddy, I met a big white dog named Boomer at the hospital. Boomer's a service dog, and I think Hypatia should be a service dog because his owner told me you just need the dog to be calm and not bite . . ."

As she rattles, Ethan picks up the note to Evie, folds it up, and slips it in his pocket. Alex either doesn't notice or doesn't care.

". . . also met a baby named Jackson whose nose and lip were all messed up but he was really cute, because, Daddy, did you know that people smile with their eyes? Jackson's mom gave me some chocolate because I was so nice to him, and oh, I met a *girl* clown, and can you please, please, please send me to circus camp this summer? And guess what, on the way home Mommy stopped at a rest stop that had a McDonald's *and* a Honey Dew Donuts, and she let me get something from both, and Daddy, where's your *hair*?"

Ethan leans down, tells Alex to feel his head, and then his daughter's hands are all over his scalp.

Zo enters, suitcase in her left hand, crumpled McDonald's bag in her right. "Hey," she greets him. She drops the suitcase on the floor. She does not approach him. Ethan watches as she takes in his shaved head.

"You're home so early," Ethan says. "I . . . I planned to have dinner ready." He watches himself lie.

"Yeah, they didn't make Alex do the last couple of tests," Zo explains. Her voice is more weary than angry. "I stupidly forgot the medicine, so by lunchtime, she couldn't focus on anything. The doctors said that by then they'd seen what they needed to see, and that—this is a quote, mind you—they're 'not in the torture business.'"

"Oh. Well, what else did they say?"

Zo glances at Alex. "Later," she says.

"But everything's okay?"

"Everything's okay. It is what it is." Zo crushes the McDonald's bag, lifts the lid from the trash can. She pauses. "Huh."

"What?" He knows what.

"My crock," she says. Just taking it in.

"Oh, that," he says. "Sorry, I was looking for something, and I knocked it down. Pizza cutter. I couldn't find the pizza cutter."

Yes, he is a liar. A monkey man lying from his monkey mouth. Look how casually he lies.

Zo drops the McDonald's bag on top of the broken ceramic, turns to Ethan. "Hon, I'm going to need you to take Alex out of the house for a little while."

Ethan touches his pocket, feels Evie's note through the denim. "Sure, in a little bit. I've got a couple of errands I need to run first."

"Please." Zo's voice is flat. She's not asking him to do this. She's telling him. It's like she somehow knows what he did last night, what he wanted to do, and now he owes her and they both know it.

Alex throws herself against Ethan a second time. "Mommy said you'd take me out for ice cream!" she says. She starts panting like a dog, then pumps her fist and chants. "Ice! Cream! Ice! Cream!"

"It's important, Ethan," Zo says. Ethan stares at her, tries to think.

Fine. Okay. There's a handmade ice-cream shop over by the Humphrey, one of those foodie places where they charge a thousand dollars a cone, or thereabouts. If he has to, he can make this work.

But for the record, he doesn't exactly feel amicable about it.

✦

Before leaving the house, he goes over the plan in his head:

Coneheads with Alex. Get the kid a massive bowl of ice cream, something that will last.

While she's eating, jog up to the Humphrey.

In the parking lot, find a blue Prius with New York plates. XTP-334.

Slide the note under a windshield wiper.

Slip away quickly, then return to Coneheads to pick up Alex.

The only thing that gives him pause is this: Isn't the whole world filled with hidden surveillance cameras these days? If so, might Evie, after discovering the note, ask to see security footage from the parking lot? Would she recognize him? Not likely. But is there some kind of facial recognition technology that might identify him? Is his image stored in a database somewhere, his features, like his thoughts, reduced to ones and zeroes?

Just how much of the twenty-first-century dystopian nightmare has made it to this corner of the Berkshires, anyway?

Sunglasses. Maybe he needs sunglasses. Or wait. No.

He picks up Zo's balaclava from the new sofa. Slips it into his back pocket.

"Okay, Alex," he calls. "Let's go! The ice cream train is leaving!"

Coneheads Ice Cream is locally made; the milk's from humanely raised grass-fed cows, everything certified organic, fair trade, sustainably sourced. Some of the flavors are ironic, like Wilbur at the County Fair (bacon bits and cotton candy suspended in strawberry ice cream), or All-American Breakfast (doughnut chunks and soda-bottle gummies in coffee-flavored ice cream). Others speak to the sort of earnest back-to-the-land purity that's accessible these days only for $7 a scoop: Clear Blue Sky (plain old blueberry), 'Tis a Gift to Be Simple (vanilla bean, hint of lavender, a wholesome nod to the Shaker community that once lived just a few miles from here), Spring Thaw (maple syrup with a touch of goat milk).

Behind the counter, a bored-looking Millennial watches videos on her iPhone. Ethan has to clear his throat twice before she looks up. "Dirty Leprechaun, please," Alex barks at the girl. Coneheads' version of mint chip.

The ice-cream girl sighs audibly, as if scooping ice cream isn't literally what she's being paid to do. She sets the phone down in slow motion. "Cup or cone?"

Ethan says "cup" exactly as Alex says "cone." The server looks back and forth between them, apparently decides that Alex is in charge. She lifts a cone, starts to scoop.

"Rainbow sprinkles," Alex tells the server. "*Lots* of rainbow sprinkles!"

"Sure, fine." Her tone implies the mere prospect of sprinkles is exhausting.

Next to the cash register is a sign, framed in acrylic: HARASSMENT OF OUR SERVERS WILL NOT BE TOLERATED. Ethan points to it. "What's up with this?"

"Why?" The girl lifts her eyes to his. "Do you plan to harass me?"

"I don't. No."

"Yeah, well. It's pretty bad sometimes."

He looks around. "But this is an ice-cream shop. For *families*."

"And?" The server hands Alex a towering cone.

And now that Alex is taking her first licks, Ethan no longer has time for conversation. "Listen," he tells the girl, "I'm just going to zip out while my daughter eats that cone. Quick errand. I'll be back before she's finished."

The girl raises one eyebrow.

"Five minutes," Ethan assures her. "Ten, tops."

And when she just stares back—she's an attitude problem on two legs, this one—Ethan opens his wallet, pulls out his last bill: $20. "This is all I've got," he says.

She examines the twenty. Then she shrugs, takes it, and stuffs it in the pocket of her cutoffs. She picks up her phone and starts playing her video again.

"Be right back, Alex," Ethan says. He kisses his daughter on the head. "You stay here and be good for the nice lady, okay?"

✦

ETHAN RESTS AGAINST a tree near the Humphrey parking lot. He catches his breath—he ran here, not in the shape he used to be—scans the cars.

There: Prius. Blue. New York plates, XTP-334. Bingo.

He slips the pink balaclava over his head, straightens it out. The acrylic's itchy against his skin. It traps his hot breath. He pulls the note out, gives one last look at his own shaking, left-handwriting in bright green.

> *EVIE EMERLING:*
>
> *I AM A FRIEND. WE ARE CONNECTED. I AM WRITING TO HELP YOU. THERE ARE THINGS YOU DON'T WANT REVEALED. WILL YOU TRUST ME ON THIS? DROP THE LAWSUIT. IF YOU DO ALL WILL BE WELL.*

He refolds the paper. Deep breath. He tells himself that when his Bränd check finally comes in, he'll donate a bunch of it to the women's shelter in Bettsbridge. Make sure some good comes of this.

He moves toward the Prius.

A voice behind him then. Impossible. "Daddy?"

He turns around, sees Alex standing there. Again, he has that strange sense of dissociation, like his daughter has split in two. She's at Coneheads—he just bribed the impudent twentysomething to watch her. But somehow, inexplicably, Alex is also *here,* her face crinkled in confusion. Like Schrödinger's cat, these mutually exclusive possibilities that are somehow, for the moment, equally true.

"Alex, I told you to wait."

"Yeah, but I dropped my cone. Just after you left. The lady said she'd make me another one, but you had to pay for it, so I followed you. You run fast, Daddy! And why are you wearing Mommy's dance mask? And can I have seven dollars?"

"I was cold," he says. Alex stands there in her shorts and T-shirt.

He pulls the mask up to his forehead. Leaves it there, absurdly. "Look," he pleads. "Just go back and tell the lady I gave her the last of my cash. Maybe she can pay for your cone from that."

Alex's jaw hardens. "Mommy said you'd get me ice cream."

Ethan digs in his pockets. He sees himself, a ridiculous animal, creature of flesh and fur, looking for money that he already knows is not there. Pink hat sticking up off the top of his near-bald head like a glow-in-the-dark condom covering only the tip.

Dickhead. He's become a literal dickhead.

Then a different voice: "Ethan?"

He turns around. Standing there is a college professor. A woman, middle-aged, wholly unfamiliar to him. How does she know his name? The woman's unusually stylish for an academic: in chic black attire and tortoiseshell sunglasses. Expensive-looking, those shades. The professor lifts them, squints a little. "Ethan . . . Frome?"

That's when it hits him: *Evie.*

Of course it's Evie. It's just a twenty-years-older version of Evie, that's all. Evie's aging like everyone else, time hurtling forward for her just as it is for Ethan. As soon as her features click into place, the years fall away entirely. Yes. There are Evie's slight freckles, the angle of her jaw, the telltale way she tucks a loose strand of hair behind her ear.

Evie hesitates, like perhaps she made a mistake, maybe she's confused, could be some other penis-man digging in his pockets for loose change.

"Evie? Evie . . . Emerling?" he says, as if he's not quite sure he remembers the name, as if her IMDB page isn't six miles long.

"Wow!" Evie laughs. "What are the chances?"

God, that smile of hers. A twelve-million-dollar smile, really.

Evie steps forward awkwardly, hugs him. One of those professional, "lean in at the shoulders but keep the torso at a distance and don't you fucking come near my pelvis" hugs. "What are you even doing here, Ethan? Do you teach college these days?"

"I, uh . . ."

I'm here to blackmail you, Evie.

Oh, nothing, just creep-stalking you in a ski-mask!

Warning you of a nefarious plan to ruin your career! That's all!

"We live nearby," Ethan explains. "My wife and I. Over in Starkfield. Wow, Evie. This is . . . such a crazy coincidence." He is stuffed full of lies. He is spewing lies. His blood and bones and organs and tendons: all of these things are built from lies on top of lies, which were constructed from yet more lies.

"I just finished up a play reading," Evie says. "I was just about to drive back to New York. Gosh, I almost didn't recognize you with that beard . . . you look terrific, Ethan."

He looks like a giant wiener, that's what he looks like. He reaches up to the top of his penis head, removes the balaclava, shoves it in his back pocket.

Evie glances at Alex, then back at Ethan.

"Oh. Uh, this is my daughter, Alex," he says. He turns to Alex, "And this is . . ."

Evie extends her hand. "I'm Evie," she says. "I'm an old friend of your dad's. It's lovely to meet you, Alex."

Alex blinks up at Evie. "You're pretty." Ethan feels his face flush with heat, as if he's the one who gave the compliment. Then Alex, oblivious, asks, "Do you like Coneheads ice cream?"

Evie smiles. "I've never tried Coneheads ice cream. Is it good?"

"Sooooo good!" Alex tells her. "You *have* to try the Dirty Leprechaun, it's the best flavor you'll ever have in a million trillion years. Except I dropped my cone, and my dad didn't bring enough money to buy me a new one, so now I don't get any."

Evie laughs. "Well, how about *I* get you some ice cream, then? I've got a few minutes before I have to get on the road. I'd love to try this Coneheads."

She's still so beautiful.

Sure, Evie's older, fine lines around her eyes. But once you get used to that, once your eyes adjust, account for the years that have

passed, she's somehow just as lovely, as she'd been back in the
'90s.

The girl behind the counter lifts her eyebrows in genuine surprise as soon as she sees Evie walk through the door. *That's right*,
Ethan thinks to himself, not without satisfaction. *Look who this ol'
dad brought to your shop: Evie Emerling. Weren't expecting that, were
you?*

Evie pays for the ice cream: another mammoth cone for Alex,
peewee dishes for the adults, Dirty Leprechauns all around. The
girl scoops more enthusiastically this time, passing herself off as a
moderately adequate server, while Alex babbles away like Evie's
her newfound best friend. Alex tells Evie about school, about Mr.
Pancake FuzzyPaws, about Hypatia. "She's *mostly* a good dog, except for all the times when she pees on the floor. We clean it up,
but sometimes when it rains, the whole house smells like pee."

Evie laughs. "Is she old?"

"Getting there, yeah," says Ethan. "Like most of us, I suppose."
Because surely Evie sees his lines, too, his middle-aged girth.

Alex bounces in her seat as she shovels another scoop in her
mouth. "We got the dog from the shelter—well, my parents did,
before they even had me. My mom says she has PTSD."

"The dog does," Ethan clarifies. "Not her mom."

Evie laughs. "What's her name?"

"Dog's name or my mom's?" Alex asks. And when Evie says,
both, Alex answers, "Hypatia and Zenobia."

"Dog, Mom, respectively," Ethan clarifies.

Alex is already popping the last of her cone into her mouth.
"Daddy, can I have the dance mask?"

Ethan ignores the request, but Alex ignores his ignoring.

"Daddy. Daddy. Daddy. I want the dance mask. Daddy. I know
you hear me. Daddy."

Fine. He pulls the balaclava from his back pocket. "Phone,"
commands Alex. She opens her palm, and when he hands this
over, too, she adds, "And earbuds."

Alex puts in the earbuds, then slips the balaclava over her head,
begins twirling around the ice-cream shop. Evie treats the whole

thing like it's the most normal behavior in the world. She turns back to Ethan. "Is your dog's name really Hypatia?"

"Yeah," Ethan says. "She's named after a Greek philosopher from about 400 B.C. . . ."

"I know who Hypatia is. Actually, I've always considered Hypatia to be history's first woman celebrity."

Ethan looks at her curiously, unsure of her meaning. Evie shrugs. "Everyone loved her, until they didn't. Then they stoned her to death."

Ethan coughs. "So you're doing that David Mamet play?" He catches himself, and adds, "I mean, I heard they were staging a Mamet reading this week."

Evie shakes her head. "Lauren Gunderson."

"Who?"

"Lauren Gunderson? She was the most produced playwright in America last year."

"Oh. No kidding. Excuse my ignorance, then."

"Well, it was supposed to be Mamet, but the organizers pulled his play."

"Why?"

"He slapped a twenty-five-thousand-dollar fine on any theater that held a post-show discussion of his work. A lot of people were pushing back against some of his messages during talkbacks, and I guess he didn't want to subject himself to that kind of criticism. So he issued the fine, and the theater canceled that reading, and we read Lauren's latest instead. It was terrific, actually. But tell me, Ethan, what are *you* up to these days?"

"Hashtag Dad Life, I guess. Breakfasts and laundry and teacher conferences."

"Well, your kid's fantastic."

He glances over: his kid, at this moment, looks like a miniature bank robber. She's moving her hips from one side to the other while making some martial-arts move with her fists.

"Well, she's *something,* anyway," Ethan says. "What she's *not* is easy."

Evie keeps her eyes on Alex. "Trust me. That's a good thing."

"Is it?" he asks. And he realizes that the question is real. He wants Evie to tell him, yes, it's a great thing, that someday the world will see and appreciate what he and Zo see on a good day, that there is room in this world for a girl who talks too much, who interrupts, who can't sleep and who struggles to read social cues, a girl who slaps Valentine stickers on classmates, and doesn't care about multiplication, and sings like Janis Joplin, and sometimes gets so angry that gray rings form beneath her eyes. He wants Evie to reassure him, to cast a definitive judgment, just as Maddy did the other night.

Yes, Alex is great. No, Ethan, you don't need to worry.

But there's no guarantee that Evie will answer the way he wants, and that's not her job anyway, so he blurts another question over the first one. "You uh . . . You ever see Randy out in L.A.?"

Evie says nothing, just keeps watching Alex dance.

"My old partner, I mean. Randy Riverstone. Remember him?"

And then: "Kind of a colorful guy, Randy."

Evie looks down, jabs her ice cream a few times with her spoon but does not take a bite. "I don't see Randy. No."

Is there some warning in her voice? *I don't know if you know what's happening, but if you do, back off.*

"Oh," Ethan says. "I just figured, you know, L.A. Anyway, he and I have mostly lost touch. Different worlds these days."

Don't worry. I don't know anything about anything.

Ethan shifts in his seat, glances around the shop. He can tell that the girl behind the counter is pretending not to listen in on their conversation. He lowers his voice a little. "So . . . what's it like being famous, anyway?" It's a dumb question, and maybe a rude one. Didn't she once have a stalker? Maybe the guy killed Evie's cat? Maybe that happened to someone else.

"Being famous . . ." says Evie. She hesitates, then says, "I'm very fortunate."

It's a practiced answer, and Ethan senses there's more she wants to say. "But . . ." he prompts.

"But, to be honest, it also feels like being wrong all the time.

It's like . . . if I dress for the cameras, people say I'm trying too hard. But when I dress for myself, I'm frumpy, a slob. I did one interview where I talked about the books I love; some people got mad at me because they didn't like those particular books. Other people said I was putting on airs for talking about books at all. And then there was still another group that insisted I was lying, because I'm clearly too stupid to read books. It feels like I'm always doing one thing wrong, or another thing wrong, and whichever it is, people insist on telling me." She shakes her head. "I shouldn't complain. I really am incredibly lucky, and I know it. But on a bad day, and I have plenty, being famous feels like the worst voices in your head came to life and started a Twitter account."

Ripples of sadness. Ethan can feel them coming off of Evie, too, just as they did from the trees, the grass, last night. Funny: you'd think that Evie Emerling and the guy in the UPS Store, and maybe even Ethan himself would have nothing in common, but they all have sorrow in common.

Alex comes over, rips her mask off, pauses the music. "Here's what I don't understand." She plops down on her seat, peers into Ethan's ice-cream bowl, sees it's empty, then frowns. Evie slides her own bowl, still almost entirely untouched, across the table to Alex, who digs right in. "Why didn't Elphaba pretend she was going along with the Wizard? If she'd pretended to be on his side, she could have fought the power from the *inside*."

"Alex, not everyone wants to talk about *Wicked* all the time," Ethan warns.

But Evie leans in toward Alex. "You know, I've wondered that too. I suspect Elphaba knew that fighting from the inside would never be enough. Because some people need to see others being brave, in order to become brave themselves. Or maybe it's even more basic than that. Maybe if they never *see* anyone standing for what's right, they won't know the difference between right and wrong."

Alex takes a bite of Evie's ice cream, pondering. "But it didn't *work.* Because people didn't think Elphaba *was* brave or right. They thought she was wicked and sent her away."

Evie nods. "That's true. I guess that's the risk she had to take. It's a predicament."

"It's a dilemma," Alex responds.

"A conundrum," says Evie.

"A pickle," says Alex.

"It's a quandary." Ethan laughs. It strikes him how absurd this all is. He's at an ice-cream shop with one of the world's most bankable superstars. Twelve million for her last film, and here she is, discussing with his daughter the morality decision matrix of the Wicked Witch of the West.

When Alex finishes Evie's ice cream, she offers Evie one of the earbuds. Evie takes it, then the two of them dance, sharing some song he can't hear. Ethan watches them move. It's like Evie, too, is split into multiple parts. She's in front of him now, this midlife version of herself, no longer ethereal, maybe, but still gorgeous. At the same time, he can also see all those other Evies: the barely-out-of-girlhood version who first walked into the Bränd office. The flickering ingenue who captivated New York in the "Heaven Is a Gal named Audrey" campaign. The woman who stood with him in Columbus Circle, telling him she wished he would move to L.A. All those versions from the movie posters. The Evie who understood that Randy's audition script was wrong. The Evie who read it anyway. And another Evie too: the one who exists only in a life he did not choose. All these Evies are together, all at once, like a mirror image reflecting toward infinity, except that every reflection is a little different.

Ethan notices the server behind the counter pick up her phone, pretend to read something, but Ethan can tell by the angle: she's trying to get a video of Evie dancing. He clears his throat, shoots the girl a warning look.

Just this once, let the woman be. Let her dance without the rest of the world offering up their opinion on it.

◆

ETHAN AND ALEX walk Evie back to her Prius. Alex skips ahead, nearly running over an octogenarian shuffling along the street in bright-green chinos.

"Alex!" Ethan hollers at her. "Careful!"

"Sorry!" Alex glances back at the man without slowing down, and only narrowly avoids running into a parking sign.

"See what I mean?" Ethan says. "I can barely keep her from running into large inanimate objects. How am I supposed to help her navigate a world like ours?"

"Well," Evie says. "I never got the chance to be a parent. But I'm pretty sure you're just supposed to love her. Be there for her if she gets hurt." A pause. "*When* she gets hurt."

At the car, Evie gives Alex a generous hug. "I'm so, so glad I met you, Alex!"

Evie hugs Ethan, too, warmer than before. "It's been really nice to see you, Ethan. You seem happy. I'm glad. You were always one of the good ones."

WHEN HE AND Alex get home, Ethan finally looks at his phone.

Randy: *how did it go?*
Randy: *????*

And then a few seconds later:

Randy: *???????????????*

And then:

Randy: *E, YOU ARE KILLING ME HERE.*

Ethan thinks about standing at the parking lot, absurdly, note in his hand. The ultimate weenie, world's biggest prick. He sets the phone down on the kitchen counter, walks outside to the far edge of the yard. He pulls the B-movie ransom note from his pocket, stares at it. Already, it looks unrelated to him, an artifact from another world. This can't possibly be his.

He tears the whole thing into pieces, holds the fragments in his hand until he feels a gust of wind. Then he opens his palm. The torn paper scatters, a bad idea dissolving into nothing.

It's time, he knows, to talk to his wife.

2 2

He finds Zo in the bedroom, hand-lettering a poster-board sign. She's only got the first letter down: a *B*.

Blackmail, Ethan thinks.

Botched.

Better off, probably.

Bad karma. Seriously bad.

Zo sets the Sharpie down. "Thank you for taking Alex out of the house, Ethan."

He nods. "Everything okay?"

Zo shrugs. "Sort of. Listen, Alex doesn't know this yet, but I just told Maddy she had to leave our home."

So Zo's seen it all apparently, everything he's done, everything he wanted to do, everything he almost did. She knows the whole of it, of course she does. Zo's always been smarter, more observant, than he, why did he think he could get away with anything?

"But where will she go?" he asks.

"Frankly, that's her problem." Zo picks up the marker again, begins moving her hand over her poster board, up and down, up and down. A downward curve, then up again.

U. This letter is a *U.*

BU, she's writing.

Buffoon, maybe.

Bungled: absolutely everything.

Bullshit, this is fucking bullshit.

"I don't think it's Maddy you're mad at, Zo."

His wife presses her lips together, begins tracing out a new let-ter. A straight vertical line. She's like Madame Defarge and her knitting right now. Zo and her poster board, writing messages about the revolution, inscrutable to most. Or to him, anyway.

"This is about me, right?" he asks.

Zo lifts her eyes. "You think this is about you, Ethan?"

"About me and Maddy . . . having dinner or whatever?"

Her hand freezes in the middle of making a right-facing bubble. The next letter is a *P* or another *B,* maybe. "This is not about your little infatuation, or whatever it is."

So there it is. All this time, she *was* watching him, making men-tal notes. Waiting for just the right time to spring it on him.

Zo returns to the poster, then adds, "But I do hope your eve-ning together was, ah, a *trip.*"

That last word lands. He swallows. "So you know, then. About the mushrooms."

"I know about the mushrooms, yes."

But how?

"It's not such a big deal," he tells her. "Did you know that Har-vard research shows mushrooms are a breakthrough for PTSD and anxiety? There's this one study with cancer patients, and they found—" He can't exactly remember what they found, actually, or if Maddy ever finished telling him.

Zo keeps her eye on the poster. "If you want to know the truth, Ethan, that's the worst part of Maddy leaving, because Maddy's been my supplier, too. And no, this is definitely not about you wanting to sleep with her, or who knows, maybe you already have."

"I *don't* want . . . We never . . ." Then the first part of Zo's sen-tence sinks in. "Wait. Your *supplier?*"

"Yes, Ethan." Eyes on him now, a look he can't read. "I've done mushrooms. Nice to meet you."

She looks down, finishes the letter. It's an *R.*

B-U-R

Burden.

Burned the hell out.

Bury me now, just fucking put me in the ground already, will you?

"So, like . . . Maddy's your *dealer*, Zo?"

"Was."

He thinks about what Maddy said last night: *It's possible, Ethan, that you and your wife don't exactly tell each other everything.* He understands that he is talking to a stranger right now, that he doesn't know Zo at all.

That's all over now.

He waits in silence while Zo finishes her poster. Finally, she looks up, sighs. "You really want to know what this is about?" He nods. She gets up, moves to the bedroom, leaving him alone with the sign.

BURN IT ALL DOWN, it says.

Zo returns with her laptop, open to a YouTube page. Some video queued up and ready to go. The title: "HEY, PROFFESSOR: HERE'S WHAT THE WORLD THINKS OF YOU!"

Zo sits down next to Ethan, hits Play.

He can't make sense of what this is. A bunch of faces. Men, women, black, white, young, old. Mostly English-speakers, a few subtitled phrases. All of them are saying more or less the same thing.

"A liar."

"Definitely a liar."

"She's a skanky liar is what she is."

"*Miente*"

"*Tā shuo huang.*"

"That rachet-ass woman ain't nothing but a lying bitch."

"She's a lying liar who tells dirty lies."

And then, incongruously, there's Maddy's face on the screen, still with her long blue hair. She's got a wry smile. She's in her bedroom, the one right here, in Starkfield.

"She's a fuckin' liar, that's what she is," Maddy says.

Zo hits Pause, freezes Maddy's face.

By now, Ethan understands: they're talking about the woman from the hearing. The professor, the one who accused the Supreme Court nominee of assault. This film, posted yesterday, already has 1.9 million views, a near-equal number of thumbs-up and thumbs-down ratings.

"This video was made by a guy named Christian Ariosopher," Zo explains. "Not his real name, but that doesn't matter. The kid's a Nazi. Or alt-right leader, or *far-right provocateur,* or white nationalist, or free-speech activist, or whatever it is they're calling Nazis these days."

She types the guy's name in, brings up a Wikipedia page, passes her laptop to Ethan. At the top of the page is a guy in his late twenties. Good-looking kid: clean-shaven, dimples. Preppy look to him, Brooks Brothers type. Ethan scans the Wikipedia subheads: Role in Gamergate. Inciting Violence on College Campuses. Doxxing of Rape Victims. He clicks back to the video, watches it again.

Anything. Maddy's profile said she'd do anything.

"How did you find this?" he asks.

"Through that site of hers."

"Ten-Spot." Of course Zo knows about Ten-Spot too. Jesus.

"Yeah, that. As soon as she told me about it, I decided to make my own account, started following her. Not a huge thing, I just wanted to keep my eye on it, you know? So every time she had a transaction, I got a notification. I'd do a little digging about the person. I mostly didn't care, I just wanted to make sure she wasn't putting Alex in any danger, that's all. But this." Zo shakes her head. "I just can't believe she'd do this."

Ethan knows: He might as well have fucked Maddy, because this, for Zo, is the uncrossable line. Only eight words, *She's a fuckin' liar, that's what she is,* but there will be no going back. Not for Zo.

"When?" Ethan asks.

Zo closes her computer softly. "The video was posted early this morning. I don't know when she recorded it."

"No, I mean when does Maddy have to leave?"

"I gave her until tomorrow morning to be out of the house."

He nods, and they sit in silence for a long time. Alex's voice, singing, drifts in from time to time. Finally, Ethan says, "So can you tell me what happened in the appointment? At Children's?"

"Honestly, they didn't tell us anything we didn't know already. Alex is impulsive. Inattentive. Oppositional. Her executive functioning and working memory are for shit."

"And?"

"Well, there's some skills training they recommend. Memory games and such. Expensive, all of it. But even with that support, she is who she is. She's going to have a harder time with some things, in school, and also in life. Honestly, that's it. I was like, 'Tell us something we don't already know.' "

He nods. Lets this sink in.

After a while, Zo says, her voice quiet, "Ethan, do you remember when I lost my cool the other night?"

He waits. There could be so many times.

"After Parents' Night. When Alex refused to go upstairs, and she just kept flopping around on our bed?"

He nods. He does remember. Zo's reaction to Alex, like all her reactions to everything these days, seemed out of proportion to the circumstance. *Opposite and amplified.* "It was late," he reassures Zo. "You were tired. I lose it with Alex all the time."

"No. You don't. Not like I do. But . . . can I tell you what I was thinking about as I watched her flopping around like that?"

"A jumping bean? A fish out of water?"

She smiles sadly. "I wish. No. I was thinking about this game I heard about. It's called Rodeo. You ever hear of it?"

He hasn't.

"It goes like this: a guy goes out to a bar, picks up a woman who seems lonely. He tells her she's beautiful, funny. Whatever it is he has to say to get her to come home with him. They start fooling around. Then as soon as she's naked, he ties her arms and legs to the bed. That's when he calls in his buddies. They all take turns trying to fuck her while she flails. Whoever can ride on top of her the longest as she resists wins the rodeo. You know, a fun game that guys can play together."

Ethan feels a wave of nausea. At this game she's describing. At the fact that Zo thought about this game near their child. He doesn't want that game—even the idea of it—anywhere near Alex. "Zo, how do you even *know* about something like that?"

"It happened to Jackie. Well, almost. The guys were so drunk that she was able to get away. But she says it feels like they're still coming for her, all these years later. Like they're right behind her, and they're ready to drag her back."

Ethan pictures the version of Jackie he knows: wire-thin and running like hell through Starkfield, her face hard as stone.

Zo closes her eyes. "The thing is, Ethan, Alex is going to go out there into a world where stuff like that happens *all the time*. And I don't know how to warn her. I don't know how to teach her everything she needs to know: who she should be wary of, how to keep herself safe. There's not enough information I could possibly give her that could protect her. I *love* Alex, love how fearless she is, how unself-conscious. But I'm scared for her, too, I really am. I'm scared all the time."

Ethan nods. He is too. But maybe not enough.

"Some days, it feels like I'm trapped inside a soundproof building," Zo continues. "And Alex is outside, I'm watching her, and she's moving through all of these dangers, they're right next to her, and they're coming for her, and she doesn't even *see* them. I keep trying to warn her. I'm banging on the window and screaming her name, but she can't hear any of it, and I just have to watch and hope. I swear to God, sometimes I think I'm going crazy. I'm trying so, so hard to stay sane."

Ethan sits there for a while, lets this sink in. He thinks about the furniture she's been buying, the carpets and throw pillows.

There are worse ways, he supposes, to try to stay sane.

Zo seems to understand what he's thinking. "I have so little control. Over anything. All I can do is shake a sign, and howl my rage at the sky, and spend money we don't have on home decor we don't need. But I tell you what: when someone in my home does business with a Nazi like Christian Fucking Ariosopher, when someone I live with deliberately contributes to making the world a more terrible place, I can draw a line. I can ask that person to leave. That is one tiny thing I can do."

UPSTAIRS, ETHAN RAPS on Maddy's door.

Maddy throws it open so hard it makes a dent in the wall. *"What?"* Her suitcase is on the bed behind her, and clothes are strewn all over the floor.

Ethan thinks about those Rainbow Seed Rules.

Tell the truth.

Listen as much as you talk.

"So . . . this is a really big deal," he says. "To Zo."

"Yeah." Maddy's voice has gone flat, a little snippy. Pissy. Like a teenager, like a kid. "I can kinda *tell*."

Ethan takes a deep breath, leans against the door frame. *Assume good intentions.* "I don't think I'm going to be able to fix this, Mad."

She lifts her eyes to his. Her purple lips twist into something ugly. "Don't worry. I already knew you couldn't."

A dig. She's calling him weak, ineffectual.

Maddy turns away from him, starts rolling up clothes, pitching them into her suitcase. "It's fine," Maddy says, a little less bitterly. "I contacted an old buddy in Burlington. Maybe I'll give Vermont a try."

"Vermont." He smiles. "I can kind of see you there."

"But I don't know. I'm thinking that if I can scrounge the cash, I'll head out to Los Angeles."

"L.A., wow. City of Angels. Quite a place, L.A."

The last time Ethan was in L.A. was a dozen years ago. Randy had scored invites to the Oscars. He'd called Ethan last-minute to say he had an extra ticket, and did Ethan want to fly out? *I want you to see what you helped start,* Randy had said.

So Ethan had flown to California, paying a nauseating sum of money for a room at the Four Seasons. There, he rode in an elevator with Alan Arkin, sat in the lobby in a rented tuxedo watching makeup artists wheel carts filled with cosmetics and brushes and hair dryers and spray bottles in and out of the elevators. When the time came, Ethan sat in a limousine with Randy and a bunch of strangers. He clinked his glass against theirs and listened to them talk about campaigns they'd done on behalf of films he hadn't seen. Outside the limousine, the streets were lined with chain-link fences, the crowd at least five people deep, everyone craning their necks. The Westboro Baptist Church was in that crowd, too, shaking signs that said GOD H8S HOLLYWOOD and YOU'RE GOING TO HELL and YOUR SINS HAVE DOOMED AMERICA, and all the while, there had been a buzzing in the background, some kind of low-grade hum, like a swarm of mosquitoes.

Ethan had been the first to step out of the limo. When he did, the crowd erupted into anticipatory cheers, then instantly quieted. They'd expected a star, but they could see he was a nobody, he was nothing, and that's when he understood that the mosquito buzz was, in fact, a fleet of helicopters, circling overhead with cameras trying to catch views of somebody famous, anybody but him.

That night, a toilet at the Kodak Theater exploded, sending filthy toilet water all over someone's gown; Randy had laughed when he heard. "Nobody important," he said—the mother of someone nominated in the short-doc category, the category for which Zo had heard a rumor, many years ago, that she might be shortlisted, then wasn't. Then Randy went off to his seat (rear orchestra) and Ethan to his (third mezzanine), and for the rest of the night, he sat alone among strangers, watching the awards from so far away it was like watching a dollhouse version of an award show. Halfway through, Randy texted him to say he was at the bar on the first level, and Ethan should come downstairs to join him. But Ethan's ticket didn't provide Level One access, and Randy didn't respond to his texts, so in the end, Ethan had finished out the ceremony at a nosebleed bar, talking to some kid bartender about his walk-on roles on *Law & Order*. Ethan left for the airport from there, and flew home on a redeye. That was the last time he'd seen Randy in person.

"I dunno," Ethan says to Maddy now. "L.A. is weird."

She shrugs. "Or who knows, I might even decide to stick around this stupid town. Arlo says that after he gets his recreational license, he's going to start an apprentice program for new growers. So maybe I'll get really rich farming weed."

He tries to imagine running into Maddy on Main Street—the Coffee Depot in the morning, maybe, as she heads off to work at an Apple Store that doesn't sell anything electronic.

Maybe it's not fair, but he hopes she'll stay away.

Ethan sits quietly, listening to Alex's voice from some distant corner of the house: she's moved on to singing a mash-up of *Wicked* and her pyroclastic-flow rap.

> *Vesuvius erupts!*
> *It's defying gravity*
> *Ash fills the air!*
> *It's defying gravity*
> *Everyone, everywhere!*
> *Defying gravity!*

Ethan looks out the window. The sun is already down below the hills, the light everywhere growing gray, too quickly, like a slow-mo version of what those fuckers in Pompeii must have seen.

After a while, Maddy says, "I didn't have a choice. Just for the record." Her voice is still flat, but less hostile. "I know you think it's super-crummy or whatever, but it's not like I knew what the guy was doing. I was hired to say a single sentence, that's all I knew. Whole thing took about twenty seconds. I didn't know what it would be *for*."

He nods. Lets that sink in. "Did you know who he was?"

She shrugs. "I mean, I'd heard of him."

"Well," Ethan says. "Anyway, I don't think there's any convincing Zo."

"Zo's a bitch," Maddy says.

"But *ten dollars,* Mad." The words don't quite come out as he intends them. The specific amount of money isn't the point. The point is . . . well, it has something to do with what he experienced last night, the way all those boundaries between people, between categories—self, others; past, present; here, out there—just sort of disintegrated.

"It wasn't the ten bucks, Ethan," Maddy insists. "It was the algorithms."

And when he doesn't understand, she explains. "If I break a contract even once, it tanks my ratings. Those ratings feed the algorithms, which means I fall off the list. Just like that, I'm not a Verified Ten-Spotter anymore, which means I don't appear on the first page of search returns, I don't appear on the second page, I don't show up *anywhere*. My whole profile gets fucking buried, and nobody ever finds me, and that's it. I *vanish*, might as well not even *exist* as far as the site goes. And, poof, there goes my income."

"You could have explained to them why you needed to break the contract."

"Them? Who's *them*, Ethan?"

"The people who run Ten-Spot. Customer service, I don't know."

"There *is* no them. There's no 1-800 number with sites like this. There's no contact information for anyone, no human resource departments, what world do you think we're living in here? You think I can explain to *computer code* that sure, I broke a contract, but hey, my reasons were righteous? The algorithms don't give a shit about right and wrong. They're soulless, that's their whole *point*."

"Well, then get off Ten-Spot, Mad."

"Right. Sure, okay, thanks for the tip, Dad."

The sarcasm. The condescension. Dismissing him like that. Pointing out, what? That he's old? Like old is something you *choose*, something you *are*, instead of something that happens to you against your will? As if Maddy and everyone she knows won't someday look around and, like Rip Van Winkle, no longer recognize the world they see?

"You know what?" he snaps. "All that stuff people say about your generation? They're not wrong."

"Whatever, bro."

"You have all these expectations, like life's just gonna—"

Maddy snaps, "What are you *talking about*, Ethan? What are you even *saying*? 'My generation,' as you call us, expect *nothing,* we've never been able to expect anything. Not to be able to go to school without being shot in the fucking face, or to learn anything that wouldn't appear on a standardized test. We didn't expect to be able to pay for college without racking up a quarter of a million dollars in student loans that everyone knew we'd *never be able to pay back,* or that anyone in power will ever listen to us unless we happen to work for Monsanto or Bank of America. We expect floods and wildfires and endless wars and dystopian hellscapes, and *that's it.*"

Floods and wildfires and endless wars and dystopian hellscapes. Ethan thinks about the moment last night, when he understood—or convinced himself—that humans wouldn't be around much longer. He wonders now: Is this what it looks like when people lose their faith? Is this the world that emerges when a society, a nation, a species, gives up on itself?

"I'm serious," Maddy says. "You laughed when I told you I was never going to settle down. But you know what? It's not a *choice,* because I'm never going to be able to *afford* to settle down. You think I'm going to be able to afford a *house*? Or to have kids? I'm twenty-six, I'm more than a hundred thousand dollars in debt for a degree I never got and that wouldn't have mattered anyway. Back in Colorado, I sold plasma for cash. Ten-Spot *helps.* It gives me back a tiny bit of control. So, yeah. I accepted a contract to say one sentence, and by the time I understood what it was for, it was already too late. You want better? Then maybe *your* generation should have left a world that's a little less fucked."

Maddy's not wrong, he knows. But she's also not entirely right either. It's like Zo saying she was arrested for speaking up without explaining the context. Like Mr. McCuttle saying that Alex was struggling at the Rainbow Seed School, without mentioning that Shreya Greer-Williams was pressuring him to kick her out, to make room for some other, easier kid. Like Ethan telling Jarrett at the UPS Store that Elastic Waist didn't exactly like him, without explaining more about how they knew each other. Like Dr. Ash promoting some studies over others. Or Evie Emerling's audition tapes. These things aren't untruths, but they aren't exactly truths, either. They're truth twisted inside out, turned into whatever evidence you need in the Choose Your Own Reality game that the world has become.

And, sitting here with Maddy screaming at him, he realizes: he's got some of his own half-truths too.

HE REMEMBERS A different hotel. This was years before, when Bränd was still based in New York, when Ethan's life felt like pure possibility. They were pitching an indie movie studio way the hell out in Irvine, California. Randy had flown the whole team out—by this point, the staff included a receptionist, a graphic designer, a PR assistant, and a crusty old office manager, in her fifties and thrice-divorced, named Flo—to make Bränd look bigger than it actually was.

They'd pitched a marketing campaign for a new horror film. A stupid movie, set in an eerie forest of living dolls. Randy had dazzled the studio with Bränd's plans. Sure, Bränd would do the usual branded billboards and web ads, that's fine, anyone could do that. But they'd also prime the market by creating six straight months of *unbranded* creepiness: Unexplained air drops of plastic baby-doll parts, pink limbs and blinking eyes raining down from the sky. Ancient dolls with missing limbs appearing mysteriously on hundreds of doorsteps with no explanation (they'd target celebrities, influencers, folks with unusually large platforms). Performers dressed as giant dolls wandering the sides of highways, or metropolitan train stations.

All of these things would happen before the movie was announced, so that by the time anyone saw the trailer, the world was ready for full doll horror.

By the end of the pitch, the studio was drawing up the paperwork.

The campaign would turn out to be a disaster: one of the doll parts that fell from the sky would smack a sixty-six-year-old woman on the head; there was a dubious concussion, and an all-too-real lawsuit. Several of the influencers Bränd had targeted with dolls had previous run-ins with stalkers; they'd taken the dolls on their stoop to mean that these stalkers had returned. One of the doll performers turned out to have been on the newly formed sex-crime registry, something it hadn't even occurred to Randy or Ethan to check.

But that night, celebrating in the hotel room, the only thing they knew was this: Bränd had done it. They'd landed their first movie studio. They were, at last, on their way.

Randy had ordered room service, and gathered the Bränd team into his suite for a toast. He was freshly showered, wearing only a pair of shorts, talking a mile a minute about leveraging the deal, catapulting forward, infinity and beyond, he was already looking at leases, they'd be on the West Coast next year, maybe even by fall, Bränd's sensibilities are more Hollywood than Madison Avenue anyway. When room service arrived, it was Ethan who answered the door. He greeted the hotel staffer—a young woman, in slacks and a black vest, her hair pulled back into a bun. The woman handed Ethan the bill and wheeled the tray in.

Ethan had barely put pen to paper to sign his name before she was rushing out the door. No thank you, no goodbye. She hadn't even stopped to take the receipt.

Ethan turned around, confused, and there was Randy: standing on the sofa, shorts around his ankles, nothing underneath. His arms were spread wide like Jesus on the cross. "Behold the new kings!" he bellowed after the departed hotel worker, the same phrase he loved to shout in college.

The others were laughing—everyone, even the women. Flo had thrown a pillow at Randy's naked form. "You asshole," she'd said as Randy hopped to the floor and began doing a stumbling victory lap around the hotel suite, shorts still at his ankles. Everyone agreed: yes, Randy *was* an asshole. He was a hilarious, unpredictable asshole who was going to make them all really fucking rich.

Now, two decades later, Ethan sits on Maddy's bed, her words turning over in his ears. *You want better? Then maybe* your *generation should have left a world that's a little less fucked.*

Ethan imagines Starkfield post-Maddy: no more evening walks, no more feeling whatever it is he's been feeling lately. Alive, maybe. Distracted from his own tedium, his lonely slog.

"I liked having you here," he says. And it strikes him that maybe that's as true as anything ever gets. You meet someone, you connect with them. They brighten your world for a little while. They shake you up, *wake* you up, make you laugh when you need it, remind you that you're alive. And then they're gone, and you're left alone with your own life.

Which isn't, it turns out, how you had hoped.

THE ONES WHO tell themselves stories, and believe them. The good guys, the affable ones, the ones whom everyone loves. The ones for whom it is enough to not be one of the Worst.

The ones who aren't wrong about that. It is enough, nearly every time.

2 3

ETHAN AND ZO take Alex out for dinner—anywhere she chooses. She picks Dunkin' Donuts, so the three of them huddle together in a plastic booth, under too-bright lights, eating egg-and-cheese sandwiches wrapped in foil. Alex tells Zo about meeting Evie. Zo doesn't ask what they were doing up at the Humphrey. She doesn't say much at all. Ethan looks over toward the bright racks of bulging donuts, more like a pop-art painting than anything edible.

If Maddy's there when they get home, she doesn't make any noise. Her door remains closed.

Ethan gets Alex to bed, and then he gets her to bed again. Alex sings. She leaps out of bed and does her Janis Joplin impression and wears him out as she always does. Ethan thinks about how, right at that moment, a grown woman is plotting against Alex, scheming to push her out of the Rainbow Seed School, and it will probably work, and the kid has no idea, because how could she? She's an eleven-year-old with impulse-control issues, an eleven-year-old who can't keep track of socks or complete a single math problem without distraction, an eleven-year-old who's been definitively diagnosed as someone who will have a harder time in this world.

He wishes he could press Pause, give Alex just a little while longer to stay safe, protected by their love, their care.

◆

TONIGHT, WHEN ETHAN enters his bedroom, Zo looks up. "So, they're expecting a big crowd tomorrow," she tells him. She bites her lip. "Maybe really big."

"That's what you wanted, right?"

"No. I don't know. Honestly, I never expected the whole thing to explode the way it has. Now strangers are fighting online about my arrest. I'm either a communist or a fascist or a narcissist or a snowflake, or I should run for Senate. Also, I might not even be real. And people keep asking me to talk at the rally. To 'speak my truth.'"

A pause. "Will you?"

"I don't know. What would I say? I wanted to feel like I was *doing* something, speaking truth to power, bringing attention to a cause that matters. Or who knows. Maybe I just wanted to feel like *I* mattered. But you were right, Ethan: none of this should have been about me."

And now that Zo's said the thing he wanted to hear—*You were right, Ethan*—it doesn't feel very good at all.

"Anyway," she finally says. "I was selfish, and I made everything worse, and now I'm in over my head. But I'm not sure I want to say that to the crowd."

She glances back down at her phone, bites her lip. He checks his own phone, but the only thing on his screen is a message from Randy: *FINE, FUCK YOU THEN.*

"Can I ask you something, Zo?" he asks. And when she nods, he tries to figure out how to ask the thing he wants to know. "Is there . . . Did something . . ." He wants to ask her how personal the Supreme Court accusations are to her, if perhaps there are things that happened to Zo, too, things she has never told him. But maybe the question is tautological. Maybe the mere fact of asking is proof that he cannot understand. So finally, he goes to his drawer, pulls out the scraps of paper he'd salvaged. *The ones who* . . . "What are these?"

"Those. Oh. It was this idea I had," she tells him. "For a book."

"A book?"

She nods.

"You want to write books?"

"Maybe. I don't know. I wanted to write *this* book, anyway. Except it was never really a book. Honestly, it wasn't even an idea for a book. It was more of just . . . an urge. Words that kept popping into my head. So I wrote them down figuring once I saw them on paper, I'd know what to write next. But they never went anywhere. I guess they were just lists, really."

He takes this in. A book.

"Stupid, I guess," she adds. "But it seemed like a good idea at the time."

It seemed like a good idea at the time. That's what he'd said to Maddy just the other night. He'd been talking about moving to Starkfield, him and Zo. But he could have been talking about so many things: being out there with Maddy in the first place, the note to Evie, all the dubious parenting choices he's made. And going further back: tying his own fate to Randy's, deferring again and again to Randy's judgment, simply because Randy was lucky enough to make everything look easy. All those moments, all those decisions, big and small, which seemed once to make sense but which unraveled with time. Maybe life is just one grand unraveling, like pulling the loose thread of a sweater until all you're left with is a single strand.

And then along comes one of the Fates with her scissors.

Zo smiles. "Ethan, did you really do mushrooms with Maddy?"

"I did," Ethan answers. "Did *you* really do mushrooms with Maddy?"

"Not with her," Zo says. She sits up a little straighter. "But with her mushrooms, yeah. A couple of times, actually. Jackie sent around an article that said they're good for anxiety. So a bunch of us decided to do them together. Just one more attempt to get through these crazy times."

He takes that in. Zo sitting around with her witch friends, tripping her brains out by day, then going to bed with him that night without saying a word. Maybe she felt then like he does now—like something profound is fading into memory. "Where did you do them?"

"At Vicky's. The painter? You went to her art show last year, remember? She lives on a hundred and twenty acres out by Lang-ford Road. We all met one morning in August and spent the day wandering the woods and just . . . I dunno, *looking* at things. Elaine—you know, the older witch?—was our guide."

Elaine. Elastic Waist. Her name is Elaine, and she was his wife's psychedelic guide, and there is so much in this world that can still surprise him. "I wonder," he says, "if in some language, there's a word for two people having the same experience, but separately. The Sharing Room, maybe."

Zo smiles. "Or Marriage."

It's some sort of offering, this. An acknowledgment, perhaps, of a truth that neither of them has said aloud. Maybe just that it's hard. That marriage is hard sometimes.

"Ethan, I have to tell you something." Something about Zo's voice, the pause that follows. The way she looks down, swallows, steeling herself.

An affair. It must be.

Ethan pictures the whole thing: some progressive activist dude more in touch with his inner Bono than Ethan is. Maybe it's some guy she met at the Women's March in D.C., a man so secure that he's not embarrassed to put on a pink hat and shake those signs. Or maybe it's not a man at all.

Either way, the entire story takes shape in Ethan's mind in a fraction of a second: the exchange of numbers, the texts, then wink emojis, then flirtatious GIFs, and then real-life meetings.

Ethan takes a deep breath. He will be understanding. He will try, anyway. He will explain the whole fidelity-as-a-window the-ory, and maybe Zo will cry, maybe she will say that she just needed a little bit of fresh air. He will tell her about what the jackal said, the warning, *That's all over now*.

Will Ethan forgive her? He will. He's pretty sure he will any-way.

But also: How could she?

But also, also: Why *shouldn't* she? After all, as long as they're being honest, wouldn't *he* have had an affair, given the chance? He wants to say no, he wouldn't, but of course he almost did, just last night.

All of these thoughts pass in a flash. It doesn't take more than a second or two for his whole world to branch out like a river into tributaries, like an artery into capillaries, all those possibilities forking and re-forking, a hundred visions and revisions, each carrying him toward some different ending of their shared story.

"I got fired," Zo says. "From the Lionel Trilling project."

This is so not what he expected to hear that it takes him a few seconds to understand. "Fired? When?"

She looks down at the bed, picks at a loose thread. "About three months ago. They said they wanted to go with someone who had a 'fresher' voice."

Three months ago. Just after Maddy arrived.

"They gave the job to some kids in Detroit. College dropouts. Maddy's age, tops, but somehow they're already filmmakers *and* web designers *and* they make video games. Oh, and they're also a hip-hop group."

"Huh. Hard to compete with that, I guess." He's making a joke, but there's not much mirth in it. Without Bränd, and without Lionel Trilling, and without Dr. Ash, and without something else— some mysterious other project that could miraculously find them here in Starkfield, some idea for the Next Big Thing (which would be what, exactly? What does the world need that it doesn't already have?), they're going to have to scrape together a living from tiny, crappy jobs, whatever they can get, not unlike the way his parents did after the factories closed and the world they'd counted on vanished for good.

No more home construction.

No more Rainbow Seed tuition.

No more lives expanding. Only contraction from here, life's possibilities growing narrower and narrower, until all that is left is a dot, a singularity, no mass or width or depth or shape, and then nothing.

Ethan knows this is the part where he should tell her about

Bränd. But as he's trying to form the words, Zo says, "I'm sorry, Ethan. I'm really, really sorry."

"Well, it's just one project."

"I don't just mean the Trilling thing," she says. "I mean everything. I'm sorry about everything. You are a good husband and a great dad, and I know things are hard for us right now. I just feel so angry all the time—I'm angry about the Supreme Court, I'm angry about the White House, I'm angry about the nonstop stream of horrors that fill my timeline, I'm angry about stupid little things that aren't even important. There are days I can't even think straight, I'm so furious. But I'm trying. I want you to know that: I really am trying. None of this is personal. I'm doing the best I can."

He imagines himself holding these words like they were a physical thing. He imagines all the truths that compose them: that nothing about this, their life together, their marriage, the fact that maybe *That's all over now,* is personal. Zo, his wife, is doing the best she can. Maybe he is too.

It's not quite infinite truth—it's more like a fever breaking—but for the moment, it is enough. He nods, and when that doesn't seem sufficient, he reaches for Zo's hand. Her fingers curl around his, tighter than he expects.

They sit together like that on the bed, holding hands—not so much husband and wife as two human beings who've known each other a very, very long time.

He doesn't know who leans forward first; it's almost like neither of them does, as if what happens next isn't so much an idea that either of them had, but simply an inevitability. Their lips meet. They kiss for a while, still sitting up, like teenagers, like the end of that John Hughes movie, a still-sweet scene in a film that the starring actress recently wrote in *The New Yorker* now seems too racist and rapey to show to her own kid.

Who knows. Maybe it's not *all* over, or maybe they don't need to know, at least not yet.

After a while, they lean back together, back against this bed that they've shared for some seven thousand nights, this bed on which they've made love again and again. Zo touches his shaved head, laughs about the rough feel of his beard against her skin.

Just like he always knew she would, eventually.

LATER, IN THE quiet dark, Zo slips on her underwear, and his T-shirt, and she puts on music on her phone and begins to dance. She does this sometimes. After. Queues up some song, whatever she's in the mood for, and dances alone.

A few bars of KC and the Sunshine Band's "Give It Up" fill the room. And just like that, Ethan is back on the quad outside Old Kenyon, and Randy's pumping a keg and playing just-the-right song, never the one you expect, never the one you thought you wanted to hear, but somehow always—invariably—exactly the one you needed.

"Mmmm . . . no," Zo murmurs. "Too fast." The music stops, and the room is quiet. Zo scrolls, and then another song comes on: Still KC and the Sunshine Band, but one of their other hits: "Please Don't Go." The music is slow and steady, and it feels like waves lapping on a calm shore.

Ethan watches his wife move in the dark. He feels sleep falling over him.

It's good, this song: better than he remembers. He listens to a swell of violins, a pounding piano. Zo sways her shoulders back and forth.

Somewhere upstairs, he thinks, Maddy is packing.

Somewhere in New York City, Evie is probably curled up on a sofa, just trying to live her life.

Somewhere, on the other side of the country, Randy is probably pacing, trying to think his way out of a bad situation he created himself.

After KC, Zo puts on another song he hasn't thought about in years. Wings: "A Little Luck." Ethan closes his eyes, and he's a kid again, rolling through Pennsylvania, in the backseat of his dad's station wagon, watching the world, the only world he knew then, roll by. He opens his eyes again, and there's his wife, moving alone.

He'd forgotten how much he loves this song. He'd forgotten how easy it could all be.

And then a familiar guitar lick, like a long-dead friend coming to him in a dream: Fleetwood Mac, "Rhiannon."

In the darkness, in her underwear, illuminated only by her phone, Zo could be twenty-five all over again. They could still be in Brooklyn, their whole lives ahead of them. He smiles, imagining that in the morning they'll walk to that café over on Fifth Avenue. He can still see Zo sitting across from him, drinking coffee and reading the Arts section, nothing but time ahead for both of them. What was it called, that café? The name is gone. The moment alone remains, like the afterimage that appears inside your lids when you close your eyes.

Past. Present. What's to come.

I'm doing the best I can.

There will be a final time that they sleep together, he and Zo. And when it happens, whenever it happens, they almost certainly won't know it's the last time. Maybe an afterimage of this moment, right now, will remain. Or perhaps this, too, will have dissolved to nothing.

Taken by

Taken by the sky.

He could have fallen in love with Maddy. He could have fallen in love with Evie.

Taken by

Taken by the sky.

He knows, the way he knows anything at all, that Zo isn't dancing for him. That if he weren't here, if he suddenly disappeared, if he had never existed, Zo would be doing exactly what she's doing now: moving the same way, to the same song, every motion hers alone. He recalls—faintly, like a flicker of light from some faraway star—that this is one of the reasons he fell in love with Zo in the first place, this sense that he was peering in at her from the outside, glimpsing someone's private self, the kind of unself-conscious realness that no one ever shows you on purpose. Except she did.

Taken by

Taken by the sky.

Zo's eyes are closed. Her hands make slow swirls. It looks as if she's conjuring the music herself, like the chords are streaming from her fingertips. Ethan allows his own eyes to close too. When they do, he sees, on the inside of his lids, Zo's afterimage: his wife, moving alone through this still, velvet night.

SATURDAY

24

Ethan wakes early, Zo by his side.

He leaves her sleeping, splashes water on his face, heads upstairs.

Maddy's room is empty. The sheets are twisted haphazardly, the closet is empty. Aside from a single towel on the wooden floor, there is nothing left of Maddy's presence. He sits down on the bare bed.

I heard the mermaids singing each to each. In the Prufrock Bränd campaign, he and Randy had paired that line with a man's silhouette, tiny and lonely against a vast, empty sea. No one, it was clear, would be singing to Prufrock.

Clever, that campaign. Everything Bränd ever did was so damn clever.

He peeks into Alex's room. She's asleep on the floor, on top of a mountain of laundry. Hypatia's curled up next to her. As soon as Hypatia sees him, her tail starts thumping. The dog gets up—she seems creakier even than yesterday—follows him downstairs, panting. *I need,* Hypatia's saying. *I need, I need, I need.*

"Okay," he sighs. "Come on."

Clank of the radiator. Scoop of dog food. Bulb flickers.

Smell of butter in the cast-iron pan. Crack of the egg.

Drive downhill, over the Ledge, toward downtown, where everything, for now, is still.

◆

It's Saturday, so only Willie Nelson sits in the window. He's the stalwart creature of routine, the only member of the trivia gang who's consistently there on weekends.

"Where the heck were you yesterday, Encyclopedia Brown?" Willie greets him. "We could have used you." Ethan has the feeling that thermonuclear war could wipe out the entire human race this afternoon, and tomorrow, Willie Nelson would still be sitting right here, perched in his window seat, thinking about trivia.

"Yeah, what was the question?" Ethan looks out to the central square, at all those handmade signs.

BELIEVE WOMEN.

NO SCOTUS PREDATORS.

JUSTICE FOR ZO.

Justice for Zo, who is doing her best.

Willie Nelson shows him the question: *In this '70s Oscar-winning film, the title character's first words are "Why did you go to the police? Why didn't you come to me first?"*

This one's obvious. "*The Godfather.*"

Willie Nelson throws his hands in the air. "Ah, I really wish you'd have been here. None of us got the damn thing."

Zo's still asleep when he returns home, still in his T-shirt, the sheets tangled around her legs. He sets down her coffee on the bedside table.

The first time he watched Zo sleep was in Iowa. They were there for a wedding, some college friend of Zo's. This was back when everyone started pairing up, marching two-by-two into the future as if boarding Noah's Ark. While in Iowa, he and Zo visited the Field of Dreams, the one from that movie. It was real, a real goddamned baseball diamond, in the middle of a real goddamned cornfield. He and Zo lined up behind home plate, waiting for a turn to bat. In line with them were muscled marines, knobby seven-year-olds, rickety grandmas, pimply teenagers. There was a toothpick-thin engineer who'd just finished his final chemo treatment, a group of wine-sloshing divorcées on some First Wives Club road trip. There were far more batters than outfielders, but it didn't matter. No one was impatient, everyone cheered for everyone else, because (as one of the First Wives slurred) *everybody plays at the Field of Dreams*! It was America, that crowd, and also it was better than America, like the stories you hear about previous generations, the ones whose mythology holds up only if you don't look too closely.

On that trip, Zo had purchased a bumper sticker, only half ironically: IS THIS HEAVEN? NO, IT'S IOWA. They wouldn't have a car for years, and by the time they did buy one, the bumper sticker would be long lost.

But here he is, decades later, watching Zo sleep, just as he had that morning in Iowa.

He wonders if there is a word, in some language, somewhere, for glimpsing a person you knew and loved when they were young, inside their older self, the way you can go back and forth, like one of those optical illusions (is it a couple kissing or a glass of wine? An old crone or a young maiden?), the line between past and present curling into itself, as if time is merely a jump rope whose handles you can make touch.

He wonders, too, about a word for the moments before you tell a person something you wish you didn't have to—that fragile bubble of peace that you know you're about to pop.

Zo doesn't wake all at once. When Ethan places a hand on her back, she opens one eye, then closes it again. Then she inhales, opens both eyes, sees the coffee on the bedside table. "Mmm," she says. "You got me coffee."

"Still hot."

Zo rolls onto her back. "What time is it?"

"Eight-thirty."

She nods. "Saturday?" This is how she's always woken up after

a heavy sleep. She pieces together the details of her world a frag-
ment at a time, as if she's snapping jigsaw pieces into place.

"It's Saturday."

She closes her eyes again. "The rally."

"Yeah. You have some time, though."

She props herself up on her elbows, reaches for the coffee, takes
a first sip. "God. There's nothing like the first hit of coffee, is
there?" And then, when another piece of the puzzle clicks into
place: "Ethan, I don't think I want to be here when Maddy leaves."

"She's gone. She left before I woke up. Listen, Zo. There's
something I need to tell you now." And then he begins to tell her
about Bränd. About Randy.

"Randy," she says when he finishes. "Of course. Randy. We
probably should have seen that coming."

"Randy asked me to do something to make the accusations go
away. Something crummy." Ethan doesn't say what it is, and Zo
doesn't ask. "I didn't do it. But I *could* have done it, I almost did.
And I think I probably could have gotten away with it too." He
knows that's not how it's supposed to be. Had this been a movie,
and he'd gone through with Randy's plan, the decision would
have bitten him in the ass. There would be some sort of karmic
retribution. But in the real world, the consequences almost certainly would have been Evie's alone.

You've always been one of the good ones, Evie had said. She'd been
wrong. If he really wants to be honest with himself, he would say
this: there were signs. Not just long-ago signs—the hotel room in
Irvine, *behold the new kings,* the occasional actress he saw scurrying
away from the audition room a little too quickly—but more recently too. As a partial owner, he still got to see, from time to
time, the Bränd ledgers. He saw the occasional lump-sum pay-
ments, usually described by Randy as *avoiding a nuisance lawsuit,
that's all, you know how it is.* Ethan didn't ask questions, because he
thought he *did* know how it was. He'd taken fragments, crafted a
version of the world in his mind, and then convinced himself that
this world he'd invented was the real one.

"Anyway," he tells Zo. "I'm pretty sure Bränd is dead."

"Bränd is dead. Long live Bränd." Zo lifts her coffee cup to his.

When Zo finishes her coffee, she pushes the covers back. "Okay." She places her feet on the floor, rubs her eyes.

Zo stands, heads toward the bathroom.

"Hey hon?" he calls. He wants to ask what she'll do at the rally, whether she'll speak, and what she'll say. But when she turns around, he simply says. "I think we've done all right, you and I. All things considered."

"Yeah," she says. "All things considered. We have."

HE SHOULD BE there. This is what he realizes after Zo departs with her poster-board sign. He's standing in front of the mirror, razor in hand, ready to shave his beard, at long last—this symbol of his pettiness, his selfishness. He'll make a mess of the sink, then he'll clean it up, and he'll try a little harder, maybe manage to do a little better, tomorrow. But before he brings the blade to his chin, the knowledge is everywhere at once: he should be there.

At the rally. With his wife.

He should be there, because he is the one who knows Zo the most, the best, who has spent half a lifetime caring about her—not as a symbol, not as a political ally or enemy, not as a hashtag, but as a *person*. He should be there, because if there is any hope left for this world, it will come from meeting people in the real world, face-to-face, standing by a loved one's side in actual time and space.

Ethan sets the razor down. He'll shave later. Right now, he'll do what he should have been doing all along: he will join his wife, and he will stand with her, and he will bring Alex along.

If this is what they need to do to be a family, then this is how they'll be a family.

Ethan finds Alex in her pajamas watching TV. She's eating Froot Loops on the sofa, droplets of oat milk spilling onto the new upholstery. "Alex," he says. She ignores him, slurps a spoonful of pink liquid. "We have to go."

She keeps her eyes on the screen.

"Alex."

She growls at him in response. Difficult today. Irritable. Dark. He makes a mental note: *Get those stupid pills*. He will. As soon as the rally's over.

"Get dressed. We're going to find Mommy."

"No thanks." Alex's eyes are already back on the TV. "I'll stay here with Maddy."

"Maddy's not here. Maddy's . . . not going to be living with us anymore." If this bothers Alex, she doesn't show it, or ask any questions. *"Alex,"* he snaps. "Come on, get up. We're going to help Mommy fix the world."

"I don't *want* to."

He takes a deep breath. Patience. He needs to have patience.

"Listen, Alex. What matters to Mommy matters to us. Everything we do to others, or *for* others, or *refuse* to do to and for others, we're doing or not-doing to and for ourselves."

Alex looks at him like he's insane, and he can't blame her. Even he can hear how convoluted that was.

"My point is, we're a family. So let's go."

Yes, from now on, he'll take charge. He'll be firm *and* loving, give Alex whatever help she needs. He'll give Zo the help that *she* needs, too. The world isn't post-narrative. It isn't post–happy ending. They just haven't yet written the next part of their story.

Alex stands. Puts her hands on her hips. *"Okay,"* she says, then stomps upstairs.

Yes. He's going all-in. Even if it means standing next to his wife on a village green in a tiny town in the middle of nowhere, holding signs that few will read, at a protest that is based on a half-truth. Maybe it's the bigger truths that matter anyway. And *his* big truth is that he still believes in this family. He wants to give it everything he's got. One hundred percent. Forward motion only.

He's starting today. He's starting right now.

WHILE ALEX DRESSES, he picks up his phone. He reads all the messages he's gotten from Randy in the last couple of days. The final messages or so are something to behold.

Randy: *Hello*
Randy: *Still not there?*
Randy: *Hello*
Randy: *Talk to me*
Randy: *Hello*
Randy: *I'm not going away*
Randy: *at least answer me*
Randy: *hi*
Randy: *hola*
Randy: *ni hao*
Randy: *motherfucker, answer.*
Randy: *FINE, FUCK YOU THEN.*

Ethan starts to type out a final response, then stops. No. He wants to talk.

Randy picks up on the first ring. "E."

From somewhere in the distance, Ethan hears a distant snare drum strike up a beat. He pictures Zo out there, holding her sign: BURN IT ALL DOWN. She said the protest was going to be big. What does that mean in a place like Starkfield? Forty people? Fifty?

"Randy, I'm sorry," Ethan says. "I can't help you. I just wanted to tell you that."

On the other end of the phone, Ethan can hear Randy's television. A voice says, *Republicans managed to get the nomination through the Judiciary Committee with an eleven-to-ten vote.* Ethan pictures Randy sitting in front of his television in Bel Air, the place like something out of a David Hockney painting: all bright colors and pool views and clean lines. *Now the confirmation is in the hands of the Senate.*

Or who knows. Maybe Randy's in an airport, or at a bar, or standing in the middle of Best Buy, and the voice is playing on forty different screens at once. What does Ethan know of Randy's life?

The drum downtown sounds like a regiment marching toward battle.

"And if I refuse to go quietly?" Randy asks.

Ethan thinks about what will happen if Randy releases Evie's tapes. The tsunami of fury she'll face. He pictures action and reaction, opposite and amplified. Then he imagines stepping into the fray himself to tell the truth about those tapes. The way all the world's invective will suddenly be aimed straight at him. "I guess I'll have to explain what those tapes are," he says.

"They're your tapes, too, you know," Randy says. "You were an equal partner."

And then: "You'll become radioactive, E. You'll lose everything and everyone."

"Yeah," Ethan says. "I think that's probably true."

Randy's voice is bitter. "Still playing the part of the good guy, I see."

"Not so good, Randy. Not really very good at all."

Randy doesn't do any fast talking. He doesn't try to convince Ethan of anything. Five seconds pass. Ten. Twenty. Finally Randy says, "Well. I guess it would have been a Hail Mary pass anyway." The statement hangs there, somewhere between Los Angeles and Starkfield, or maybe everywhere, all at once.

Ethan walks to the window, gazes out at the apple trees Zo fell in love with a lifetime ago, back when they first looked at this house. They're half-dead, these trees, more empty branches than leaves. Just another species struggling to survive the coming collapse.

"Rand? You still there?"

"Yeah. Just sitting here thinking."

"About?"

"Honestly? I'm thinking about my first-ever record player. Christmas present. Was under the tree when I woke up. I must have been, I don't know, seven or eight years old? Made of plastic, you could fold the whole thing up and carry it around like a suitcase. For some reason, it was a *Welcome Back, Kotter* record player. Huge photo of Kotter and his Sweathogs plastered on the outside. Can you believe that? Nineteen seventies, and someone's all, *Hey, you know what will help us sell this hunk of plastic? We'll put Gabe Fucking Kaplan's ugly mug on the outside.* I didn't even *watch* that show, that's the funny thing. But the thing is, it worked. My parents stood in a store looking at that record player, all, *Should we? Maybe we should.* And they did. They bought it for me, and they wrapped it in Christmas paper and Scotch tape, and I tell you what, I was as happy as a pig in shit. I played my John Denver on that thing, I played my John Lennon, my James Taylor. Figured I'd never need anything else to be happy."

John Denver: almost choked his wife, the woman about whom he wrote "Annie's Song."

John Lennon: admitted to beating women. In his words, "any women."

James Taylor: no assaults to Ethan's knowledge, thank God for that.

"I don't even know what happened to that record player," Randy says. "Must be at the bottom of the Great American Landfill by now, probably leaching noxious shit into the soil as we speak. Made me happy, though. I'll tell you that. For a while, it made me really, really happy."

Ethan smiles. "Sometimes it's the little things."

More silence, then Randy asks, "Hey, remember that time we out-Baudrillarded Baudrillard?"

"I sure do. Behold the new kings."

"We *were* kings then, weren't we?"

"Hey. You're still a king, Randy."

"No, I'm not. Not anymore. I guess I thought I'd always be one—that once you get the crown, it's yours to keep. But it turns out, they get to just take that crown away. Anytime they want. I didn't know that part of the deal."

"You'll come back. You're Randy Fucking Riverstone. You always come back."

A pause. "Yeah, maybe." But Randy's voice sounds deflated.

"You know, we should get together one of these days," Ethan says. "Maybe take a trip back to Kenyon, walk the old path, see how the place has changed."

"Yeah, sure," Randy says. "That sounds fun, actually, I'll look at my calendar, get back to you with some dates."

But Ethan knows that it won't happen, that Randy won't send him dates, that they'll never again walk together beneath those grand trees and Gothic buildings. Instead, Ethan has a feeling, a *knowing,* really—like this, too, is already a memory, even though it hasn't happened yet—that one of these days, maybe sooner than later, Ethan's phone will ring. The call won't be from Randy, but it will be about Randy. The voice on the other end will tell him that he's now in a post-Randy world.

Maybe he's already in a post-Randy world. This phone call, right here, is just the stray threads, the loose ends, the wispy, cold feeling of a ghost brushing by.

The king is dead, long live the king.

"It's gonna be okay," Ethan says. "You take care of yourself, all right?"

Randy doesn't say goodbye when he hangs up.

Alex bursts into the room: she's wearing red sneakers and a green plaid flannel over one of Zo's T-shirts: GET IN WITCHES, WE'RE GOING HUNTING. She stands there, crosses her arms.

"If I'm going to this rally," she bargains, "then will you *at least* take me out for a Conehead milkshake when we're done?"

2 5

THEY WALK TOGETHER toward the sound of drums. Or rather, Ethan walks. Alex hops around, making movements that seem equal parts interpretive dance and martial arts. She stops occasionally to pluck plants from the ground.

"What are they protesting today anyway?" Alex asks. Her eyes scan a patch of grass. "Is it the shooting?"

"Not the shooting. Wait, which shooting?"

"The one in Maryland?"

"I don't know about that shooting. Remember I told you about the guy who wants to be on the Supreme Court? Who might have done something bad?"

"Oh." Alex punches the air in front of her, makes an attempt at a karate kick, spins in a circle. Then she nods. "Okay, the Supreme Court thing."

The drums grow louder. Ethan hears chanting now, too, though he can't make out the words. Just how many people are down there anyway? Alex stops again, picks something small and green from the earth. Bent over the grass like that, she looks like a very young child. Age eleven: both little and big, all at the same time.

"Alex, was there really a shooting in Maryland last week?"

"Yup." She stands, keeps walking. "I read about it on a website, where you can look up whatever mass shootings happened that day." Ethan adds this to his mental list: *Pay more attention to what Alex is looking at online.* Yes, he'll do this too. "It happened at a warehouse. One of the workers cut in front of another as they were punching the clock in the morning. The person who *got* cut made a comment, so then the person who *did* the cutting went home and got a gun."

"Are there shootings every day?" he asks.

"Mmmm . . . not every day, but sometimes there's more than one on the same day." Alex is matter-of-fact about the whole thing, but of course, why wouldn't she be? She's never known a world where she didn't have to rehearse for the moment someone shows up at her school to hunt her like an animal. "But what I don't understand, Daddy, is why they would punch a clock at all. That's such a weird thing to do."

That's the thing she doesn't understand.

"It's an expression," he explains. "It just means reporting for duty. Did anybody die?"

But Alex is focused on the grass again. She brightens. "Hey, there's another one!" She reaches down, plucks something from the ground. She holds it up for him.

It's a clover. With four perfect leaves.

"Alex," he says. He takes it into his hand, and examines it. "Holy cow. You did it. You found an actual four-leaf clover."

"I found four, actually." From her pocket, she pulls three others, already starting to wilt. "You can keep that one if you want, I'm really good at finding them. Anyway, I think three people died. Also, Daddy, I decided: I think witches are most like gas."

"Like . . . gas?" The drums are so loud now, maybe he misheard her.

"Yeah. That's what I'm going to write in my science report: that becoming a witch is like heating water. It's like, when you put a pot filled with water on the stove, all those water molecules start moving around." She begins moving her fists—slowly at first, and then rapidly. "And after a while, it's just too much heat, they can't take it. That's when they rise into the air as steam."

He stares at her. "What did you say?"

"I think maybe that's what happens with witches, too: they get all agitated, so mad about stuff that they just . . ." Alex's hands flutter toward the sky, indicating a witch lifting off from the ground.

"It's a *metaphor*?" Ethan asks. "Your science project on witches is a *metaphor*?"

Alex makes a face. *Dad the dumbfuck.* "What did you think it was? Anyway, do you think that's a good idea? Mr. Boorstin says that if we do a good job, we'll get a good grade in English *and* Science." She doesn't wait for his answer. She skips ahead, does a few more karate/dance moves, *kapow, kamchaka, pew-pew-pew,* until they reach the Ledge. That's when she stops, brightens.

"There they are!" She points toward the village green, this clear, unobstructed view. "*Whoa.*"

ZO WAS RIGHT: there are a lot of people down there. So many that he can't believe he's still in Starkfield. So many that they're spilling over the green, into the street, onto the sidewalks, blocking the storefronts.

Who *are* they all? Some look like college kids, but he sees people of all ages. It's like the whole *world's* come to Starkfield today. There must be hundreds of pink caps. And so many rainbow flags and equality flags and protest signs it's hard to keep up. *Tell me what democracy looks like!*

This is what democracy looks like!

But it's not only protesters who are down there. Judging by the signs, an almost equal number have come to protest the protesters, to assert a different view about what this world, this country, is and should be. Ethan scans the signs, looking for Zo:

DON'T SILENCE WOMEN

CONFIRM NOW

#METOO HAS GONE #TOOFAR

STOP POLICE OVERREACH

PREVENTING CRIME IS NOT A CRIME!

YOU ARE ON STOLEN LAND

DON'T LIKE AMERICA THEN GET THE HELL OUT

STOP THE WITCH HUNTS

TIME'S UP

A picture of a machine gun: COME AND TAKE IT

DEFEND LIFE

WOMYN'S RIGHTS = HUMAN RIGHTS

LEFTIST MORANS

HALF OF WHITE WOMEN VOTED FOR THIS PRESIDENT

Ethan thinks of Baudrillard, wonders what the philosopher would have thought of this scene—the way a single protest, grounded on a half-truth, has become an opportunity for people to assert their own dot-to-dot reality.

Welcome to the hyperreality. Will the real America please stand up?

All of these people, all of this energy, all of this human potential, and somehow the only thing this crowd seems to be able to do *together* is hold up traffic. A steady line of cars waits to take their turn around the rotary. A few lay on their horns.

Drums. Screams. Chanting.

Tell me what democracy looks like!

Next to him, Alex asks, "But where's Mommy?"

This is what democracy looks like!

Ethan searches the crowd for Zo's BURN IT ALL DOWN sign, but there are too many signs, too many people, he can't find his wife. It's like Zo's been absorbed into something larger than herself, has ceased to exist as an individual self.

Near where he and Alex stand on the Ledge, two teenage girls stand hip-jutted, surveying the scene. "Yeah," says one of them in a bored voice. "My mom is basically the Buddha. She meditates, like, *every day*." The girl's holding a sign that says, I'M PRO-LIFE AND I VOTE, though there's no way this kid is old enough to vote. Nearby, a couple dressed in black, goth-like, marches past. "But, like," the woman says, "what if Satan was trying to *save* Eve from, like, blind authority? Since when is *knowledge* such a bad thing? And how do we know Eve wasn't being, you know, *raped*?"

Alex points down the hill. "Oh! There's Mommy."

Ethan searches, but he can't find Zo. "Right *there*," Alex says. "Don't you see?"

He gazes down at Alex, this miracle kid who can look down in a patch of clover and spy the one with four leaves, like it leapt right out at her. Brilliant girl who can look at this chaos and find the one person who matters most to her. That's what Shreya Greer-Williams has no interest in seeing, it's what Mr. McCuttle had promised he'd see, but didn't.

He will, though. From here on forward, he will.

At the bottom of the hill, a car, stuck in place, lays on its horn. Futile.

Ripples of sadness, of grief: they're here too, they rise from this crowd, from these streets, they bend the air. But sadwaves don't remain sad, that's the problem: they refract, become something else altogether. That's what outrage is, isn't it? A passing back and forth of despair, *You take this grief; no, you,* like the tide sloshing back and forth between shores, eroding everything in its path.

Someone starts banging out a rhythm on a cowbell.

Ethan turns to Alex. He wants to tell her that the world doesn't have to be this way. He wants to tell her that sometimes what looks inevitable, or organic, or accidental, is anything but: that someone's *doing* this. That right now, as they stand here, invisible forces are churning away, cold calculations written in code, ones and zeros designed to transform *E Pluribus Unum* into *Show Me the Money*. Soulless, these calculations: devoid of compassion or judgment or wisdom, or hope, but it doesn't have to be this way, and she needs to understand this.

"This isn't how we were meant to live," he says. But Alex isn't next to him anymore, she's already moving slapdash into the crowd. The hill is steep and her strides are long, and with every step she looks certain to fall but she doesn't.

"Alex, wait," he calls, but his voice is drowned out by the crowd, a new call-and-response. *What's up? Time's up! When's it up? Now!*

Red shoes landing hard, one leap, then another. Plaid flannel ripples behind her. Ethan knows Alex would be just a tiny bit less impulsive if she'd taken her red pill, but still: there is something exhilarating about this moment, this child, her energy and fearlessness. The sheer force of her will.

Yes. Now he sees Zo. Green COAT, BURN IT ALL DOWN. He feels light, like he's being lifted above the crowd. He takes one careful step down the hill, then another.

Alex ducks between two protesters facing off with signs held high in the air: THE FUTURE IS FEMALE, says one. FEMINISM IS CANCER, says another.

At the bottom of the hill, an engine revs. Ethan shifts his gaze to the line of cars. One of the vehicles, the one revving its engine for a second time, is the truck he's been seeing around town, the rusted pickup with the enormous flags and the bumper stickers. The driver's-side window of the truck is down. To his surprise, Ethan recognizes the person sitting behind the wheel.

It's Jarrett K, from the UPS Store.

Oh, Ethan thinks. Another puzzle piece of the world snaps into place. *Of course. Of course that's Jarrett's truck.*

He'll tell Zo about Jarrett, too, when this is all over. He'll tell her that he'd known she wouldn't have liked the guy, but he'll also tell her about Jarrett's lost friends, the kid's sorrow. The way he reminds Ethan of the guys he grew up with. Ethan will tell his wife so many things, all of the things he hasn't yet told her, and maybe tonight, Zo will dance again by the light of their bedroom window. If she does, he'll sit up and watch. This time, he won't drift off to sleep, he'll watch until she's done, until she crawls into bed next to him and he can feel her heat becoming his own.

Ethan nears the bottom of the hill, he's almost to the truck with the flags and the bearded kid whose four friends rode the comet, who were more real to him than real people, and it's as if Jarrett can feel Ethan's gaze, because he stops looking forward through his windshield, shifts his eyes directly to Ethan.

Ethan nods at Jarrett, who offers a slow, serious nod in return. They are two humans acknowledging each other, two animals with monkey bodies, nodding their monkey heads as a kind of hello, but also as an acknowledgment of some bigger truth: the world is weird. It's changing fast. They happen to have landed here together, at the same surreal moment in space and time. They are witnessing this weirdness together.

Jarrett's eyes return to the crowd in front of him. It's hard to hear over the drumming, and the cowbell, the call and response, but yes, there's the engine revving for a third time. And there must be a break in traffic at last, because Jarrett begins rolling forward.

Something funny about the movement. Some anomaly. Hard to make sense of.

No, wait. The traffic isn't moving. It's only Jarrett who's moving. He's cranking the wheel, moving around the car in front of him, even though there's nowhere to go. There are people to the left, people to the right—signs, motion, commotion everywhere, but somehow that's not stopping him. Jarrett's over the curb now, two wheels on the green. Moving slowly at first, then faster.

Too fast.

There's a fleeting moment where it's Jarrett's safety for which Ethan is alarmed.

And then he understands. In a sudden rush, the stuff of nightmares, Ethan understands, and then he's running, his long legs taking enormous strides downhill like he could possibly stop this, but he loses his footing. He gets up, tries to run and falls again, and now it's too late, he's helpless to do anything but watch.

From the grass, he begins to calculate. It's a terrible calculation, the worst possible: the truck's angle, its velocity, the people in front of it, the direction they're facing, who sees, who doesn't see. Where his daughter is now.

Red pill meets no-red-pill, and what happens?

This. This is the thing that happens.

THE ONES WHO are lonely. The ones who feel like a joke. The ones who assuage their loneliness by making jokes. The ones who like how the joking feels. The ones who find community in these jokes, then find themselves nudged, one click at a time, deeper and deeper into something that is no joke.

The ones who think that perhaps they've found it, at last, the explanation that makes all mismatched puzzle pieces of a life click together.

The problem is obvious. The problem is Them.

The ones who are no longer joking, who begin to see the world as a sinister, zero-sum game. The ones who are determined: if this is a game, it's one they won't lose, can't lose, refuse to lose. No matter what it takes.

The ones who will do anything.

LATER, WHEN THIS moment has morphed into the past, when the whole world has heard of Starkfield, Massachusetts, Ethan will look in the mirror. He'll see what Jarrett himself must have seen in those final moments of the Before: the man with the shaved head and long beard, the trace of "RED PILL" still on his pale skin. Only then will he understand: Jarrett saw himself in Ethan. And while Ethan saw a part of himself in Jarrett, these things, bewilderingly, were not the same.

The nod the two shared was no friendly greeting, no benign acknowledgment of the world's weirdness. Jarrett was having a different conversation entirely, just as he had been all along.

Punching bags for the whole world.

Kissing American soil faster than you can say make me a sandwich.

People coming in just to make trouble.

Refuse to accept the decline of our own lives.

Ethan will learn, too, surreally, that Jarrett K wasn't even the kid's name. He'd been wearing another employee's shirt, someone who no longer worked for UPS. These misunderstandings will be enough for Ethan to convince himself at times that maybe none of this was real, that perhaps it never actually happened, *That is not what I meant at all.*

But all of that will come later. Because right now, there's no more sound. No more meaning. There is nothing but that truck, going where no vehicle ever should: into the crowd. And moving on the edge of that crowd is a child in plaid, craning her neck to find her mother.

Unaware, unself-conscious. Unprepared for the world that is.

There is nothing but terrible distance between them. Not big enough, and closing fast.

JUST BEFORE IT happens, from his helpless spot near the bottom of the hill, Ethan sees Zo's face. Or maybe this is something he invents later in his mind. Either way, when he looks back at this, the final instant before he crosses over into some new thing, he will remember Zo's expression as twisted, monstrous, expressing the full horror of what is happening.

And that is when Ethan understands:

No out there, separate from here.

No they, separate from I.

No one else, nowhere else.

What happens in the world happens, too, to him.

get in, witches

there will be time, there will be time

we're going hunting

welcome to the

decisions and revisions a minute

hyperreality

will erase

Wind in the trees, sun through the leaves.

A cloudless sky, crisp and perfect, and beneath it rises a child. She soars upward, arms extended to her sides. She's unreasonably high, impossibly high. She looks like she could rise forever.

Time slows, then ceases altogether.

She dangles, plaid rippling, red sneakers against blue sky. She is a scrap of linen suspended on an invisible clothesline.

Alex will never write that report for science day. *That's all over now.* Because witches are real, and right here is all the proof Ethan will ever need: his daughter, his miracle child, finder-of-four-leaf-clovers, hider in attic stairwells, belter of showtunes.

Alex, doing the impossible, the thing she alone seemed to know was possible.

Alex: His daughter, a girl in this world, propelled by forces she can't possibly understand.

Taken by

Taken by the sky.

Alex: a speck in space, moving farther and farther into the deepening blue, all of Starkfield immeasurably below her.

Alex: Defying, at long last, gravity.

EPILOGUE

The photograph, that sunny image of smiling faces, was still in my hand when I heard Ethan's voice behind me. "What happened?"

Instantly, reality began piecing itself together again, LEGO bricks slotting into place: the flat tire, the car ride, this torn-apart living room crammed with boxes. The stacks of furniture, the weary man, the *me* and the *him,* the Technicolor reality of here and now. I must have started when he spoke, because Ethan apologized, took a step backward. A way of reassuring me, probably.

How long had I been standing there? When, exactly, had Ethan stopped searching for the car jack? *What happened?* It was unnerving, frankly, his asking that question. Like the man could read my thoughts.

Maybe he *could* read them, actually. He probably could.

I glanced down at the picture in my hand. "Looks like a happy family," I said. In the photo, a girl, somewhere between young and old, sits flanked by her mother and father. Both parents' heads are tilted back, mouths open, their faces captured in a burst of joyful surprise. The girl wears an impish, delighted expression. She appears to have said something funny and unexpected, made her parents laugh, the instant—just one of the seemingly endless string of instants that somehow combine to form a life—made indelible with a single click of the camera.

What had the girl said? I almost asked; I opened my mouth to form the question, but the words stuck in my throat. I set the picture down, turned around. Behind Ethan, streaks of sun, the last of the day, streamed through the window. Inside, they were absorbed into stacks of furniture, all those open, overflowing boxes. Long shadows stretched across the floor: lumpish beasts slouching their way toward who-knows-where.

"Anyway," Ethan said, "I found the car jack."

Yes. There it was: on the arm of a gray sofa that was supposed to be blue.

I didn't want to see that sofa. I didn't want to look at Ethan, didn't want to watch light and shadow duke it out inside this cramped, chaotic space. All I wanted—and I wanted it desperately, hungrily, the way a drowning person must crave air—was to escape. I longed to return to *This Is Genius,* to disappear into my book, lose myself in big ideas, in human aspiration. I wanted to push this whole mournful scene so far into the periphery that I could forget, just for a bit, that any of it existed.

Call me heartless. But if you'd seen that room through my eyes—the shadows, those boxes, that earnest, broken man—you'd have needed out too.

Ethan's voice was quiet when he spoke again. "She had a good day today." He offered no more explanation.

I nodded, walked to the pillow where the old dog lay. The animal lifted her head, thumped her tail. When I bent down, she rolled onto her side, exposing the soft pink of her underbelly.

Be careful, Hypatia. I'm not to be trusted.

I pressed my hand against the dog's chest, felt her heartbeat. I closed my eyes, tried to imagine all it takes to keep a body going: the pumps and proteins, the cell factories deep inside marrow, the electric jump of nerves, the tiny coils of genes, all those rushing currents of blood.

Ethan moved toward the door.

So it was done at last, this visit. Now we'd head out into the cold March afternoon, climb back into my car, head down the hill, return to that dented Subaru with the flat tire. Maybe I'd wait with him in the cold—long enough, anyway, to be sure he got the spare on. Then I'd flee.

But Ethan's hand rested on the doorknob, didn't move. "Svetlana," he said. And when I didn't answer, didn't understand, he explained: "The thing that made us laugh. Just before Maddy snapped that picture. Remember?"

And then I do. I do remember. It wasn't long before Alex started sixth grade. We'd asked Maddy to take a photo of the three of us, something the Rainbow Seed School could put into their family directory. After several closed-eye attempts, Alex had begun, out of the blue, speaking in a Russian accent. "Vahht?" she'd purred, when I asked what she was doing. "Dees is how Svetlana always speak, you no like?"

It's like a fever breaking, that memory.

I move toward Ethan. We wrap our arms around each other, his hand on my back, my head against his chest. "Zo," Ethan whispers to my hair. Then he says the thing we have said again and again, each to the other, and to our child, and to whatever forces govern this world: *I'm sorry I'm sorry I'm sorry I'm sorry.*

"Shhh." This time I am the one who comforts. Next time it will go differently. Because solace, too, moves back and forth, like waves between shores: his then mine then back again, world without end. "She's okay," I remind my husband. "She was lucky. We're so lucky, remember? Alex is going to be okay."

THE SMELL OF Steris, the smell of lilies, the smell of bacteria festering beneath hard cast, of unwashed hair, of hospital meals ordered and left uneaten on plastic trays until some girl in red scrubs clears them away. Bouquets and Mylar balloons and oversized stuffed bunnies, too many gifts, so many that the nurses must carry them elsewhere, to other rooms, to strangers, the lonely and the lost, the ones who don't get visitors, the ones whose faces aren't plastered across televisions on six continents, who haven't seen their still-short lives turned into a national tragedy, or—depending on who you are and what websites you visit—a meme.

Tubes in the nose, tubes in the arms, tubes in the bladder, the throat, the lungs. Mysterious fluids drip-dripping, don't ask too many questions about what's in those IV bags or why they're needed, no one's got time for good answers, and anyway, you probably don't want to know. The endless beeping: machines that measure oxygen, temperature, heart rate, pressure on the brain, respiration—touch and go, that, but the kid's still respiring, thank God.

Thank God.

Nurses spread balm on cracked lips. Some days, those lips fade to ghostly gray. Again and again: the surgical waiting room. Never alone in there (what, you think you're special?). Some families weep, huddle, hold hands, pray. Others stare at the television with dull eyes. In the hallway just outside the door, the chaplain hovers. He doesn't enter, but he never strays far.

No. Like your shadow, like your nightmares, like the grim reaper himself, the man's never far off.

THERE WAS A moment, eleven and a half years ago. Just after Alex was born.

Those early days of motherhood were hard for me—harder than I ever expected, or confessed. Maybe the problem was chemical—a precipitous drop of hormones after a long and harrowing birth. Maybe it was exhaustion, my desperate lack of sleep combined with the strange, driftless tedium of new motherhood—all those shapeless days of cluster feedings and diaper changes, up-the-back poops and stained onesies. Or perhaps it was that I'd become, overnight, an *it,* not so much a person as an object that existed solely to meet another's needs.

Make no mistake: I adored this child, loved her wholly, unconditionally, boundlessly. But love, it turns out, can be complicated. Sometimes it takes the form of a stone on a chest: the bigger it is, the more difficult it becomes to breathe.

I think it was a month after Alex's birth, maybe two. One of the bad days. I'd announced (my voice strong, I was almost sure) that perhaps I'd go out for a walk. Would Ethan mind so much holding the baby for a while?

It was late summer then, late afternoon. The world outside was green, lush, unnervingly alive. The air smelled ripe and grassy. I looked up as I walked, saw hundreds of thousands of leaves, palms up, drinking the sun. I glanced at my hands, noticed with a strange sort of detachment that they seemed to be shaking. I moved them in and out of the dappled light, watched my flesh turn pink, then gray, then back again, and when I finally returned home, I found Ethan sitting on the sofa beaming at Alex.

It was a nothing moment, a plain, ordinary thing: a father gazing at his infant daughter, light in his eyes.

"How is she?" I asked. He answered with one word: *perfect*.

He meant it too. Alex was perfect in his eyes. Everything was perfect, nothing more was needed, and in that moment—almost shocking in its simplicity—I was able to glimpse the world as my husband saw it.

His was a world uncomplicated. He had no reason to believe that this baby, this little girl in his arms, needed anything more than What Is. Ethan was, as humans go, relatively whole: unscathed, unbroken, unashamed, undiminished.

For him, love wasn't merely sufficient. It was everything, the only thing.

I sat down next to them. I kissed my daughter on her tiny forehead, let my lips linger on her skin. She smelled of lavender, of Desitin, of baby powder, of herself.

Yes, I thought: *Yes. It can be this simple sometimes.*

It's a fact: Ethan has always been my better half.

IN THE HOSPITAL where Alex lay after the smash-up—Schrödinger's child held in the balance by medicine and machinery—the sheets smelled like glue. The odor, formaldehyde maybe, was so thick I could taste it when I got too close. The windows didn't open, but perhaps that was just as well: on the other side of the glass I could see the news vans, the endless, awful news vans that filled the parking lot.

Sometimes the president of the hospital made statements to the assembled press corps. He fumbled his words, was skewered online. He wasn't made for this.

One season drifted into the next. The leaves outside turned red, then brown, then—like the cameras, who eventually left to chase some new headline—they disappeared entirely.

I AM TRYING to tell you what happened. I am trying so hard to explain.

ETHAN STAYED BY Alex's side after the smash-up. He refused to drift more than a few feet from her bedside. He barely ate, slept only in short bursts. Mostly, he read to her, chapter upon chapter of whatever books nurses could find for him, as if his voice was a life buoy that could haul Alex back from the depths.

I was drifting in and out of sleep near Alex's ICU bed, when Ethan stopped reading midsentence. "Well, hey there," he said. He sounded like he was talking to an ordinary kid waking up from an ordinary afternoon nap, and not to someone who'd been unconscious nearly forty-two hours.

I rushed over. A nurse was there, and a physician, too, and the four of us leaned in, peering at Alex's bleary confusion. Ethan asked gently, "Do you . . . know who we are?"

Alex blinked. Her eyes drifted, vaguely to his face. Slowly, she said, "Eenie." She paused, took in the nurse, the doctor. "Meenie . . . miney . . ." Her eyes came to rest on me as she finished:

"Zo."

One side of her mouth curled into a half smile. Then she closed her eyes again, and returned to sleep.

◆

HERE WAS THE official count: thirty-three distinct fractures, almost entirely on Alex's right side. One lung punctured, then collapsed, then repaired through surgery. Two spleen ruptures, requiring three separate surgeries. Fourteen surgeries in total, which took place over a combined thirty-nine hours.

It could have been worse.

It *would* have been worse, in fact.

FIVE DAYS AFTER Alex woke, Ethan and I left the hospital together. Dressed in black, we drove to the First Congregational Church of Starkfield. Once again, our sleepy little town was transformed—filled with strangers holding handmade signs. On this day, though, the visitors were quiet, somber. On this day, their signs bore messages not of anger but of love.

Someone else—I don't remember who—parked our car. Ethan and I walked up the church steps, ignoring the cameras, the microphones, the reporters, the gawkers. Inside the vestibule, a stranger handed us a program.

On the cover was a photograph: Elaine.

Elaine of the Witches, of the elastic waist. Elaine, who somehow understood what was happening at that protest before I did, before anyone. Elaine, who had, it seemed, been anticipating this moment, practicing for it, her whole life.

I'd been talking with her, trying to explain myself. Telling her I wouldn't speak that day, why I shouldn't, couldn't possibly. Elaine was right there in front of me, and then she wasn't. By the time I'd made sense of what was happening, Elaine had already moved away from me, toward the oncoming truck. She'd managed to throw Alex a few feet backward—not enough to protect her completely, but enough that my daughter was hit from the side rather than straight-on, which would have been certain, instant death.

As it was for Elaine.

◆

ELAINE HAD BEEN an attorney, a lifelong activist. She'd helped organize protests against Vietnam, then the Iraq War, then the WTO.
She'd briefly been among the higher-ups at the National Organi-
zation for Women, where she'd been one of the leading voices for
the Violence Against Women Act. She had, also in the 1990s, co-
authored a groundbreaking, data-rich tome about women's influence in politics. That book, still widely used in wonkish circles,
would, within five weeks of her death, help usher in an unprece-
dented wave of new women congressional representatives, something I wish desperately she'd been around to see.

Elaine, it seemed, had an instinct for being at the right place at
the right moment, for nudging history forward the way it's usually
done: in tiny increments. A modern-day Sisyphus who maybe, just
maybe, got a little further with each try. *Bit by bit, then all at once.*

She was, said the pant-suited, pink-haired nun who officiated
the funeral, a genius.

I'd been asked to speak. When it was my turn, I stood at the
pulpit, looking down at the words I'd prepared. Something about
the word the nun had used—*genius*—had jarred me, thrown me
off my game. I cleared my throat, looked out at the packed church.
The witches filled the front two pews. Behind them sat Ethan,
wearing a face I could not read.

I knew at that very moment, the Supreme Court nominee
whom we'd been protesting was at his swearing-in ceremony,
right hand raised, left hand on the Bible.

I folded up my prepared words. I spoke, instead, about the first
time I'd met Elaine.

A WOMAN DRIVES through a small town. It is the second week of
November. Something happened a few days before, something
unexpected, unbearable. All attempts to reassure her have failed.
She is weeping, this woman. She feels very much alone.

As she passes the village green, something catches her eye: a lone figure, a little hunched. It's an older woman, bundled in a heavy coat, holding a cardboard sign: HOPE OVER FEAR. There is no further explanation, no context.

The weeping woman continues driving.

Two days later, the hunched figure appears again. This time her sign reads: FIGHT FOR THE VULNERABLE. The day after that, there are three figures, three signs:

LOVE ONE ANOTHER.

HATE HAS NO HOME HERE.

I BELIEVE IN HUMANITY.

The weeping woman isn't so sure she believes in humanity, not right now. But still. She pulls the car over.

And that is the answer to the question Ethan used to ask me: What, exactly, is the point of a tiny protest in the middle of nowhere, seen by almost no one?

The point is that the person who *does* see might need exactly this, exactly now. The point is, her individual grief can become part of a collective one. The point is, this may or may not change the world, but it will almost certainly change *her*.

WHAT HAPPENED IS people were hurting. What happened is people were afraid. What happened is that anger is stronger than fear, and so, for that matter, is hate.

But it is easier to know what you want to burn down than it is to imagine what you might grow in its place.

AFTER THE SMASH-UP, I was deluged with calls: film producers, screenwriters, book agents, important ones, all clamoring for Alex's life rights, for mine. I ignored every one.

But after the funeral, I kept thinking about what that nun had said: that Elaine was a genius. I cycled over the word again and again, in the same way I'd been cycling over *what happened*.

Genius. Something about the word crawled inside me, got stuck, repeated itself, like a groove in a record. *Genius.*

It occurred to me that I had a very specific image of what a genius looked like, and it wasn't Elaine. I thought of professors I'd known, poets I'd loved, novelists I'd cherished, filmmakers and artists and scientists who had influenced my work, my life. Had any of them been called a genius out loud?

The idea came to me just after Alex's fifth surgery: a book, an encyclopedia of sorts. Filled with grand ideas from world-changing geniuses at work today—not unlike other "great minds" books, except for a single twist: these pages would be filled only with those who didn't look the part, many working in fields too often ignored.

I'd call the book *This Is Genius.*

I emailed one of the book agents, sent her a proposal. At the last minute, I attached an idea for a second book, something totally different: a half-listicle, half-journal called *Goodbye and Good Riddance: An Eviction Letter to the Ones Who Have Been Living Rent-Free in My Brain* (the first half would be filled with descriptions, each beginning *the ones who* . . . The second half would be left blank for a reader to fill in her own experiences. The whole thing, I suggested, could be printed on materials that are easy to burn).

The agent sold both books within four days.

It's possible the publisher genuinely liked these ideas. But it seems just as likely they hoped to be first in line should I ever decide to tell that *other* story: the one about Alex, about me, about what happened, about what it's like to be the mother of the new national symbol of our fight against hatred.

But this I will never do.

The day after I signed the contract, I told Ethan I planned to move out.

WHAT HAPPENED IS that each of us can see only so far. What happened is that we are graceless and blundering, like selfish toddlers who reach out to touch something beautiful and shatter it.

Curious, how a single, simple sentence—"I hurt"—simultaneously holds two, opposite meanings. *I myself am hurting.* And also: *I am hurting someone else.*

Or, no. Not opposite. In fact, maybe not so different after all.

IT WAS ABOUT the work, that's how I explained our separation to Ethan: I needed to get the books done quickly, we needed the money. If I could just write fast enough, without distractions, perhaps I'd complete both projects before Alex came home.

This explanation was both true and not true. Like much of my life, it was a half-truth, a simulacrum, a dot-to-dot picture that could be drawn in infinite other ways. The full truth, like all complete truths, was a tangled jumble, knotted so tight a person could spend her lifetime trying to unravel it and never fully succeed.

It had something to do with the way Ethan and I had been moving around each other, guessing at the other's *what happened,* both of us almost certainly more wrong than right. It had something to do with a sense I couldn't shake: that there was someone I had yet to become, but to find her, I'd first have to *unbecome.*

It had something to do, too, with what my research on genius was beginning to reveal: New ideas, new worlds, new truths, new selves, always begin in negative space. Unlike the groaning heft of What Is, possibility has no mass of its own—no force, no shape or structure, not yet. To most eyes, What Could Be looks like nothing at all. It takes faith to discern this invisible thing, to protect it and tend to it, until the day it comes screaming into the open, startling everyone with the plain fact of itself, a truth that's suddenly clear as day.

TWO WEEKS AFTER the smash-up, Mr. McCuttle stopped by the hospital. He told us the Rainbow Seed School was there for Alex, whenever she was ready to return. Faculty would tutor Alex, help her catch up, *whatever Alex needs to return to the classroom with all her wonderful friends.* I watched his mouth move, and I was struck by how small he looked.

How inadequate any one person is, really, in the face of all the world's need.

I thanked Mr. McCuttle for the visit and explained that whatever money we had would surely go toward Alex's medical needs. Then the following week, Shreya Greer-Williams visited. She stayed just long enough to deliver a stack of hand-drawn cards from Alex's classmates and the world's largest teddy bear (wearing a Rainbow Seed T-shirt, of course). Then she pressed into my hand an envelope. Inside was a folded-up piece of paper: a printout of the total from a GoFundMe campaign she'd organized, which had raised enough to cover the next three years of Rainbow Seed tuition. More, she said, was coming in by the day.

After she left, Ethan and I stared at each other.

"Well," I said. "That Shreya certainly knows how to get things done, doesn't she?"

"Huh," said Ethan. He rubbed his bare chin, looked like he was thinking hard. "For some reason, I always thought her name was Stacy."

It was the first time we laughed together since the smash-up. Maybe for a long time before that too.

AND THAT'S WHERE we are. It's been nearly five months. In this time, Alex has moved between acute care and rehab, back and forth, again and again. But her stretches in rehab are getting longer, and soon, she will come home.

Will she live with both parents then, or just one of us?

All Them Witches bring dinners to Ethan three times a week, and to me when I'm not traveling. They leave the dishes covered in foil, often with gifts: a book of Ada Limón poetry for me, some Mary Oliver for Ethan. Meetings are now at Jackie's house, but the witches continue to do what witches have always done: refuse to accept the world as it is.

It will take eighteen months, maybe longer, before we are done with this phase of our lives. Alex will be a young woman before she's fully recovered. But recover she will.

I cannot wait until she starts driving us crazy again.

SO HERE ARE: Me and you, Zo and Ethan, husband and wife, standing in the doorway of the home we shared, breathing in each other's exhalations. Still and always inextricably linked. Your arms are curled around my back. They feel good there, comfortable. You smell of sweat and spice and Tide. You feel like forgiveness, you feel like home, which is to say comfort and shame and anger and love and failure and hope, all together, all at once.

Soon, I will drive you to your car, help you change a tire, wave goodbye. Then I'll return to my rented apartment, where I'll tell my landlord, the Widow Hale, about seeing you. She'll pepper me with questions: how did it feel to be back at the house, how did he seem today, did he like the casserole I left?

And the big question too: Oh, Zo, don't you think you'll ever go back?

I won't answer that last question, not out loud. I won't say, I hope so, even though that is the truth. The Widow Hale will frown at my silence, pat my arm, and tell me I'm a very complicated person, which of course is her way of saying she doesn't much care for me.

But all of that will come later.

Right now, though, as I breathe your skin scent, I am thinking of a dream I've been having lately. It comes in the early morning: after the nightmares, before the dawn, in that dim, gray, formless in-between place. Between waking and sleeping, night and day, what was and what might yet be.

The dream always begins the same way: I'm rising. At first it's more of a hovering, feet dangling, against all physics, as if asking, Do I Dare? And then: unexpected weightlessness, a stomach drop. Like a roller coaster, almost, whoosh.

I'm never alone as I rise. Others are there too. Sometimes it's people I know—Jackie, or Alex, or Elaine (this time she does not fall beneath tires, this time she does not disappear forever in an instant I can never erase). More often, though, I'm with strangers, sometimes thousands of them, stretching as far as the eye can see.

It's some strange sort of rapture, this. But for whom? And why?

Up, up we go. We move past rooftops, beyond trees, we rise until we can make out the ridges and contours of our lives, the truths that are harder to see when gravity has us in its grasp: that we are, all of us, part of something much, much bigger than ourselves. That we are, each of us, a holy miracle, filled with potential.

The air around us becomes thinner, purer.

We rise until we arrive in some new place, or some old place, maybe. It's familiar, anyway, and soon we understand why: it's scattered with bits of ourselves, like some sort of forgotten mannequin factory. Look: here, and here. Here are the parts of us that we've lost along the way. We left these fragments of ourselves behind in school hallways, in alleyways, in the backs of cars, in childhood bedrooms, or offices, or back alleys, or basements. We left them behind closed doors, or right out in the open, in full sight of others. No one had noticed our loose parts falling away, not even us, but here they are.

We pick up these pieces, try to slot them into place, make ourselves whole again. Some search furiously, selfishly, hoarding more parts for themselves than they can possibly carry. Others hold up pieces for others: Did anyone lose this, or this, or this?

I search frantically, desperately. But it is the same thing, every time: there's some piece that I cannot find, some essential thing that will make everything click into place.

This morning, though, that changed. From the faceless crowd, from all those anonymous parts, you emerged, Ethan. You and Alex. Alex saw me first. She brightened, pulled you forward, and when you saw me, it was just like that moment, years ago, when a look in your eyes as you smiled at our daughter gave me a glimpse of a world where love—simple love—might be enough.

What would that world require?

What might it produce?

Just for a moment—fleeting, but no less miraculous for its ephemerality— I could see it: Skylines morphed, becoming at once familiar and not at all. From darkness: new philosophies, films, technologies exploded into being. I saw Aristotles who aren't Aristotle, Shakespeares who aren't Shakespeare,

Newtons who aren't Newton. Symphonies began to blare, hallelujah choirs never before heard. All around me, people dropped to their knees, listening.

Ethan, did you see it too? Did you witness this great expansion, this big bang, this cosmic smash-up, matter and art and understanding and ideas filling the space where empty void has always been? Can you see now, by contrast, how twisted this old world is, how distorted—like a tree growing in shadow, straining toward the sun? Everything down here is flat, a little too gray: a world that's missing not some, but rather most, of its parts.

Perhaps love is its own kind of genius. Maybe, like all genius, it has the potential to remake the world, if we just give it the space and time to do its work.

We have been through so much together, you and I.

I pull back now, look at you, and a new question forms on my lips. It's a simple, two-word query, not unlike what happened. *But instead of moving us backward, into all the places we've already trod, this one propels us forward, into what might yet be.*

Not what happened, not that anymore, but instead, simply, What's next?

ACKNOWLEDGMENTS

With thanks to:

My agent Mollie Glick and editor Kate Medina, as well as Noa Shapiro and Lola Bellier. The entire team at Random House, especially Gina Centrello, Andy Ward, Avideh Bashirrad, Benjamin Dreyer, Rebecca Berlant, Cindy Berman, Sandra Sjursen, Joe Perez, Diane Hobbing, Maria Braeckel, Susan Corcoran, Carrie Neil, Leigh Marchant, Barbara Fillon, Jess Bonet, and Matthew Martin.

All those who helped in ways large and small: Jennifer Berry, Sheila Boyle, Molly Burnham, Leslie Connor, Rónadh Cox, Sam Crane, Lisa Cushman, Marisa Daley, Jackie Davies, Caspian Dennis, Jessica Dils, Joe Finnegan, Tracy Finnegan, Elinor Goodwin, Kerry Hoffman, Lita Judge, Karen Kelly, Molly Kerns, Grace Lin, Shari Marquis, Jon Riley, Mariko Sakurai, Noah Sandstrom, Michael Schaeffer, Alexis Schaitkin, Geraldine Shen, Amy Simon, Matt Syrett, Cathy Thompson, Cynthia Wade, Tom Wade, Meredith Walsh, Heather Williams, Kim W, the Tunnel City coffee/ trivia crew, my GT family, and of course my actual family, especially Blair, Meredith, and Charlotte.

Edith Wharton, for the inspiration.

Dr. Christine Blaséy Ford, and Anita Hill before her, for telling the truth.

ABOUT THE AUTHOR

ALI BENJAMIN is the author of the young adult novel *The Thing About Jellyfish,* an international bestseller and a National Book Award finalist. *The Next Great Paulie Fink* was named a top children's book of the year by *Kirkus Reviews, Publishers Weekly,* the New York Public Library, and the Los Angeles Public Library. Her work has been published in more than twenty-five languages in more than thirty countries. Originally from the New York City area, she now lives in Massachusetts. This is her first adult novel.

alibenjamin.com
Instagram: @alibenjamin

ABOUT THE TYPE

This book was set in Bembo, a typeface based on an old-style Roman face that was used for Cardinal Pietro Bembo's tract *De Aetna* in 1495. Bembo was cut by Francesco Griffo (1450–1518) in the early sixteenth century for Italian Renaissance printer and publisher Aldus Manutius (1449–1515). The Lanston Monotype Company of Philadelphia brought the well-proportioned letterforms of Bembo to the United States in the 1930s.